Praise for *Into* ...

'It was impossible to put down t...
G. D. Wright is a star – another ...., ..., ...,
and deeply moving story with a twist that hits like a
sledgehammer. I loved it!'
LISA JEWELL

'*Into the Fire* is G. D. Wright's sizzling hot thriller that
starts as grippingly as it means to go on. One man's past
bleeds into his present as he fights for his family's future.
A gripping tale that explores the flip side of heroism, and a
rollercoaster ride you will not want to get off!'
JANICE HALLETT

'Such humane and compelling writing, I couldn't
put it down. Move over, crime giants, there's a new
giant in town! And if this doesn't become a TV series,
I will eat my own Netflix subscription.'
JO CALLAGHAN

'A remarkable book. Genuinely gut-wrenching and the
very real reactions of ordinary people thrust into an
extraordinary situation is handled sensitively without ever
letting up on pace, plot or tension. A joy to read – I can't
wait to see what G. D. Wright does next.'
M. W. CRAVEN

'A novel that picks you up and sweeps you along
to the most harrowing, devastating conclusion;
I couldn't turn the pages fast enough.'
JACKIE KABLER

'Authentic, compassionate, and beautifully written, *Into the Fire* is an emotional rollercoaster of a thriller with a shocking finale.'
SARAH CLARKE

'A powerful, deeply emotional and gripping crime drama. This high-octane rollercoaster of a novel shows, in dramatic detail, just how far a man can go for the people he loves. My heart still pounds when I think of that ending. Highly recommend!'
LISA TIMONEY

'I don't know how G. D. Wright topped the excellent *After the Storm*, but he has! It's astonishing and the most gripping, emotional and addictive book I've read since I don't know when. If you only read one book this year, *Into the Fire* has to be it.'
GRAHAM BARTLETT

'A hugely gripping, tense and emotive read, with a shocking end that hits you like a gut punch. My jaw was on the floor. G. D. Wright delivers a masterclass in characterisation and a taut, intricately crafted plot that will consume you long after you turn the last page. Simply brilliant. A brave, haunting and accomplished read that will grip and shock you.'
A. A. CHAUDHURI

'G. D. Wright is so good at writing characters you empathise with, who are so normal and everyday, but who harbour such toxic secrets! I felt all the emotions reading this, and absolutely tore through it. A compelling, human, heart-wrenching read that I could not put down!'
RUTH IRONS

'A gripping read from start to finish. Wright has managed to create a captivating story that will stay with readers long after they finish the book. The plot is intelligent and emotionally taut. One to look out for.'
RHIANNON BARNSLEY

'Heartbreaking, gut-wrenching and tense: *Into the Fire* is an emotional rollercoaster ride you don't want to miss.'
HEATHER J. FITT

Praise for *After the Storm*

'Amazingly fearless and a pure adrenaline ride! Totally addictive. I nearly fainted due to not breathing for the last half hour. This is one of the most tense and gripping thrillers I've read in ages. When it gets its claws into you, you'll be gasping for air.'
LISA JEWELL

'A beautifully written, emotional thriller about loss and consequences. So compelling and tightly plotted I couldn't put it down.'
CLAIRE DOUGLAS

'Tense and emotional . . . A dark beating heart of a novel, a murder mystery but also an examination of the pressures of the police and justice system: those who come up against it, but, more importantly, those who work in it and bear the consequences of that trauma . . .'
GILLIAN McALLISTER

'What an absolute rollercoaster ride of a book. Reminding me of *Broadchurch*, with its small town feel and its taut, propulsive plot, *After the Storm* is truly gripping.'
JENNIE GODFREY

Gary Wright joined Kent Police at the age of eighteen and worked in a variety of uniformed roles. At the age of twenty-nine, and completely out of the blue, he suffered two cardiac arrests that led to the diagnosis of a life-limiting and incurable disease of the heart. Following the implantation of an internal defibrillator into his heart, he was unable to continue policing and retired at the age of thirty. He bought a coffee shop in Ramsgate Harbour, and spent years looking out over the sea and dreaming up stories. He now writes full time, committing those very stories to paper.

Also by G. D. Wright:

After the Storm

INTO THE FIRE

G. D. WRIGHT

avon.

Published by AVON
A division of HarperCollins*Publishers* Ltd
1 London Bridge Street
London SE1 9GF

www.harpercollins.co.uk

HarperCollins*Publishers*
Macken House, 39/40 Mayor Street Upper
Dublin 1, D01 C9W8, Ireland

A Paperback Original 2025

1

First published in Great Britain by HarperCollins*Publishers* 2025

A catalogue record for this book is available from the British Library.

ISBN: 978-0-00-870243-4

Set in Sabon LT Std by HarperCollins*Publishers* India

Printed and bound in the UK using 100% Renewable
Electricity at CPI Group (UK) Ltd

This book contains FSC™ certified paper and other controlled
sources to ensure responsible forest management.

For more information visit: www.harpercollins.co.uk/green

For Nay

Content Warning:

Into the Fire, although fictional, tackles some events and issues that some may find distressing. If you'd like to find out more, please read the 'Content Warning' note at the very back of the book, but please be warned it does contain spoilers.

According to most industry standards, there are four stages of a fire:

1. Ignition
2. Growth
3. Fully Developed
4. Decay

The National Fire Protection Association

Prologue

A full moon it may have been, but it didn't stand a chance of penetrating the canopy of blue lights that shimmered and bounced around the neighbourhood.

DS Willmott stood sentry on the pavement at the front of the house, watching, waiting, and breathing it all in. It was a street much like any other. Residential housing, with small driveways or gardens at the front of each home. But this street would forever be tarnished now by what had happened here. Death's aroma permeated all around her. It clung to her skin, seeping into her pores and coursing through her veins. She'd smelt it before, too many times to remember, but this was different. This one would endure, in the deepest, darkest recesses of her mind.

A symphony of sounds filled her ears. The distant sirens as further reinforcements were assembled. The low, almost excitable murmurs of those who were gathering to watch, being held at bay by a handful of cops who were doing their level best to keep the scene sterile. The click, click, click of camera phones as everyone sought to snatch their own, morbid snapshot of everything that was happening, flashes breaking through the darkness. And her colleagues' voices, on edge, as orders were barked and the airwaves were flooded with a deluge of jigsaw pieces that, as yet, were failing to come together as a completed puzzle.

'No chance of life.'

'One in custody.'

An ambulance was in front of her, half on the pavement. The blue lights that twinkled from its roof complemented those of the police cars that had been abandoned all around it and, as its crew returned to their vehicle, with their faces drooped low, DS Willmott nodded at them. It was a sympathetic smile that ran halfway up her cheeks, but it wasn't returned. Shock, she guessed. It was understandable.

The crowds grew as the bigwigs with pips and crowns on their shoulders began to arrive, turfed out from their beds as the balloon went up.

Police cordons were established. An inner one, close to the house, and an outer one further down the road, which the onlookers were shepherded towards.

Scene logs were filled out as uniformed officers tried to work out who had been where, and at what time. Every movement needed to be logged, every action accounted for.

And, for whatever SIO it was who was going to be in charge of that mess, a policy book was instigated.

DS Willmott looked on, from the sidelines. She'd watched it all unravel as the weeks had passed by but, as the chill of the late autumn night pierced through both her jacket and shirt, she shivered, partly from the icy air that froze her bones, but mostly from her internal reflections. She hadn't seen *this* coming, that's for sure.

Hours passed by, the dead of night giving way as the light of a new day dawned overhead. Camera crews turned up en masse to complement the throngs of locals who had braved the hours of darkness to be in amongst it all. The media caravan had not long gone from Beachbrook, not long put what they thought had been the finishing touches to the story that had gripped them all and yet, there they were, back in town once more.

As the sun breached the horizon and sent early shards of light in every direction, there was a gentle buzz in the air. This was a new chapter. Hell, it was a whole new story, and it was going to run and run.

'Gently.'

'Steady.'

'Easy does it.'

Words, uttered with clarity by an all-seeing and all-knowing undertaker.

A metallic clatter followed from just inside the hallway as a stretcher was erected and the wheels locked in place. Moments later, that very trolley, loaded with its cargo, emerged from the front door. A silence descended, save for the incessant clicks of those camera phones, and the hushed murmurings of producers in the earpieces of their respective news reporters.

The trolley was wheeled down the path, but the body bag it carried didn't reflect those early-morning rays of sunlight. Instead, the beams were absorbed by it, trapped in the black fabric and lost in the morbid bubble that tracked its route all the way to the black private ambulance parked outside. DS Willmott flanked it, every step of the way.

The undertakers loaded their freight with ease and, as she stood back, watching as the non-descript van departed, she squinted, trying but failing to dispel the growing migraine from her temples.

'DS Willmott?' a voice called.

She looked up. A suit. She thought she knew all the SIOs in the region, but obviously not. They all looked the same, all carried themselves in the same way. She could spot one a mile off. As she nodded, the suit marched towards her and offered a hand. She shook it. Good grip. Nice and firm. Just how it should be. His face, though, told a different story. From the jagged frown lines that streaked his forehead, to the way his top lip twitched ever so subtly as he spoke, the scene upstairs had clearly got under his skin.

She was glad she hadn't been the only one.

'It's a bad one,' he muttered.

'Worst I've seen,' she replied.

She looked at him as he puffed his cheeks. No matter how hard he tried, though, it seemed the colour wouldn't return to them.

'I understand you've got some knowledge of the players?' the SIO asked.

DS Willmott sighed and nodded once more.

'Let's get a coffee,' she said. 'Might take a while.'

PART ONE

Ignition

/ɪgˈnɪʃn/

noun

1. the action of setting something on fire or starting to burn

Source – Oxford Languages

3 Weeks Earlier

Chapter 1

STEVE

'PLEASE, NO!'

Sleep. His old enemy.

'PLEASE, NO!'

His body writhed as his bedsheet dampened, sweat filling the fibres until it was one pooling mass.

'PLEASE, NO!'

A deep slumber. Normally his mind returned him to reality with haste. Not tonight, though.

'PLEASE, NO!'

On and on, again and again, the same nightmare. The years may have turned into decades, but that voice hadn't aged. The clarity, the tone, the pitch, all undiminished.

'PLEASE, NO!' he shouted, returning serve with a volley of his own.

'Steve?' Sarah yelled.

Her fingers groped at his ribs, her nails digging into his skin, and he tensed his shoulders. He was still stuck in that haze in his mind where sleep met reality, and his wife's voice didn't rouse him.

'Steve,' she repeated, louder. Firmer.

His eyes opened, but he only saw darkness. It's how she liked to sleep. He fumbled for his bedside lamp, bringing the night to life.

'Again?' he asked, as he wiped away a bead of sweat that dribbled onto his top lip.

'Again,' Sarah replied. He squinted through misty eyes as she sat up and stared at him, the edges blurred as he struggled to focus on her. Where he had drips of sweat on his forehead, hers was dry. Where his fingers trembled, hers were still. He may have woken from one of those recurring nightmares that had only intensified as the years had gone by, but she hadn't. Hers had been a presumably peaceful slumber, and to have dragged her from it? Her loud sigh as she slapped her pillow into shape spoke more than words.

'Sorry,' he said. He had nothing else.

'You've got to see someone,' she said.

'Change the record,' he whispered, so delicately that she couldn't hear.

'What's that?' she asked.

'Will do,' he replied. They both knew he wouldn't.

Her sighs drifted into his ear as he reached for the lamp and flicked the switch, once again plunging the room into darkness. Within minutes the softest of purrs floated from her lips. While she slept, his eyes stayed open, staring into the black.

It was going to be a long night.

Summer had breathed its last and the gentle nip in the air signalled that change was coming. The holiday season was over, the beaches deserted as holidaymakers returned to their own distant realities. The sun still shone, of course, but with less brilliance, its intensity dimming as the weeks passed by. Autumn, and all the variables that it brought, was due.

The changing weather, though, couldn't take away from the aesthetic of Beachbrook. From the bright white cliffs that guarded its sands, to the town centre that was a throwback to the heyday of the 1990s, it lived and breathed as though it was a tribute to a time gone by, one not necessarily more innocent, but certainly more attuned to the values of the past. It was a place where community was front and centre, where tourism ruled, where people still gathered for their own slice of nostalgia from yesteryear.

Autumn? It was the time of year that locals loved. They breathed in the last embers of summer, free from the madding crowds that assembled at the height of the season. They came out of their reverse-seasonal hibernation, keen to reclaim their beaches. Their promenades. Their sea and their sand.

Their Beachbrook.

And Steve? He was right at the centre of it all. Owning a coffee shop on the promenade next to those golden sands may have been 'work' on paper, but it was the dream job of so many around him.

When he climbed from his bed, though, after a night that had been spent tossing and turning as usual, his steps were heavy as he trudged down the stairs. '*PLEASE, NO!*' Those two words only stalked him when he slept. Only in *his* dreams.

Scrub that.

Only in his nightmares.

'Daddy!' Oscar shouted, flecks of cereal spraying from his four-year-old mouth as he welcomed Steve into the kitchen.

'Morning, kiddo,' Steve replied, ruffling Oscar's hair. 'All right, Gracie?'

His daughter had her back to him, but Steve knew where Gracie's focus was: her iPad.

'Mmmm,' she replied, her eyes remaining firmly planted on the screen.

'Gracie . . .' Sarah said.

'Morning, Dad,' Gracie said. Her voice was quiet as she turned around and looked up at him, barely returning the smile that he flashed at her.

'Seven going on seventeen,' Sarah said. 'Morning, love.'

He looked at her, and her eyes widened.

'You look awful,' she blurted out.

Her bluntness never failed to make him smile and, in spite of her words, he couldn't help but look at her with the giddy feeling he always had. She was his rock. His best mate as well as the voice of reason in his day-to-day, who made him laugh as much as she made him smile. That she had the movie-star looks to match only sweetened the deal. He might look awful but she was the dead opposite. With naturally blonde hair that had been bleached a unique shade of gold by the Beachbrook sun, she had drawn him in and never let him go.

'You were snoring. I couldn't get back to sleep,' he replied. He'd already seen his face in the bathroom mirror and, though she had phrased it without much tact, she was right. They weren't rings around his eyes. They were saucers.

It was a lie, of course. She wasn't a snorer. With a smile on her face, she whacked him on the shoulder.

'I'll get you some of those nasal strips if you like,' he said, provoking another whack, another smile.

'Are you taking them this morning?' Sarah asked, looking at the kids who were sitting at the kitchen table, eating cereal and each now utterly engrossed in their respective tablets.

Steve nodded. Their school was on the way to the beach, and it tied in perfectly with his opening hours.

'Course,' he replied, ruffling Oscar's blond hair. It was getting far too long, and Steve had hinted plenty of times for it to be trimmed, but it hadn't cut much ice with his wife.

14

She'd argued that he was a beach boy, that his tanned skin and flowing locks complemented his sister, Gracie, so well. Steve had given up with the hints. It was on the 'to-do' list, but he wouldn't tell Sarah. He'd just go and get it done, then face the consequences afterwards. Sometimes it was better to apologise afterwards, than to ask permission in the first place.

He sat at the table with the kids and fiddled with some toast while they finished their breakfast, nibbling at an edge but barely letting the crumbs pass beyond his lips. He watched Gracie and Oscar, each of them with more technical nous in their fingertips than he possessed in his entire body. It was true that children picked things up a lot quicker than adults, but they had both been proficient in all things 'iPad' since before they could even talk. Steve almost chuckled to himself as he remembered, pre-children, how he and Sarah had always insisted that their kids would NEVER spend the majority of their time using technology, how they would insist on there being family games, reading sessions and time spent outdoors. Oh, how naïve they were, he thought. Kids playing up? Give them the iPad. Kids tired? iPad. Kids arguing? iPad. Kids won't sleep? iPad. Essentially, the answer to anything child-related? iPad.

He was an analogue man who was struggling to embrace a digital world, amazed at how instant everything had become, at how quickly news could make its way across the world and how everything was available at the merest click of a button.

'Alexa, music on,' he said. Within a second, the kitchen was filled with some inane tune that was just a bit too loud.

'That's too noisy,' Gracie said, putting her fingers in her ears, and she had a point.

'Alexa, turn it down,' Steve said and, as the volume lowered, Gracie's fingers resumed their place on her iPad.

Steve wandered over to the kettle, passing the day calendar

on the kitchen side. Sarah had already ripped yesterday away, and in big, bold letters on today's agenda was something they'd been looking forward to for ages.

MUMMY AND DADDY 'OUT' OUT WITH PHIL AND EM!!!

As he flicked the kettle on, his smile was real. It had been too long. Far too long.

'Come on, you two, time to get ready,' Sarah said, ushering the children from their seats.

Gracie groaned, and Oscar smiled. His daughter's slow and weighty footsteps were a marked contrast to the way his son bounced from one foot to the next.

Steve chuckled. Gracie's apparent apathy towards school had only come on in recent months. A teenager before her time, they'd joked. If only she knew there was at least another twelve years of education left to navigate, he thought. He knew the value of time, and just how long it could take for those years to pass, particularly when carrying the baggage he did.

'Daddy?' Oscar said. He was standing in front of Steve, Sarah watching from the kitchen door.

'Steve?' Sarah said. 'All right, love?'

He shook his head, vigorously. It wasn't an answer to her question, just a means of stirring himself back into the present. He had lost himself again.

'Sorry, miles away,' he replied, climbing to his feet and grabbing his keys.

'Miles away now,' Sarah said, 'jumping outta your skin in bed . . . What's going on with you?'

'We'll chat later,' Steve replied, cutting her off as he ushered Oscar out of the kitchen door and into the hallway. 'Gracie,' he shouted up the stairs, 'time to go.'

He didn't see Sarah shaking her head, but he knew one thing was for sure: he wouldn't be speaking about it later.

Like countless parents all over the country, the school run was part of the routine for Steve. Not only did he get to wave the kids off to class, but it meant that he could ensure a regular and consistent opening time of 09.00 at Coffee and Cream. It provided structure, familiarity, routine – principles that a lot of people live their lives by . . . His early morning patrons among them. He had regular customers who he could set his watch by. If he was even ten minutes late opening then they would let him know about it.

Steve adjusted his rear-view mirror so that he could see both kids. Gracie, slouched and staring out of the window, indifferent to the world as it passed her by. Oscar, sitting upright with a smile on his face, his book bag on his lap and his hands clasping it with ever-whitening knuckles. The contrast between them couldn't be more marked. Steve remembered how excited Gracie had been for school not more than three years before, when she had been sitting in Oscar's place. He wondered how long it would be before his little man's shoulders started to slouch, before the realisation that school wasn't just a passing phase would hit him.

He gave it two months.

'Cheer up, Gracie,' he said.

'How long 'til the holidays?' She turned to look at his eyes in the mirror.

'You've only been back a couple of weeks,' he replied, laughing.

Gracie reassumed her position vacantly staring out of the window.

'Are you excited, little man?' Steve said, turning his gaze to Oscar.

'Yeah, Daddy,' Oscar replied, smiling so wide that Steve could see his milk teeth in their full glory.

Steve grinned. Maybe he'd give it three months.

It was unusual to find a space close to the school gates, but he pulled up right outside the gates just as another parent was driving away. A good start to the day, he thought. Gracie was out of the car and through the gates before Steve had even finished undoing Oscar's seatbelt.

'Bye then,' Steve called after her as he stood up with his boy in his arms.

Gracie turned around and looked at him sheepishly. She walked back slowly, meeting him just as he got to the gate with Oscar.

'Sorry,' she said quietly.

'You all right, darling?' Steve asked.

She nodded, then smiled.

'Love you, Daddy,' she said.

'Love you more, princess,' Steve replied.

He reached down and wrapped his arms around her. She gripped him in return, just a bit tighter than normal, and for a second longer than usual, then she turned and walked back through the gate without looking back. With Oscar still by his side, Steve tracked her as she walked alone before disappearing through the main doors. The playground was full, but she hadn't stopped to play with anyone. Steve stood for a moment, before approaching one of the teachers who was standing on the gate.

'Can I help?' the teacher said. Steve recognised her, but didn't know her name.

'Don't suppose you can get Mrs Adams to keep an eye on my daughter, can you?' Steve replied. 'She seemed a bit down in the dumps going in just now.'

The teacher smiled. A normal request at the start of a school year. 'Of course,' she replied. 'What's her name?'

'Gracie Minchin,' Steve replied. 'Thanks.'

The teacher nodded, as Steve turned to Oscar.

'You have a great day, little man,' he said, kissing his son on the forehead.

Oscar ran through the gates and went straight to the play area where most of his friends had already gathered. He smiled, then turned and headed back to his car, where he reached for his phone and composed a message to Sarah.

Kids dropped. Gracie seemed a bit off. I told the teacher on the gate and she's going to get Mrs Adams to keep an eye out – can you call them at lunchtime to check she's okay?
Xx

He saw that Sarah had read it straight away and was typing a reply, so he waited for that to come through before he started the engine.

Yep will do. Have a great day xx

Steve put his phone to one side, and pulled away carefully, returning the waves and smiles of several parents as he did so. His work set him at the heart of the community, and the school was no different. He had once been asked to consider being a parent governor, and he had looked into it more out of a sense of duty than anything else, but any interest that had been piqued within him had immediately dissipated when he found out that he would need to be DBS-checked.

Police checks.

Not an option. Who knew what that would entail, after all?

Of course, he had made up a reason to explain his sudden change of heart. Couldn't commit the hours. Busy business to run. Baby Oscar to look after. Excuse, excuse, excuse. With Oscar now starting his educational journey at the school, however, he wondered if there would once again be any noise about him stepping up. He hoped not. He didn't know if he could think of any other plausible reasons not to.

As troubling as all those thoughts were, it was something that he had become accustomed to. All he could do was take everything day by day. Eventually, he had found, those days had turned into weeks, the weeks into months, and the months into years.

Many years, in fact.

Decades.

As always, he pushed it into a part of his mind that he tried not to access in the hours of daylight.

He knew that when it was dark, and when sleep came, it would confront him.

It always did.

Chapter 2

DS SUE WILLMOTT

Another day, another dollar. DS Willmott had been threading the days together for so long that it felt like she should be a millionaire. Even so, though the sun had barely begun its rise, she still jumped from her bed with the same enthusiasm she always had. A bit wiser, sure. A few more lines on her forehead and wrinkles around her cheeks, naturally. Each of them told a story of their own, though, and she wore them with the pride of a battle-hardened veteran.

She hadn't heard her mum creep through the front door, but she knew that she'd be downstairs waiting. It had been like that since forever. An early shift for her meant an even earlier start for her mum.

She showered and watched as the steam formed rivulets on the glass enclosure. With the softest of touches, she drew a heart onto the glass and watched as it steamed over in seconds. She drew another and, before it had the chance to disappear, she wrote her initials above and LW beneath. People had told her she was mad to not formalise Lottie's name as 'Charlotte', but it had never been an issue to her. More importantly, though, her late husband, Alfie, had been on board with it. She smiled as the steam spread over her scribblings once more, and she flicked her short hair back with a deft touch. As she turned the shower off and walked from the enclosure, she was a woman refreshed and ready to face whatever the day threw at her.

'Mummy!' Lottie shouted, as DS Willmott walked into the lounge. She may have recently started Year Four at school, but her voice still contained enough youthful exuberance to make her mummy smile. The early bird gene had always run in the family. It didn't matter if it was a weekday or a weekend, Lottie would always rather watch the sun rise than set. On schooldays, it didn't half make it easier.

'Morning, Sue,' DS Willmott's mum said. On the lounge table there were two vessels with steam pouring from them – a mug for her mum and a travel cup for her. It was her fuel for the morning, and no one made it quite like her mum did.

'Cheers,' DS Willmott said, as she lifted the coffee to her lips and tilted it upwards. It didn't matter that it was like magma pouring through the small hole in the lid; the caffeine hit was almost instant.

'Cheers, love,' her mum said, raising her mug and pointing it at her.

Lottie ran up to DS Willmott and clung to her and, as Willmott ran her hand through her baby girl's golden locks and picked at knots that had tied themselves in her sleep, Lottie buried her head further into her thigh. Leaving any child at the crack of dawn was hard, as any parent would attest, but DS Willmott was pragmatic about it. There was work to do, money to earn and bills to pay. Besides, if she had to leave Lottie in anyone's care, then she couldn't and wouldn't choose anyone other than her mum. The maternal flames were strong and, particularly since Mr W had gone, they had extended across the generational gap to Nanny.

'Normal shift today?' her mum asked, as Lottie pulled herself away and took a seat on the sofa, reaching as if by instinct for her iPad. DS Willmott smiled and met her mum's gaze, their eyes rolling collectively.

'Sure is,' DS Willmott replied, rubbing away the tiniest bit of dribble that Lottie had left on the black trousers of her two-piece suit. 'On call tonight, though . . .'

She looked at her mum, who nodded. She understood her assignment, DS Willmott knew. On call meant a Nanny sleepover, just in case. It was in moments like those that she appreciated just how much her mum had stepped up to the plate. She just got it. DS Willmott's dad had died too young and, when history had repeated itself, her mum had been the rock to guide her through. DS Willmott fiddled with her finger. The wedding ring may have been long gone, but its absence had indeed made the heart grow fonder.

'Right then,' she said, taking another sip and rolling her shoulders, 'let's get this show on the road. See you later, pickle.'

'Bye, Mummy,' Lottie replied, actually looking up from the iPad and even giving a wave.

'Thanks, Mum,' DS Willmott said.

'Always,' her mum replied.

Though summer had gone, and despite the sun still being low in the sky, DS Willmott kept the window down as she navigated empty roads on her way to Beachbrook Police Station. Its place atop the cliffs afforded the very best of views on the drive around the coast and, as she took a moment to look out to sea, the sun sent diamond shards in a million directions and more. It was something that she'd never get bored of looking at, no matter how many times she saw it. As always, she flicked off the radio in the car and listened. The sea purred, barely registering above the revs of the engine. Sometimes, it was wild. Sometimes, it was tame. Today it was gentle, and she nodded. The sea demanded respect and, from too many bitter experiences, she was more than happy to afford it.

As she swung into the rear car park of the police station, the resident seagulls scattered to the sides of the tarmac. She wove through them, as they caw-cawed at her, their squawks another overture to the symphony of life in Beachbrook. Sleepy-eyed uniformed officers milled about, their night shift nearly over as the folk of the town began to rise from their slumber. As she climbed from her car, she breathed it all in. The salt of the surf intertwined with the fresh morning air, and she felt alive.

The CID office was deserted. She was the first in, at least half an hour before the first of her DCs would begin to filter through the doors and slump at their desks. Her coffee had maintained its warmth for the entirety of the journey and, as she walked into her office, sat down and flicked on the computer, she took another sip. The temperature was perfect, and it flowed down her gullet like nectar from flowers.

There was nothing of note from overnight. A couple of burglaries, a few assaults, the usual drunk and disorderlies playing up in the custody suite but, all in all, Beachbrook had slept well. The town had rested nicely, ready for whatever Friday and the weekend was going to throw at her. She sat back and watched as the clock on her desk ticked away the seconds, sipping at her coffee until, as she drained the last dregs, thirty minutes had passed by.

'Morning, Sarge,' DC Robson said as he poked his head around her office door.

'Vinny,' she replied, with a smile.

'Top-up?' he asked.

'Please,' she said.

He always seemed to turn up at the exact right time, when her cup was empty and when a fresh one was needed more than anything.

As the door creaked on its hinges, and more and more of her DCs shuffled in and sat at their desks in the open-plan office, she walked amongst them. They were her charges, her officers, and she treated them accordingly. Do well, and you'd be showered in praise. Mess up, and you'd be warned.

Cross her? You'd be out on your arse before you even knew what had hit you.

Chapter 3

STEVE

As mornings go, it was pretty special. The shutters of Coffee and Cream were up, and Steve was sitting in the sun, looking out to sea. It was glorious, one of those autumnal days when everything seemed right in the world. The sun rode gently on the crest of the waves and the sand glowed golden; there was little else in the world that would have rivalled its aesthetic. It was picture-postcard-perfect. For Steve, though, there was something else. It was a view that he could draw blindfolded yet, for him, it wasn't entirely untainted. Looking out to sea had always provoked conflicting emotions in him. It was glorious, on the one hand, and filled him with a peace that was difficult to describe. Yet, on the other, it had the power to evoke memories of the past. Rarely, when combined with that briny smell in the air and the soft, rolling waves on the surf, it was the perfect storm that made his knees buckle.

Steve's legs ached – a sure sign that it had been a busy season, but the wind-down weeks were nearly as much fun as the winter months of closure. Seasonal businesses were a hard slog, but the rewards were more than worth it. In Steve's case, it meant having six months off in the low season. He would say that he earned it, that working seven days a week and missing out on the kids' sports days and weekends away and everything else that 'normal' workers did in the summer months was the price that he paid, but it wasn't a secret to anyone who knew him that he wouldn't be caught dead in any other job.

It was the time of year that he liked the best. Behind him, six hot and sticky months of hard graft. Ahead? A blank canvas to make more memories with his wife and kids. To complete the 'to-do' list that had been building up over the summer. To smile while others slogged their lives away in an office, grinding out a living on the nine-to-five ticket to a distant retirement. That wasn't for him.

He checked his watch. He had a few minutes to finish his coffee before the first of his regulars arrived, so he sat back in his chair and drank in the majesty of his surroundings as he swallowed the last few dregs of his drink. The splendour of the sea was something that he was permanently in awe of: how it could be calm and flat on a day like that, but also how quickly it could change to exude malevolent violence. Working on the beach every day, he had seen it first-hand. It commanded respect and he gave it in droves.

'Morning, Steve,' a voice said, approaching him from behind.

'Morning, John,' he replied. He didn't need to turn around to see who it was. John was always his first customer. 'Usual?' he asked.

'Please,' John replied.

Steve got to his feet and walked towards the side door, pausing on the way to stroke John's black Labrador.

'Morning, Lex,' he said.

Lex jumped up at him, keen for attention. Steve grinned, then pushed him down.

'Would love to have a cuddle, mate, but the health inspector wouldn't like it,' he said.

'So how's things?' Steve asked, his voice loud as it fought against the whistling sound of the milk steamer.

'Yeah, all good,' John replied. 'Family well?'

'Yeah, all good as well,' Steve replied.

He was used to this type of conversation, words being exchanged, but minimal substance contained within them. Indeed, this conversation played out every morning between the two of them. Even so, he liked John. He had been coming to Coffee and Cream for years and was part of the furniture. As his coffee was passed to him, he repeated his oft-said words.

'Best coffee in town,' he said, taking his first sip. 'You must tell me where you get your beans from.'

Steve chuckled. 'Trade secrets,' he said.

They both stood and looked at each other. They'd covered the usual bases. A greeting. An enquiry about the family. A joke about the coffee beans. There wasn't really a lot else to say.

'Come on, Lex,' John said, throwing a ball onto the sand.

Lex needed no second invitation, and he shot off into the distance.

Steve stood outside and watched as John trudged away, the sand seeming to weigh heavily under his feet. The contrast between Lex's bounding strides and John's rather more sedate progress was marked. He watched as they disappeared around the corner to the next bay, listening as the sound of seagulls and the gentle rippling of waves provided the soundtrack to his morning. It was a beautiful duet.

So attuned was he to the majesty of what was in front of him, that he didn't hear more footsteps approaching from behind. It didn't matter that the hand grabbing his arm was gentle, nor that it was from friendly quarters. It still made him jump out of his skin, and caused his heart to pump just a bit quicker than it should.

'Come on, you lazy old sod,' the voice attached to the hand said, 'less sitting and more brewing.'

'Me lazy?' Steve said, turning around. 'Why aren't you at work?'

A beaming smile on a sun-kissed, forty-year-old face greeted him and, as his handshake with Phil quickly turned into one of those man-hugs that are all testosterone and yet still meaningful, he grinned. If his interaction with John had been superficial, then this with his closest ally was much more meaningful. Friends. Real, true friends.

'Working from home,' Phil said, 'flexible hours . . . take your pick.'

If a person and their job were the embodiment of chalk and cheese, then it was Phil and his role as a computer boffin of some description. Apps or something. Steve had once asked, but got an answer that he didn't understand. Whatever it was, though, Phil was very much an extrovert, who could out-tech the geeks of the world with one eye closed.

'Hard old life,' Steve replied, smirking. 'Coffee?'

'Go on then, you smooth-talking bastard,' Phil said.

Coffees made, the two men sat down and looked out to sea.

'How's things?' Steve asked.

'Usual . . . Eat, sleep, wake, repeat.'

'That good, eh?'

'You know it.'

They both chuckled and, though there was a silence, it was a comfortable one. Nature's percussion was melodic enough for them to maintain that silence, listening as beach life played out in front of them. Today, it was peace that hit

Steve in waves, as the sea rolled in front of his heavy eyes. He didn't mean to close them, but base human instinct took over.

The terrors that normally stalked him when he closed his eyes at night didn't care for the fact it was daytime, nor did they take into account the total tranquillity of the surroundings. Sleep, it seemed, was where they thrived, come what may.

'PLEASE, NO!'

He sat bolt upright. Wide and wild, his eyes darted left and right, seeking the source of the voice. It was louder than normal but, given the location, perhaps that was inevitable.

His mind. It was just his mind.

'All right, mate?' Phil asked.

'Yeah, sorry,' Steve replied, lowering himself back into the seat, 'must've dozed off.'

'Tired, mate?' Phil asked.

'Always,' Steve replied.

He stood up and took his mug back into the hut.

That voice. Though years may have passed, it was still as crisp and clear as ever. His hand shook. Time had taught him that nowhere was safe, that what ailed his mind could and would pop up anywhere. It was all a part of his penance, all a part of the sins that had stalked him across the decades.

He looked at his hand. The adrenaline had passed, but it was still shaking. He breathed deeply, willing it to stop but powerless to make it do so.

'Steve?' Phil said, peering in through the serving hatch.

'Just washing up,' Steve said.

'Need a hand?' Phil asked.

'You're not qualified, mate,' Steve replied, turning around and forcing a grin.

Phil appeared by his side, tea towel in hand. Steve's smile

endured. The years of dealing with it all had caused him to develop the thickest of skin, and had never allowed his inner turmoil to be exhibited externally. It was something he was proud of, in a macabre way.

Steve ran the taps and put his mug in the washing-up bowl. He had committed to doing it, so he had better see it through.

'Finished yours?' he asked.

'Yeah, cheers,' Phil replied, placing his mug in the sink. 'What do I owe you?'

'Same as always,' Steve replied, washing both the mugs with the deftest of touches and handing them to Phil, who dried them just as quickly.

Phil smiled. 'Thanks, mate,' he said. 'I'll see you tonight.'

'Can't wait,' Steve replied, his northern twang leaning heavily on the last syllable.

'What's the plan?' Phil asked.

They both looked at each other with vacant eyes, before smirks developed fully across their chops.

'Girls sorting it?' Phil asked.

'Girls sorting it,' Steve confirmed.

They nodded at each other before Phil walked away. Steve stared into nothing, his mind absent before he was brought back to reality with another voice summoning his attention. Another regular. Another order. Another exchange of faux pleasantries.

Another part of an otherwise normal day in his life, the rest of which passed off without further incident. It had been a bumper day for a Friday in September, and being busy had certainly helped the hours to pass by quickly.

In the height of the summer holidays, there had been nothing to distinguish one day from the next for Steve. The routine for each was set in stone. Get up early, get ready, leave the house, work all day, get home just before sunset, go to bed. Repeat. Then repeat again.

Now that it had all calmed down a little bit, and the end of the season was in sight, the days and weeks had begun to take on a different structure. Weekends were busier than weekdays. Children were back at school and the societal need for ice cream had been dampened by the changing of the season. On the final gallop to his six months off, it was hot drinks all the way.

The late afternoons blended into an evening routine that was consistent in the Minchin household. Sarah would pick both kids up from school and ferry them home. The kids would gravitate straight to their respective iPads, of course, while Steve and Sarah would try to prise them away for the homework that had invariably been set by their class teachers. It was the only time that an outright ban on technology was enforced in the house and, despite their protestations, both kids knew it was futile to argue.

Tonight, though, the routine was out of the window. Tonight, Mum and Dad were on the tiles. Tonight, the glad rags were out. As any parent will attest, the chance to go OUT out was one to be grabbed with both hands and clung onto, and even Steve was looking forward to it.

Chapter 4

SARAH

The front doorbell rang half an hour early, and the smile that came across Sarah's face was matched by Steve's as they rose in uniform synchronicity from the sofa in the lounge. They'd both been ready for ages, not wanting to miss a second of an ACTUAL night out. The babysitter was normally on time, sometimes a few minutes before, even, but half an hour? They'd won the jackpot before they'd even walked out the front door.

Spontaneous nights out had become a fabled thing of the past, a hazy memory of their life pre-children, when they'd been young, carefree twenty-somethings whose eyes had met as they'd each been slamming a tequila. Sarah didn't mind though, in all honesty. Evenings spent in with the kids had long been the dream. From those heady days where the two of them had floated through life, to the lingering apprehension about whether or not she'd ever have kids as the years seemed to pass them by, their drifting days had become focussed with the arrival of Gracie. Oscar had completed their tribe a couple of years later, and it was perfection – the sheer, unadulterated realisation of a dream come true.

From quick-stepping up the rungs to success in the world of marketing, she'd jacked it all in to be a mum. Maintaining a small portfolio of local clients still gave her some skin in the game but, in being a mum, she had found her true calling and she revelled in it.

Even so . . . as Friday afternoon had dissolved into evening she couldn't help but feel a tingle of excitement floating through her. An adult night out. No iPads. No one asking if it was time to go home. No hair pulling, no screaming fits, no tantrums. Just a meal with Phil and Emma. A meal and drinks. And a handsome hubby in tow. Tonight, the Sarah of the time before kids was coming out to play.

'I'm in the mood, for dancing . . .' she sang.

'Who sings that?' Steve asked.

'The Nolans.'

'Let's keep it that way, shall we?'

The gentle thump on his arm was well earned.

As they made their way out of the front door, deaf to the kids' protestations about something or another, Sarah watched Steve as they climbed into the car. He may have looked older than his forty years, but the frown lines suited him. The greys that were creeping through were something he'd embraced. They were distinguished, even as they'd spread across his cheeks and chin in the designer stubble that he always wore, giving his face definition. The blazer and chinos he wore were in keeping with the man. HER man. Smart. Modern. On point. And, more importantly, maybe, he looked up for it. His sleepless nights hadn't gone unnoticed, nor had his moments of absence when the lights were on but nobody was home. Seeing him with a smile on his face warmed her soul.

Those thirty minutes had presented them with an opportunity – time for a livener, perhaps. Either way, it was thirty precious minutes that they hadn't been expecting. They were out of the door in a heartbeat. As Sarah parked her car in the town's multi-storey car park, it wasn't even close to being dark.

They certainly didn't waste the extra time that they'd been afforded. In fact, by the time Phil and Emma arrived, Sarah and Steve were already two drinks in, and she was beginning to feel the effects of it.

'You've got some catching up to do,' Sarah said, as she stood up to give Emma a hug.

'Love the highlights,' she said.

Emma reached for her hair, where streaks of blonde blended in perfectly, and smiled.

'Thanks, love,' she replied.

The two men were close, and the women had forged a strong bond, too. Sarah had never forgotten just how many friends had dropped away as the kids had come along. Where some had fallen, though, others had remained. Emma had been there for Sarah through thick and thin. They were a foursome where, they'd joked, the women were the rock stars and the husbands were the groupies and, it had to be said, neither of their husbands had been particularly shocked when someone had told them both, in the very recent past, that they had each been punching above their weight.

'How are the babies?' Emma asked, as she sat down and picked up the menu from the table.

'All good,' Sarah replied.

'I need a squeeze soon,' Emma said.

'They love their Auntie Em.'

'And me!' Phil said.

'Yes, and you.' Sarah rolled her eyes, but it was all in jest.

In the absence of blood relatives, they had become as close to the children as any aunt or uncle would and, given the amount of time that Sarah spent helping Steve at Coffee and Cream, there had been enough sleepovers with Uncle Phil and Auntie Emma across the years to formalise their honorary titles.

The usual cut and thrust of a well-established friendship was soon in full flow, more than aided by a few bottles of wine. Phil and Emma soon caught up and, with food cravings sated and moods buoyed by alcohol, they found themselves in Sarah and Steve's local pub, not too far from home, doing shots.

At their age.

It was a good idea at the time, of course. As Sarah crooned on the karaoke machine with the verve and panache of a youthful Meat Loaf, time simply got away from her. Last orders were called and, through the haze of whatever it was she'd been pouring down her neck, Sarah screwed her eyes shut in confusion. She could've sworn it was only about ten o'clock.

It was beyond midnight when they finally stumbled out onto the street. The air was fresh and, though it was calm, it slapped her on the cheeks. Drunk. She was steaming drunk. And, in the silence all around them, she couldn't find the mute button to stop her giggles.

'What's so funny?' Steve asked, as their collective footsteps stumbled a path home, echoing in every doorway, under every car, in every corner.

'What's so foony?' Sarah slurred, gently mocking his accent. It may have mellowed over the years, but it was still a thick, northern twang that sprung from his lips and sounded totally at odds among the southern folk of Beachbrook.

'Piss off,' Steve replied, smiling as her giggles evolved into a laughter that carried with it a snort, setting everyone else off.

In the absence of streetlights, the only thing that guided her path was the moon, ambient lighting from the occasional house with curtains open, and her ingrained knowledge of the exact route home. She could've done it with her eyes shut, in all honesty. They had spent many a night in that pub, before the kids had come along, and this was a journey they could repeat from habit alone.

'Coming in for a quick one?' Sarah asked, as she walked unsteadily.

'A quick one isn't a quick one, is it?' Emma replied, laughing to a tune of her own.

Curtains twitched as the four of them stumbled along, Steve and Phil up ahead and Sarah and Emma lagging behind. The residents were used to being woken up by drunk people walking home from the pub. It didn't mean that they liked it.

It was still calm. It was still . . . still.

Steve stopped dead in his tracks up ahead; her zigzagging footsteps soon caught him up.

'What's the matter?' she slurred, but Steve's raised hand was the only reply she received.

'What's up, mate?' Phil asked.

'Hang on,' Steve said quietly.

Sarah looked around, trying desperately to focus, to make her inebriated eyes cut through the haze with clarity, but everything was a blur. Edges were fuzzy, and colours mixed together. Whatever it was Steve was seeing, whatever it was he was noticing, it was entirely lost on her.

'You smell that?' he asked, sniffing the air.

'Smell what?' Sarah asked.

'Shhh,' Steve replied, putting his finger to his lips.

Sarah shushed as instructed, but was still none the wiser.

'Look!' Steve screamed, shaking his hand towards a low, glimmering light on the other side of the road. 'Over there!'

Chapter 5

STEVE

He had smelt it first. He could hear it, too. It was only a gentle crackling noise, but – having spent so long living on the edge of his wits – his senses were so incredibly attuned to any sign of danger.

As his eyes worked their way towards the source of the noise, towards the seat of the smell, he was the first to see it.

He didn't wait for the others to look. He was gone before they were able, a figure in the dark, his flight in tandem with the instinct to fight.

It started as the dullest glow of orange with only gentle wisps of smoke floating on the crisp night air but, as he reached the mid-terraced house on the other side of the road, flames were already beginning to lick the side of the property. Their ferocity increased by the second, the intensity magnified when set against the stillness of the night.

'Christ's sake!' Steve shouted.

It took seconds to spread and, in the merest of moments, it was crackling no more. Instead, roars of fire set the world around Steve alight. The heat was unbearable. It forced him back into the road itself where he bashed the back of his thigh against the bonnet of a car, his proximity to the flames dictated by the searing, burning air around him. Even there, he could feel the hairs on his chin singeing in the face of what he was staring down. He raised his hand to cover his nose and eyes, an instinctive act perhaps, but one that allowed him to fully digest the messages that were being sent to his brain.

Mid terrace. A front door. A window to the left of it, presumably the living room. Flames pouring from that exact window with thick, choking smoke billowing upwards. Upstairs, two separate windows, each distinct from the other. Two separate bedrooms. One of the windows was decorated with shapes and stars and all of the things that his own children would have chosen, once upon a time. A child's bedroom. Directly above the window with the flames. On the cracks of the blind inside that child's bedroom, the faintest of orange glows.

There were no sirens in the air, there was no one else coming to help. He didn't turn around to look for the others, as adrenaline tore through him.

He ripped his blazer from his arms and held it over his head as he ran forwards, fighting with everything he could against the flames that were attempting to hold him back. He tried the front door but it was locked. With a strong kick near the latch, though, it gave way easily. The hinges and UPVC were no match for a man possessed by a need to get in, driven by the will to get up to that bedroom.

Into the fire.

The air around him was a toxic cocktail that he choked on as it clung to the lining of his throat. His task, though, was clear. Simple, even. Get upstairs. Get to that kid's room. It was pure instinct, his mission being driven by something paternal, something deep within, his inhibitions no doubt dulled by a night of drinking. Whatever. It wasn't a conscious decision, more one summed up simply as *how could he NOT go in?*

He heard Sarah shouting his name, but the raging flames soon drowned out her screams.

The heat battered him, and he found himself on his knees as it threatened to overwhelm him. Holding his blazer to his head, and feeling the loose fibres on it fizzle as the strength of the flames dissolved them into little strands of nothing, he looked up.

'HELLO,' he screamed, scrambling to his knees, coughing and spluttering as he fought to regain his footing.

There was movement, in his periphery. A grease of colour against a glowing backdrop, scampering into view at the sound of his voice. The pants of the dog were unlike any he'd heard before, but they were translatable. In many ways, they were universal. It was fear. Undiluted, total fear. And as the golden-brown baby cockerpoo launched itself towards him, it took every ounce of dead-eyed balance that he could muster to stop himself from toppling over once more.

The dog's hair was steaming hot, its coat covered in what felt like clumps of split ends where it had been scorched by the embers. As one, Steve and the dog tremored, their horror united across the mammalian divide. He held his blazer to his face once more with one hand, while holding the bundle of heated fur in the other.

'HELLO!?' he screamed once more, and the dog cowered into his chest.

The stairs were directly in front of him, and – through pockets of smoke and the distorted waves of heat – he could see the same, ominous glow of orange up there that he had seen from outside. Heat rose. He knew that much. If it was like a furnace on the ground floor, what was it like up there? He had seconds to choose. No one would blame him if he gave up. No one would say a word. They would talk of the heat, of how the flames licked with acidic verve. They would say that it was impossible. They would say he couldn't have known if anyone was up there, that he had done everything he could. He might even be feted as a hero just for trying. What they WOULDN'T know, though was that in that moment he had the strength to go on. He had the will, the desire.

They wouldn't know just how much he NEEDED to do it.

He would know, though. And that was enough. He couldn't face anything being added to the burden that weighed down on him every day, with every breath, with every sleepless night.

'HELLO,' he screamed again, his voice muffled and lost in the material of his blazer, as he inched closer to the bottom stair.

The dog, it seemed wasn't having it. Not when there was an open front door. It scrabbled at Steve's chest, its claws drawing scratches on his skin through his top. Steve tried to cling onto it, but the puppyish spring in the cockerpoo's legs was just too quick for him.

He watched as the dog bounded out of the front door, losing sight of it the second it passed the threshold into the safety of the street beyond.

Steve looked up the stairs, as flames took hold of the banister next to him, then back to the front door. Stairs. Front door. Stairs. Front door. Heart versus head. Right there, and right then, there was only one winner.

'Jesus Christ,' he whispered to himself as cloying smoke weaved a path through the finely knit cotton of his blazer and made him gag.

He forced one foot in front of the other, completely focussed and oblivious to anything else. If there was a dog, then there was a family who may still be at home, and he had to get up those stairs. As he climbed each of the thirteen torturous steps, he navigated the normal clutter associated with family life. A handbag. A magazine. A couple of books. A baby's toy. Evidence of life. Proof of family. Of parents. Of children.

He reached the top. It was quieter, almost eerie, and the cloak of the thick and vanquishing smoke enveloped him. The melting heat of downstairs had yet to find its way up there, but the smoke had laid a trail for it to follow. Through its haze and murk, Steve could taste the acridity and, as he breathed through the cloth of his blazer, trying to filter out the worst of it, he retched and coughed. Those fumes were suffocating. They were crushing.

They were lethal. Murderous.

He looked back from whence he'd come. It was only a matter of minutes before upstairs would be engulfed as well. Indeed, as he surveyed the scene, he could see that the flames had chased him up the stairs and were wrapping themselves around the wooden, decorative spindles that adorned the staircase, pushing higher, harder and faster and leaving nothing but burnt embers and black ash in their wake.

Minutes? No way. He had seconds.

'Anyone up here?' he shouted.

No reply. Just wisping and crackling as the fire stalked him.

He looked ahead of him, at an open door. The bathroom. Not where he needed to be. He pivoted on the spot and saw two doors. To his left, an open door leading to a room plunged into a darkness so black as the grim veil of smoke swamped inside. To his right, a closed door, one that the draughts of death were breathing against, but were being repelled. On the door, a picture of a bunny. Of random stickers, collectively painting a picture to him of exactly what it was that lay beyond. A child's room.

The flames were kissing his feet now, but their tongues were forked. There was no affection, just a spitting, hissing wickedness. It was malice, pure and simple, and he was out of time.

He made his choice and barged through the closed door, slamming it shut behind him. It was dark and, despite the fire raging in the building all around them, quiet. The only light radiated from a battery-powered LED light strip on the wall. Its colour? Orange. Glowing, vibrant orange. It wasn't the glow of flames or fire that he had seen from the outside, it had been the sparkle of light that helped a child to sleep.

Only it wasn't a child's bedroom.

It was a nursery.

And, in the opposite corner of that nursery, a cot.

Steve stood still for mere milliseconds before he ran across the room, removing his blazer from his face as his eyes remained fixed on the baby's crib. The bitter taste of smoke still cloaked the air around him, but it wasn't nearly so strong as it had been outside the room. The closed door had bought him time, but that was of the essence. The fire had already chased him up the stairs. It would be relentless in hunting him down.

He bashed into the side of the cot as the alcohol of a night out that seemed decades prior combined with the effects of the fire and the adrenaline in his veins. It was an internal cocktail that made his knees buckle. He held his hand on the side of the crib, steadying himself, and looked down.

To race in, to face down the flames, to chase up the stairs and to do what he'd done – in an instant, it was clear that it had been the right choice.

He guessed eight months old. He guessed boy. He saw that tiny chest rising and falling, and those delicate lips quivering. Eyes closed, sure, but the fire hadn't won. Yet. There was still a fighting chance.

If only he could get them both out.

He tried to be gentle. He tried to do it with care, with the nurturing parental instincts of raising his own kids guiding him, but with that cocktail of alcohol and adrenaline interfering with his every action, it was impossible. Covering the baby's face with a muslin wrap and lifting them from the safety of dreamland into a waking nightmare provoked the expected response. The screams, Steve recognised. The tone and pitch, he didn't. Babies cry for many reasons, as any parent will attest. A grizzle spoke of an illness or annoyance. A whelp normally indicated pain. This scream, though, Steve hadn't heard before. It was one of abject fear.

He held the baby tight against his chest as he made his way across the room but, in those few seconds he had been in there, smoke had begun to billow through the crack at the bottom of the door. He didn't need to open it to know that fire was taking hold on the landing as well. Even so, he reached for the door handle, the sweat on his hand fizzing as he took hold of it. He grimaced as he cracked the door, his eyes widening as they processed what was happening. The flames out there weren't licking. They were spitting with rage at anything and everything that crossed their path.

Steve closed the door and kicked some cuddly toys that were lying on the floor against the base of it, stamping on them until they were wedged against it, and temporarily stopping the smoke from seeping in.

'Think,' he said to himself, 'think, think.' The haze of smoke in the air matched the fog of desperation in his mind. He had to find a way out, and quick.

The baby's screams rung heavily in his ears, only adding to what Steve already knew: it was grave. So desperately grave. The tiny one wriggled, desperate to free themselves from both Steve's grasp and the muslin that was protecting their precious, vulnerable lungs.

Steve made for the window and, in the absence of clarity, ripped the blind from the wall. It crashed to the floor, but the noise was dampened both by the carpet underfoot and the flames that had come knocking on the door outside.

He saw out, onto the road and beyond. Sarah. Phil. Emma. The tarmac and pavements were alive as a sea of people watched, neighbours in nightclothes, patrons of the pub they'd been in only minutes prior, and all of them with their mouths collectively agape. Steve looked one way, then the other. People, everywhere. Blue lights, absent. There was no help arriving.

He needed to find a way out of there because the flames . . . They were finding their way in.

He fumbled with the window, but only managed to open it a few inches. Child-safe. It wasn't enough to squeeze his hand out of, let alone the baby or himself. He looked around. Soft furnishings. Cuddly toys. Books, with cushioned covers and edges. In every way, it was a safe nursery. There was nothing hard in it, certainly nothing that could break double-glazed glass.

'PHIL,' he shouted through the gap in the window.

'STEVE,' Phil shouted back.

'You've got to smash it,' Steve shouted. 'Bricks, anything.'

His words may have been intended for Phil, but they came across as a collective call to arms. Neighbours and onlookers swarmed towards the fire, armed with whatever they could find.

'STAND BACK,' Phil shouted, as the onslaught of missiles began. As Steve stood with his back to the nursery door, he could hear the flames beginning to announce their imminent entry as they flickered around the edges of the doorframe. The LED light on the wall extinguished as the heat intensified, but that dim glow was replaced with a far

45

more sinister source of orange as the inferno crept into the room. It had found him.

It had found them.

Objects began bouncing off the window, thudding as they failed to penetrate.

'Come on,' Steve said, his voice laced with desperation as the baby continued to scream and writhe.

The thudding continued as the flames spread. Louder. Harsher. Louder. Harsher.

The air, though, was like the inside of a sauna, but where the oxygen was thin, and the taste bitter. He could feel the oxygen being sucked out of his lungs. For the first time, he closed his eyes as panic began to rise from the very depths of his being. Was this it? He couldn't help where his mind was taking him. Was *this* it?

The useless thud, thud, thudding continued as the flames began to roar around him. He was at the coalface. He was in a furnace. This *was* it. He knew it.

He resolved to keep his eyes closed until it was over, that when he inevitably went down to the floor he would do so with the baby under him. It would give the baby the best chance, after all. He just hoped that his weight wouldn't suffocate them.

Had he done the right thing? He thought of his own children. How would they deal with being fatherless? He thought that he knew pain, but nothing compared to his feelings of anguish as he stood there, right on the precipice. His children. Oh, how he loved them. He had always said that he would do anything to make sure they never felt sadness, yet there he was, in a position that would cause them the ultimate heartache. Had he done the right thing? He couldn't breathe. He couldn't think. It was overwhelming, and he was utterly powerless. Useless.

Time stood still. The thudding dulled as his mind took him to another place, one where fire didn't rage and smoke didn't billow. It was one where he cuddled his children and breathed in the essence of their very being. As he held the baby closer, and felt those wriggles of distress limpen, he was ready. If it was time to go then surely he'd done what he could to atone for the sins in his past. Surely, this counted.

He sank to his knees. How many breaths would it take? he wondered. How much of that caustic air would need to be breathed in for it to be over? Would he feel pain? Would he be conscious for his last breaths, aware enough to do what he could for the baby to have a chance?

As he pondered the end, and all the questions about it that are avoided while living, his senses dampened to the point of redundancy. He didn't hear the window smash. Instead, he felt a shard of broken glass skim across his arm, opening a small wound that brought him back into the real, living world. He opened the very eyes that he thought had taken in their last images.

Freedom beckoned in the form of a shattered window.

Clouds of smoke were being sucked from that very opening and, as Steve got to his feet and stumbled forwards, still clinging on to the now silent baby, he took a mere nanosecond to look down.

'WAIT,' screamed Phil, as droves of onlookers and neighbours ran forward with cushions, pillows, bean bags sofa furnishings, anything that they could lay their hands on in their own homes.

Steve looked around. He couldn't wait. It had to be now. With the baby in one arm, he grabbed its blanket from the crib and wrapped it around his own fist, punching through the sharp shards of glass around the edge of the break in the window, making the gap large enough for him to climb through.

As the props for a safe landing rained down beneath them, he leaned forward and jumped into the night, into the beyond, feet first and the baby tight to his chest. As he fell, he mouthed a silent prayer to a deity he didn't believe in that the baby would survive the fall, even if he didn't.

His knees bent as his feet moulded into a cushioned landing. He lurched forwards, rolling into a ball while still clinging onto his precious cargo, who was wrapped up in his arms and still held tightly against his bosom. That they'd landed without injury was a miracle, one that he'd pleaded for with the gods above.

As his lungs filled with the sweet, fresh air of liberation, he turned to look up from where he had jumped. Roaring flames now fanned the platform.

He may have been breathing clean air, but the stench of death was all around him.

Chapter 6

SARAH

'STEVE,' Sarah screamed.

Graceful landing or not, the fire was still trying to claim him and, as she ran into the front garden, dancing on the fringes of the furnace, the flames pouring from the downstairs windows were reaching with all their might to try to find them. With Phil by her side they took an arm each and, as they dragged Steve away together, Sarah grabbed the screaming baby from his chest. Those flames licked them as they ran across the scorched earth beneath their feet, and it was only when they had reached the relative sanctuary of the kerb on the opposite side of the road that the thermostat was turned down to something approaching bearable.

'Steve,' Sarah whispered, as her husband sank to the ground and pulled his knees close to his chest. His cough was hacking, as though every toxin that his lungs had been subjected to was trying to escape all in one go, and he didn't respond.

'Jesus,' he mumbled, on repeat. 'Jesus.' Cough. 'Christ.' Cough. His was a broken record, playing on repeat as Phil handed him a water bottle passed forward through the crowd.

Sarah cradled the baby in her arms, but there was no soothing the wriggling limbs, nor the screams that came from the depths. She wasn't his mummy. She turned to face the hellhole from whence Steve had barely escaped, and she gasped.

The house was gone.

The structure still remained. But, as a liveable house it was obliterated. As a home, it had been annihilated. The window that Steve had jumped from was still completely awash with flames while the roof was now aglow with leaping balls of fire and, all around her, burning ash floated on the gentle breeze.

In the distance, she could hear wails of a different kind filling the night air. Those sirens told her that the cavalry was on the way, and they were rhythmic . . . Melodic, even. The baby, though? His screams were brutal. They were laced with a terror that she understood but could do nothing to pacify. She shushed and shushed, but it would never be enough. Regardless, she continued anyway and, as she did, she couldn't help but notice the number of people all around them. Her senses may have been slow – she could still feel the shots working their way through her system, and they sat heavily in her stomach – but she had her wits about her, all right. How could she not?

It was like an audience, and those who weren't focussed on the fire had their attention dialled firmly in on her husband. Steve was bent over the kerb wheezing, with Phil and Emma by his side so he wasn't able to see the number of camera phones trained on him. Sarah could, though. She saw them. And she could hear the not-so-subtle beeps and clicks of photos being taken and videos being recorded.

Steve didn't know anything about social media, but Sarah did. She was one of the those who used every platform. It's what she did for a living, after all, and she knew all about the soaring highs and the cavernous lows that came with each social media platform. As she looked around, at fingers dancing on bright screens around them, she could sense tweets being sent and stories being uploaded.

And all the while, her husband was still doubled over, rendered breathless and gasping for air to soothe his burning lungs. It didn't matter that the baby was screaming, that those maternal instincts had reached across some kind of divide and taken the helpless bundle into her arms, she simply *had* to be in two places at once. She *had* to divide her attention. Her husband needed her, and that mattered.

The sirens? Louder, but still nowhere near close enough. The burning embers flushed a deathly silence across the street as the joists began to cave. It was one of those mid-terraced houses that had been thrown up in a hurry and, as Sarah stood over Steve and the flames roared with such vividity that they made her squint, the structure was tumbling down.

'Steve, love,' Sarah said, her voice cutting through the air to the tune of the cavalry that were getting nearer, getting closer.

She received a mumble and a wheeze in response.

'Steve,' she repeated, bending down to her knees and stroking his forearm, trying desperately to soothe the singed skin where his fine, blond hairs had been reduced to nothing. He flinched, and pulled his arm away. Too painful, presumably, too sensitive.

'The baby,' Steve rasped.

Right on cue, the baby screamed. Steve fumbled with his hand, grasping at Sarah. He pulled her closer and, as she took hold of his fingers, she felt tremors. An earthquake had exploded inside him, and the aftershocks were kicking in.

'It's all right, love,' she said, as he removed his hand from hers. Though he was still struggling to catch his breath, to suck down enough of the night air to cleanse his lungs, his fingers moved gently up and down the baby's back, just like she'd seen him do a million times and more with Gracie and Oscar.

Her soul was full, yet empty at the same time. She was torn between the pride that she felt in that very moment, and the grim spectre of death that hung all around them. Steve and the baby had been the only ones to make it out. As she looked up once more, it didn't take a fireman to know that no one else would.

The road, previously so dark, was as bright as dawn as the flames continued to wreak havoc. That glow was supplemented by a sea of blue lights as a fire engine finally pulled into the street. Sarah's mind wandered. Who else had been at home? A mum, perhaps. A dad, maybe. She whispered a quiet prayer that there were no other children and, though she wasn't religious by any stretch of the imagination, hoped with everything that she had that those pleas would be answered.

Two ambulances arrived in convoy and pulled up behind the fire engine. Paramedics got out and spoke with the lead firefighter at the scene.

'Injuries?' a firefighter shouted.

'Here,' Sarah called back.

Two of the paramedics hurried over. One of them took one look at the baby in Sarah's arms, smelt the smoke that was seeping from the cotton baby suit and winced before jogging towards his ambulance.

'Are you mum?' The paramedic shouted, as he climbed into the rear door.

'I . . . No,' Sarah replied.

'Tell me what happened,' the other paramedic said, his eyes planted firmly on Steve.

Steve coughed and wheezed. That alone told the paramedic what he needed to hear.

'Can you walk?' the paramedic asked.

Steve, still wheezing, reached for Sarah, who was only too happy to help him to his feet. They followed the paramedic to the second ambulance, as the first one performed an abrupt three-point turn and disappeared back down the road, its blue lights still illuminated. Steve stopped abruptly.

'The baby . . . ?' he said, his tone guttural.

'Your baby?' the paramedic asked.

'Not ours, he got 'im out of there,' Sarah whispered, as her shaky finger pointed to the mass of fire behind them.

The three of them looked beyond her extended digit, at the scene of destruction that was now a major operation for the fire crews in attendance. The paramedic paused before his widening eyes slowly fixed upon Steve.

'Jesus, mate,' he said quietly, gently patting Steve on the back. 'Good job.'

Inside the ambulance, and under the artificially bright lights it provided, Sarah sat to the side in a bubble of her own as Steve coughed and spluttered beneath the protection of an oxygen mask that sat affixed to his face.

'You did great, love,' she said, patting him on the leg. *Great?* It wasn't enough . . . Nowhere near . . . But she was struggling to find a summation of exactly what it was that her husband had just done that would do it justice.

He, on the other hand, just lay there. His hand was limp in hers, and his expression vacant. In between coughs, he stared into . . . Sarah didn't know what. Was he in shock, maybe? A brush with death knocking the sense out of him? Understandable, obviously, but even so . . . he was a *hero*.

Sarah watched as he reached for the elastic on the face mask, pulling it to one side.

'Was there anyone else?' he asked the paramedic. His voice was like Sarah had never heard before. A rattled whisper, gripped by something akin to naked fear.

'Not sure, mate,' the paramedic replied. He smiled. 'You're a hero, you know?'

'I'll say,' Sarah whispered.

'We'll get you in and checked over properly, all right?' the paramedic said, his initial assessment complete. 'Can't see anything to worry about, just keep breathing that oxygen.'

Steve nodded as the paramedic banged on the wall separating them from the driver, indicating for them to leave the scene.

'The kids!' Steve said, frantically pulling his mask from his face.

'It's all right,' Sarah replied. 'Phil and Emma are sorting them.'

The rear windows of the ambulance were heavily tinted but, as the driver performed a three-point turn, Sarah could see the fire still burning. Through the tints in the glass the embers looker duller, but she knew it was an illusion. Beyond the safety of the ambulance door, it was still raging.

As the ambulance drove away, Sarah looked at Steve. He shook his head gently as tears began to fall. She knew exactly why. Their bond was strong, their link almost telepathic. He knew, and so did she, that no one else was coming out of that building. Not alive, anyway. As one, they were weeping for an unknown person, grieving for someone they had never met and would never know.

'I should have got them . . .' Steve began to say, his words muffled from under the oxygen mask, but Sarah shushed him with a simple, raised hand.

'You did everything you could,' she said. A cliché? Sure. But it was the truth.

Her tears weren't just for an unknown soul, though. She had seen him disappear into the flames. Those moments had been pure purgatory, her anguish intensifying in tandem with the flames as they had grown. Her hope had almost gone when she had seen him at the upstairs window. She had thrown everything at it to try to break it, to try to release him from that hellhole. She'd even thrown her shoes, hoping against hope that the pointed heels might have penetrated the glass. They had simply bounced off, just as everything else seemed to. Again, she had felt her hope seeping away when someone had managed to strike the window at the right point, at the right angle, with the right strength and with the right missile. Him jumping from the fire into the safety of the night sky had provided her with the greatest relief of her life, bar none. Nothing even came close. And yet, how close he had been, to . . .

'You feeling okay?' the paramedic asked.

Steve nodded, but didn't speak. The rest of the journey passed in silence. The sirens weren't on; the blue lights weren't flashing. The driver was keeping to the speed limit. It gave Sarah the exact reassurances she needed about Steve's prognosis.

The ambulance pulled to a gentle stop at the rear entrance of the Accident and Emergency department at Beachbrook Hospital. Steve tried to stand up, but the paramedic shook his head and indicated for him to sit back down on the trolley.

'Got to roll you in,' he said.

Steve looked like he was going to argue, but a sharp look from Sarah soon made him sit back down.

'Let them do what they need to do,' she said, holding his hand. It was unnaturally warm but then, she supposed, it had been cooked in something akin to an oven.

Despite the late hour, or perhaps because of it, the department was alive with activity. House fires were a rarity, after all. There were doctors milling around who rarely set foot in A & E unless it was absolutely necessary. Consultants. On-call specialists who usually drove a desk in between meetings. Word had gone around that someone had jumped from a burning building with a baby in their arms, the stuff of legend that was surely embellished. Now, he was here in the flesh. Now, they could hear his story.

Sarah clung onto Steve's hand as the paramedics did their handover, though she couldn't take in everything they were saying.

House fire.

Inhalation.

Fell from first storey.

She wouldn't let go of his fingers, even as he was wheeled into a private side room.

'Excuse me, nurse,' Steve said quietly, pulling his face mask away as a blood pressure collar was placed on his arm, 'but you couldn't find out how the baby is who came in before me, could you?'

'It's true, is it?' the nurse replied, smiling.

'What's that?' Steve asked, confused.

'You pulled a baby from a burning house?'

'I . . . Errrm . . . I guess so.'

Sarah stroked his cheeks as they flushed red.

The nurse paused, then let the cuff rest on Steve's arm. She leaned in and gave him a hug.

'You, sir, are a hero,' she said.

Sarah looked at Steve, and he at her. She wore a contorted smile, one that she knew he was unable to translate. It was part pride, part anguish, and total relief.

'The baby, he's doing fine,' the nurse added.

'Do you know . . . anything else?' Steve asked.

'I'm afraid I don't,' the nurse replied, 'but they might.'

Sarah heard the police officer's radio before he entered the room. It was blaring with indecipherable chaos, presumably from the scene of the fire. Voices were laced with urgency but, it seemed, everyone was talking over everyone else. She tried but failed to tune her ears in to the noise, to pick out key words, but she was unable. In any case, as the police officer walked into the room, he turned the volume down to barely above a whisper.

'I'm sorry, but I don't even know your name,' the police officer said as he approached Steve's bed.

'Steve,' Sarah replied, 'Steve Minchin.'

The police officer looked at her and smiled, before turning back to Steve.

'Sounds like you've done something pretty special tonight, Steve,' the police officer said.

Sarah nodded, wholly in agreement.

'Was there anyone else in there?' Steve asked.

The police officer held his hands up. 'We don't know yet,' he replied, 'we just don't know. It's . . .'

'A hellhole,' Steve muttered.

'Pretty much,' the police officer replied.

They sat in grim silence with only the beeping hospital monitors and the garbled, muted transmissions on the police officer's radio penetrating the bubble of melancholy that fell upon them.

Sarah had seen it. Her husband had barely got out alive. For anyone else in there? No chance. None, whatsoever. Those conflicting feelings intensified: pride, at what he'd done; relief, that he'd emerged unscathed.

And utter desolation at what, she was sure, was yet to be confirmed.

Chapter 7

DS SUE WILLMOTT

Her vibrating phone lit up DS Willmott's bedroom like a lighthouse in the gloom but, before she'd even roused herself sufficiently to answer it, the faintest whiff of smoke that had crept into her bedroom through her ever-open window told her what the call-out was going to be.

'DS Willmott,' she said, rubbing the sleep from her eyes as she held the phone to her ear. 'Where am I going?'

'It's a bad one, skip,' DC Vinny Robson replied. That one phrase got her full and undivided attention. A bad one. It sounded churlish to say that she lived and breathed for the bad ones. It was in the bad, though, that she could help the most. That's what kept her on her toes, what made the constant sleepless nights worthwhile. It's what made her the first through the office doors and, with only the rarest of exceptions, the last to leave. And it's that which focussed her mind as Vinny's voice filled her ear.

Lottie slept through it. She always did. DS Willmott's mum, though? She was awake, as usual.

'All right, Sue?' her mum said, as she crept down the stairs. DS Willmott looked up and forced a smile.

'House fire,' she whispered, 'persons reported.'

'Oh God,' her mum said.

DS Willmott nodded. Oh God, indeed.

'All right to get Lottie sorted?' DS Willmott asked.

'Go, on,' her mum replied, nodding, 'scram.'

And scram, she did. As she walked from the front door, the whiff of smoke that she had picked up in traces when she'd woken had grown stronger. It wasn't overpowering, more a perfume on the air but, still, where there was smoke, there was fire and – at its source – something terrible had happened.

She had the address and knew the area. A six-minute drive from her house but, then, in small communities such as theirs, everything seemed to be on the doorstep. As she drove from her road, where the houses were smart semis with driveways, the houses became tighter as she navigated away from the beach and further inland. As she did, she pulled the car window down and let the night air in. It wasn't the nip in the breeze that she was looking for. She didn't need waking up. Instead, it was the wafts of invisible smoke that she was seeking. It was the scent of the night, and she needed it to sharpen up her senses for what was to follow.

Those neat semis transformed into rows of tight terraces as the smoke grew stronger. They were the first rung on the ladder for many, the first dip of a collective toe into house ownership. In the distance, she could see the lights of the police cars and fire engines and whoever else had turned out. It wasn't just one set, either. The sky above them was a murky haze, almost like mushroom clouds that were lit with a baby blue glow. She took a deep breath and coughed. That smoke? Those invisible vapours? They were rancid, and she closed her window.

She knew not to park anywhere near the scene. What little evidence would be left was chief in her mind, of course, but she knew that the closer she left her car the more chance there was of it being blocked in by any number of personnel who were yet to arrive. Instead, she rolled to a gentle stop in a street several roads away, and climbed from her car. It may have been called a day book that she carried in her hand, but it seemed that it saw most service when the hour was late and the moon was high. As she looked up now, though, that moon wasn't visible, and it wasn't because of any rain clouds in the sky.

She was a detective's detective. One of those who looked, who listened, who took it all in before acting. As she stood at the end of the road, peering around the corner and watching as the tarmac and pavements bustled with onlookers all glowing under a canopy of blue lights, phone screens and a mid-terraced house that was being systematically gutted by the flames that were still billowing from it, she took a deep breath.

And coughed.

With her day book tucked under her arm, she walked forwards, nodding at the uniformed bobbies that she recognised and beating a path that didn't get in the way of the firefighters who rushed around with an urgency that she only ever saw at scenes such as the one that presented itself to her.

'What have we got?' she asked, as she sidled in next to Vinny. He was standing on the opposite side of the road, next to a couple who were looking on with horror in their eyes.

'I didn't catch your names,' Vinny said, looking at the couple.

'Emma,' the lady said.

'Phil,' the man followed up.

'A baby's come out,' Vinny said, looking down at his own day book, 'rescued by . . .'

DS Willmott looked at him, at his squinting eyes, and she cast hers down to his day book. It was pure scribbles. He'd never had the best handwriting, let alone in the middle of the night and fuelled by the adrenaline of an incident in progress.

'Steve,' Phil said, 'Steve Minchin.'

'Parents?' DS Willmott asked.

The silence that greeted her question told her all she needed to know. She turned and looked at the building, at the flames, at the firefighters doing their damnedest to beat them back. With every hose that they trained on the house, though, it just seemed like they were pouring petrol onto the inferno.

'Baby gone?' DS Willmott asked.

'Gone?' Emma whispered.

'To hospital,' DS Willmott said, very quickly. 'Gone' could be interpreted in too many ways.

'Yeah,' Vinny replied. He was quiet. Respectful. And that's what DS Willmott loved about him the most. He had the right tone, at the right time, and the right attitude to boot. 'There's a video,' he said.

DS Willmott's ears prickled. A video? Of what?

'Over here,' Vinny called, beckoning one of the many onlookers towards them. He pointed at the phone in their hand and, with the merest flick of a finger, DS Willmott was watching in 6.7-inch form what everyone there had witnessed in real life, oh so recently.

A burning building.

Flames, licking a smashed upstairs window.

And a man, emerging from the fire, baby in arms, and plummeting into the night sky.

'My God,' DS Willmott mumbled.

Vinny nodded.

'Where is he?' she asked.

'Hospital,' Vinny replied.

She looked at the fire again, at the window from where he had jumped. Flames still leapt out, but beyond them it was black, the kind of darkness that meant only one thing.

Death had come knocking, and it had found its way inside.

Chapter 8

STEVE

Tests, tests and more tests. Sats. Blood pressure. ECGs. Bloods. Chest X-rays. All of them, and even more. The police officer sat in the corner, his face perfectly still, and put in an earpiece as he listened to all of the radio transmissions. Steve couldn't tell if the copper was holding a pair of bullets or two-seven off suit – there was no read and no tell. Whatever had happened, and whatever updates were coming through, one thing was clear – the copper had been told to say nothing.

The cough lingered, but the intensity diminished. After a few hours it was no longer hacking, more a tickle in the throat. He couldn't argue with the VIP treatment he was being afforded – it was a revolving door of consultants, all eager to lend their expertise no matter how irrelevant to his ailments their specialism was.

Yet, despite all the fanfare, all the proverbial bunting and all the nods of reverence that came his way, there was one inescapable fact that was running across his mind on repeat. Two words, in fact.

If only.

If only he had gone into the other room at the top of the stairs first.

If only he had taken just a few seconds to think, to rationalise, to strategise.

And so it went, on and on, his brain taking him to places he simply didn't want to go, an unwilling passenger chasing tails and following circles.

'Mr Minchin?'

He looked up and knew that they were coppers approaching him. The woman had an aura, the kind of no-nonsense impression that simply clung to whatever space it was she was inhabiting. Yet her voice . . . It was smooth. Laced with concern, with a kindness ringing through it.

'Steve?'

'Yeah,' he replied, with a cough. The single, solitary word had prickled his throat as it'd come out of his mouth.

'I'm DS Willmott,' she said, 'this is DC Robson. How are you doing?'

'Was there anyone else in there?' he replied. There'd be plenty of time for niceties, he was sure. Right now, he had to know.

DS Willmott smiled gently, but it was one that conveyed only sadness. Steve knew what was coming. So, it seemed, did Sarah, as her fingernails dug into the skin on the back of his hand.

'There was,' DS Willmott said. God, her voice was gentle. 'The baby's parents. They . . .' Her words trailed away and, as Steve stared into her eyes, he could've sworn that the tears that had formed in his were reflected in hers.

'The parents died,' DC Robson said, quietly finishing her sentence for her. 'They were in bed.'

Steve shuddered, rocking the hospital bed that he lay on so much that the joints creaked.

'You couldn't have done anything for them,' DC Robson said.

Cliché bullshit.

If only.

If only.

IF ONLY.

Sarah's whimpers didn't even register in his ears. Nor, for that matter, did any of the follow-up conversation with DS Willmott and DC Robson, nor with any of the medical staff. He'd been in there. He'd gone into the fire and, though he'd come out with one, he'd left two behind. It was an inescapable fact, one that he couldn't get away from, no matter how many more of those nods of appreciation came his way.

It was almost light by the time they left the hospital. No injuries. Unbelievable, really, the doctors had told Steve. It had washed over him as he lay there, wondering. Pondering. Contemplating. Why hadn't he just gone through that open door first? Why hadn't he just checked it out? Why had he been so hellbent on getting in the room with the closed door without taking just half a second to check out the other room first. Why? Why? Why?

As the police car made its way slowly towards Sarah and Steve's road, his senses awakened as the stale stench of smoke in the air grew stronger. Steve shuddered once more. They lived nearby, where the rows of terraces morphed into an area of a little more affluence, yet he simply hadn't appreciated that there would be such a stark reminder of what had happened to confront him so soon after. The smell of smoke had always been something he'd liked. A good bonfire. A decent burn-up. Now, it just provoked pure horror.

They arrived home and, as they got out of the police car,

Steve looked at his vehicle. There was a very thin layer of something coating it and, as he wiped his finger over the bonnet, a film of dust and ash filled the ridges on his skin. There it was, physical evidence of something life-changing. Something orphan-creating. Deep within, it ate away at him.

Jack. That was the baby's name, he'd learned. Nine months old. And the parents? Those who'd died? Adam and Louise. They were just in their early twenties. Kids themselves.

Their whole lives had been in front of them, theirs a blank canvas to create the most beautiful of lives with their baby, and it had all been taken away from them. A normal family. A normal life. A normal house, on a normal street, on a normal Friday night. Such a waste. Such total, utter devastation.

'What will happen to the baby?' Steve asked, as the police officer walked with them up the driveway.

'Hospital for a bit, just to check him over, then it'll be down to the local authority,' the police officer replied. 'Hopefully there's some family about.' Steve closed his eyes, grimaced, and nodded with forlorn sorrow. 'You take good care, Steve,' the police officer added. 'I mean it, mate. You did good last night.'

Steve opened his eyes. That poor, poor baby. He could feel his eyes welling up again. What would become of little Jack, he wondered? He knew only too well how the social care system worked. He'd been there. He'd lived it. He winced as he pushed those old, miserable memories to one side, and silently prayed that there was a family out there to care for Jack. He felt an attachment to him, a bond so deep but one he would never be able to adequately explain.

He shook his head and was consumed by melancholy as Sarah guided him through the front door. It was just after 06.30 and, after the chaos and turmoil of the hours prior, the total silence when the door closed seemed deafening.

Steve's eyes felt heavy. He hadn't slept, of course, and the effects of the alcohol from the previous night had taken hold. His actions may have sobered him up, but they didn't take away the physical symptoms. The headache, the dry mouth, the unquenchable thirst. He must've drunk three pints of water while he was at hospital, but still he needed more.

He walked into the front room and found Phil lying on the sofa, snoring.

'Phil,' he said quietly, but it wasn't enough to rouse him from his slumber.

'Phil,' he repeated, louder.

'Gracie?' Phil said, coming to with a start. 'Oh, Steve, all right, mate?' he said, rubbing his eyes and trying to clear away the mist of alcohol-disturbed sleep.

'Where's Emma?' Steve asked.

'She's been with Oscar since we got here,' Phil replied, sitting up before getting to his feet. 'Little man woke up when we knocked on the door.'

'Gracie slept through?' Steve asked.

'Yeah, good as gold, mate, not a peep,' Phil replied.

The two men stood opposite each other, only feet apart. They looked at each other, as the musty smell of smoke from their clothes began to bleed into the air around them. As Steve stepped forward and buried his head into Phil's shoulder, that smell only intensified.

'Baby's parents died, mate,' Steve said, his voice barely audible and quivering with emotion.

'No way,' Phil mouthed.

It was a few rare seconds of affection as Steve's head rested on Phil's shoulder, and a soft sob crept from his lips.

Friends for years.

Brothers in every way but blood.

Emma came into the room and stood by Sarah's side.

Their hands linked as all four adults in the room were unified in mourning, for two young parents who they'd never met before.

Saturday mornings at any point in the working season always involved an early start. Steve would be up, dressed and out of the door before the kids had even woken up. He liked to get to the cash and carry as soon as it opened so that he could stock up for the weekend. On that particular Saturday, however, work didn't even enter his mind. How the hell could it, after what had happened? For the first time in many years, Coffee and Cream would remain shuttered during the working season. There were things he had to do, chief among them attending the police station to see DS Willmott and give a statement.

Sarah made a pot of tea and passed a packet of paracetamol around as they sat on the sofas in the lounge. Almost by habit, Phil picked up the remote control and flicked the television on.

'What the . . .' Emma said, staring at the screen, wide-mouthed.

A large 'LIVE' logo was emblazoned on the top left-hand corner of the screen and a news reporter was standing outside the smoking shell of a house. All of the adults immediately recognised the scene.

'Details are still sketchy, and the authorities say they have launched an investigation, but we have extraordinary video footage that has been passed to us of the fire at the height of its intensity last night,' the reporter said, staring directly at the camera and speaking, Steve felt, exclusively to him.

The live broadcast gave way to a clip that had been recorded the previous night. No longer was such bystander footage grainy and unclear. Mobile phones had evolved to such an extent that everyone in the land was now a budding film producer and director. What they were watching had been captured in stunning clarity.

It felt like an out-of-body experience. Steve sat with his mouth open, not knowing what to feel. His emotional state was already frayed to the limit, and this was exacerbating it.

It looked like something out of a Hollywood film as he ran and jumped from the window, babe in arms. The landing wasn't captured, but the collective gasp from the assembled crowd was. Bleeped swearing was audible from the person videoing the action. As if for extra flourish, a flame had shot across the window just after Steve had jumped. If it had been a work of fiction, it would have been criticised for being overly dramatic.

The reporter appeared on screen again, but now with a banner at the bottom of the screen in bold red, with words in capital letters:

'LOCAL HERO RESCUES BABY FROM DEADLY BLAZE'.

The reporter appeared momentarily speechless.

'Wow,' she said before pausing. 'Well, I'm not sure I can believe what I've just seen, but that seems to show the moment when a local man rescued a baby from this fire, which appears to have tragically taken the lives of two adults. Amazing. Simply amazing. Back to you in the studio.'

The news station cut back to a studio shot, where two presenters sat with their mouths wide open.

Steve got up and walked over to Phil, taking the remote control from him, and turning the television off.

He felt anything but the hero that he was being described as. It was a tragedy. A total, gut-kicking tragedy. People had died, and he might've been able to stop it.

'Steve, love,' Sarah said.

'I need to lie down,' he said, walking out of the room and

slowly ascending the stairs. Each step he took was a reminder of the thirteen he had navigated in the fire. He remembered it with precision. The handbag. The clothes. The normality of it, and how it had all burned around him.

Gracie's door was open. Poor little lamb, he thought. It was always closed. She must've woken up in the night. Not surprising, really. Kids always knew when something was wrong. He poked his head around the door. She was curled up on her double bed, facing away from him. He was just about to close the door when she turned her head to look at him. It seemed like she had been crying.

'Daddy?' she said.

'Daddy's here, princess,' Steve replied, walking into the room and sitting on the bed.

Gracie cuddled into him.

'You weren't here, Daddy,' she said quietly.

'Sorry, darling,' Steve said, kissing her on the forehead and running his hands through her beautiful blonde hair. 'I'm here now. Want me to lie with you?'

Gracie nodded vigorously.

'You stink like a bonfire?' she said.

'Let me get changed and I'll be back, okay?' Steve said gently.

'Can I come with you?' Gracie asked.

'Oh, darling,' Steve said, 'of course you can.'

He climbed out of bed and Gracie followed him closely. He undressed and tossed his clothes to one side. Only good for the bin, he thought. He put on some pyjamas and brushed his teeth. He was going to have a shower, but Gracie needed him more.

'Come on, princess,' he said, leading her back to her bedroom.

She cuddled into his shoulder as they lay on the bed.

'You'll always be my baby, you know?' Steve said. 'I won't leave you again if it makes you sad, all right?'

Gracie nodded.

Steve closed his eyes.

'PLEASE, NO!'

The past. It was still there. His eyes opened wide, as they always did. Through thick and thin, it would still haunt him.

'Not now,' he said quietly.

He put a pillow over his head and, for the first time in forever, drifted into a deep, dreamless sleep.

Chapter 9

SARAH

And while Steve was upstairs, Sarah sat in the lounge. Emma and Phil had gone and, apart from Oscar's iPad churning out the jingle of whatever game it was he was playing, there was silence. She sat back on the sofa as the adrenaline in her system slowly drifted away, leaving the after-effects of all those drinks from the evening before, coupled with an entire night where sleep had been the last thing on her mind.

Her eyes were heavy, but she didn't shut them. Instead, she looked all around her, taking in the normality in which they resided. Oscar, sitting on the sofa, focussing on the screen in front of him. The four walls, which afforded them security. Protection. Warmth. Comfort. Framed photos, little snapshots of life through the years. Aesthetics. Fake flowers, in vases. A canvas on the wall. A couple of lamps. Matching oak furniture. It was all so ordinary, so average.

And yet, so wonderful.

Gracie's gentle footsteps on the stairs announced her arrival before she wandered into the room and, as she closed the gap towards Sarah, Mum held her arms wide open. Gracie fell into them but recoiled.

'Why do you smell of bonfires too?' she asked.

Sarah's smile wasn't real, but it was enough to convince her daughter.

'Long story, kiddo,' she said. 'Let me go and have a wash and we'll do some baking. Deal?'

'Deal,' Gracie replied.

Sarah snuck up the stairs as Steve's snores drifted on the air around her. At least he was sleeping. She walked into the bedroom on tiptoes, avoiding that one floorboard that always creaked, and looked at him. From those giddy and carefree days of the past, through everything and beyond, never before had she been so enamoured with him.

The shower may not have taken the smell from the inside of her nose, nor the prickling feeling from her throat, but it did the job so far as Gracie was concerned and, as mother and daughter sifted flour and weighed butter, it was another slice of normal life that Sarah revelled in. After a night so extraordinary, so tragic, it was perfection.

The morning drifted past and the smell of cookies filled the house. As the clock ticked over into the afternoon, there was still no sign of her husband emerging. He'd want to be woken, she was sure. Besides, she'd seen what was going on in the world of social media. Insta? TikTok? Facebook? It was everywhere.

'Steve?'

'Mmmm.'

'Steve, love.'

He sat up, and Sarah saw the disorientation writ all over his face. It was the juxtaposition, she supposed, between a room that was bright and a mind that told him it was the middle of the night. He looked around, his hands grasping at the sheets, duvet and pillows that were surrounding him.

'It's all right,' she said, walking towards him with a mug of coffee in her hand.

'What time is it?' he asked, rubbing his eyes.

'Just gone midday,' Sarah replied, 'didn't think you'd want to sleep all day.'

'No, thanks,' Steve said.

'I've got to show you something, love,' Sarah said. Her voice was gentle. Soothing.

She gave Steve her phone. He squinted at it, as the video that had been on the news earlier in the day played on repeat.

'It's everywhere,' Sarah said.

Social media wasn't for Steve. He'd told Sarah that countless times before, when she'd told him about this happening on Facebook, or that happening on Instagram. He'd always joked that he lived in a time gone by, where phones were meant to be used for making phone calls.

'What do you mean?' he asked.

'Facebook, Instagram, even TikTok,' Sarah said quietly. 'It's gone viral, love.' Social media was her world. It's what she did. In any other circumstance, in any other situation, the professional in her would have seen it as a marketing dream. This, though? It was as far removed in her mind from being something to exploit as was possible.

Steve sat in silence. Viral. It normally had negative connotations. Something done for likes, attention or notoriety. Seldom did something take off like that, something positive, something . . . heroic. She couldn't help being impossibly proud of him, but the limelight? That wasn't for him.

'Have they named . . . Do they know it's me?' His voice shook, and he faltered as he asked.

'I've not seen your name anywhere but I honestly don't know,' Sarah replied.

Downstairs, the front doorbell rang. Sarah looked at Steve, and his face screwed up in a tight grimace.

'You're a hero, love,' Sarah said. There was an edge to

her voice, a firmness that suggested her diktat wasn't up for discussion or negotiation. 'I'll get it.'

She walked out of the room, leaving Steve's coffee on the bedside table, and went down the stairs. The doorbell rang once more, just as she reached the front door and, as she pulled it open, kindly smiles on two faces greeted her. Between her and the two detectives on her doorstep, there had barely been an hour's sleep in the preceding twenty-four hours. Still, DS Willmott and DC Robson looked as fresh as daisies, while Sarah felt hung over, bedraggled and as though she'd been hit by a bus.

'Sarah, isn't it?' DS Willmott asked.

'It is,' Sarah replied.

She stood and looked at them both, as her brain fought to keep up with her body.

'Can we come in?' DS Willmott asked.

'Sorry, of course,' Sarah replied, taking a quick step back and beckoning them both inside.

They walked into the lounge, where Gracie and Oscar were sitting playing on their iPads. For once, Sarah was glad for their little minds to be distracted from everything that had happened and, in all likelihood, was about to happen.

'Steve about?' DS Willmott asked, as she and DC Robson hovered near the sofa.

'I've just woken him,' Sarah replied. 'Please, sit down,' she said, throwing a hand towards the cushions that were scattered atop the throw rugs that protected the fabric from whatever milk and food the kids might spill over it.

DS Willmott smiled as she perched on the edge of the sofa, closely followed by DC Robson as he sat next to her.

'Won't be a sec,' Sarah said, as she walked into the hallway. 'Steve, you need to come down,' she called up the stairs.

She waited, but there was no movement. Just silence.

'Steve, love, you coming down?' Sarah called again, louder this time.

Movement, this time. The creaking floorboards. Slow, thudding footsteps. The groaning hinges, as the bedroom door opened slowly. The carpet on the landing dulled his steps, but they were so much heavier than she'd heard before.

'Who is it?' he asked, as he trudged down the stairs.

'Police,' Sarah replied.

Steve sighed, and followed as Sarah led him into the lounge.

'Daddy!' Oscar shouted, running up to him and cuddling his leg.

Gracie's eyes remained fixed on her iPad, apparently oblivious to anything going on around her.

'Up to your rooms, kiddos,' Sarah said. 'Mummy and Daddy just need to speak to the nice lady.'

Gracie ran to Steve and grabbed hold of his other leg.

'She's not taking us away, is she?' she whispered, only just loud enough for Sarah to be able to hear.

'Of course not, sweetheart,' Steve said. His smile was a forced one that Sarah rarely saw but recognised. He ruffled Gracie's hair. 'Go on, go and play and I'll come up in a little bit, okay?'

Gracie didn't look at DS Willmott as she grabbed hold of Oscar's hand and ran out of the room. Sarah pushed the door to as the sound of young footsteps running up the stairs thumped in the background.

DS Willmott and DC Robson stood up, and each of them walked towards Steve, each of them shaking his hand with such a flourish that it oozed respect. Sarah breathed deeply. With each and every show of admiration that came her husband's way, her pride swelled. Steve, for his part, appeared unmoved and said nothing.

'Please, sit down,' DS Willmott said. It was weird, Sarah thought. Surely she should be the one playing host in her own home, not a police officer who had been there for only a matter of minutes. Regardless, she obliged, sitting next to Steve and instinctively reaching for his hand.

'I just wanted to come to give you an update,' DS Willmott said, as she resumed her seat on the edge of the sofa opposite Sarah and Steve, 'and to give you the tiniest bit of good news amidst all the bad. Little Jack, the baby you . . .'

Steve shifted uncomfortably.

'. . . rescued,' DS Willmott continued, 'we've found his grandparents. Lovely couple. And while they're . . .' Sarah looked at DS Willmott closely as, once again, the detective's eyes appeared to fill. It was obvious that she was choosing her words carefully, selecting the right ones with precision. 'While they're bereft . . . with everything that's happened,' DS Willmott said, 'their grief is . . . tempered . . . by having little Jack with them. Safe. Alive.'

DS Willmott looked directly at Steve, and his hand squeezed Sarah's until she winced. Whatever. No amount of squeezing could take away from her the resounding and overwhelming jolt of relief that the baby had family, had grandparents, had someone who could love him, dote on him, give him an upbringing in the face of what had gone before. THAT meant everything.

'And, while it's obviously incredibly sad, it could have been even worse,' she added. 'What you did . . . Well, I have no words.'

'I'll second that,' Sarah said.

'Have you seen the news?' DS Willmott asked softly. She shifted in her seat but not uncomfortably. Sarah guessed that this wasn't her first rodeo. DS Willmott was sitting with her legs uncrossed, her arms wide and an enduring, if sad, smile on her face. As posture went, it was as open as she could possibly be.

'Yeah,' Steve said, nodding.

'Has anyone tried to speak to you yet?' DS Willmott asked.

'No,' Steve replied.

'We can help with that if you like,' DS Willmott said. 'Sometimes it's better to get ahead of the game. I can imagine they'll be trying to find you as we speak.'

Steve's face contorted, part anguish, part anxiety.

'Sorry, Steve,' DS Willmott said, 'I'm not trying to worry you. Trust me, you've got absolutely nothing to worry about. I just want to be open with you. That's why it might be worth putting a statement out through us, so that it's manageable.'

'Okay,' Steve said.

'So . . . would you like me to put something together and get back to you?' DS Willmott asked.

'That'd be great, thank you,' Sarah said.

'Have you spoken to the grandparents?' Steve asked. His voice was barely above a whisper. Sarah sucked down a lungful of air. It hurt every inch of her to hear such pain in Steve's voice.

'Yeah,' DS Willmott replied.

'Can you . . . Please can you tell them I'm sorry?' Steve asked. His words were so faint they were barely audible.

'You're sorry?' DS Willmott replied. Her eyes narrowed, as confusion spread across her face. 'Sorry for what?'

'Sorry I didn't get them out,' Steve replied. Though his voice was louder, it was laced with no less agony than it had been before.

Sarah grasped at his fingers as he pulled his hand away from hers, and she wasn't sure if her wet palm was a result of his sweat or hers. Steve got up and walked out of the room before DS Willmott could reply and, though Sarah got up to go after him, she responded to DS Willmott's calming hand that urged her to remain where she was.

'Sometimes, people just need a minute,' DS Willmott said.

'I hear you,' Sarah replied kindly, grateful for DS Willmott's consideration of Steve's feelings, 'but sometimes they just need their wife.'

'That's understandable,' DC Robson said. 'I'm the family liaison officer for the grandparents,' he continued, 'and you can rest assured that I'll be helping out wherever I can with baby Jack and his needs.' He looked at Sarah and, as if to emphasise his point, repeated the crucial part. 'Wherever I can.' His voice dripped with an empathy that, Sarah could only assume, came from years of having dealt with all kinds of bereavement. His words were warm, yet laced with reason. In an instant, she was at ease.

'Thanks,' Sarah said and, though her voice was hollow, her gratitude was pure. She hovered above the sofa, keen to get to Steve and trying desperately to transmit that the conversation was over without being rude.

'We'll be getting off,' DC Robson said, taking to his feet at the exact same time as DS Willmott, as if their thoughts and processes were aligned.

'Please do get in touch if you need either of us,' DS Willmott said, as both detectives reached into the inner pockets of their jackets and produced almost identical business cards, 'any time.'

Sarah took the cards and placed them on the table in front of them.

'Thank you,' she said, as she ushered the detectives from the front room with as much respect and deference to their good intentions as she could muster. Farewells done and formalities complete, she closed the front door, turned around and walked into the kitchen. No Steve. She walked into the dining room. No Steve.

She crept up the stairs, finding him on the landing. He must've ghosted up there, for his footsteps had been silent. He was sitting, with his back to the banister, his knees tight to his chest and rocking ever so slightly backwards and forwards. In the background, Gracie and Oscar were making all the noises that playing children made, behind the closed door to his bedroom and, as Sarah sat down next to Steve, she got it. She understood. She knew why tears were leaking from his eyes, what was silently eating away at him as Oscar's innocent giggles were met with Gracie's 'big sister' orders and instructions.

It was the privilege of being there, of basking in exactly what it was that being a parent meant. Those poor, lost souls never got to hear their little boy speak, never got to see him walk, would not see him grow and develop into the child that they no doubt had great plans for. Theirs had been two lives snuffed out before they'd even had a chance at life, at family.

Sarah grabbed at his hand once more and stroked his palm as his tears continued to roll down his cheeks. She knew. She really, really knew, that no matter how many times anyone praised him for his actions, he would never feel worthy of it. He breathed deeply, his inhalation mired with the judders that sobs inevitably provoked, as he opened his mouth to speak.

'All right?' he asked.

'She said she'd take your statement another day,' Sarah replied.

Steve nodded.

'And she's going to email us in an hour with a press release,' Sarah added.

Steve nodded and, as Sarah found herself snuggling into his armpit, not even the whiff of the smoke from the night before could put her off. His quivers were expected, in her eyes at least. The tremors in his bones, too.

What was going through his mind, though? She couldn't even begin to imagine.

Chapter 10

DS SUE WILLMOTT

PRESS RELEASE

Contact:
DS Willmott
Beachbrook Police Station

The circumstances surrounding the tragic death of two adults following a fire in Haybrook Road, Beachbrook, are being investigated by detectives from Beachbrook Police Station in conjunction with Fire Investigation Teams from the Fire Service.

I would encourage anyone with information, or who may have witnessed the fire, to please make themselves known to police by calling 111 or, anonymously, Crimestoppers on 0800 555 111.

I would urge the public not to share photos or videos from the scene.

In response to intense speculation by the press and members of the local community in relation to a video that has been widely shared on social media, I can confirm that we have identified and spoken with a witness who will remain anonymous at this stage.

ENDS

She read it once, twice and three times, before calling Vinny into her office. He entered, bearing two mugs of double-strength coffee.

'Reads okay to me,' he said.

DS Willmott pursed her lips. No matter how many times she put together a press release, nor how many times she dealt with the aftermath of something so tragic, it never failed to impress upon her the fragility of life. And . . . it never got any easier. From the first time, she'd encountered death on the job, all those years prior, through unimaginable tragedies along the way, each one of them took a toll in their own way. The mounting hits across the years had only stiffened her resolve to be the best damned detective that she could.

It wasn't so much the facts of the case that hit home. A fatal fire, sure. It was more the human aspect that gnawed away at her, the recognition that what had happened could have befallen anyone else. *But for the grace of God, there go I,* went the saying, and she could only draw comparisons with her own life. What if . . . it had happened to her? She was already a single parent. What if Lottie was orphaned? It was those thoughts that drove her forwards.

Not more than twelve hours before, Adam and Louise had probably tucked baby Jack in to his cot, read him a story, fed him, sung to him, watched him as he drifted off to sleep. It'd probably been like any other night, ones that DS Willmott remembered well herself. She may have been a much older mum than Louise, but maternal instincts didn't diminish as the years passed by. Louise would have gone to bed, probably listening to the soft purrs of Jack's contented slumber as she drifted away herself. What came next? Unmitigated, horrific tragedy.

'Anything from the scene?' Vinny asked.

DS Willmott shook her head. One thing she'd learned, long ago when she'd investigated her first house fire, was to leave the professionals to do their job. This was one for the crime scene investigators and the fire investigators to piece together. If they said there was more to it than what appeared to be a tragic accident, then she'd be the first to get her teeth into it.

She'd stood by earlier in the day as the fire had been extinguished and the dampening down had begun. No sooner had the last flame been put out, than the investigation had begun in earnest. She'd called in CSIs from wherever they were, even if it meant a cancelled rest day. She'd deployed Vinny as a FLO where her peers would perhaps not have done. Hell, she'd even authorised the uniform crews to work into a rest day to ensure that her scene was preserved to the fullest. For her, life mattered most and, when it was snuffed out in the blink of an eye, the circumstances surrounding it almost didn't matter.

'They'll be trying to find the seat of the fire,' DS Willmott said. 'God knows how they do it.'

'Second that,' Vinny sighed, by way of reply.

DS Willmott closed her eyes. She cared too much, and she knew it. It was a part of her DNA, a piece of her internal fabric.

'Any steer?' Vinny asked.

'Not yet,' she replied, opening her eyes and rubbing them with the heels of her palms. She held her mug to her mouth, and let it linger beneath her lips as she inhaled the fresh wafts of coffee. The caffeine may have been in the liquid, but the vapours certainly brought a bump of their own to her system.

She reached for her computer and flicked onto the internet tab that had been sitting idle in the background. It was X, or Twitter, or whatever it was called, that had kicked off the most and, as she and Vinny watched in real time, the comments, likes and retweets were going off the charts. Steve's video hadn't just gone viral; it was an epidemic sweeping across social media. There was no doubt in her mind that the other platforms would have been responding similarly.

'What do you make of him?' Vinny asked, as if reading her mind.

'Hero,' DS Willmott replied, the word leaving her mouth before Vinny had a chance to finish his question.

Of that, she was in no doubt. It was the thing of movies, to run into a burning building, to rush up a flame-licked staircase, to kick open the door to a baby's bedroom, to hold them to your chest as you leapt from the inferno and into the night air beyond. That it had all been captured on phones, documentary evidence for evermore, only added to the legend that was being created online, across the whole country.

The video played on loop, before it auto-scrolled to the next. It was a different user sharing it, but the exact same content.

'It could have been another dead kid,' Vinny mumbled, to himself as much as DS Willmott.

'Should've been,' she whispered, as Steve's leap from the window played again, and again.

She closed her eyes. It was always the children that got to her the most. Always had been. Always would be. Adam and Louise were barely adults themselves, but there had been so many others who lurked in the memories of her past. Each of them had their own place in her mind, in her heart, but a few were seared in her subconscious, so much that they were fundamental to who she was and why she did what she did. There was Joe, the boy from the sea. Sweet, innocent Joe. She'd solved that one, all right.

And then there was Charlotte, the girl from all those years before, way back when DS Willmott had been a green-eyed beat cop with only a year of uniform service under her belt.

Charlotte.

Sweet, innocent Charlotte.

The girl who went out one afternoon all those years before, but had been returned to her parents via the morgue.

Charlotte. A girl she'd never met to say hello to, but knew so well.

A girl with whom she shared a connection so deep, she'd furtively named her own daughter after her. But it was DS Willmott's own silent tribute to a child who was forever stuck in time as a thirteen-year-old victim.

Chapter 11

KEVIN

There is no word for a bereaved parent. No title afforded to them, no moniker. When a parent dies, a child is an orphan. When a spouse dies, the living half is a widower. A parent bereaved, though? A parent left behind, one who has buried their child? No word would ever be enough, so none apparently exist.

Kevin only stayed close to be near her. His only link to Beachbrook was now one that resided in the past, decades beyond. His wife had left in the aftermath, unable to cope with what had happened so close to their front door, making tracks up north and escaping the hell that confronted her whenever she walked outside. Him, though? He may have lost his marriage, but it was a sacrifice he'd been willing to make. There was no way he'd ever leave, no way he'd ever be apart from whatever memories of his baby girl still remained.

His house was the one all the neighbours talked about. An inheritance, and one that was prime real estate on the clifftops of Beachbrook. To those who lived near him, though, the aesthetic may have been a stain on their community, but they all understood. They all got it. Not one person ever complained about the overgrown bushes, the tall grass, the rats that would sometimes come with the territory. Hell, on occasion they'd even give the outside a once-over, as much to maintain their own house prices as anything else.

His routine was set in stone, and he rarely deviated from it.

Wake up, whenever his brain allowed. When your life is governed by anything other than normality, circadian rhythms are rare – ultradian, infradian, whatever. He slept when he needed to, and functioned the same way. If he needed fuel, he ate. If he needed liquid, he drank. He'd given up living long before, a deathly shadow of the man he'd once been. Back then, family had been everything. Back then, Charlotte had been the centre of his universe. Now, she still was, but not in the way that any child should be.

No breakfast. His body rarely needed food when he'd just awoken. He always washed, always shaved. It was a strange juxtaposition, the way he kept himself clean and tidy but allowed the gardens to grow into jungles. There was a simple enough explanation, though. He'd grown a beard once and Charlotte had hated it. It was enough to ensure that not even a millimetre of growth adorned his cheeks.

He'd always spend the first hour of the day sitting in the lounge on the same threadbare chair that had been his throne for years gone by. A spring or two may have popped, but it moulded to his shape in a way that no replacement would ever be able to. He'd read the papers and catch up on whatever had been going on in the world. Always had done, always would. A creature of habit, he'd have the same two dailies delivered to his door, one from the left and one from the right. Reading between the lines, it helped him to find the centre ground. He'd flick on the TV, too, just to keep abreast of anything that might have happened overnight. He'd never be able to explain his fascination with the news, save to say that it was all he had, really. Never one for sport, never one for films or those banal television shows that catered to the masses, the news was all he was interested in. Besides, one day might be THE day when . . . And he always stopped himself. It was torture, if that train of thought progressed.

Then, come what may, he'd go for a walk. He'd nod to his neighbours, give them a friendly smile and sometimes even a kindly word. They'd always return the compliment, too. Long gone were the looks of sympathy, the rabbit-in-headlight gazes that came his way when people saw him approaching. He was a part of the community, in his own little way. He wasn't so stupid as to think that people wouldn't talk about him, about how life had gone on but he'd been unable to, about the tragedy that had happened within spitting distance of his house, about how – to a person – in his position, they'd have had to move away, lest they be confronted by it every day when they walked out of their front door.

For Kevin, though, he needed it. Even all these years later, he craved it, in fact. To wade through the overgrown grass where there had once been a driveway, to look at that lonesome bench that sat on the clifftop, and the vast sea stretching beyond? It helped him, in some deep and dark way, to be close to her. To feel her spirit. Hell, if he closed his eyes, he would sometimes swear that he could hear her gentle voice, drifting on the breeze when it floated in from the sea.

It was THAT that kept him there. It was THAT that had led him to where he was. Everyone knew someone like him, of course. The bachelor who lived alone, apparently in a permanent state of shabbiness, a benevolent man who looked older than the years he was approaching, weighed down by life but who nodded and smiled and lived an existence apart.

Behind the façade, though, behind the aesthetic, stories abounded. Kevin's, and Charlotte's, was a tale that had needed no exaggeration, no embellishment. It was the simple story of a father and a daughter, separated by tragedy. No more, no less.

But today, as Kevin went about his routine, it felt a bit different. There was something in his bones, something he couldn't explain, but he was a bit more alert, a bit . . . Happier.

The news caravan had come to town. A hero. A local, real-life hero, leaping from the flames and rescuing a child. A baby. The papers might not have printed it yet, but the TV had been running it relentlessly. And, though his heart had been shattered decades before, it thudded with something that he couldn't put his finger on. Deferred pride? Maybe. Whatever it was, the man had done something special. Something incredible. And, as Kevin walked the clifftop, there may even have been a little spring in his step. Good news stories were far better than the usual misery that normally adorned the front pages, after all.

Chapter 12

STEVE

'What do you think?' Sarah asked.

'Not sure it'll hold them off for long, will it?' Steve replied.

Sarah was sitting in front of her phone, her fingers poised to type a response to the press release that had just arrived in her inbox from DS Willmott when the doorbell rang.

Sarah climbed to her feet, just as the doorbell rang again. As she walked towards the lounge door, it rang once more. Steve looked towards her, their eyes meeting. It was followed by a rattle of the letterbox, a thud against the door, and another ring of the bell. And another. Another. With every press of the doorbell, the chime's volume seemed to rise. Thud. Doorbell. Thud. Letterbox. Doorbell. Then, a voice.

'Mr Minchin?' It was a shout, amidst a clamour of other voices.

'Steve . . .' Sarah mumbled as she looked at the window and pointed with a trembling finger.

A photographer was peering in, his camera around his neck and his hand raised to his forehead as he strained his eyes to see something beyond the protection that the nets covering the windows afforded them. It didn't matter that he couldn't see them. They could see him. His presence, his intrusion, it was like a dagger striking Steve in the place he should've felt safest.

'Mr Minchin, are you in there?' The voice outside the front door shouted. It was louder, now. Whoever it was, they'd got down on their knees and were blasting their enquiry through the letterbox. Intrusion? It didn't even come close.

'Daddy?' Gracie called from upstairs. Her voice trembled.

Steve jumped up and ran from the lounge into the hallway. He was confronted by a set of eyes peering in through the letterbox.

'Mr Minchin?' that same voice called. 'Have you got a minute?'

Steve didn't look or respond as he double-stepped up the stairs. His children were on the landing, and their faces were screwed up, a mishmash of confusion and worry.

'It's all right,' Steve said, with as much reassurance as he could muster, 'let's go in here.' He guided them into Gracie's room and closed the door.

Downstairs, the incessant ringing of the doorbell had been replaced with a constant and almost rhythmic banging on the front door.

'Daddy,' Gracie said, as tears began to fall down her face.

'Who is it, Daddy?' Oscar asked, his bottom lip quivering, all while the thuds on the front door grew louder in the background.

Sarah opened the bedroom door and let herself in, closing it quickly behind her and shutting out the commotion on their doorstep as best she could. Even so, Steve could still hear it. If anything, it was getting louder and showed absolutely no signs of abating. The press had seen him. They knew he was there. They'd been looking for him and, like wolves hunting prey, they'd picked up the scent. So much for the quiet life.

91

And still, the children's eyes leaked tears of apprehension. Still, the knocking intensified.

The more people dug, the more they would find. His head was a pressure valve, building and building and building and building until, decision made, it was about to blow.

He stood up, opened the bedroom door and closed it firmly behind him. Walking down the stairs, he didn't know what he was going to say but, by God, he needed to say it. The clamour from outside had only increased in those minutes he'd been upstairs. That wolf he'd been trying to keep away? It was now firmly at his door.

He paused for a second, perhaps to compose himself. Even he wasn't sure. His mind was scrambled and rational thought had long since gone.

He threw the front door open. A sea of light greeted him as cameras flashed and popped from all directions. His eyes burned as he forced them open in spite of the onslaught of light, but soon turned into squints as the flashes continued, wave after wave, photographs being captured and disseminated instantly to news feeds across all manner of social media. He tried to listen but all he could hear was a cacophony of noise as questions were shouted at him from countless reporters. It was a frenzy. He was a lamb to the slaughter.

He could see television cameras. He could see microphones. As instantly as the still images were being relayed across the world, so too was the live feed.

'How does it feel to save a baby?'

'What was going through your mind?'

'What do your family think of it all?'

'Are you proud of what you've done?'

'You're a hero, Mr Minchin, how does it feel?'

'Hero.'

'Hero.'

'Hero.'

It's all he could hear after a while, that word recurring again and again in his head, spinning through the fog of anxiety that had taken root. Amongst the yells of strangers, and in the face of chaos, he heard a welcome, familiar voice that grew louder as it got closer.

'Out of the way, come on, move,' Phil shouted as he fought through the gathered throng to get to Steve.

In an instant, a kindred spirit was by Steve's side, reaching across his face and slapping a microphone away before ushering him back inside.

'You lot should be ashamed of yourselves,' Phil shouted as he slammed the front door shut behind him.

The quiet inside the house seemed magnified when contrasted with the noise there had been outside. Steve was breathing deeply, again forcing his heart rate to return to a normal level. He could still hear the crowd outside, but the intensity and volume of their demands was diminishing by the second.

'What were you doing out there?' Phil asked.

'I don't know,' Steve replied, shaking his head.

Both men walked into the lounge. Phil went over to the window and looked outside.

'Unbelievable,' he said, with a whistle.

Steve sat heavily on the sofa, his mind still without focus or clarity. After a while, there was silence. No noise coming from outside. No conversation inside. Just total and utter silence, interrupted only by the creaking of the stairs and the opening of the lounge door as Sarah walked in, carrying one child in each of her arms.

'Phil?' she said, surprised. 'What are you doing here?'

'Just came to check on you guys,' Phil replied.

'Saved me from the mob,' Steve muttered.

'All right, kiddos?' Phil said.

Oscar squealed with excitement and wriggled free from Sarah's grasp. He ran over to Phil and gave him the biggest of high fives, while Gracie turned her head away and looked out of the lounge window.

'You want us to take the kids for the night?' Phil asked.

Steve looked at Sarah, who nodded her head almost imperceptibly, mirroring Steve's own thoughts. He'd seen the fear in his kids' eyes. Who knew, he wondered, when the press would be back? They'd yet to be sated, yet to have their pound of flesh from him. That they were feting him barely crossed his mind. It was attention, and it is what he'd sought to avoid ever since the troubles of his childhood.

Besides, nothing mattered more than his kids. Their safety and wellbeing were foremost in his mind, with the exception of nothing. This was a scenario unlike any he could have ever imagined. With Phil and Emma, they were safe. Entirely out of the firing line.

'That'd be great if you could,' he said, 'just until this all blows over.'

He walked over to Gracie and scooped her up in his arms before blowing a raspberry on her tummy.

'Get off!' Gracie shouted.

'Everything all right with her?' Phil asked, as he set her down and she scuttled out of the room after Sarah.

'She's been a bit off all week,' Steve replied.

With Gracie's protestations still ringing in his ears as they waved the children off, Steve followed Sarah into the lounge and sat on the sofa. His leg bounced with nervous tension as they spoke and, though Sarah reached across to hold it, she simply couldn't soothe what ailed him.

'This isn't going away,' she said. Quite the opening

gambit, he thought, but it was true enough. 'Everyone, love,' she continued, 'everyone thinks you're a hero. Me too, you know?'

He closed his eyes and, in his mind, he was walking up the stairs. Flames were chasing him.

'Who else went in there?' Sarah asked. 'Who else ran into the fire?'

Those flames were licking him, singeing the hairs on his arms. He could feel them, as they tried to get him. To claim him.

'You're going to have to accept it, love,' she whispered.

And, as he reached the top of the stairs, he once again saw the two doors. Not even in his mind, where it wasn't real, could he find a way to choose the one on the right. He just couldn't do it. It was like a nightmare, where he wanted to walk through the open door, to shout, to scream, to plunge himself into the darkness and to try to find life within. They were just kids, and he could've done more. He opened his eyes, and looked at Sarah.

'It was all . . . so quick,' he said.

'Fight or flight,' Sarah countered, 'and you fought like hell.'

'Could've done more,' he said, 'should've done more.'

They were at an impasse, one where she wouldn't hear him beating himself up, and he wasn't happy playing the role of hero that she'd designated him.

Sarah reached for her phone, and Steve looked across to her as soon as the sharp intake of air crossed her lips. He hadn't a clue when she'd last been on it but, as she held the screen in his direction, it took a second to let the numbers filter from his eyes to his brain.

Thirty-two missed calls.

Forty-eight messages.

Countless notifications from Facebook, Instagram and X. Hell, as he squinted, there was even something from TikTok flashing up on the screen. She didn't say anything, but her face gave her away as she clicked on her tagged posts.

'What's up?' Steve asked.

'Errr,' Sarah replied.

Steve looked over her shoulder as the scene on their front door played out on screen, only from a perspective on the other side of the divide.

She clicked a different link. Same scene, different angle. And another. And another. All of them from the cameras that had been pointing at Steve as he opened the front door, many with captions asking who the mystery hero was.

They weren't so blatant as to suggest that they would welcome any information on Steve, but the implication seemed to be clear. *If you know this man, then get in touch*.

In Sarah's messages were news articles that had been sent to her with Steve's face at the front door emblazoned across them.

It was leading on all the news websites. Rescuing baby Jack had, it seemed, evoked a collective sense of pride in the public at one of their own. It had captured their imagination. An ordinary bloke. A run-of-the-mill fella. A have-a-go hero. Someone who had risked it all and had rescued a baby. The kind of thing that you'd see in the cinema but that didn't happen in real life.

Only it had.

Sarah reached over to the remote control and turned the television on. She dropped the remote as the 'breaking news' caption boldly flashed at the bottom of the screen, and the clatter on the floor startled Steve.

BREAKING: BEACHBROOK HERO NAMED LOCALLY AS STEVE MINCHIN

'Oh for crying out loud,' she said, as a photo of Steve flashed up on the screen.

'What's up?' he asked.

'That's from my Facebook,' she said, pointing at the image on the screen.

Steve's digital footprint was non-existent, so they must have cast their net wider and found her social media feeds. Cold chills washed over him. What else could they find? Sarah snatched her phone back from Steve and began furiously tapping at the screen, with an urgency he'd never before seen. Her fingers were working double time, the taps on the screen so quick that they were an almost solid chunk of noise.

'What are you doing?' he asked.

'Setting everything to private,' she muttered.

Steve didn't quite get it but, in Sarah's eyes, it felt like naked intrusion, as bad in a virtual sense as the hounding at the front door had been physically.

The image of Steve shrank to fill the right-hand side of the screen as the 'live' logo reappeared on the top right-hand side of the display. On the left side of the screen, a news reporter was still standing outside the house where the fire had been. In the background, firefighters could be seen training their hoses on small pockets of fire, but the sense of urgency had long since gone. A police cordon was clearly still in place and, as the camera panned around, it seemed that every news media outlet in the land had descended on the town. The camera fixed upon the reporter as she turned to face her interviewee.

'So, how do you know Mr Minchin?' the reporter asked.

'Oh, I'm a regular at his coffee shop,' the interviewee replied.

It was John. He couldn't be sure, as it was only a head shot, but Steve would have put his mortgage on him having

Lex with him as well. He'd never seen him without his dog by his side.

'So tell me about Steve, the man himself,' the reporter said.

'Well,' John said, 'he's a good one, he is. Family man. Doesn't surprise me in the slightest, what he's done here.'

'And what would your message be to Steve, if he's watching now?' the reporter asked.

'Well, I didn't get my coffee this morning,' John replied, 'so I expect to see you tomorrow!'

The reporter chuckled in unison with John.

'They're laughing,' Steve whispered. 'Show some respect.'

He stormed out of the room.

Sarah was right. It wasn't going away. And with exposure came interest. With interest came exploration. With exploration, of his life, of his past, came threat. Came danger. Came everything that he'd spent decades trying to escape from.

And as one day turned into two, the doorstepping didn't stop. The collective clamour may have ceased, but it didn't stop individual reporters trying their luck. Steve had given up answering the door and begging them to leave him alone and, before long, it didn't matter anyway. They'd gotten hold of his phone number somehow. It'd rung so much that he'd had to turn it off, as journalists of varying levels of scruple offered him everything from money for an exclusive interview through to the chance to tell his story to a screenwriter. The embers still burned hot, and the ash had yet to settle, but it seemed people were queuing up to cash in on the tragedy.

It took those two days for the worst of it to pass. Steve didn't dare leave the house, no matter how many times John appeared as an interviewee on various news channels, leading the acclaim. John had become a hybrid of spokesman and cheerleader, yet Steve watched it through his fingers, cringing at what his eyes were showing him. Sure, they spoke on a daily basis through the summer, but it was what Steve would refer to as popcorn conversation. It didn't mean anything. Their exchanges were just empty words, a hollow, almost formulaic script that they followed each day, thespians playing their part in an act where real life was temporarily suspended.

And yet there John was, blowing Steve's proverbial trumpet. The media lapped it up, of course, as John's rhetoric soared to stratospheric levels of hyperbole at Steve's deed. He didn't quite refer to him as the Second Coming, but it wasn't too far a bridge to leap.

And still . . . No matter the lofty acclaim, no matter the acclamation, the praise, the universal approval of a community united behind him, there was still the clear and present danger, lurking in the background, and it was bearing down on him like a weight from the heavens.

His melancholy was for Adam and Louise, of course. But, in the corner of his mind, something else was eating away at him.

Was it only a matter of time before he was exposed? Before he was outed?

Before the sins of his past caught up with him?

Chapter 13

DS SUE WILLMOTT

The weekend had passed by in a flash. DS Willmott had barely had a chance to snatch two minutes with Lottie, given the need to make progress in the fire investigation, but she'd made sure that she'd been home by bedtime on Sunday night. Even when her mind was stacked, and it seemed the world had thrown everything it could at her, putting her baby girl to bed could always take the edge off. As soon as those eight-year-old lips began to purr, though, she was back out of the door, back to the grind, back to the coalface. Her mum might as well have taken up permanent residence.

As Monday morning arrived, and after she'd attended strategy meetings with those who worked on the upper floors during office hours, DS Willmott sat down with Vinny to take stock, him as the FLO and her as the OIC. In her hand, she had Steve's statement, obtained after she'd fought her own way through the throngs of reporters at his house the day before, but the words on the paper didn't tell them anything other than what they already knew, and what the videos all over the socials had already shown.

'How was Steve?' Vinny asked.

'Hard to tell,' DS Willmott replied. 'Putting a brave face on it all but it's always in the eyes, isn't it?'

'He can't be feeling guilty, can he?'

'He's beating himself up about Adam and Louise,' DS Willmott said, quietly. 'The mind's a funny old thing – plays tricks on us sometimes. He'll get there.'

Vinny nodded, and DS Willmott sighed. If life had taught her one thing, it's that resilience was everything. Keep on keeping on, and the cards tended to land the right way up.

'How are the parents?' she asked.

'Bearing up,' Vinny replied. 'They want to meet him, you know?'

'You said.'

DS Willmott paused for a second, as inspiration struck.

'Tee it up,' she said.

'Already?' Vinny replied.

'If they're up for it? If he sees what good he's done, it'll help him . . . Right?'

'I guess.'

There was a moment of silence, and DS Willmott looked at Vinny.

'Now?' he asked.

'No time like the present,' she replied.

Vinny reached for his phone and, within thirty seconds, had made the necessary arrangements.

'They're home all day,' he said.

Chapter 14

STEVE

Steve had spent his whole adult life putting on a show, concealing a hidden angst. He was masterful at it. Now, those feelings were more intense than ever.

The weekend had dribbled past but, as Monday morning arrived, the circus out the front had all but disappeared. It was barely first light when the doorbell rang but, this time, it was one that he'd been waiting for.

Gracie and Oscar stood in front of Phil, the very finest of deliveries to start the working week.

'How was your holiday?' Steve asked as they ran up to him and melted into his body.

'Good!' Oscar shouted.

'I wanted my own bed,' Gracie said.

Steve picked her up and wrapped his arms around her, holding her close in a paternal embrace of pure love. Gracie snuggled in, her little arms enveloping her daddy.

'Missed you too, princess,' he said, rubbing his nose against his daughter's. 'Let's get some brekkie, kiddos.'

Life had to go on, regardless of his internal machinations. It simply had to. For the kids. For Sarah. And even for him. No matter how guilty he felt about those who had perished. No matter about the emotions it stirred up. No matter, even, about how it had all left him feeling nakedly exposed, like his past had collided with his future. All he could do was get on with getting on. Stoic. Stiff upper lip. Belt and braces. Typically British. He pulled on his Coffee and Cream polo shirt, and stood at the bottom of the stairs.

First things first. The school run.

'Are you ready?' he called. In moments, the kids were in the car. Normal as could be.

Steve adjusted his rear-view mirror so that he could see them both. It was like déjà vu. Gracie was slouched and staring out of the window while Oscar was buoyantly upright, smiling with all the innocence of his tender years.

'Good weekend, Gracie?' he asked.

'Yeah,' she replied, not turning to look at him. Instead, her gaze was fixed yet unfocussed as the world passed her by.

After he dropped the kids at the school gates, Oscar strode with swagger to his play area as usual, but it was Gracie who Steve was watching. He tracked her as she walked slowly across the playground. She tentatively glanced left and right, before looking at a group of children who Steve recognised. Gracie's friends.

'Go on, kid,' he whispered to himself.

As if on cue, she turned and went over to them. Steve smiled as he watched her begin to play with them.

He barely noticed as assorted shadows assembled behind him. He heard whispers. Hushed, reverent murmurings. Not gossip, not tittle-tattle, just the deferential purring of a grateful mob. He turned around, and the shadows that had been behind him had grown into a crowd of about thirty parents. His cheeks turned red as they burst into a spontaneous round of applause, the noise attracting the attention of even more parents who, recognising Steve from the sheer saturation of news reports and attention that had been focussed on the town, joined in the chorus of acclaim. It was like a domino effect. The more people who clapped, the louder it got. The louder it got, the more attention it drew and the more people who joined in. And so it continued. Steve looked to the ground, praying for a sinkhole to open and swallow him up, but all he could do was smile inanely and nod his head. He was well versed in faking it. The whole road was at a standstill. The children on the playground had stopped playing and were joining in the clapping, most totally unaware of why, but wanting to join in, nonetheless.

The clapping finally died down, but that wasn't the end of it. Not by a long shot. Steve was approached by a seemingly endless stream of other parents, some of whom he knew, many he didn't, offering their own personal compliments and tributes. His back was slapped, his hand was shaken. He was hugged, and he was kissed. It seemed never-ending and, as he finally extricated himself, and found sanctuary in his car, he looked at his fingers. They were shaking.

As he drove along Beach Road on autopilot, he barely noticed that there were a lot more cars parked in the vicinity than usual. He rolled to a gentle stop, a distance away from where he normally parked, and got out of his car. He heard the same reverential murmurings that had been present outside the school gates, although amplified. The air was filled with a crackling tension, so palpable he could almost taste it. From his vantage point up on high, he could see snakes of people queuing up outside Coffee and Cream and, as he squinted his eyes, a few media types. They may have left his road but, it seemed, they hadn't left town. The hum of noise coming from the assembled masses was almost carnival in atmosphere. Squinting more, he could make out John and Lex at the front of the queue, John once again being interviewed on camera.

'You're kidding,' he said to himself.

What could he do? Turn around and walk away? Of course that was an option, but they'd only be back tomorrow. It was almost as if he needed to give them a part of himself to get back to the normality that he craved.

Taking a deep breath, he slowly walked down the slope and along the promenade. It may have been tarmac underfoot, but his heavy footsteps felt as though he was trudging through quicksand. The crowd noticed him long before he got to the bottom and, before he knew it, they'd hotfooted over to him. He was surrounded by backslappers and well-wishers, each wanting to impart to him their own words of praise and, amongst them all, he recognised a news reporter. She was the one on the news channel, presumably doing whatever she could to get her exclusive with him. Now, perhaps, it was time to get it out of the way. That way, maybe it would all pass by.

With expert ease, she burrowed a route through the crowds and appeared at his side with her cameraman in tow.

'How does it feel to be a hero?' she asked. Her voice was calm. Measured. Yet laced with a natural authority that was born of years of doing the job.

Steve squinted, momentarily blinded by a dazzling studio-style light shining on him from behind the cameraman. The sun, it seemed, wasn't enough.

'I'm not a hero,' he replied.

'I'd suggest that this crowd who have gathered thinks otherwise,' the reporter said, smiling, as the crowd murmured their assent.

'Look, I did what I did,' Steve said quietly. 'But let's keep it in perspective and keep our thoughts with that poor family.'

The reporter allowed the seeds of melancholy to grow, infiltrating the hush that had descended upon them as people in the throng craned their necks to see and hear what was happening. She had been expecting a triumphant interview, but from Steve's initial answers, she knew it wasn't going to be that kind of exclusive. A veteran at conducting interviews, she immediately changed tack.

'Of course, and I'm sure everyone would echo that,' she said, with a tender flourish. She paused before continuing. 'How are you feeling?'

There was a sense of genuine sympathy loaded in her question. It hadn't been something that Steve had anticipated and it caught him off guard.

'I . . . Well, I don't know actually,' he replied.

It touched him, deeply. He hadn't been expecting something so personal. He had seen many people interviewed on television before, and everything had always seemed so detached, so formal, so . . . scripted. Yet, here he was, being asked to bear his soul on a matter that was still so raw to him.

'We've all seen the camera footage, Steve,' she said, gently. 'Have you seen that beautiful baby since?' Her voice soothed him and his mouth, though initially as parched as a barren desert where the words had run dry, moistened. The beads of sweat on his back dissolved into the fabric of his polo shirt. He wasn't comfortable – far from it. But there was something about the way she framed her questions that brought on just a hint of ease.

Steve shook his head. 'No,' he replied.

He had thought about asking, but there was no way that he wanted to intrude on the private grief of a suffering family. Jack still had his grandparents. That had mattered to Steve, a hell of a lot. He would have a chance at some kind of family life with blood relatives.

'Would you like to?' the reporter asked, gentler still.

'I . . . I don't know. I guess so,' Steve replied.

A deep and respectful silence had developed amongst the crowd as the interview continued, punctuated only by the gentle crashing of waves in the background. The words of both interviewer and interviewee had them spellbound.

'So, the big question here,' she said, 'is why did you do it?'

Steve had been repeatedly asking himself that very same thing. The truth was that he didn't have an answer. He wondered if, deep down, there was a part of him that had been attempting subconsciously to repay the sins of his past, that an act of heroism might in some way square the debt that he had morally encumbered himself with. Would he have done it had he been stone-cold sober? He wouldn't know. He couldn't know. It was just something that he had done instinctively.

'I'd love to be able to tell you why, honestly I would. I just can't,' he said.

'Well,' the reporter said, 'I think I speak on behalf of everyone here and, probably, the entire viewing public when I say, simply, thank you.'

Steve nodded, his eyelashes fluttering as he blinked on repeat. What came next, he could barely have expected.

In normal times, and in normal interviews, there was an invisible divide between the one asking the questions and the one with a microphone thrust under their nose. He'd never seen it be breached on TV before, that was for sure. Now, though, the reporter reached across that unseeable barrier and wrapped her arms around him. It threw him so much that he flinched.

'Thank you,' she repeated.

Was it too much, he wondered? Maybe. Probably. But, in that moment, it touched him in a way that he simply couldn't explain.

In the background, a small ripple of applause began. It grew in volume and intensity until it cut through him from side to side, bottom to top, and everywhere in between. His lips juddered and, as the bright lights bore down on him, a solitary tear fell from his right eye. It was captured perfectly on camera, of course.

And in amongst those crowds, watching on, was the man who had lost his child on the clifftop above, all those years before. Steve didn't see him, didn't know he was standing on the fringes, but Kevin had watched with a smile on his face, one that the world seldom saw.

Chapter 15

FIONA

'That was special,' Fiona said, as the blinding light above them went dim and the red light on the camera extinguished.

'I . . . don't know what to say,' Steve replied.

'You did good,' she said, 'real good.'

She thrust her card into his hand, as the crowd took their chance to swallow the pair of them whole. In seconds, she had lost sight of the subject of her exclusive, but it didn't really matter. She'd got what she needed. With the slight nod of her head at her cameraman and producer, they slinked backwards, for once not the centre of attention. It suited her just fine and, as they retreated to their news van at the top of the slope, the crowd below were showing no signs of releasing Steve from their grip.

Hot-desking had become the norm and, as Fiona sat at a soulless pod in one of her company's satellite offices that had sprung up all over the country, she yearned for her old office. Four walls and a door. Her own space. Something she had put her own stamp on, her own identity and personality shining through with photos on the shelves, awards aplenty and certificates on the wall. Still, it didn't really matter. What did was what she'd just committed to camera and, as her instincts had suggested as she'd conducted the interview with Steve, it had been televisual gold. One of those moments, in fact, that shone through as the very best of journalism. Personable. Relatable. Totally newsworthy.

She thought of the interview on the promenade itself and smiled. She'd taken a punt on him going to Coffee and Cream, and it'd come off.

She had seen him arrive and had stood back while the crowd had surged towards him, his Messiah status all but confirmed. The interview itself? It couldn't have gone better. Her hug at the end? It had been genuine, both in appreciation at what he had done and that she had got the scoop. His tear falling? It being the parting shot on camera? A money shot that would be forever priceless.

A loose curl of perfectly fashioned hair straddled her cheek, and she fiddled with it as she opened her laptop. She stared at the picture of Steve that filled the screen, and then she scrolled down. She'd already put the feelers out to her colleagues, to her sources, to anyone who might be able to do a bit of digging but, as she reached a tab that was headed 'background information', it was decidedly blank. No whiff of a past, no hint of a backstory. All she had was what was already out there: a married man, two kids, his own business – just a normal family man.

Her lips pursed. Who in that day and age didn't have a digital footprint of any sort? She'd always prided herself and her team on being able to dig up anything on anyone, but not Steve. With him, it was dead end after dead end.

On a news item as big as that one, a backstory was crucial. Essential, even. What had made Steve into the man he was, what had driven him, what was it that had guided him to do what he did? For a story that was destined to run and run and run, she knew what her viewers wanted. It was context. It was depth. It was the fabric of his existence, and what stitched it together. And she wasn't so naïve as to think she wasn't the only one looking for it, the only one searching for the background information. Sure, she might have been the only one to have thought to show up at the beach, but there were other reporters out there. It was a cut-throat world and she might be ahead of the game now, but it was only a matter of time before the others caught up.

For now, though, she could bask in the familiar glow of a job well done. This was a story that would rumble on. There was still the outcome of the police investigation to come, the funerals of the two who had perished. And they had barely even touched on the baby at the centre of it all, either.

She stared at her screen, as a million and one thoughts ran through her mind. She had seen it all, done it all, and been at the centre of it all so many times before. Public interest stories such as those she was dealing with were good for the soul. So many times she had dealt with murder and mayhem and misery but, once in a while, something like this came along.

In a world where celebrity was a status or title obtained by sometimes nefarious or obscure means, Steve's story had cut through to the common person. She had seen it coming, and had ridden the wave to the very crest and beyond and, as sure as night followed day, she was certain that those waves would just keep on coming.

Chapter 16

SARAH

'Turn it off,' Steve said as Sarah rewound the interview and played it again.

'I know it's you, but I've never seen anything like it,' she replied. She shook her head in disbelief. 'It's like it's not you at all.'

He may have still been wearing his Coffee and Cream polo shirt, but the clock had yet to hit midday. Normally she'd rib him for keeping the shutters down, but not now. Everything, it seemed, was different.

The news presenters on television were engaged in conversation, analysing Steve's actions. There'd even been behavioural and psychological experts on air, imparting their opinion as to why Steve had acted the way he had when he saw the fire. Sink or swim. Fight or flight. Darwinism. It had all been discussed.

Steve took the remote control from her and put his thumb firmly on the power button.

'I thought that would've calmed it all down,' he muttered but, as yet another notification popped up on her phone, Sarah murmured her dissent.

The silence was broken by the soft tapping on the front door, followed by the bell ringing. Sarah peered out of the window as Steve walked out of the lounge.

'It's the detectives,' she called.

In a matter of seconds, DS Willmott and DC Robson had joined them inside. They all remained standing, and the two detectives smiled kindly at them. Sarah looked closely at DS Willmott. How did someone bear that kind of load, she wondered? How did someone deal with things like that on a daily basis, and still manage to stand with a benign, placid smile on their face. She looked at the lines that tracked the detective's forehead, only able to imagine the story that each of them might tell.

'How are things?' DS Willmott asked. Her voice straddled the delicate line between humane and professional, and her face was engaged. It was a question she seemed to have a genuine interest in the answer to, not one just asked out of courtesy.

Sarah shuffled over to Steve and stood next to him.

'Okay,' Steve replied.

'I saw your interview today,' DS Willmott said. 'Touching.'

'It was, wasn't it,' Sarah replied.

She slipped her hand into Steve's, pride abounding.

'Let me ask you a question, Steve,' DS Willmott said, taking a step closer to him but seemingly being careful not to invade his space. 'It doesn't matter how many times you hear people tell you how special what you did was, Adam and Louise are weighing on your mind. Am I right?'

Sarah looked to her husband, at his bowed head, and his lack of words provided the answer.

'And I reckon that's all you can focus on, right?'

Sarah gripped Steve's hand as his head slowly lifted. His nods were subtle.

'The parents,' DS Willmott continued, 'they'd like to meet you.'

As DS Willmott's words bounced around between Sarah and Steve, his clammy palm tightened around hers.

'They're a decent family,' DC Robson chimed in, 'bearing up well, given everything that's happened.'

Sarah looked at Steve. He was stunned and, she guessed, unable to put together a coherent sentence. In the absence of words from him, she asked the questions she was sure he'd want answered.

'How would it work?' she asked.

'There's no playbook for this kind of thing,' DC Robson replied. 'It's pretty simple really. I'd take you around there and just let it play out.'

Steve squeezed Sarah's hand once more, then released his grip. With her hand swinging by her side, he seemed to find his voice.

'Jack's grandparents, the ones he is with. Are they the mum or dad's parents?' he asked.

'Louise's,' DS Willmott replied. 'Adam's aren't with us anymore.'

Steve sighed, and it was a noise Sarah recognised. It was the one where he might not necessarily have wanted to do something but, regardless, was about to acquiesce.

'Yeah,' Steve whispered.

'Yeah?' DS Willmott said.

'I'll do it,' Steve murmured. 'When?'

DS Willmott didn't say anything. Her gesturing towards the door answered the question.

'Now?' Steve cried. He was whispering no longer.

DS Willmott nodded.

'I . . . I need Sarah with me,' he stammered.

'I'm right here,' she said.

In a matter of minutes, Sarah and Steve were walking down the pathway to DS Willmott's car, with both detectives in tow.

Sarah looked at her husband. Like a child lost in the corridors of a new school, he bowed his head as he climbed into the vehicle. She knew what he was thinking because, in a way, similar thoughts were crossing her mind. What could they possibly say to Louise's parents? Was there anything? Her pride in what her husband had done was tempered only by the knowledge that bereaved folk don't always see things rationally. Would they be angry? Would they be hysterical? Would they shout, and scream, and holler? Or would they be appreciative, grateful even? Facts were facts and, in her eyes, they wouldn't even have Jack with them if it weren't for Steve's actions. THAT was the truth of the matter and, as she sat and let the world pass her by, THAT was what mattered, in her eyes at least.

'Here we are,' DS Willmott said, pulling up outside a detached house in a nice part of town.

It had been a mere ten-minute journey. Steve gulped down a lungful of air and, as he climbed from the vehicle, Sarah was by his side as they followed DC Robson and DS Willmott up the driveway. There was a front doorbell but, instead of pressing it, DS Willmott gently knocked on the front door.

'Jack might be asleep,' she said.

Sarah nodded, as a dog scrabbled at the other side of the front door.

Soft footsteps informed her that the inside of the house was thickly carpeted and, as those paces came to a halt, her heart started to thump. Inside those four walls, tragedy had struck and, here they were, about to bear witness to it. She reached for Steve's hand once more. If her heart was racing, then God only knew how he felt. She looked at him, but his chin was still tucked into his chest.

A simple Yale lock was undone with the merest twist of a latch. The door opened on freshly greased hinges, not making a sound. Standing in front of them was a man of late middle age. Sixty, she guessed. Grey hair, and deep creases in his forehead.

At his feet? A golden-brown baby cockerpoo, with matted fur and a croaking wheeze when it panted.

And in his arms? A baby. Nine months old. Dressed in a babygrow and with a smile on his face. The last time she'd seen him, a paramedic had taken him away. Now, here he was, in the flesh.

Baby Jack.

Living, and breathing, because of what her husband had done.

Chapter 17

STEVE

The panic rose within, first in his stomach, then ascending through his chest and into his head until it raged throughout his upper body. His heart rate spiked. *Breathe,* he told himself. *Deep breaths. Breathe, Steve. Breathe.*

'You must be Steve,' the man said.

'That's me,' he mumbled.

The man held the baby in his left arm with the ease and deftness of someone who had done it countless times before.

'And you must be Sarah,' the man said, looking towards her and nodding.

'That's me,' she said, parroting Steve's words.

'Please, please come in,' the man said.

Steve crossed the threshold into the house, followed closely by Sarah and the two detectives. He looked around. It was just a normal house, in a normal road. Everything screamed conventional, from the pastel blue shade of the walls to the light, sandy-coloured carpet, from the shoes neatly arranged on a cabinet to the photos that stood proudly on a sideboard.

Photos. Steve stopped and looked at them. He'd never met Louise or Adam but, instinctively, he recognised them.

They were just kids themselves, and the pictorial evidence only reinforced that point. He looked at them both in a snapshot that, perhaps, encapsulated their spirit. She was beautiful, him handsome. In her arms was Jack, and both Mummy and son were wrapped up in the protective embrace of Daddy. They had been a family. They had been alive, with hopes and dreams. Now, in the flash of a flame, they were no longer. He winced as Louise and Adam, previously faceless and unknown, had seared another image into his memory that was sure to haunt him.

Deep breaths. In through the nose, out through the mouth. Repeat. He moved forwards, following the man, keeping his breathing level and his thoughts as rational as he could manage as his hushed footsteps moulded into the shaggy carpet beneath them.

'Just in here,' the man said, leading Steve and Sarah down the hallway and into the lounge.

Steve rounded the corner and, as he did, a woman stood from the sofa to look him in the eye. Hers were red, with bulging bags beneath them. Her skin was the type that had got thinner as the years had passed by, and those cheeks were raw from all the tears that had leaked. Grief. It was etched on every crease, in every pore. Still, she forced a smile. Still, she walked unsteadily to him. Still, she wrapped her arms around him and squeezed him tightly. More tears fell, rivers of heartache trailing their way down well-worn tracks, but her words were full of poise. Dignity. Grace.

'For Jack, thank you,' she whispered in Steve's ear.

Steve pulled his head back so that he could see her eyes. He nodded as, through tears of his own, he held her in a clinch that blurred the line between deference and reverence.

'Steve, Sarah, thanks for coming,' Louise's dad said. His voice was deep and gravelly, a tone moulded by days spent mourning. 'I'm Bob, this is Pam.'

Pam tightened her grip around Steve, and he found himself reciprocating. Whatever atmosphere there was in the room, it wasn't one of recrimination or bitterness. Instead, there was warmth, a feeling of acceptance and, dare he think it, gratitude.

'And this,' Bob continued, 'is Jack.'

As if on cue at hearing his name mentioned, Jack cooed in Bob's arms, and Steve's heart melted. It was a sound so familiar, a baby satisfied. If he closed his eyes, he could remember his own kids humming the same babyish melody.

'Please, sit down,' Bob said.

Pam removed her arms from around Steve as he sat down on the sofa with Sarah next to him. Pam sat on the other side of him with Bob in the armchair opposite, half fussing over Jack and half looking beyond the baby to Steve and Sarah. DS Willmott turned to DC Robson and nodded to the door.

'We'll be in the kitchen if you need us,' she said, and they both walked out, closing the door behind them.

And then, there was silence.

Steve looked around the room. More photos on shelves. Various mementos and ornaments, each with a memory attached. Each, no doubt, intrinsically linked to Louise. As with him and Sarah, while houses may be owned by adults, if there were children in the family then they made it a home.

He looked closer. A stone that Louise had decorated as a youngster that had been on show for years. A set of handprints from when she was a baby. A framed certificate informing the world that she had passed a grading from her dance school. A graduation photo from her university days. A garish teddy bear that looked out of place, which no doubt had a story of its own to tell. Pictures. Artefacts.

Memories.

'Have you got children?' Pam asked, her voice soft.

'Yeah, we've got two,' Steve replied quietly. 'Gracie and Oscar. Seven and four.'

Pam looked into Steve's eyes and nodded, her expression vacant. Steve could only guess what she was thinking. Had her mind wandered back to a time and place when Louise was seven years old, he wondered? Had she been a happy and outgoing little girl who always had a smile on her face and the sweetest tooth of any child she had ever known? That was the seven-year-old Steve knew and loved, and he wondered if those qualities were universal.

'At Beachbrook Primary?' Pam asked.

Steve nodded.

'Louise went there,' Pam said softly. 'She loved it.'

Bob slowly stood up and passed baby Jack to Pam. He walked towards Steve who, without knowing why, but letting instinct guide him, stood up as well. They faced each other and stared deep into each other's eyes. Man to man.

Father to father.

'I want to shake your hand,' Bob said. He spoke softly, but his words echoed around inside Steve's head.

A handshake, it seemed, wasn't enough. Almost as soon as their hands touched, their respective left hands reached around the other's right shoulder. It was an embrace born of mutual, paternal emotion. Steve could feel Bob's grief. He could taste it. It bled from every inch and sprung from every fibre of his being. Daddies and daughters. It just couldn't be described. Steve closed his eyes as his head rocked back and forth.

'I'm sorry,' he whispered.

Bob pulled his head back and looked directly at Steve.

'Sorry?' he asked, his face taut with confusion.

'Sorry I didn't get them out,' Steve said, his eyes still closed.

Bob nodded and smiled the very saddest of smiles.

'You have nothing to be sorry about,' he said, gripping Steve's shoulder with a tightness that exuded admiration. 'The police said they were probably already gone when you got in there. Smoke. Their door was open.' He sighed and closed his eyes. 'They didn't stand a chance.'

Steve remembered it with clarity. The open bedroom door. The burning and mortal fog of smoke therein. Were they already dead? Had his screams not been answered because they'd already passed? It all made sense, didn't it?

'Nothing to be sorry about at all,' whispered Pam.

'It's just, I've thought of nothing else since, really,' Steve said. 'You know, I was up the stairs, and the fire was coming, and I knew there was a kid's bedroom. I just went straight in there. I should've gone in the other room first.' His voice got louder and louder as the memories flooded back.

'Shhhh,' Pam said, raising her finger to her lips and stopping him mid-flow. She pointed down to Jack and tickled his ribs, sending him into fits of hysterics.

'You see, Steve,' she whispered, 'if you hadn't done what you'd done, then this little man wouldn't have stood a chance.'

'Ifs and buts don't even come into it,' Bob added, 'all I know is that we're forever in your debt. And, I mean this from the bottom of my heart, Louise and Adam would've thanked you a million times over for it.'

'They might not be able to,' Pam said, 'but we can.' She stood up and squeezed his hand. 'And we do.'

Steve's lips trembled. It was truly overwhelming. Their solemnity, their grace, their poise. The way they conducted themselves. The way they spoke. The way they grieved. Everything.

'How is he?' Steve asked.

'Louise was still feeding him.' Pam sighed.

'Is he going to . . . I mean, are you . . .' Steve said, but he couldn't get the words right.

'Is he staying here?' Bob said, finishing Steve's question for him.

'Sorry,' Steve said.

'Don't be sorry,' Pam said. 'Yeah, he'll be with us now.'

The three of them stood in silence. No words were needed. Instead, Jack's continued giggles filled the air around them with the innocence of youth. Though two lives had been so heartbreakingly and suddenly taken away, there had been some kind of recompense. Life had balanced the books, in a way. Death had claimed two, but not three.

Those chuckles washed over Steve and, once more, he closed his eyes as Pam and Bob's selfless benevolence finally allowed him to find peace with his actions in the fire.

The ice hadn't just been broken, it had been thawed entirely. The conversation flowed. It was smooth, it was relaxed, it was . . . easy. And as an hour passed, and Sarah and Steve noticed the time, promises were made that they would stay in touch. Phone numbers were exchanged. Bob and Pam even asked for a photo of Steve with Jack, and he'd obliged without so much as a second thought. In that moment, in that bubble, everything seemed fine.

It was when Bob motioned for Steve to walk out of the room ahead of the ladies that the two of them found themselves alone in the hallway. Able to talk. Man to man. Father to father.

'I don't know how I'll ever be able to thank you,' Bob said. He looked down at his feet, and the way his words had trailed off gave Steve notice that tears were on their way.

'Honestly . . . I'd do the same again tomorrow,' Steve replied.

'And we'd love for you to come to the funerals, too.'

Steve paused, but it wasn't dread that filled him. It was something else. Warmth. Acceptance.

'Of course,' he whispered.

Bob slowly lifted his head, and fixed his gaze on Steve.

And Steve almost recoiled.

It was the look on his face. One, presumably, that Bob had been unable to share with anyone since it had happened. Not with his wife. Not with baby Jack there. Not with the police. No, he had saved it for someone who would understand. For someone who he shared a bond with, something deep and intrinsic, something unbreakable. It was the look of a man who had lost a daughter. The look of total, utter desolation. The knowledge that a bond had been broken, a bond that Steve himself shared with Gracie. A bond between daddy and baby girl that is beyond sacred.

That look. That grief. Those eyes, and that broken bond. He'd seen it before, all those years ago.

'PLEASE, NO.'

It had been another girl, another dad, from another lifetime. But that expression? That paternal feeling of loss, of futility, of not wanting to go on without your baby girl by your side? A dad bereft, mourning a life so tragically cut short with only a yawning void left in its place.

Oh, he'd witnessed it all right.

All those years before, he had caused it.

Chapter 18

KEVIN

The walls in his lounge were filled with pictures. Not the type that were bought at the shop, but instead ones that had been drawn and painted in real life.

Charlotte had always loved the arts. Kevin had always been one for sport but, for every ball that he'd try to put into her hand or roll to her feet, she'd counter with a paintbrush or a pen . . . And he kept every single scrap of paper that she'd ever doodled on, from her three-year-old scrawls with crayons, all the way through to the much more accomplished vistas and horizons that she was beginning to perfect as a teenager. *Way ahead of her years*, her art teacher had said. *An eye for detail*, someone in the know had agreed. *You could make a career of it*, a professional had told her.

Now, Kevin lived among them, the patterns and pictures that she'd created, framed and immortalised all around him. Better that than the generic garbage that most people hung on the walls, he reasoned. These had meaning. They showed the advancement of craft, the development of technique and ability as the years had passed. That there were no more frames to be filled, though, cut him to the core.

Well, there was one more, but that was a whole other story. Just thinking of it made his blood pressure rise, just a fraction higher than was good for him.

He'd asked the police so many times for them to return it to him, but they'd always declined. Even now, more than twenty years hence, they still said it was needed as evidence, and he got it. He understood. But, even so, there was just one hole left to plug on the wall, one space left to fill.

He'd seen it, of course. He'd even taken a photo of it, and tried to blow it up, to enlarge it so that he could at least have a filler of sorts, but it would never be as good as the real thing. Brushstrokes were always missed in a photo. Colours were warped. The intensity of the sea was diminished, not magnified.

And yet, in a police store it remained, presumably gathering dust in a drawer, its vividity leaking into the bag it was sealed in as each day passed.

Charlotte hadn't even had the chance to finish it. She'd been on that very bench, opposite his house, painting the great beyond, when . . . it . . . had happened. She'd finished the outline, and even begun to fill in the gaps with heady blues for the sky and a more tranquil turquoise where the horizon blended the heavens with the sea.

'It' had happened then. What that 'it' was, he still didn't know. He only knew the end product, the police activity, the commotion and sirens outside, the loose pieces of A3 paper scattering in the breeze as he ran across the road, across the grass, to the clifftop bench when his baby girl was lying on the ground.

The past was curious, he'd always thought. All those years had passed by, but he could still remember with vividity the taste of the salt in the air as he'd sprinted full speed towards her, being stopped at the last hurdle by a burly police officer who said something about a crime scene and preserving evidence. He could remember the wails of his wife as she followed apace, and her being stopped by a young-looking female officer who had gone on to be a friend. He could remember looking at his daughter, his baby girl, her hair fluttering in the wind, her eyes still open as she faced him, the tiniest trickle of blood dribbling from her mouth.

He'd known she was dead, right there and then. There was no need for paramedics, no need to rush her to hospital, to plug her in and keep her turned on. He'd seen it in her eyes. They'd always been so full of life, so vibrant, so luminously blue yet, as she had lain there, whatever spark had once been within her had gone.

As he looked at the pictures on the wall, he smiled. And as he walked out of the front door, he looked across the road, across the grass, to the bench. He'd paced it out enough times to know that it was sixty-two strides away. About fifty metres, all in, from front door to where Charlotte had breathed her last. The original bench had long gone, seized as evidence by the police but, in its place, he'd made sure there had been a replacement. Today was usually his day to go and sit there, but he'd had a last-minute change of heart. It took a lot to change his routine on a Monday, or any day for that matter, but the hero of the weekend worked at the main sands just around the coast, he'd heard. He didn't know why he was drawn to so radically alter his daily plans, but something drew him to wander along the cliff-top path for a good twenty minutes. It was a pretty route, one that walkers took in on a daily basis.

'Morning,' he said.

'Good morning,' came the reply, every single time. Some had dogs, some had prams, some were in couples and some were alone. Each of them offered a smile in return for his own, and it warmed his soul.

He arrived at the top of the slope down to the main sands, and whistled. He'd never seen so many people congregated together on the promenade. There were camera crews, too. With a deep breath, he joined the masses. It was odd. He'd spent so long trying to avoid people, yet – when something like that happened – you just had to tip your cap and go with the flow.

He stood on the periphery as the man arrived. He wasn't one of those who swarmed him. Instead, he kept his distance, unable to hear what the woman reporter was saying to him, nor the responses. Instead, he let their actions speak for themselves. Head bowed. Reverential. A cuddle. Respect. A hand raised to the face, to wipe away a tear. Personable. Relatable. Totally human.

It was those things that Kevin spoke of, only an hour later, as he stood by Charlotte's grave. In stark contrast to his surroundings outside the four walls where he lived, not a blade of grass was out of place there. Hers was prime real estate in the middle of Beachbrook Cemetery.

She had been cremated. It wasn't a tomb, or a long grave, but instead a white, granite stone, with words inscribed in a delicately stylish font. It was so clean and tidy that a casual passer-by would have been taken aback had they read that she had lain there for more than two decades.

Charlotte Hitch
Taken far too soon.
Earth's loss is Heaven's gain.
Sleep tight, angel.

'Should've seen it, love,' he said, 'jumped from the flames with a baby in his arms. Proper hero.'

He bent down and picked a late-blooming daisy from the

grass beside him. He pulled at the white florets and flicked them in the air, watching as they scattered in a variety of directions, and smiled. When the head was empty, and just the yellow centre remained, he placed it gently onto her stone.

'You take care up there, you hear me,' he said, as the daisy was dragged away by the wind, 'and give your mum a big hug from me, okay?'

He knew better than to expect a response. How many times had he left a sentence lingering, waiting for some kind of acknowledgement? How many times had he looked around, waiting for a sign? A sudden gust of wind, maybe? A bird to swoop past him, a feather to float nearby? A drop of rain, or a bolt of lightning? Too many times he'd had his expectations dampened and, now, he was wiser. He was sure that his words were getting through, transcending the invisible divide, and that was enough.

And it didn't matter that Charlotte's mum was buried all those miles away. Cancer, they'd said, but he knew it was a broken heart that had never healed that had made her leave the world. It may have seemed perverse, and he'd never have voiced his opinion, but he was so happy that Charlotte had one of them with her.

One day, he'd be there too, but only after he'd found out what had happened to her.

No matter how long it took, he just had to know.

Chapter 19

STEVE

His shift in mindset was so fundamental that it shook Steve, but not in a bad way. The opposite, in fact. And all it had taken was the benevolence afforded him by two wonderful people.

As he tucked his kids into bed later that evening, the events of the weekend finally began to sink in. The very fleeting and precious nature of life was manifest in his thoughts and actions. He spent just a few extra minutes by each of their bedsides, reading each of them just one more story than he usually would, then one more when they begged for it. The lights went out later than normal. He sat silently and listened as they gently snored. He would never, ever get tired of listening to his children sleeping.

Gracie begged him to lie with her, not to leave her side, and he was more than happy to oblige. After everything, she didn't need to ask twice. He'd lie with her until the end of days if she wanted.

He closed his eyes.

It was dark.

And it was silent.

No words from his past.

No flash of the spectre that haunted him.

Just darkness, just silence.

He opened his eyes, then closed them again. It was the same. Just the liberating and deafening sound of silence against the backdrop of nothing. Never had emptiness felt so good.

He heard a noise at the door. Gracie was sleeping next to him, and Sarah stood in the doorway, looking in. The smile on her face spoke volumes to him, a silent message that was pure gold. He stood up and rubbed his eyes, softly kissing Gracie on her forehead, before he tiptoed out of the room and pulled the door to. He followed Sarah downstairs to the kitchen.

'Sorry, I didn't mean to wake you,' she said.

'Was I asleep?' he asked.

'Snoring like anything,' Sarah replied.

Snoring. He had been asleep. He had done it. It had been one thing just to close his eyes and not be confronted by that voice, those images, but to actually fall asleep without having that recurring, ever-present menace looming large? It was on a different scale altogether.

'You all right?' Sarah asked, as a grin spread across Steve's face.

'Oh yeah,' Steve said. His senses were on fire as euphoric thunderbolts of relief washed over him.

He'd saved a baby. He'd saved a life, and it was something to be celebrated. He could see it, now. Like DS Willmott had said, Adam and Louise had been weighing on his mind and, in a way, they still were. Of course they were. How could they not? But . . . his eyes had been opened to the good that he had done and, as Sarah approached him with a well-deserved beer, it was the good that flooded his mind.

'You deserve this,' she said, as she clinked his glass with her own.

You know what, he thought. Damned right he did. It was like honey as he worked his way through the frothy head of his drink to the liquid underneath, the first sip saccharine as it worked its way down his throat. That sip turned into a slug, the first beer into a second, then a third.

By the time they made their way upstairs, God only knew how many hours later, he wasn't seeing just double. There were three Sarahs in front of him, which ironically made it easier to select which one to take hold of. The Sarah in the middle made the two either side of her disappear and, though his head was spinning on its axis, he looked her square in the eyes as they lay side by side.

'I love you, babe,' he slurred.

'Love you more,' Sarah replied, her words not much more coherent.

In many ways, it was just like they'd met all over again . . . And not just in Steve's mind, but in the way their bodies shifted closer to each other. All those years before, the lust in their minds had overridden the love in their hearts and, as their lips slipped together, history repeated itself.

As they lay afterwards, their arms wrapped around each other's bodies and both in a happy but boozy state of exhaustion, everything seemed right.

Steve closed his eyes and felt himself drifting away into one of those drunken slumbers, just on the edge of nausea but not quite. There were no screams in his ears, though. No haunting images. Just a void. Just blankness. Just quiet.

It was the sleep that he had long dreamed of.

Waking up the next morning was painful. The clock had barely ticked past 06.00 and one thing was for sure: after just a few hours' kip, and with the alcohol still working its way through his system, it was going to be the longest of days. He

131

rolled over and bumped into Sarah, who grunted at him. No words. Just a groan, a grumble, and a back turned to him.

'I'll sort the kids,' he said, sitting up and wincing. It didn't feel like sewing needles that stabbed him in the temples, more the knitting variety.

'I'm coming,' she moaned.

As he sat downstairs, nursing a mug of something dark and strong and decidedly non-alcoholic, it seemed she wasn't. Instead, half an hour later, a sleepy Oscar wandered down the stairs, followed a few minutes later by an equally lethargic Gracie.

'Morning, kids,' he said. He'd already brushed his teeth, but he couldn't get rid of the taste of aniseed. Whose idea had been the sambuca? It was so potent in his mouth he could almost chew it.

Sarah did eventually materialise, physically if nothing else. She was as white as a sheet.

'I'll take the kids,' she said, but her words were hollow.

'Don't worry,' Steve replied. 'I'll do it.' Insofar as being grateful for small mercies, it was that if he was feeling bad, she looked worse.

She nodded and, as their bloodshot eyes met above the kids' heads at the breakfast table, neither of them could resist a smirk even in spite of their pounding heads. Drinking on a school night? It was like old times.

Steve dropped them off with less of the fuss than twenty-four hours prior. There were still a lot of smiles that came his way, but the rapture that had greeted him at the school gate the previous day was tempered down to something much more comfortable . . . Dare he think it, something he almost enjoyed.

'Hey, Steve,' someone said, with the biggest of grins.

'Will be down for a coffee soon,' someone else chimed in, going out of their way to cross his path.

'We should do drinks,' another dad said.

And, unlike before, Steve took it all in his stride, smiling and nodding like royalty as he climbed back into his car and began the five-minute journey home. Coffee and Cream could wait another day. He had sleep to catch up on.

He normally stuck to the speed limit. He really, really did. He was averse to any transgressions of the law, such was his ingrained fear of bringing any attention to himself. But this wasn't like any other morning. His senses weren't in tune with his actions, so dulled had they been rendered by the previous night's shenanigans. In truth, he wasn't looking at his speedometer as he drove the route that he had taken many, many times before. It was a journey that he could make on autopilot and never before had he seen a police patrol carrying out speed checks.

Until now.

'No,' he muttered, as a police officer in a yellow tabard indicated for him to stop.

It wasn't the hangover, he reasoned, as he hit the kerb when he pulled over to the side of the road, braking abruptly with an unusually heavy right foot. It was nerves, pure and simple. He didn't know what to do. Should he get out, or should he wait for them to come to him? The policeman moved slowly, looking at the reading on his speed-checking device before looking up at Steve and shaking his head. His face was firm, his annoyance obvious. Steve stayed in the car. He wasn't sure if, had he got out, those nerves that had caused him to bump the kerb would render his legs jellylike. He wound down his window as the policeman finally approached and lowered his body so his head was within touching distance.

'Good morning,' the policeman said with the firmest of voices.

'Morning officer,' Steve replied. His voice was bright, but a bead of sweat dribbled down his forehead.

The officer had heard enough. Or, more appropriately, he had seen and smelt enough.

'Out of the car,' he growled, reaching in and removing the keys from the ignition.

Steve obliged. He would never be so reckless as to drive drunk, but the morning after? He'd barely even considered it could be an issue, until now. And yet, as he blew on the hand-held device that the police officer presented to him, the 'fail' reading seemed inevitable. As the handcuffs ratcheted around his wrists, the waves of nausea that rode roughshod over him were nothing to do with the alcohol that was yet to dissipate from his system, and everything to do with what came next.

It was a slow drive back to the police station, time aplenty for those queasy undulations to make him wheeze in the back seat.

The police officer kept his eyes on Steve as they waited at a red light.

'Are you all right?' the copper asked.

Steve nodded, a little too vigorously, as the police officer took the green and drove on. When they approached the next crossing, the car stopped once more, and the copper's eyes lingered on Steve again. There, they remained, as Steve looked everywhere but ahead.

'Don't I know you from somewhere?' the police officer asked.

Steve didn't answer.

Chapter 20

DS SUE WILLMOTT

A 9 a.m. start afforded DS Willmott the rare luxury of making Lottie's packed lunch fresh rather than the night before, of spending precious moments with her little girl before they had to leave, and of doing the school run itself. It was always the little things that meant the most.

She stood in the kitchen, spreading butter on a couple of slices of bread, before putting a layer of cheese inside.

'How very domesticated.' She chuckled to herself, as she cut the sandwich in half. The metal handle on the knife chimed gently against the wedding ring that she still wore on her finger. She did it again, then once more, until she found herself tapping out the basic tune of Mendelssohn's 'Wedding March', with a smile on her face. In order for there to have been bad times later on, the good times had to have been there first. It was those memories that always kept her going when times were tough.

'Cheese okay?' she asked, as a freshly dressed Lottie ambled into the kitchen in her Beachbrook Primary school uniform.

'Got any ham?' Lottie asked.

'Cheese is made, poppet.'

'Why did you ask then?'

A good point. For a woman who made a career out of interviewing and putting away the bad guys, her line of questioning was slack when it came to her own four walls.

'Ham it is,' she said, putting the cheese sandwich in her own lunchbox for later.

Lottie had never been one to hang around at the school gate. It didn't matter that it was one of those gold-dust moments when Mum was dropping her off; she was across the playground without so much as a look back. DS Willmott loved that little streak of independence about her. Like mother, like daughter . . . And then some.

As she walked back to her car, she saw Steve climbing from the driver's seat of his own car on the opposite side of the road. Funny, she thought, how she'd never noticed him before on the school run. Their paths must have crossed, even though it was normally her mum who did the drop-offs and pick-ups. But then . . . why would she have noticed him? She barely knew any of the other parents by sight. She wouldn't call herself an absent mum, but it was Nan who did the parties, Nan who did the after-school clubs. As she watched him walk towards the school gate, unsteady of foot as he struggled to coax both his kids along under the weight of school and book bags, she was about to call out to say hello before thinking better of it. Boundaries, and all that. Instead, she climbed into her car and looked at herself in the rear-view mirror.

Something about those thoughts had stuck in her craw, and it wasn't letting go. Something nagging.

Was she absent too much? As she drove away, and checked herself once, twice and three times in the same mirror, it was a question that remained unresolved in her mind, all the way until she was sitting in her office and staring out of the window as the troops filed in.

She flicked at the mouse on her computer, trying to digest the overnight handover and to work out a plan of action for all the prisoners in the bin who would need dealing with, not to mention the various emails that had found their way into her inbox with updates from various investigations. Most notably, it seemed, was one from the fire investigator, which she clicked on first.

'Vinny,' she called, as she skimmed over it.

He wandered into the office, and looked over her shoulder. It was long-winded, full of technical jargon and words that wouldn't have looked out of place in a chemist's notebook, but the crux of it was contained at the bottom, in the concluding paragraphs.

. . . the team determined that the fire originated in the kitchen, located at the rear of the premises. This was an electrical system that was circa forty years old, and had not been updated. The insulation properties of the wiring were found to have degenerated, notably brittle and cracked, and the fuseboard showed clear evidence of arcing and burn marks. A short circuit was the likely cause.

'Such a waste,' Vinny said, quietly.

'Terrible,' DS Willmott replied, as her mind turned to what came next. There may have been no crime, but there would still be an inquest, and His Majesty's Coroner could be even more demanding than a CPS prosecutor. It was one of the things about being a DS. Not everything she investigated ended up in the criminal courts. Her findings would still be interrogated but, instead of a 'guilty or not guilty' verdict, it'd be one that determined the cause of death. This one had 'accidental' written all over it.

'I'll update the family,' Vinny said, walking out of the office and putting on his jacket. She watched as he left, a bounce in his every step, and smiled. He was one of the good ones.

An hour drifted past as she dished out the work and spoke with the detectives in her charge and, as she sat back down at her computer, she clicked on the Custody Whiteboard to see if there were any new prisoners in custody.

A single take.

Then, a double.

MINCHIN, Steve. Time of arrest: 08.57. Time of arrival: 09.12. Offence: Excess Breath Alcohol. No trace PNC. Biometrics required.

'You're kidding me,' she whispered. A mistake? Another Steve Minchin in the district? As she clicked on his photograph and it flashed up in front of her, she saw that it was no error. Not at all. There he was, with bloodshot eyes and puffy cheeks, a look of horror strewn across his face from chin to forehead. She bundled down to the custody suite and found Steve with the arresting officer in the fingerprint room.

'All right?' she said.

Steve looked across to her, as the arresting officer rotated one of his fingers over the digital pad on the fingerprint machine. His cheeks were taut and white, and his eyes glazed. He was, clearly and decidedly, not all right.

'It's not like on the TV,' the arresting officer said, as he carried on with the fingerprinting, 'none of that wet ink and paper anymore. It's all digital now, sent off on the computer and we get results straight away.'

'Results?' Steve asked.

'Yeah, it lets us know if your fingerprints have been found at any crime scenes, or if you're already on the database,' the arresting officer said.

'Righto,' Steve replied.

Steve looked her square in the eye and nodded.

DS Willmott watched as the arresting officer worked with deft precision, taking Steve's fingerprints with the ease of someone who had done it a thousand times before. She hadn't even looked at the Livescan machine, let alone used it. This was as much an education for her, as it was for Steve.

'Results will be back soon,' the arresting officer said, as he typed a few details in and sent the fingerprints off.

'Soon?' Steve asked.

'Before you're released,' the arresting officer replied. 'DNA next.'

'Does that come back straight away, too?' Steve asked.

The arresting officer looked at DS Willmott, and they both smiled.

'Not that advanced yet,' she said.

Steve nodded and, though he smiled, it wasn't quite the same as hers. As the arresting officer scraped the inside of his cheeks with a stick that would be a good substitute for a cotton wool bud, she made small talk.

'Kids all right?' she asked.

'They're good,' he replied.

'And Sarah?' she asked.

'Good too,' he replied.

It was monosyllabic, like a robot answering, but she understood. He'd seemed nervous enough when she'd interviewed him as a witness, God only knew what he was going through now.

'Good night, was it?' she asked.

'Steady . . .' the arresting officer said, as he sealed the second of the two samples in its pot, and sealed the tamper-proof bag shut.

'Sorry,' she said. It was fair enough, after all. Any questions about the offence should come formally in interview. It wasn't that she didn't know that, of course, it's just that she was finding it hard to differentiate between the Steve who she'd placed on a metaphorical pedestal, and the Steve who would likely end up in court over this.

'Right then,' the arresting officer said, 'intoximeter time.'

Steve looked at him, and, as DS Willmott looked on, he wore a face she'd seen so many times before. He was resigned to his fate. It was manifest in the way he nodded, in the way he bowed his head, the way he shuffled forwards with meek steps as the arresting officer led the way.

While the fingerprint technology had evolved from the Dark Ages, the intoximeter machine was still a relic from the past. Steve provided two samples of breath and, as the machine did its thing, the wait for the results was purgatorial.

'You're kidding,' the police officer said, shaking his head.

Steve looked at him. He hadn't been listening.

'Your lucky day,' the police officer said. 'You've blown thirty-three and thirty-one. Legal limit is thirty-five.'

'What?' Steve replied.

'You're on the way down,' the arresting officer said.

Steve still looked blankly at him.

'I'll put it another way,' the arresting officer continued, his eyes narrowing as he stared at Steve. 'The amount of alcohol in your system is below the limit. Now.'

'I can go?' Steve whispered.

'As soon as all the boxes are ticked, yeah,' the arresting officer muttered.

'You lucky, lucky thing,' DS Willmott whispered, nudging Steve on the shoulder.

He looked at her, but the expression of resignation was still etched on his face from cheek to cheek.

'Cheer up,' she said, as the arresting officer bundled out of the room.

'Yeah, good news,' Steve said. His expression didn't mirror his words, though.

'Let's see about getting you out of here,' she said, beckoning Steve forward and leading him out of the intoximeter room and back down the corridor to where the arresting officer was standing in front of the custody sergeant at the podium. DS Willmott stood next to him, with Steve in front of them.

'Your lucky day,' the custody sergeant said.

'So everyone keeps saying,' Steve mumbled.

The custody sergeant tapped away at his keyboard, while the arresting officer ripped open a bag containing Steve's property.

'Belt,' he said, handing it to Steve, 'wallet, cash . . . £21.20 . . . mobile phone . . . car key . . . that's it.'

Steve pocketed it all, not taking the time to fit his belt through the loops of his trousers.

'Livescan results . . .' the custody officer said.

Steve looked up, and DS Willmott looked over.

'No trace,' the custody officer said.

Steve sighed.

'Any questions for me before you go?' the custody officer asked.

DS Willmott walked around to the front of the podium, ready to lead Steve out of the custody suite, but he hovered. There was clearly something on his mind.

141

'Just one,' Steve said, quietly.

'Go ahead,' the custody officer replied.

'The DNA, does it still get sent off, even though I'm not getting charged or anything?'

'Absolutely,' the custody officer replied. 'If you get arrested, we keep your prints and DNA on file forever.'

PART TWO

Growth

With the initial flame as a heat source, additional fuel ignites.

Source – www.nfpa.org

Chapter 21

FIONA

As the days had passed and merged into a week gone by, the news caravan had, indeed, moved on to other stories in different towns and far-flung cities.

Fiona, though, had stayed local. While her peers and colleagues had disappeared to other duties elsewhere, she had no pressing engagements, and what she did have to do could be done at one end of a computer, wherever that may be geographically.

She'd been taken in by Beachbrook, in any case. She'd heard just how mesmerising the little towns dotted around the coast could be, but she'd rarely visited them. Most of her work was found in the cities and larger towns but, now that she'd walked amongst the townsfolk of Beachbrook, she'd developed a certain affinity for them.

How many places had she stayed where people said 'good morning' to you, after all? How many times had people walked past and nodded with a smile, rather than having their head buried in a phone, or tuned out from the world around them with earbuds in? Beachbrook was a throwback, in many ways, to a time gone by, when life had been simple and where community was king.

And yet . . . There was something still nagging away at her. Something, about her digging yielding no treasure. Something about Steve that just didn't add up. It was a running joke amongst her and her producers that they could find anything on anyone, whether it was by a conventional source or something off the books. Steve, though, was proving a tough nut to crack. No social media. No news articles. A sparse record on Company House. Even voter checks were coming up without a trace. It was almost as if he was trying to be as inconspicuous as possible, making a conscious effort to be anonymous . . . And, in her world, the more someone tried to be a ghost, the more she felt duty-bound to dig.

Besides, in her mind, she had grand plans for Steve. Have-a-go heroes were journalistic gold dust and, if she could just get an 'in', just find an angle, then the sky was the limit, and not just for him. If she could build something from scratch, create a legend from the ashes, then she knew exactly what it meant from a professional standpoint . . . Not just ratings but acclaim. The perfect duo.

In the absence of anything to build a picture for her, she'd learned across her career that, sometimes, the best thing to do was to ask. To seek answers from the horse's mouth, so to speak. As she arrived at Coffee and Cream, just as the sun was reaching its mid-morning position far above the horizon, the shutters were still down. She frowned, as dog walkers and others cascaded past her on the promenade and the warmth in the air made her skin moist. It wasn't a day to be closed, was it?

'Not sure where he is,' someone said as she looked around the back of the kiosk.

She turned around and put on her best fake smile, the

one she'd worn more times professionally than she cared to remember.

'Haven't had my caffeine fix today,' the man grumbled, as he trudged past with a dog in close quarters. 'Come on, Lex,' he said, as he walked away.

She certainly wasn't going to get any answers there and then. She sighed and walked back along the promenade, reaching the slope and climbing it slowly. The gradient was enough to have her out of puff when she reached the top and, as she reached to her forehead and mopped her brow, she felt every single one of her fifty years.

She stopped at the road, waiting to cross. There was a steady stream of traffic in each direction and, just as she thought she had time to get to the other side, a car pulled to a stop, blocking her path. Never one to remonstrate, she stood back and, as she did, she did a double take as Steve climbed from the passenger side of the vehicle.

'Thanks for the lift,' he mumbled, as he shut the door behind him.

Fiona stepped back, hoping to find a shadow to hide in and, as the driver said something incomprehensible back to him, she saw her face. It was the detective who'd been investigating the fire. That made sense, she supposed. He'd been giving a statement or something. It gave a perfectly logical reason why he hadn't been open, why his day had been delayed. And, as he walked towards her, looking down at his feet and muttering something under his breath, she was about to say hello, to lay some of the groundwork, to do the chatty, 'off-the-record' bit that – in all honesty – she could do with her eyes shut.

He didn't see her, though. He didn't look up even once, as he stomped a path past her, still chuntering something under his breath that she couldn't make out, but she didn't need to be a fluent linguist to work out he wasn't happy. Bitter experience across the years had told her when to pick her battles and to choose her moment, and this was clearly not one of them.

Steve stood at the top of the slope, staring out to sea, his back arched. It was like the weight of the world was on his shoulders, and Fiona stood down.

Her time would come to speak to him, be it on the record or off, but this wasn't it.

Chapter 22

STEVE

Steve stopped at the top of the slope and stared at the great, wide sea beyond him. He closed his eyes and listened to all the familiar sounds, the seagulls cawing, the late-summer beach revellers on the sands beneath them, the gentle roll of waves lapping into shore, but it didn't bring peace. Far from it. The serenity of it all only exaggerated the fear within. Just when everything had seemed so good, it had all come crashing down around him.

'What are you doing here?' he whispered to himself.

With his head bowed, he performed an about-turn and stared at the ground as he marched back along the road, hoping and praying that he wouldn't bump into anyone, that no one would ask where he'd been and why Coffee and Cream wasn't open. He turned his phone on, wondering if the couple of hours he had spent in police custody had set any alarm bells ringing anywhere. Had Sarah been trying to get hold of him? Phil? Anyone? As the seconds passed by and the phone remained silent, it seemed that his absence hadn't been noticed.

As he plotted the half-hour walk back to his car, sweat

poured from him, and not entirely as a result of the sun that beat down upon him. Nor, to that point, was the ache that pounded him between the temples just a result of the hangover from the night before. Everything that had happened that morning had served to open up the rawest of wounds from yesteryear with the precision of a surgeon's scalpel.

He knew what was coming. It was a ticking bomb waiting to explode.

As he tried to unlock his phone, his fingers trembled. It took three attempts to type a four-number PIN, and four tries to open an incognito tab on his in-phone browser. He needn't have searched for the news article from all those years before. He knew it by rote, and could recite it with his eyes closed, but he needed to see it in black and white, just to confirm in his own mind the winds of change that were coming his way. Crouching in a driveway, hidden from sight, his eyes tracked the words on the screen, and his senses went numb.

BEACHBROOK KILLING: SLAIN CHILD NAMED

Police have named the child who was killed in Beachbrook last month as thirteen-year-old Charlotte Hitch.

Police were called to the scene, atop the cliffs on Beach Road at 17.30 hours on Friday 26th May, where Charlotte was found in a critical condition having sustained a serious head injury. She was rushed to hospital where she remained for two weeks until life support was turned off and she passed away.

Detective Chief Inspector Tom Jefferson has issued the following statement:

'This was a tragic and appalling incident, and I am appealing to members of the public to help us find out what happened. Charlotte's life has been cut short in terrible circumstances, and we want closure for her family, however it may come. I would implore anyone with any information to contact us, either through your local police station or by calling Crimestoppers.'

Charlotte's parents, Kevin and Anna Hitch, added the following:

'We remain utterly devastated at the senseless killing of our beautiful and talented little girl, Charlotte. She should've been safe. No parent should have to bury their child. We have to live with this for the rest of our lives.'

Everything written there, he knew. How many times over the years had he searched for that article? How many times had he read it? How many times had he looked at the picture of Charlotte that adorned the top of it, perfectly dressed in her school uniform, with tassels of light-brown hair that fell down in front of her rosy cheeks? It had always been a part of the penance that he'd self-imposed, to never forget, to remind himself of what had gone before. Now, though? It wasn't so much a kick in the guts that he was feeling, more a nausea so crushing, so overwhelming that the contents of his stomach rose through his throat and deposited themselves on the driveway next to him. The acid burned his mouth, and he welcomed it.

He stumbled as he walked on, caught in a purgatorial state of knowing what was coming, but being an onlooker until it arrived. His phone flashed at him. A weather warning. Amber. Not yellow, where the peril was less; not red, where the risk was grave; but amber. Be aware. Be prepared. The winds of change were coming.

He arrived at his car. The custody sergeant's words rung in his ears, finding their way through the fog. *Don't even think about driving home.* The alcohol content in his system may be fluctuating, and he had no intention of finding himself back in handcuffs. He needed his house keys, though.

The walk had at least cleared the physical effects of his hangover. His keys retrieved, he turned around and retraced his steps, walking in the direction of home. His home. The home he had made with Sarah, Gracie and Oscar. He stood outside the house and looked up at it. Bricks and mortar did indeed make a house, but it was the memories created inside those four walls that made a home. He crept in through the front door, unsure if Sarah was still awake or had gone back to bed.

'Steve?' she called, walking from the kitchen into the hallway. 'Where have you been?'

'Bloody car broke down,' Steve replied, thinking on his feet.

'You're kidding,' Sarah replied.

'Think it's the battery or something,' Steve said. 'Was waiting for recovery but they're snowed under so I just left it.'

His knowledge of cars was terrible, but his only saving grace was that hers was worse.

'You should've called,' Sarah said, gently slapping him on the arm.

'Yeah, I didn't even think,' he replied.

'Tea?' Sarah asked, as he wandered into the kitchen.

'Coffee,' Steve replied. He slumped down at the table as Sarah flicked the kettle on.

'Seen the weather that's coming in?' she asked.

Steve nodded.

'Thursday or Friday they reckon it's going to hit,' Sarah said.

Again, he nodded and, with a weary sigh, unlocked his

phone. He opened another incognito tab in his browser, and searched for another news story that, once again, he could recite by heart. He clicked on the link, as the kettle boiled.

BEACHBROOK KILLING: POLICE HUNT CONTINUES

Two months after the crime, police hunting for the killer of thirteen-year-old Charlotte Hitch have issued an update in relation to their investigation.

Detective Chief Inspector Tom Jefferson said in a statement: 'A thorough and extensive examination of the crime scene on Beach Road has yielded a significant array of evidence, including forensic capture in the form of DNA. I am appealing to anyone with any information to contact myself, my team or Crimestoppers.

I'd like to assure Charlotte's family, and the community at large, that we will not rest until Charlotte's killer is brought to justice.'

DNA. DNA. DNA. DNA. It wasn't a surprise, of course, but it ripped through him like a bolt of lightning through clouds, nonetheless.

It took him two clicks of a button to open yet one more incognito tab, to search for the answer that he'd avoided since he left the police station. And, as it stared him squarely in the face, it wasn't just the storm that was due to make landfall in the next few days. His time was running out. DNA results weren't turned around in a matter of weeks or months.

He had days.

A couple at most. Before everything crashed and burned.

Chapter 23

SARAH

Wednesday was grey but muggy. The fine drizzle in the air had Sarah running from the bedroom into the garden at far too early an hour to rescue washing that she'd forgotten to take in the night before, but she was far too late to save it from being sodden.

As she dumped it back in the washing machine and set it on a quick wash she chuckled to herself. How many people put clothes in the washing machine to make them drier? As the drum kicked into action, she felt hands wandering down her back and, as she turned around, Steve was there. She pecked him on the cheek. She hadn't heard him come down the stairs or into the kitchen, but she was glad to see him.

'Morning, love,' she said.

'Morning, you,' he replied.

'Opening today?' she asked, looking out of the window at the flat calm sky that was uniformly bleak as far as the eye could see.

'Not a chance,' he replied. 'Can I take you out for lunch, instead?'

'God yes!' Sarah beamed, combing her hands through her

hair. 'Be nice to get away from the phone for a couple of hours!'

And it was true. Since news had broken of Steve's deeds, her phone had been ringing off the hook. She wasn't so naïve as to think it was anything other than people wanting to tap into Steve's fifteen minutes of fame but, whatever the case, it had led to a hell of a lot more work, and *that* was always welcome.

Steve put his hand into hers and, as she looked at him, there was something in his eyes, something in his face. Something . . . contemplative. Good or bad, she wasn't sure, but his next sentence cheered her no end.

'You know I love you, right?' he said, quietly.

'And you know I love you too?' she replied.

Morning breath didn't matter. The kiss he gave her was one for the ages, one of those that made the fine blonde hairs on her arms stand to attention. As she pulled away, the smile he gave her was one she couldn't decipher. Happy? Sad? She could normally read him like a book, but now the words were all jumbled up.

'What's up?' she asked.

'Nothing,' he replied, and she took him at his word. Maybe it was all just part and parcel of the 'new' Steve who had come through everything that the past week had thrown at him, who seemed to be embracing the good that he'd done since they'd met with Louise's parents. Maybe moments of depth, of gravity, of solemnity made up the sum of his parts, now. Whatever it was, she liked it.

'I've just got a couple of socials to update, then I'm gonna skip over to Em and Phil's before we do anything,' she said, as she pulled away and flicked on the kettle, 'take them some flowers or something for having the kids for us at the weekend.'

'Good shout,' Steve replied.

And, as she walked up Phil and Emma's driveway an hour or so later, with a drab bunch of roses from a corner shop in her hand, that fine mizzle weighed down the petals and dampened her hair. Emma answered the door, looking equal parts surprised and happy to see her best friend standing in front of her.

'All okay?' Emma asked.

'Surprise!' Sarah replied, bundling inside without the need to be asked. In all honesty, Emma was lucky that she'd knocked and hadn't just let herself in.

'Just caught me,' Emma said, as she fixed the top button on her two-piece suit, off to work in a mo.'

'Early for you!'

'Early bird catches the worm and all that . . .'

Sarah eyed her closely. She may have worn the mask of a confident solicitor who was entrusted with contracts and the like where the number of zeroes on the end were boggling, but it was a façade that Sarah had always been able to see through. Behind that tough exterior there was a vulnerability. It didn't matter how much concealer she had applied to her cheeks that morning, the tear tracks were still obvious.

'You okay?' Sarah asked.

Emma sighed and nodded for Sarah to come in.

Sarah ambled into the back room of the house. It was one of those where the kitchen and living space were merged, the new-fashioned way of doing things with brilliant whites and sleek greys, which would have been the perfect camouflage for the skies outside. Phil was standing over the kitchen island, nursing a cup of something, wearing boxer shorts and a T-shirt. In every respect it was a normal morning in a normal house, the like of which would be playing out in towns and cities all across the country yet . . . There was

156

something. An atmosphere. A tension. Something that Sarah couldn't quite put her finger on. In spite of the mugginess in the air, there was an ice all around them.

'Hey, Phil,' she said. Was she imagining it?

'Hiya,' he replied. Nope, she wasn't. Phil's single word was as cold as the weather was forecast to turn.

'Brought you flowers,' she said, walking towards the island and popping them on the counter, wondering if the petals would wilt under the strain.

'What's that for?' Emma asked.

'Just . . . everything,' Sarah replied.

'Come on,' Emma said, 'let's go in the front room.'

Sarah nodded at Phil and flashed the biggest smile she could find and, though he reciprocated, it didn't have the blazing intensity and authenticity of the man they all knew and loved. She wandered away, pretending to be oblivious to anything while, at the same time, noticing everything. As she walked into the front room and pulled the door shut, she looked at Emma, at the frown lines that seemed just a little bit deeper and at the almost imperceptible shake of her head as she rolled her eyes, the bags under them sagging as she did.

'Don't worry about it, you've got enough going on,' Emma said.

'What's up?' Sarah replied, completely ignoring her best mate's instruction.

Emma chuckled and, for good measure, rolled her eyes once more. If the first one had been aimed at Phil then, Sarah was sure, the second was entirely hers.

'Marriage shit,' she sighed.

'Marriage IS shit, or marriage . . . shit?' Sarah asked.

'Marriage shit,' Emma replied.

They looked at each other and, for no reason other than the confusion between whether the word 'is' should have been present in a sentence or not. A little giggle soon turned into the pair of them laughing like hyenas. Sarah didn't hear the stomps up the stairs beyond the front-room door, but she couldn't fail to feel the vibrations as the bathroom door upstairs slammed shut. She looked to Emma, but all she got in return was a third roll of the eyes.

Theirs may have been a friendship that had come about through Steve and Phil, but it was one that had developed a life of its own. They had their own closeness, their own alliance.

'Talk to me,' Sarah said.

Emma's lips pursed.

'We're just going through it at the moment,' she said, quietly. 'Life though, eh?'

It was a kick in the guts, truth be told. Emma and Phil had always been solid. Now? There was a frailty that she'd never seen coming.

As she told Steve all about it later, with a voice low enough to avoid back-seat earwiggers, her husband seemed unbothered about it. His response was monotone . . . Uninterested, even.

'Ups and downs of life, I suppose,' he mumbled.

'Phil said anything to you?' she asked.

She looked at Steve, who indicated right before turning into the car park. It may have only been a chain restaurant they were going to, but it was time spent together that mattered. It could've been McDonald's and it wouldn't have mattered . . . too much.

'Nothing,' he replied.

'Weird,' she said, as Steve slotted the car into a space.

As they sat at their table, which was upgraded to a booth in the window after the owner recognised Steve, and Sarah set about analysing everything on the menu, her heart was full. Friendly nods came their way from all quarters, and someone even came over to shake Steve's hand. She was so proud of him and just wished he'd be able to allow the enormity of what he'd done to sink in properly.

She looked at her husband and, as he nodded in appreciation, his lip twitched and his simple 'thank you' was delivered in a tone she hadn't heard before. It wasn't a squeak as such, just a bit more high-pitched than she was used to, and with a quivering overture, too. Was it the new-found depths of emotion, she wondered? He was different now, all right. Good different. Great different. She reached across and brushed her hand against his, not taking hold of it but imparting as much adoration as if she had. He looked up at her and, if she didn't know better, she'd have said there were tears in his eyes.

Chapter 24

DS SUE WILLMOTT

What a difference a day made. From the glorious sunshine and unseasonable warmth of Tuesday through to rising winds and apocalyptic forecasts, Wednesday and Thursday were the rest days that DS Willmott needed. Though the rains outside were precipitating the storm that was on its way, inside her four walls there was love. There was happiness. There was tenderness, as three generations of Willmott women shared dinner on Thursday evening.

As night fell and darkness came, she tried to sleep, but it was no use. The winds were whipping up, finding gaps in the frames of her bedroom window that she never knew were there, and whistling through. What started off as the faintest of hums grew louder as an hour passed until, finally, she gave up. Nature's percussion was too much, even with a pillow planted firmly over her head.

The clock showed 23.14 as she poked her head into Lottie's room and, save for the soft melodic tunes purring from her night clock, there was silence. No winds seeping in, no cracks in the edges of the windows being taken advantage of. She gently pulled the door to and crept downstairs. As she looked

160

out of the front-room window, it was one of those 'once every couple of years' types of storms that seemed to blow through town. The news media had been salivating over it all day on the telly. It had even been designated a name. Storm Isabella was forecast to make landfall on the south coast early in the morning. The gusts and rains that were hitting now were a mere entrée, the antipasto to whet the appetite. The main course was going to come to town soon.

She flicked on the TV, stabbing furiously at the volume button to keep it from waking Lottie. The overnight news channels were full of red 'breaking news' banners and presenters slavering at the prospect of what was to come in the following hours. Satellite imagery showed a mass of red heading their way and, in the centre of it all, Beachbrook was fairly and squarely in the firing line. As if to emphasise the point, somewhere outside, in the distance, a bin toppled over.

She slept in fits and starts, dozing to the soft drone of the overnight news while waking every hour or so. By the time first light should have risen, it was still dark, the clouds outside refusing to let the light of the sun through.

'Sue?'

She forced her eyes open.

'All right, love?'

She looked around, momentarily panicked at waking up somewhere other than her bed, to a voice other than her daughter's.

'Hey, Mum,' she said, sitting up and stretching her arms.

'Bloody nightmare out there,' her mum said.

DS Willmott didn't laugh. It wouldn't have been fair. But . . . it was rare to see her mum with a strand of hair out of place, let alone the whole mop. Instead, the cracks at the edges of her mouth rose just a smidgen, but it was enough for her mum to see.

'You wait 'til you go out there!' she said, palming at her locks and trying to flatten them.

And she wasn't kidding. With Lottie's kiss still fresh on her cheek, it wasn't so much a breeze that cut through her as she ran from the front door to the car, more a gale. It took real effort to force the driver's door open and, conversely, to close it behind her. Even inside, she couldn't escape the winds. The car may have been stationary, but it was rocking on its axle as it was buffeted from side to side.

The drive wasn't long, but it was an adventure. She'd never done any driving courses – CID had been her goal, not Traffic – but she was sure that even those with the advanced courses, the tactical pursuit and containment, or even the instructors on the police driver training unit, would have been out of their comfort zone in those conditions. After she pulled into the rear yard at Beachbrook nick and climbed from her car, she ran into the wind until she found sanctuary in the CID office, bursting through the doors to a silence that yawned at her, given the squalls outside. She collapsed into her chair, feeling like she'd run a marathon.

As the team filtered in, at least she had the advantage of having got in first and ironing out the creases that Storm Isabella had brought upon her. Her hair was short, anyway, and had only needed fine-tuning. She wasn't one for make-up, so there were no smears on her face. A quick press of her jacket straightened it out. The others, though? Those who weren't so fortunate as to have a parking space in the rear yard? Isabella had played a game with them, it seemed, blowing long hair into a tangle and leaving cheeks windswept. Much like when she looked at her mum earlier, she couldn't help but chuckle as she fired up her computer and walked out of her office into the open-plan room beyond.

'Coffee run,' she said, as she stalked the rows of desks

where her detectives were fixing themselves up. It was the least she could do and, as the smell of instant granules filled her nose from the assortment of mugs on the tray in her hands, and she looked beyond the windows at the tree branches whipping around and the wind beating the sea into a frenzy in the distance, she shuddered.

It'd take a hand grenade going off to get her out of the office on a day like that.

As she settled down at her desk, coffees delivered and computer fired up, it wasn't a hand grenade that sat in her email inbox. It was a bomb, and the fuse was well and truly on fire.

Her hand hit her mouth. Her coffee hit the floor.

And her mind raced back a couple of decades or more, to when she'd been a rookie cop on the beat.

'Control to any patrol available to attend a flash call, Beach Road, concern for welfare?'

'Sounds like one for us,' Geoff said.

PC Willmott looked up at him, a man old enough to be her father and one who was ambling his way towards his pension with a twinkle in his eye. In every respect, he was the perfect tutor.

'Control from Bravo Bravo Two Two,' PC Willmott said, 'we're available. What have you got? Over.'

Geoff slipped the car into second and stretched the engine. With the click of a button, he lit the lights and, with the flick of a switch, the siren too.

'Sketchy at the moment, but reports of someone unresponsive on the clifftop,' came the reply.

'You need a sudden death,' Geoff said, as he navigated two sets of red traffic lights in the middle of town with consummate ease.

PC Willmott's mind whirred, as she pictured in her

development record the list of incidents she needed to attend in order to be designated an independent patrol officer. In the sudden death column, there was a gaping hole.

'Anything else?' she asked, holding the transmitter in her hand and thinking of the million and one things she needed to get right at an unresponsive person report. Scene preservation. Crowd control. First aid.

'Radio discipline,' Geoff said.

'Over,' she said quickly, into the radio.

'Good girl,' Geoff said, as the radio barked into life.

'Control to Two Two,' the radio operator said, before pausing . . . 'stand by.'

She looked at Geoff, at his 'seen it all, done it all' face that told stories of a thousand and more incidents that he'd attended across the years, and he seemed relaxed. She, on the other hand, wasn't. It was something new and, like every green copper who was learning the trade, something different was something to be nervous about.

'Control to Two Two,' the radio operator said.

'Go ahead,' PC Willmott said, 'over.'

'More reports coming in,' the operator continued, with a voice totally different to the normal, relaxed, chipper one that had been speaking only moments before. 'It's a kid. Sorry. Unresponsive person is a child. Looks like an assault. I'll get more resources en route.'

And, as those resources were assembled, and officers with stripes and pips were scrambled, she looked at Geoff, at the unflappable, resilient bloke who was teaching her everything he knew, and his cheeks were twitching. His right foot grew heavy. And they travelled at a speed she'd never experienced before.

Their sirens announced their arrival long before they arrived. As PC Willmott ran from the passenger seat, her *mind was scrambled. There was a cacophony of noise set against a backdrop of tranquillity, a clifftop where panic reigned as, just beyond, the sea purred. Screams of anguish, complemented by the wailing of yet more sirens in the distance. And at the centre of it all, a girl, no more than thirteen, lying on the ground, her blue eyes wide but with no life behind them. From her mouth, the tiniest dribble of blood fell and, as her hair fluttered in the wind, loose pieces of A3 paper floated in the air.*

'CHARLOTTE!' a man screamed.

'CHARLOTTE!' a woman shouted, in chorus.

Two figures emerged from nowhere, racing towards the bench where PC Willmott was standing, looking around, wondering what the hell she needed to do. Geoff grabbed the man and so, by instinct, she grabbed the woman.

And everything else was a blur.

'No way,' she whispered to herself.

She reached for her phone. Years, they'd waited. Years, and years, and years. It may not have been protocol but, after a couple of decades, she knew who needed to hear it first. Who deserved to hear it first. Who had yearned for an answer, who had lost everything as a result of not having one.

As the phone connected, she closed her eyes and remembered the scene, all those years before.

And those thoughts shifted in a flash, to everything that was yet to come.

Chapter 25

FIONA

Fiona was up early. Too early. As the winds slapped against the window of the clifftop hotel she'd grown rather accustomed to, she was awake long before her alarm clock told her it was time to get up. There was nothing better than that feeling, though, of being curled up under a duvet, listening to the outside world getting itself in something of a pickle. She didn't even pick up her phone once. Instead, she just lay in the dark, waiting for her cue.

Sure enough, as 05.59 rolled into 06.00, and her phone chirped into life, she climbed from her bed fully awake and ready to go. She'd always hated doorstepping someone, but needs must and all that. Besides, Steve hadn't been at Coffee and Cream, and every time she'd tried to call his phone her call had been blocked. Sometimes, it was the most direct route that got the best results and, in any case, it wasn't so much an ambush, more a friendly nudge. No cameras. No fuss, no microphones or demands on his time. Just a request for a few minutes so that she could share her plans with him.

She'd been given the thumbs up within minutes by the bigwigs at the network. Those docu-news programmes had been gaining traction as the years had gone by, the ones where current affairs were blended with background, with backstories. She'd always pitched it as giving colour to something that may otherwise have been a sea of grey. What she wanted from Steve, what she needed most, was his take on it all. What had made him stand up when others would have run away, what gave him the impetus to face down the flames and come out on top? From every angle that she stared at it, it was a story that demanded answers.

She washed and changed. Casual clothes. Jeans and a jumper. A raincoat in hand, too. This wasn't a piece for broadcast, it was just a friendly chat to lay some groundwork. First, though, she had some edits to get through, some other deadlines to hit. She'd found the perfect coffee shop that opened its doors early to catch the morning rush just in town, where the Wi-Fi was good and the noise always low but, as she looked out of the window, and the rain fell in slanted sheets, not even the lure of a decent hit of caffeine could pull her from the confines of the hotel. Instead, it'd have to be a morning of dodgy filter stuff, and Wi-Fi that came and went as it pleased.

As she kicked back on one of the sofas in the lounge downstairs, her laptop firing up on the table in front of her, she looked out of the window to her left and smiled. Coffee was coffee, and Wi-Fi was Wi-Fi, but those winds? That rain? Forget about it.

As she scrolled through her phone, the 5G at least running like normal, she laughed. Long ago, when she'd been young and keen, she'd been the one to chase the weather all around the country, reporting on it in a mac, almost praying for a fork of lightning to strike within eyeshot or rumbles of thunder to pour through the microphone, drowning out any commentary she may have been giving. Now, though, as she watched colleagues of hers whom she knew, and some she didn't, battling the elements in little snippets on X and Instagram, how glad was she that she was chasing something altogether more newsworthy, that the bosses hadn't called her and asked her to cover Isabella making landfall. It would have made sense, after all. She was in the right place, and her natural gravitas would have added a certain oomph to proceedings. Instead, though, she guessed that her years of service had worked in her favour. Instead of standing out in the rain, getting drenched and freezing cold as she waited for her cue for just a minute of airtime, she was sitting in the warm, drinking coffee, and watching it all play out in front of her. Smug? You bet.

She flicked through the draft of a document in front of her. It was her opus, the bible to the story that she'd been working on. Steve's story. Baby Jack's story. Louise and Adam's too. It was a story of tragedy, of bravery, of hope and heroism, the words that, one day soon, she hoped to bring to life on screen. She'd been toying with a title to it. *Phoenix from the Flames*. That worked.

And that's how her morning passed her by. Sitting in front of her computer, bashing out copy, searching for different angles with which to attack the story, all while looking at the worsening vista in the world beyond the window. All in all, it was a good morning's work, and the clock on the wall behind her hadn't even struck midday.

As she stood up and packed her laptop away, she reached for the rain mac that she'd stashed on the chair next to her. As her eyes lingered on the window and the carnage beyond, she reached for her phone one more time. Steve's number was littered throughout her call list but, no sooner had she dialled than it went straight to voicemail. With a sigh and a smile, she popped the phone into her pocket.

'No rest for the wicked,' she said, loudly enough to attract squinting eyes from someone sitting nearby. She nodded at them, and they looked away quickly, no doubt wary of the woman who talked to herself, she thought. Her grin grew large. People normally stared at her because there was some vague sense of recognition, not the weirdo who had conversations with themselves.

With her bag on her back, and her car keys in hand, she walked towards the hotel exit.

Out of the fire.

And into the storm.

Destination: the Minchin house.

Chapter 26

KEVIN

Much as he loved routine, over his dead body was Kevin going on his usual Friday morning walk in THAT. Instead, he watched the TV as reports of Storm Isabella making landfall and churning up everything in her wake dominated the agenda. 'Generational,' they said. 'Amber warning, bordering on red,' they claimed. As he looked from the window, and the wind bent trees sideways, it seemed, for once, that the events were living up to the hyperbole, that the clichés may actually be ringing true.

The morning passed him by, as he sat back in his chair watching the reports on the TV and, in the background, the grim view from his front-room window. He was safe inside, away from the winds and the rain and the near apocalypse that the reporters were broadcasting about from various spots across the country.

Charlotte's pictures stood sentry over him as the breakfast hours drifted towards lunch, as the weather worsened, as the news reports became even more alarming.

It took the soft, melodic tune of his phone to draw his attention away. He picked it up from the table next to him and stared at the screen. Unknown number. Withheld. It was either one of those marketing companies, a spammer, or . . .

'Hello?' he said, taking his chance and answering it.

'Hey, it's only me,' came the reply.

It was almost breathless. They were just four words, from a woman he'd met so many years before, a woman who had been a uniformed copper, who had been there when Charlotte's young life had been snuffed out, who had snuck into the back of the church weeks later at the funeral, dressed in civvies, trying to be as anonymous as possible.

A woman, who had gone on to be a detective, and who had kept in touch on such a regular basis that the line between police officer and friend had blurred. A woman who had visited Charlotte's bench with flowers so regularly that they'd shared war stories and all manner of conversations there over the years.

A woman who, when DCI Jefferson had retired, had been only too keen to take on the as yet unsolved investigation into Charlotte's killing. She was a couple of ranks too low, some had suggested, a detective sergeant in charge of an unlawful killing, but it was an argument they were never likely to win. Not when Sue Willmott had had her say.

And a woman who, in those four words of greeting, transmitted to him that she had news. Big news. News, that he'd waited decades to receive.

'Tell me,' he whispered, as he clasped the phone close to his ear.

Chapter 27

STEVE

It was a heavy knock on the door that made Steve's stomach drop. This was it, he reasoned. His time was up.

Isabella may have been pounding away outside but, in his head, the perfect storm had arrived. Sarah looked at him and, as she made to stand up, he gestured for her to sit back down.

'I've got it,' he whispered as he walked out of the lounge. His head hung like a condemned man, taking his last steps along death row.

He reached the front door and, for just a fleeting second, understood why religious people crossed their chests. He pulled it open, still staring at his toes, letting the outside world in. It was a storm out there, all right, but it wasn't a copper standing on the other side of the threshold.

'All right, mate?' Phil said.

'Phil?' Steve replied.

'Well durrrr,' Phil said as, behind him, carnage ensued as the rains poured down. 'You letting me in or what?'

'Course, mate,' Steve replied, shaking the demons from his head and moving his body to the side as Phil walked past.

He closed the door, shutting out the winds, the rains and the madness.

Phil strolled down the hallway, seemingly oblivious to the washing machine he'd just ambled in from. Steve followed, still shaking his head.

'All right, kiddos?' Phil said, as he walked into the lounge.

'Uncle Phil!!!!' Oscar shouted, dropping his tablet to the sofa and running across the room, latching himself to Phil's leg and not letting go even when Phil's fingers dug into his ribs and made him dissolve into ribbons of laughter.

'Are you mental?' Sarah asked, with a smile on her face. 'It's World War Three out there!'

And Steve made her right. As he looked at Phil, at the normal expression on his face, at the normal way he was acting with the kids, at his normal voice and his normal grin, it was all too . . . normal. And he saw through him like a cheap piece of tracing paper.

'In here,' Steve said, as Sarah prised Oscar away from Phil, whose grin disappeared as he nodded. Whatever it was, he was busted, and it took about ten seconds of probing in the dining room for Steve to get it out of him.

'Just an argument, that's all,' Phil said.

'Just an argument?'

'Just an argument.'

'She all right?'

'She's fine.' Phil's reply was short. Curt. Pointed, even.

'Wanna talk about it?'

'Not really, mate.'

'Gotcha,' Steve said. 'Tough, though.'

Sometimes, people needed a prompt. Something was wrong. Something was amiss. Phil was his best mate, and Steve was all ears.

Alas, Phil didn't get a chance to talk to him. No sooner had he opened his mouth to speak, no doubt to remonstrate, to claim that everything was okay, than there was another knock at the door. This one wasn't a tap. Thunder clapped through the house, and it hadn't come from the sky.

It was a copper's knock.

Steve looked at Phil, abject fear radiating from his eyes, before turning and near running down the hallway to answer it. No way was Sarah going to get there first. He opened it, letting the storm in once more. Beyond, it was a hive of activity. Police officers. Police cars. And DS Willmott, wearing a face of granite where before he'd only ever seen kindness. The game was up. His time had come.

And it was just like he'd expected it to be.

'You're under arrest on suspicion of the murder of Charlotte Hitch,' DS Willmott said, as a uniformed copper snapped a pair of handcuffs onto him. 'You do not have to say anything, but it may harm your defence if you do not mention when questioned something you later rely on in court. Anything you do say may be given in evidence.'

'What are you talking about?' Sarah gasped. 'Charlotte who? Charlotte WHO, Steve!? He doesn't know a Charlotte.'

'What the hell's going on!?' Phil shouted.

'Daddy,' Gracie cried.

'Daddy,' Oscar moaned.

It was a dream. A nightmare. And, as he walked out of the front door, into the storm, into the raging winds, the torrid skies, the sheeting rains, waves and waves of nausea flooded his every sense, his every sinew.

'I'm going to be sick,' Steve whispered.

And he was. Right there, as the eye of Isabella looked down on him, he brought up whatever it was that had been sitting in his stomach.

'Been nicked before?' the uniformed copper asked, as Steve stood up, before heaving once more.

'Yeah,' he replied, his voice shaking as he wiped globules of vomit from it with the back of his hand, 'a few days ago. but never for murder.'

DS Willmott walked down the path until she was by his side and, though the rain stung his eyes, he lifted his head as she read to him from her day book. Procedure, presumably. She was making sure she crossed all the t's, dotted all the i's, it seemed. Still, her words pricked his ears as painfully as the drops from the sky on his face.

'Just to clarify,' she said, 'we have forensic evidence that links you to the murder of Charlotte Hitch. Your arrest is necessary to allow us to investigate it promptly and effectively, and to allow for further forensic evidence to be obtained, namely an evidential sample of DNA. Understand?'

Steve nodded his head but, as he looked beyond DS Willmott, at a figure standing behind her on the pavement, he wasn't the only one who understood the ramifications of what she'd just said to him.

That reporter. Fiona. She was standing right there, and she'd heard it all. Worse, she had her phone in her hand, and it was pointing directly at him.

Chapter 28

DS SUE WILLMOTT

She had to say the words. She had to be the one to do it, to tell him he was under arrest, to caution him, and to see the look on his face when she did so. For Kevin, as much as her, she had to look into his eyes and search for a reason, to seek answers. And, as DS Willmott stared at Steve, looking far beyond what the surface told her, she saw a tortured soul being battered by a deluge, both from above and from within.

Good.

Steve was looking beyond her, staring at something with ever-widening eyes. Her sixth sense burned and, as she pivoted on the spot, she felt her tummy fall through her pelvis.

A journalist. THAT journalist. The one who was always on the telly, was now standing no more than four feet away from her, mouth agape, and the phone in her hand pointing directly at them. She sighed as the journalist turned around and marched away.

DS Willmott sat next to Steve on the way back to the police station, watching as he fidgeted, trying to find a position that was as comfortable as a pair of rigid cuffs to the rear could be, and she wasn't minded to help him. In normal circumstances, she might have engaged in a bit of small talk, something to help the minutes pass by and to put her detainee at ease. Not now, though. Not a chance. Any confusion that had reigned in her mind over the DNA result had dissipated in the minutes since she'd received them. Now, she had processed it. Now, she had come to grips with what she'd read in black and white. It was *his* DNA that she'd spent years searching for, and she wanted him to squirm.

To suffer.

Charlotte had.

Now it was his turn.

And, even though there was a mountain of work to do, a summit yet to be reached, closure was within her grasp. For her. For Kevin. And for everyone who had been touched by those events, all those years before. All she had to do was ask the right questions, and get the right answers. At the moment, it was foggy. But, only yesterday, it had been dark. She needed to ask the right questions, to get the right answers, to find the light beyond the haze.

'Name?' the custody sergeant said, as uninterested as the other one had been when Steve had been arrested before.

'Steve Minchin,' he replied, quietly.

This time, there was no flicker of recognition, no peering over the custody podium at him. This time, the sergeant tapped away with the jaded fingers of a veteran cop who was counting down the months to retirement.

'Offence?' the custody sergeant asked.

'Murder,' DS Willmott replied. She'd been waiting for that moment, and her heart fluttered in her chest.

That piqued the custody sergeant's interest.

'Circumstances,' he said, rising to his feet from the chair he'd sat slumped in.

It was a speech that DS Willmott had practised in her

mind time and time again. She'd long given up hope that she'd actually be able to deliver it in real life but, as the words tumbled from her lips, it all felt so very real.

'I'm the OIC on a historic case where a thirteen-year-old girl was murdered. Mr Minchin here was arrested last week for an unrelated offence and had his biometrics taken. This morning I received notification that he has been forensically linked to that historic case. He has been arrested to allow us to investigate it, to obtain an evidential sample of DNA, allow any relevant searches and to obtain evidence by way of questioning.'

The custody sergeant jabbed at his keyboard as he sought to keep up with DS Willmott's monologue, and she knew why he was suddenly so keen to seem interested. Everything was up for scrutiny in a case like this one. Everything. A defence brief would seek holes everywhere, from procedural indiscipline all the way through to how their client was treated in custody. The last thing someone on the verge of retirement needed was something like that hanging over their head.

She watched Steve as he answered every question asked of him in the same low voice that bordered on monotone. Had he given up, she wondered? Was this him throwing in the towel? Had he been expecting it, waiting for it to happen?

She cast her mind back to when it had happened, how she had pestered and pestered to be a part of the investigation team but had been laughed at, a rookie cop wanting to be involved in one of the most high-profile investigations of its time. Operation Grace, it had been called, and she'd followed it from a distance as mass DNA screenings came up blank. How had Steve slipped the net?

As she closed his cell door, and the heavy bolts slammed shut, she took a moment just to stop, to listen. Whether she was expecting a sudden breakdown from him, or a voice talking to itself asking for forgiveness, she received nothing. Instead, it was just a groaning silence that developed, punctuated only by the sound of her footsteps a few seconds later as she walked down the corridor. It mattered not. She had an interview to prepare for, paperwork to complete, and a DCI to brief.

One thing she didn't need to do was to go through the boxes and boxes of evidence that had been accumulated across the years. Everything within them, she knew. Everything they contained, she'd committed to memory long before. There was no one with a knowledge of the case that came anywhere near to matching hers, and it had been the joker in her pocket when she'd claimed ownership of the investigation.

'Is it enough?' DCI Maine asked, as DS Willmott briefed her via conference call to the Major Crime department.

'I hope so,' DS Willmott replied.

'What about that journalist?' DCI Maine asked.

'No press enquiries yet . . .'

'It's gonna go crazy.'

'I hear ya,' DS Willmott replied.

The two women looked at each other, on differing ends of the conference call. DCI Maine's credentials as an SIO were impeccable, one of those real 'been there, seen it, done it' career detectives who had risen through the ranks quickly but had stopped at three pips. Anything beyond that, she'd always maintained, was too political for her. It was qualities such as that which made DS Willmott like her so.

'Update me after interview,' DCI Maine said, as they spoke of strategy, of policy decisions, of the evidence trail that led all the way to Steve's door.

'Will do, boss,' she said. As she walked out of the conference room, down the corridor where all those with pips and crowns on their shoulders plied their trade and back down the stairs to where the real work took place, those butterflies in her tummy sprouted wings once more.

'Treat it like any other case,' she muttered to herself as she sat at her desk, walking herself through the interview question by question by question, while knowing that it was anything other than that. This one was personal. This one affected her, on a molecular level.

It was normal practice for her to let an interview breathe, to let it develop naturally as it evolved, where scripted questions were a big 'no-no' lest they interrupt the flow. Now, though, she had specific things that she needed answers to. She jotted down a list of questions before going over them with Vinny. More than once, she altered them, some totally and some technically. It took a couple of hours but, with tweaks complete, she was ready to go in to bat. Vinny was walking to the crease with her and, as they gave Steve's solicitor disclosure, they resisted the brief's attempts to coax the very nature of the forensic evidence from them.

Steve's consultation with his solicitor lasted well over an hour itself, and it did little to settle DS Willmott's nerves. They were a heady mix of excitement and responsibility, coupled with that nagging doubt that took up permanent residence in every detective's head: have I dotted the i's? Have I crossed the t's? Does everything stack up as it should?

She'd been a detective for years, and had interviewed everyone from the humble shoplifter to the serial rapist, but this was one that she'd been waiting for. As they finally lined up against each other, the man she'd feted as a hero until only a few hours before now entirely on the other side of the battlefield, it was game time. She slipped the interview discs into their respective slots in the machine without so much as looking at him, her eyes only fixing on his as the long, steady beeping sound indicated that the interview was beginning.

As the noise died and the silence grew, it was on.

Chapter 29

STEVE

Inside the cell, where the paint flaked in patches and the four walls grew closer the more Steve stared at them, the veins in his head bulged. The pressure was building within. These were moments that he'd imagined many times, but they'd just been a morbid fantasy, the type that had haunted him but that he never would have expected to happen in real life.

Yet, there he was. The storm outside may have been gathering strength but, as he sat on the plastic-coated mattress and the walls moved closer still, the tempest inside his head was raw. It was all-encompassing. It was potent. And it was going nowhere.

He'd had years to ruminate, to formulate, to cook up a plan, but the truth was nothing could have prepared him for a cell. Nothing could have made him ready to hear what DS Willmott had spat in his direction. *You're under arrest on suspicion of murder.* Just thinking of those seven words, of the way that DS Willmott had delivered them, of how Sarah and Phil had reacted, of how Gracie and Osc . . .

'I'm so sorry,' he whispered, his voice trembling. The tears that began to fall weren't for him. They were for his kids, for

Sarah, for Phil, for Charlotte, for everyone and everything that he'd done. That he'd been found out had certainly forced the issue, of course, but they weren't the tears of an insincere man.

And still, his head pounded. And still, his heart thumped against his ribcage. The more he thought of Gracie, of Oscar, of Sarah, even of Phil, the tighter the vice on his lungs became. What were his options, he wondered? What was he to do. To say nothing, and to hope it all went away, or to tell the truth, and risk losing everything?

By the time the jailer opened the door and led him to his consultation with his solicitor, his head was a melting pot just waiting to blow.

The strategy, it seemed, was clear. His solicitor was one of those faceless men in suits, his advice simple. In all honesty, Steve knew the tactics long before he'd even spoken to a brief. He'd seen enough cop shows, done enough research.

As DS Willmott stared into his eyes, and the beeping sound came to an end as the interview began, his lip twitched. He didn't mean it to, but, sometimes, a poker face was simply impossible to maintain.

As she began her opening gambit, she didn't once look away from him. And it scared him. Deep within. To the core. To his very, very soul.

DS WILLMOTT: The time by my watch is 15.23. We're in an interview room at Beachbrook Police Station. My name is DS Willmott. Also present are DC Robson and solicitor Mr Russell. Could you please state your name and address.

So far, so expected. He'd read all about the introduction to police interviews, how they were nothing like on the TV, what with all the preamble and everything. There were bits and pieces that DS Willmott needed to go through before she got into the nitty-gritty, and he knew it.

STEVE: Steve Minchin, 40 The Glades, Beachbrook.

DS WILLMOTT: Thank you. Before we get into the interview, there are some things I need to go through first. I need to caution you, so you do not have to say anything but it may harm your defence if you fail to mention when questioned something you later rely on in court. Anything you do say may be given in evidence. I'll break it down for you, so that you understand, okay?

Steve nodded. He knew what it meant, in intricate detail, but he played along. Anything to delay the main course.

DS WILLMOTT: You do not have to say anything is your right to silence. You don't have to answer my questions if you don't want to. What I'd ask, though, is that you say "no comment" so that we're not sitting with great vacuums of silence. Okay?

Again, Steve nodded.

DS WILLMOTT: But . . . if you don't answer my questions, and if this matter goes to court later on, the court might think that you've had time to think up a different story. Same goes for if you give me an account now, and then change it at court. The simplest way of explaining it is that now is your chance to give your side of the story. Make sense?

Another question and another nod.

DS WILLMOTT: Last thing, this interview can be produced at court as evidence. Next, I need to tell you that you're entitled to free and independent legal advice at all times while you're here. You've got Mr Russell with you. If at any time you want to stop the interview for a consultation, just let me know and I'll turn the tapes off so you can do that. Finally, you've got the right to consult a book called the codes of practice. It governs how we look after you while you're in custody.

She shuffled some paperwork on the desk that sat between them. Steve's stomach grumbled at him, and it wasn't just because he'd emptied it all over the pavement outside his house. It was nerves, pure and simple, a pack of cards somewhere deep within him, balanced precariously and just waiting to come tumbling down.

DS WILLMOTT: You've been arrested on suspicion of murder. For the avoidance of doubt, it's in relation to the death of Charlotte Hitch. What can you tell me about that?

Steve took a deep breath, but it was one of those that wasn't pure. It wasn't clean. Instead, it was shaky, a stuttering inhalation, followed by an outbreath that felt contaminated. What he was about to do, he knew, was the weakling's way out. He'd weighed it up in his mind and come to a simple conclusion. If there was a choice between being a coward and leaving his kids without a daddy, there was no discussion to be had.

STEVE: No comment.

His voice was barely audible and, when it passed from

his lips and struck him in both ears, he didn't recognise it as his own. It was that of a weasel, of someone who would rather run from the fight than face up to it. He looked at DS Willmott and, in her face, in her eyes, in every single facet of her, in fact, saw derision.

DS WILLMOTT: I see.

There was silence, as she shuffled her papers once more. For Steve, it was insufferable but, he guessed, it was a tactic designed to make him squirm. Whatever. It was working.

As the minutes passed, and one set of discs turned into another, there appeared to be no let-up in her questions.

Background about him, about his upbringing.

No comment.

Where he'd been living when Charlotte was killed.

No comment.

He'd been a kid, himself. Just a kid.

No comment.

Where he'd been on THAT day.

No comment.

What he'd done in the years since.

No comment.

To every question, every query, every attempt to provoke a response.

No comment.

All of the preamble wasn't what mattered, though, and everyone in the room knew it. It's what his solicitor had asked him about, what DS Willmott was pinning her hopes on, and was the very reason that he'd been arrested. Finally, after about an hour of him playing a dead bat to every question she asked, she got to the point.

DS WILLMOTT: At the scene, we found a source of DNA. Care to tell us about that?

STEVE: No comment.

DS Willmott's sigh was long. Deep. Intentionally drawn out. This was it, he knew. The nitty-gritty.

DS WILLMOTT: That's not going to cut it. Not now. DNA. Talk.

Steve's solicitor nudged him and leaned forward.
'My client is asserting his right to silence,' he said. 'Tread carefully, Detective.'
Steve looked at DS Willmott, at how his solicitor's words just bounced off her without being processed. She was in the zone, he guessed, and she launched into her next question without flinching, without acknowledging his reprimand.

DS WILLMOTT: Your DNA, Steve. Tell me about it.

STEVE: No comment.

They were at an impasse. It seemed DS Willmott was building up to the grand reveal, but it didn't matter to him. He knew exactly where it was heading. He closed his eyes, and it all came flooding back.

It was one of those halcyon days. The sun shone, the sea hummed and the sky was cloudless, the most striking shade of blue. Steve ran, and ran, and ran. Straight past the front door, straight up the drainpipe, as nimble as they came, straight into his bedroom window on the second floor that was opened way beyond its safety catch, straight into a communal lounge where the others sat and watched whatever it was that teenagers of the day watched. In that annoying way of those of his age, sprinting even that distance had barely caused him to catch his breath.

DS WILLMOTT: Your blood, Steve. Tell me why it was under her nails.

'PLEASE, NO!'

Those words echoed in his ears as he looked down at his arm, the scratches bleeding as if cut by razor wire.

It raced around in his mind as the faintest hum of sirens drifted in through the windows. They got louder. Louder. Louder. The screeching of tyres heralded their arrival, but they passed on by. As loud as they'd been, they soon receded into the distance. And so it continued. Faint sirens became loud as they screamed past the care home, then quiet as they disappeared into the distance, only to be replaced by more oncoming wails as yet more coppers raced to the scene. Faint, loud. Faint, loud. Steve didn't dare look out the window, lest the sea just beyond tell tales on him.

DS WILLMOTT: 'Tell me about the blood, Steve. You were there, weren't you. Your DNA was under her nails. What happened?'

Steve opened his eyes. DS Willmott's words were laced with a desperation that transcended the role of a detective investigating a crime. There was something else there, with her. Something deep. Something . . . intrinsic. Her eyes begged him to tell her what had happened, what had gone down, but to do that was to risk it all. He wanted to. Of course he wanted to. He'd spent years almost fantasising about lifting the weight, but each time he thought of vomiting up the words, the thought of Gracie and Oscar spending years without a daddy made him suck them back down. His cowardice was a sickening bile, but he simply had to stomach it.

STEVE: No comment.

DS WILLMOTT: Your blood, Steve. Your DNA. Talk to me.

Steve's tremoring breaths returned, but his answer was the same.

STEVE: No comment.

DS Willmott flicked over some pages with a flourish and, as Steve strained his eyes to see what she was looking at, he caught the words at the top of the page. It was the post-mortem report.

DS WILLMOTT: Cause of death, blunt-force trauma to the head. What did you hit her with, Steve?

That was a question that hit him like a freight train, square in the forehead and made his quiet, reserved voice squeak just a little higher than before.

STEVE: No comment.

DS WILLMOTT: Don't you owe Charlotte that much, Steve? Don't you owe her family? Her mum went to her grave not knowing what happened, don't you think her dad deserves the truth?

STEVE: No comment.

Steve rocked on his chair. It was gut shot after gut shot. If it'd been a boxing match then he'd have been on the ropes, clinging to his opponent with everything he had. There, though, in DS Willmott's ring, he was cannon fodder. He was her punch bag, his stomach her bull's eye and, with every question, she didn't miss a shot.

DS WILLMOTT: Did she scream, Steve? Did she cry out? Did she ask for her daddy, as you killed her?

His mouth dropped and, if he didn't know better, he'd have sworn that there were tears in DS Willmott's eyes as she spat the questions at him with quiet yet unreserved venom. He opened his mouth to answer, to say something, to protest his innocence, anything, but his solicitor beat him to the punch.

'Steady, Detective,' he said, patting Steve's knee that was tapping to the beat of DS Willmott's drums, 'don't be oppressive.'

DS Willmott's eyes remained fixed on Steve, not once wavering, nor acknowledging a word the solicitor had said.

DS WILLMOTT: Well?

Steve couldn't maintain eye contact with her. It was all too much, all too raw. He looked to his feet, as the same two words escaped his lips.

STEVE: No comment.

Chapter 30

DS SUE WILLMOTT

It was no victory dance, no stroll towards the finish line. She'd gone into the interview confident enough with the evidence she had, but answers were what she needed. Without them, what she had was fragile. She was sure she had the right person, at the very least, but knowing it and proving it were two different things in the eyes of the law. She could put him at the scene. She could show that he was there. What happened, though . . . Why Charlotte had died, how she had perished, well that was something different altogether.

'Thoughts?' she said, as they approached the conference room.

'Same as you, I guess,' Vinny replied.

DS Willmott sighed. Good detectives seldom differed on initial reactions to how something had gone and, though she'd half been expecting a 'no comment' interview, she'd really thought that she could rub the lamp and release the genie within. The questions she'd asked hadn't just been those of an officer investigating something. They'd been something she'd wanted . . . NEEDED . . . to know, for many years. That Steve had kept the genie locked away had stymied her from an evidential perspective but, that was nothing compared to the frustration on a basic level. Those questions towards the conclusion of the interview? They'd been lingering in her throat, just waiting to escape and, in the end, she'd been incapable of preventing them from slipping out.

She sat opposite Vinny in the conference room, and looked at her younger charge. Their gaze met halfway. As he spoke, it seemed, great minds did indeed think alike.

'He did it, didn't he,' Vinny said.

DS Willmott nodded, as she dialled DCI Maine in to the video call.

'Talk to me,' the boss said.

'No comment,' DS Willmott replied.

'Other enquiries?' DCI Maine asked, the SIO in her coming to the fore.

'Phone download, searches, intel checks, family background, it's all in hand,' DS Willmott replied.

'Is there anything else we can do today?' DCI Maine asked.

DS Willmott shook her head. Everything that needed to be done was being done. They were slow-time enquiries, though, nothing that could be done while Steve was still in the bin.

'Enough to meet charging threshold?' DCI Maine asked.

DS Willmott rolled her shoulders and, with the weight of more than two decades of pain bearing down on her, both her own and that conferred on her by Kevin, she pursed her lips.

'Enough to ask.'

And as she sat in her office, with the phone number of the CPS Complex Case Work Unit in her hand, she knew that the scrutiny of what evidence they had so far was going to be far greater than that of a normal CPS prosecutor. To meet the threshold was the same principle – the law was the law, no matter what level it was being applied at – but it was more than likely going to be a barrister testing the waters, dissecting her report to them. It may have had DCI Maine's name on the paperwork, but it was her investigation.

Two hours later, and a whole heap of deep diving into every avenue of evidence later, she had her answer.

'Bail,' she muttered, as Vinny floated into her office at the first sign of the phone being hung up.

'For murder!?' Vinny replied.

'For murder,' DS Willmott said.

'Is that a thing?'

'It is.'

And, though rarely advertised in newspapers and on TVs up and down the country, pre-charge bail for unlawful killings was actually more common than most people knew. In truth, DS Willmott had known there was more work to do. Steve being at the scene was never going to be enough to go to court with. Sure, it might have got them across the line on threshold, but that was dependent upon there being something else, something dynamite that they could blow up at court. At the moment she had one ace, but she needed a pair at the minimum. Three or four, in one hand? That'd be the icing on the cake.

'Bail conditions?' The custody sergeant asked, as he typed up the bail notice with Steve standing in front of him and DS Willmott to his side.

'To sign on every Monday, Thursday and Saturday here at Beachbrook nick,' DS Willmott replied.

'You heard all of that?' the custody sergeant asked, as he populated the words and ticked the boxes.

'Yeah,' Steve replied.

'Sign here, here and here,' the custody sergeant said,

producing a piece of paper from the printer and pointing at three signature boxes.

Steve took hold of a pen and hovered the tip of it over the MG4A form that was presented to him before finally penning his name.

'Back here four weeks' today,' the custody sergeant said, 'at 13.00 hours. Don't be late or we'll come and get you.' He countersigned his part of the form, and gave Steve a copy. 'And make sure you sign on every Monday, Wednesday and Thursday at the front counter until then to uphold your bail conditions.'

'Okay,' Steve replied. DS Willmott watched, as his shoulders dropped.

'Property?' the custody officer said, and a jailer appeared with a clear plastic bag, sealed at the top with a property form attached. The custody officer checked the serial number written on the form against the cable tie attached to the neck of the bag, and ripped it open.

'Belt, wallet, keys, twenty-two quid, all yours,' he said, as he passed the items to Steve.

'My phone?' Steve asked, slipping the belt through the loops on his trousers and pocketing the other bits and pieces.

'That's ours for a while,' DS Willmott said. 'No stone left unturned – I'm sure you'll understand.' Her words were cold, her tone icy.

'Gotcha,' Steve replied, but he didn't look at her. It seemed that he was all out of eye contact.

'Anything else?' the custody sergeant asked.

'Just gotta grab his evidential DNA sample, then done,' DS Willmott replied.

'Crack on,' the custody sergeant said.

And crack on she did. It was the same process as when Steve had had his DNA taken less than a week before.

Something akin to a cotton bud on a stick, scraped down the inside of his cheek but, as DS Willmott took hold of his face with one hand, and planted the swab inside, she did it with a roughness she'd never before employed. Sure, she could have claimed rustiness, having not done it for . . . well, years . . . but as Steve winced and the teeth on the stick gripped the inside of his mouth, she had meant it.

'All done,' she said, as she popped the sample into the tamper-proof pot and sealed it inside the bag.

'Good to go?' Steve asked.

'Good to go,' she replied.

And as she saw him off, through the front-counter exit, her eyes narrowed. She was sure she had her man. Proving it, though, was another thing entirely.

Chapter 31

SARAH

Within seconds, Steve had been whisked away and there were coppers searching their house. Her house. It was all too much, too surreal, like a living nightmare.

Sarah didn't have a clue how to navigate the system, but that didn't really matter. In her blind panic, she first dialled 999, demanding answers as to where her husband was, why he'd been taken away, what was happening. All she received by way of reply was an admonishment that wasn't gentle, that the 999 system was for emergencies only. Her whisper-screams down the phone that it was an emergency, that her husband had been arrested by the police, only earned her another stern lecture, and a warning that any more calls would make her liable to end up in a cell next to him.

Finally, after what seemed like hours of calling around the houses, getting put through to one department then another, with lines going dead and people hanging up, she reached Beachbrook Custody Suite.

'Custody,' the voice on the other end of the phone said. It was gruff, exactly what she would've expected from someone who worked with prisoners all day long.

'Steve Minchin,' she said, breathlessly spluttering his name for the umpteenth time in as many minutes, 'I think he's there with you.'

'And you are . . . ?' came the reply.

'Sarah Minchin, his wife,' she said.

The line went silent.

'Please, don't hang up,' she whimpered.

'Still here,' the jailer replied. The voice was softer now. Sarah wondered just how many times they fielded calls like this, from family members who weren't clued up on the system and how it worked. Sure, they must have their fair share of regular customers, but Steve wasn't like that. SHE wasn't like that. Their family wasn't. They were just normal, everyday folk.

'He's here,' the jailer continued, his voice trailing away. Sarah tried to picture it. Was there a board, or something, that he was looking at? Was it a long list of people who were in the custody suite? Were his eyes tracking down it as he searched for Steve's name?

'Is he okay?' Sarah whispered.

'He's fine,' the jailer said, 'but you'll understand I can't speak to you about what he's here for.'

'They said murder!' Sarah cried, her words escaping her lips with a volume she didn't intend.

'Try not to worry,' the jailer replied. Try not to worry. TRY NOT TO WORRY! Fat chance of that.

'Is he coming home?' Sarah sobbed as, above her, the floorboards creaked and Oscar's faint laughter tracked its way through the ceiling.

'Someone will be in touch,' the jailer replied.

She sat alone, quietly contemplating what had happened. Murder. Murder. MURDER!? What the hell? She'd watched Steve be handcuffed behind his back, watched him be led away, watched as he'd emptied the contents of his stomach all over the pavement before he'd sat in the rear of the police car. There may have been tinted windows partially obscuring his face but, as she'd walked on autopilot down the pathway towards him, oblivious to the storm that made her sway from side to side, she'd seen his face as they'd driven away. She'd seen his lips move.

Sorry.

Was she mistaken, she wondered?

Sorry.

No, she wasn't. He'd mouthed it to her and, as she stared into the mirror in the lounge, and made her own lips mimic the two syllables that he'd mimed to her, she tried to find replacements. Anything that could cast doubt on her certainty over what she knew to be true.

Help me.

No. The letter 'm' required the lips to be closed for a moment.

Love you.

Nope. The tongue rolled differently with that.

He'd said 'sorry' and, for what he was apologising, she needed to know.

Murder? MURDER!?

'What the hell, Steve?' Her whispers were slight as she stood in front of the mirror time and time again, working through all manner of double-syllabled permutations, each of them getting more outlandish than the last as she tried so desperately to make sense of it, to find reason in that solitary, individual word.

Sorry.

It implied sadness.

Sorry.

Sympathy?

Sorry.

Regret?

Sorry.

Penitence.

'Sarah?' Phil whispered. While she'd been searching around corners for answers that remained elusive, he'd been entertaining the kids. That he'd crept down the stairs and into the lounge without her noticing spoke volumes as to the extent her mind was chasing shadows in the dark. She looked up at him, and his face spoke for itself. No words were necessary. Worry was pouring from every pore of him, seeping from hairline to chin and, though she was looking at his features through his reflection in the mirror, it did nothing to dull the strain.

'Heard anything?' he asked as, upstairs, those floorboards creaked once more. Within seconds, the rumble of young feet on the stairs grew louder.

'Nothing,' she replied, as Oscar charged into the room followed a few seconds later by Gracie. She rubbed her eyes dry, but couldn't do anything about the raw streaks that stained her cheeks. She wasn't ready to field the expected questions, about where Daddy was, when he'd be home, why the police had stolen him.

Phil must've seen it in her eyes. As she looked to him, and without saying anything, a switch flicked in him and the worry was gone. He turned around to face the kids as Sarah turned away and, as he led them both into the kitchen to make mud pies, she sighed with relief.

The winds softened and the rain died out as Storm Isabella passed through and, in her wake, the sun crept out beyond the clouds just as it approached the horizon. Sarah stared out of the window as darkness approached. She stood up to flick on the lamp when she heard the faintest sound coming from the hallway. Metal on metal. Key in lock. Door opening. She was up like a shot and out of the room before Steve had closed it behind him.

She stared at him, and he at her. She opened her mouth to speak, to find a bunch of words that she could string together in a sentence that could be construed as vaguely coherent, but they wouldn't come. In any case, as Oscar and Gracie came on the rampage from the kitchen, it simply wasn't the right time. They each affixed themselves to one of Steve's thighs, and clung on for dear life, chattering excitedly.

'Uncle Phil said you were helping the police,' Oscar shouted, 'on a secret mission!'

'Were you, Daddy?' Gracie asked, as she kept her head firmly pressed against him.

Sarah looked at Phil, and he shrugged his shoulders. She got it, though. She understood. What else could he have said, after all? That their daddy had been led away in handcuffs, with the word 'murder' ringing in the air? That she'd not been the one to have been there for them, that she'd not dealt with their queries herself, that she'd been too wrapped up in it all to even think about anything other than her own inner turmoil, made a lump form in her throat. As the seconds passed, it swelled in size.

'Come on, kiddos,' Phil said, tickling each of them until they fell from Steve, and Oscar's giggles once again filled the air around them, 'let's go and finish those pies off.'

They may have been unwilling footsteps that followed Phil, but the lure of a mud pie was like a magnet to the kids. And, as they disappeared out of sight, but not necessarily out of earshot, Steve beckoned with his eyes and the point of a finger for Sarah to join him upstairs.

She stared at him before she moved.

Sorry.

What secrets was he clinging on to?

Sorry.

What had he been hiding from her, from them?

Murder. MURDER!?

Sorry.

As she stomped her way upstairs, she had questions. Lots of them. And she wanted answers.

Chapter 32

FIONA

The storm had raged around her as she'd stood with her jaw touching her chest, watching as an assortment of police officers in both uniform and plain clothes had swarmed the pavement outside Steve's house, led by the detective who she'd seen only a few days before, dropping Steve off at the beach. Now, there was nothing so friendly as THAT going on. Now, as she stood back, making herself as anonymous as she could be, she did something that separated the good journalists from the great ones.

She didn't interfere.

She didn't ask questions.

She just stood back and looked on.

Answers would come later but, for now, hers was a watching brief. She stood on the opposite side of the road, oblivious to the wind and the rain and the stormy clouds overhead that began to soak her through. She checked once, twice and three times to make sure that her phone was recording. It was only then that she took any notice of the weather, and it wasn't in the interests of self-preservation, nor vanity. No. Instead, she cradled her phone like a newborn baby, protecting the lens from any rivulets of rain, lest they blur the images they were capturing.

It was a veritable assortment of cops. Were they expecting trouble? What the hell was going on?

The images, though . . . they spoke for themselves.

Steve, being frogmarched down the pathway towards the road when he chundered everywhere. His wife, shouting after him. His kids, crying. The other bloke in the house, remonstrating with a cop on the doorstep. And the female detective, a face that sat somewhere between cheerlessness and the cat who got the cream, following behind and giving a monologue that had been caught in stunning 4K on her phone.

Every moment was televisual perfection. Every second was gold. And, as she slinked away as stealthily as she'd arrived, she knew there and then that she'd hit the jackpot.

As she sat on a Zoom call with her boss in one of those soulless satellite offices, thirty minutes from Beachbrook, there were decisions to be made. There were questions to be asked. She'd yet to change out of her drenched clothes, such was her urgency. Her requests were met with tempered responses, though.

There were answers to find, and time was of the essence. He hadn't just been nicked for shoplifting. It was murder. And not just any old murder . . . but one that had touched a nerve up and down the country so many years prior. As 'heroes turned villain' stories went, it was in a league of its own and, what was clear, whichever way she looked at it, was that she'd landed on a little mine of gold. Strike that. She'd landed on a massive pile of gold but, where there were riches, others would soon be digging away, trying to get their grubby mitts on their own share of the treasure.

Whatever it was, whatever had happened, she needed

to land it fast, before everyone came sniffing around in her wake.

'Let's talk public interest . . .' her boss said.

Amidst the adrenaline that was still coursing through her veins from something massive brewing in front of her, Fiona smiled. That very question was why she was happy she'd not progressed to the executive level, in spite of the attempts that had been made to promote her. Sure, it was her story, but to run it would require authority from above. There had been too many high-profile cases in recent times where things had gone, for want of a better term, tits-up.

'Hero turns villain,' she replied. 'And not just any villain . . . He's being plastered all over as a poster boy . . . but . . .' She let her words trail off, their implication obvious.

'All right,' her boss said, 'get digging. And when you've dug, dig some more.'

'On it,' Fiona replied, as she hung up on the call.

The tingling in her fingers told her everything she needed to know. She was on to something. What that something was, though, was as yet unknown. It was the hunt that kept her young, that kept her on her toes . . . And that's what made hers the best job in the world.

Chapter 33

STEVE

Steve had spent over a week living the life of the reluctant hero. Now, and for evermore, everyone would know who he was and what he had done.

Sarah.

The kids.

Phil.

The choice had been taken out of his hands. He had to tell Sarah before she found out some other way. That news lady . . . she'd seen enough. She'd heard enough. How long would it be before word got out, before the wolves that had been hounding his front door returned with a vengeance?

He crept upstairs feeling that, with every angst-ridden step, his life was heading towards the edge of a cliff, a precipice beyond which there was no return. How could there be? Life, as he knew it, was over.

'Today' had always been a prospect. As the days had melted into years gone by, it seemed as if he might just have gotten away with it. Alas, 'today' had arrived, and tomorrow would forever be shrouded in doubt and darkness.

As he followed Sarah into their bedroom, a little bit of

him died. She wasn't yet facing him, but she was shaking. He could see it. Her hair, flowing loose and free, was shimmering from side to side under the spotlights in the room. Her arms hung by her sides, but the tiny blonde hairs on them stood on goose bumps. This was the moment that he'd spent his adult life desperate to avoid, a moment when he had to tell her that everything was going to be different. Everything was going to change.

She turned around to face him, locking her eyes on his. He'd stopped under one of the spots, and its light burned into his skull as he tried to find some words from somewhere deep within that might explain everything to her.

'Well?' she asked. There was venom in her question, all right.

His head was numb and, as he scratched at a growing twitch on his cheek, it did nothing to alleviate the prickling feeling beneath his skin.

'I'm sorry, love,' he said. 'I'm so, so sorry.' He tried to keep his head up, to look at her, to show her that he meant every single word, but he just couldn't do it. The burden of more than twenty years of concealed sin had emptied a weight over his head that forced his eyes south . . . Eyes that sprung leaks, no sooner had they left her gaze.

'For WHAT!?' she shouted, as she crossed her arms. No matter how deep the apology, he realised, no matter how heartfelt it was, she needed to hear it.

'It's unforgivable,' he whispered, between the tears.

'What is?' she asked. Her words were still spat with a toxicity that he'd never, ever heard.

Composure evaded him and he fought to stop the tears from falling, and to form some words that would explain everything. How could he defend his past, though? How could he even begin to justify why he hadn't told her everything from the outset? There was no rational excuse or reason. He'd long known that. He'd lived with it all that time.

'I've got to tell you some things about who I was before I met you,' he began, his voice quivering, his body shaking.

'Spill,' she said, her one- and two-word entreaties making her instructions so easy to follow yet so hard to obey.

And yet . . . Was it an olive branch, he wondered, as she sat down on the bed? Was there a seed of hope, as she pointed for him to sit next to her? Was their bond, so deep, so powerful, so true, enough?

And so, he began. Or at least, he tried to. It was a speech that he'd always had in his mind, but didn't know if he'd ever deliver. And Sarah didn't interrupt him. Not once.

'I was born in Finisham, up north.' His voice quivered. 'I lived there, when I was a kid. Those days . . . my childhood . . . it was the worst of the worst.'

It wasn't that he glossed over exactly *why* his childhood had been so bad, more that those reasons were hidden, repressed, and secured deep within him. Things that remained under lock and key, no matter how much he might want to share them with her. Even now, faced with the absolute disintegration of everything he had lived for, those words wouldn't come. The utter devastation that had followed him through his childhood were memories too far a gap to bridge.

He'd been a child in need, a child in care, but one failed so terribly.

'I ended up in Beachbrook, half the country away from where I'd grown up. It was different. Better different, you know? Better people. Better chance, for someone like me.'

'Someone like you?' The venom in her voice laced his ears with a poison so acute that it made his temples throb.

'Someone like me. A broken kid.'

She didn't respond and, though her body remained rigidly still, he could sense the tension in her. It oozed through the mattress underneath them, radiating through his every sense. The silence that followed reverberated all around him as the spotlight on him grew stronger. Within a minute it was unbearable, and he simply had to break it.

He'd never said the words, though. They'd never passed his lips. Until now.

'I killed her,' he whispered. 'I killed that girl. Charlotte. I did it.'

Sarah's body remained still. Dead still. Her knuckles, though, tightened around the duvet beneath them. Steve wanted to grab hold of them, to remove the white from her balled fists, to get the blood flowing, to tell her it was all going to be all right, that he was sorry. That he was so, so sorry.

But he didn't. He couldn't. Instead, another silence descended over them and, this time, it wasn't his right to break it. He just had to sit there and suffer as Sarah's ragged breaths filled the air. He deserved it.

'A leopard never changes its spots,' she whispered, after minutes had passed by. She was still gripping the duvet, her knuckles now white.

'What's that?' he replied.

'It's one of your sayings,' Sarah said.

Steve sat in silence. He knew where this was going, but he let it play out. This wasn't about him. Not anymore. This was all her, and he had to let it run its course.

'How many times have you said that?' she whispered. 'When someone does something, and then they do it again and again and again, and you always say, "a leopard never changes its spots".'

Steve stared at the floor, at the tiny specks of dirt that

sat on the carpet around his trainers. He had nothing he could say by way of riposte, nothing to placate everything that was no doubt raging through her mind. Every second, he guessed, there was a new revelation as she tracked her way through more than two decades of memories, all of them tainted by what he'd done and the secret he'd kept from her.

'You even laughed about it,' she said.

He stayed silent.

'Look at me,' she ordered, and that's exactly what it was. An order. An instruction. Not the request of a loving wife, but a demand from someone aggrieved.

'Laughed about what?' Steve murmured.

'Spots!' Sarah spat back at him. 'Leopards and their stupid spots! I feel sick.'

'I'm sorry,' Steve said.

Sorry. He had nothing else. What good would any other words do, after all? There wasn't anything else he could say, no cleverly composed, structurally sound sentence that would even begin to repair the damage.

'Get out,' Sarah screamed, turning her quivering body away from him. Whether they were trembles of angst, or shivers of rage, Steve wasn't sure, but it stabbed him between the ribs to see it either way.

He stood up and his hand touched her shoulder. She flinched, before her body jolted as if struck by lightning. He pulled away, as the current diffused from her and flowed through him. His heart was still racing, as beads of sweat formed on his forehead and the palms of his hands grew clammy. He could feel it all falling away. Everything that he had fought so hard to build and to maintain was crumbling before his very eyes. He just wanted to hold her, to tell her that everything was going to be all right and that they could get through it together, but his very touch had provoked a reaction of fear in the woman he loved.

She had shuddered. His touch had made her recoil.

He stood up and shuffled slowly out of the bedroom, closing the door behind him. As he walked down the stairs, he heard the muffled wails of his wife being carried through the air. They penetrated deep inside him, breaching whatever barriers of fortitude he still held within. He wanted to turn around. He wanted to go back upstairs, to be the hero that he had spent the week being feted as. He wanted to be the husband he had always tried to be, the one who would make bad things good, and wrong things right. He wanted to do all of that, and more.

But she had flinched.

He opened the front door and, in the absence of Storm Isabella, it was still. It was calm. The air was flat. All around him, though, there was evidence of the carnage that had been left in her wake. Wheelie bins, everywhere. Tree branches, scattered. Sand, whipped up from the beach and deposited all over town. As he turned around, and looked at the house that they'd made a home, he knew that the ruins that he was leaving in there were just as profound.

This must be rock bottom.

Chapter 34

KEVIN

After the storm, came the calm. The clouds that had swamped Beachbrook for the day had gone and, in their place, the sky was a uniform vista of black with speckled stars in between. Only the moon brought any light, but it was a mere crescent in the canvas above him. If Charlotte was there, she could've joined the dots with her chalks, making pictures from nothing. It's what she'd always been good at. Taking nothing and making it something.

As he sat on her bench, and the still of night surrounded him, he should have felt a peace within. In reality, he felt anything but, and he fidgeted from position to position, straightening his legs before curling them up underneath the wooden slats, folding his arms and stretching them above his head. He had goose bumps on his goose bumps as he sat and waited. Waited for answers. Waited for Sue to come. It was a purgatory almost as hellish as the decades that had passed him by.

THIS had been a day that he'd yearned for, the day when the phone call came, when the last piece of the jigsaw was put in its place. His was an agitation that had been brewing for so many years. Before, it'd been a pipe dream. Had he

210

given up hope? Publicly, of course not. No chance. Privately, though? When the nightmares came and the terrors kept him awake? His will had begun to wilt, for sure. With the unscratchable itch tantalisingly in range, a fire had begun to burn inside him that had long been dormant.

Car headlights telegraphed Sue's arrival long before she walked to the bench. He guessed she'd be coming. There was no way that she wouldn't, not given everything they'd been through together across the years. The phone call earlier, he understood. He'd always wanted to be the first call that she made, when that sleeping DNA finally met its match, and she'd been true to her word. Now, though, she was visiting in person. Good news or bad? He couldn't quite decide.

'I guessed you'd be out here,' Sue said, as she sat down next to him.

'Talk to me,' he demanded. Niceties would follow. Now, he needed to know, and the bite in his voice was something that had been dormant for years.

DS Willmott sighed and, in a flash, he dug his nails into the damp struts of wood beneath him. A sigh was bad news. A sigh told him everything he needed to know. Pain shot up his hand, through his arms and into his soul as he scraped his fingers a few millimetres backwards, exposing the root skin to splinters and the like, but he didn't care. He needed words, not sighs. Answers, not silence.

'We've had to bail him,' she said, 'went "no comment" in interview. There's a lot more work to do.'

They'd discussed the evidence so many times across the years that Kevin could well have been one of those unpaid detectives who are the staple of many a murder mystery on the TV. *The DNA isn't the be-all and end-all*, he'd been told, but it would open doors. It was what lay in the rooms beyond that they were interested in. Now, though? The fact that it wasn't the holy grail, in spite of everything they'd said? His heart was shattering all over again. More than that, though, he felt anger, hard like a stone, in the very pit of his stomach.

'His DNA was under her nails.' He may have been quiet, but there was no mistaking the growl in his voice.

'It was,' Sue said.

Kevin's breath was long and slow. In through his nose, out through his mouth. He counted to ten in his mind, before turning to Sue and taking hold of her hand. His grip was just a little bit too tight.

'Who is it?' he whispered. 'Do I know them? Did Charlotte know them?' A whimper formed in the back of his throat, from nowhere. As it escaped from his mouth, it took him by surprise. He had to know. Had to. HAD TO.

Sue's hand gripped his just as tight as his held hers and, under the dull light of the moon, he caught her eye. The shake of her head was barely noticeable, as an apology spilled from her lips.

'Sorry, you know I can't tell you a name,' she said quietly. 'But no, she didn't know him.'

Kevin stood up, and stared beyond the clifftop, to the place where he knew the sky met the sea, but where it was solidly black.

'I know you can't tell me who it is. I get it.'

He stopped and stared at Sue. He wasn't finished yet.

'But I need to know. Is it him? Is it the man who killed my girl?'

He didn't care about whether the evidence simply put him at the scene, nor what the guidelines were about whether there was enough to pursue a charge. Theirs was a friendship built on the foundation of tragedy, but it was a friendship no less. If she said it was him, if she believed it, then he would too.

'I think so,' Sue replied. 'DNA doesn't lie.'

That was enough, for now. Justice would see its course, one way or the other.

It always did.

Chapter 35

DS SUE WILLMOTT

It was a job like no other, one that DS Willmott had never taken for granted when times were good but, equally, one where she thrived when the going got tough. Through peaks and troughs, up hills and in valleys, she loved what she did. Come hell or high water, she'd be there in the morning, the first one in the office as normal, with a renewed incentive to get justice for Kevin, To get justice for Charlotte. To close a book that had been open for years, where the ending hadn't yet been written.

First, though, home. She left Kevin on the bench with a peck on the cheek and a squeeze on the arm, and climbed back into her car. That he'd been on edge was only to be expected, but the strain he'd exhibited had been buried for years. She'd been the shoulder to his grief for so long, yet the anger simmering beneath? She'd heard it in his voice and felt it in his hand. She'd promised him a resolution. Now it was on her to deliver.

She'd left the office with various boxes ticked on paper after a long session with DCI Maine, but it didn't hurt to revisit them as she drove. It was when she was in her car that she could think. Not wind down. Think. Analyse. As she ploughed a route home, through debris that Isabella had left in her wake, those tick boxes filled her mind:

Steve's phone. Sent off for download. She'd once tried to learn how the tech-bods did it, but the explanations had flown right over her head. Instead, she'd just wait for the report to hit her desk.

Background checks. Still coming up negative. Intel tasked with digging up whatever they could.

Financial Crime Unit tasked with . . . anything, really. Anything anomalous in his finances. They had carte blanche, when it came to things like that.

Inter-agency work. Taskings sent to the local authority, council tax checks, NI checks, anything that might open a door, that might provide a lead.

Media strategy. The statement had been released only a couple of hours earlier. It was one of those bland ones, a generic bundle of words that said a lot but didn't actually give much away. As the hour hand on the dashboard completed another cycle, she tuned in to Beachbrook Hits Radio, and the words that she and the boss had concocted with the press office were read out by the local news reporter.

'Our headline news, police in Beachbrook have announced that they have arrested a forty-one-year-old man on suspicion of murder, in relation to the decades-old murder investigation into the death of thirteen-year-old Charlotte Hitch. The local man was taken into custody earlier today, interviewed and bailed to return at a later date.'

She racked her brains, to see if there was anything else she could have done, if there was anything else still to do. It wasn't your run-of-the-mill investigation. It wasn't like there were video doorbells back then, CCTV everywhere, people with camera phones. Charlotte's murder was a generation prior, and it made her bones ache to think about it.

But, think about it, she did.

'I need someone to go with her to the hospital,' the inspector said, as the stricken girl with the eyes staring at nothing was loaded onto an ambulance trolley.

PC Willmott didn't know the boss, but she could sense the urgency in his voice, the strain as he wrestled with the conflicting demands of bosses above him wanting answers, a radio that was barking at him, and the burden on him to secure and preserve a crime scene.

'I'll go,' she said. She looked around for Geoff, but he was nowhere to be seen, a tutor constable swallowed up in the chaos. Golden rule number one had been broken; she'd left his side.

As she climbed into the back of the ambulance, not once letting the girl out of her sight, the two adults who had come steaming over to them tripped over each other as they followed her inside. They were babbling, talking incoherently, telling their 'Charlotte' that everything was going to be okay, that they were there, that they'd have her back painting in no time at all.

PC Willmott didn't know what to say, so far out of her comfort zone was she. She didn't have Geoff there to guide her, to tell her what to do. Instead, her eyes filled with tears.

What was she supposed to do? Make notes? Take it all in? Write a PDR report about it? In the absence of all of the above, she did what she could. She stood up, and held both of the parents' hands, and told them she was sorry about what had happened. That's all she had. Sure, she was a cop, but she was a human first.

It was a bumpy ride. The sirens wailed throughout as one

of the paramedics did things to Charlotte that she didn't understand. Needles, all kinds of things. She watched through misty eyes, not really understanding what was happening but being able to recall it so vividly many years later.

She'd never been inside the A & E department at Beachbrook Hospital before, didn't know what resus was, nor what ICU meant . . . But it mattered not a jot. Was she green? Sure. Naïve? Absolutely. Totally engaged, in a way she didn't know possible? Completely.

Charlotte clung on for a couple of weeks, and PC Willmott took guard duty on her whenever she was on shift. She visited even when she wasn't.

And when the doctors held one of their multi-discipline meetings, and decided that there was no prospect of life, she was there. She held both parents' hands again.

And she watched as Charlotte drifted away.

'Mummy!'

She'd shut the front door quietly, just in case her daughter was asleep, but she wasn't. Lottie ran up to her, and wrapped her little arms around DS Willmott's waist. She was getting far too big, far too soon and, as DS Willmott looked at the clock on the wall, it didn't matter that she was half an hour late for bed. Those hugs were everything, especially after a day like that. The memories it had evoked had been visceral, from the initial call way back when, all the way through to naming her own daughter, many years beyond. To call her Charlotte would have been too close to the mark, too obvious, too . . . Deliberate? 'Lottie' had served a purpose all of its own; a tribute, sure, but a subtle one. And that's how she liked it.

'She wouldn't go up without seeing you,' her mum said, walking into the hallway from the lounge. In the background, the television hummed with the popcorn chatter of some inane soap or another. It was a slice of normal on a day that had been anything but.

'That's absolutely fine,' DS Willmott replied, lifting Lottie up with the ease that every mummy has when it comes to scooping their kids off their feet, and they nuzzled noses together.

'Come on, pickle,' DS Willmott said, 'say night to Nanna.'

'Night, Nanna,' Lottie parroted.

'Night, love,' DS Willmott's mum said.

'Say night to Daddy,' DS Willmott said.

With Lottie still in her arms, she walked over to the mantelpiece. Next to the clock sat a large picture of a handsome man in his forties, in a frame that wore thousands of lip impressions from years gone by.

'Night, Daddy,' Lottie said, as she pressed her lips against the cold, smooth glass. DS Willmott winked and smiled at the picture, hoping against hope that Lottie would never grow out of that particular ritual.

Alfie was gone, maybe, but never forgotten. Lottie might not remember him, but she knew him. DS Willmott had made sure of that. When she spoke about him, she brought him to life. When she kissed Lottie, she'd sometimes give her an extra one just from him. He lived on, just not in the conventional way.

Lottie didn't take long to go off. She'd always been a good kid, like that. As DS Willmott walked down the stairs, her legs felt heavy. It was as though the weight of the world was sitting on her shoulders.

'Rubbish day?' her mum asked.

'Long day,' DS Willmott replied. She collapsed into the sofa and closed her eyes.

'You need a hobby, something to take your mind off it. It can't be healthy, you know? All work, no play.'

'Work IS my play,' DS Willmott replied, with a weary grin, but she took the point. She'd tried, over the years. Her cupboards were full of the remnants of hobbies and pastimes that she'd tried to pick up. A badminton racquet here. A table-tennis bat there. Hell, there were even some juggling balls somewhere.

No sooner had she sat down, though, than her work phone shrilled into life. The two women looked at each other. All they could do was smile. Another day, another phone call. No rest for the wicked.

'You're not on call, are you?' her mum asked.

'No, I'm bloody well not!' DS Willmott replied, reaching onto the table and picking it up. A withheld number . . . But then, what else would it be?

'DS Willmott,' she said, holding it to her ear.

'Sue,' came the reply, 'it's Geoff in the press office. You'll never guess what . . .'

She'd wondered how long it would take for the press to come knocking, and one journalist in particular.

'Bet you fifty quid I can,' she replied. 'Fiona Strevens? Anchor News?'

'Cash or card?' Geoff replied.

Chapter 36

FIONA

The police statement was enough motivation for Fiona to chase the bosses, to give her an answer. Editorially, it was her call. Reputationally, though, it was their arses on the line. Instead, though, they stalled.

She hadn't covered the murder of young Charlotte, way back when, but it was one that lived long in the memory, no matter who you were. Some crimes stuck in the public consciousness, and that had been one.

There wasn't much that she could do, as she waited for the on-call press officer to get back to her. She'd given a deadline, as was her right. Whether it was by good fortune or not, she'd stumbled on it and she didn't want anyone else scooping her. There wasn't much she could do from that angle so, in the absence of confirmation from the police, she began a deep dive into archive footage. It was all about staying one step ahead of the game, about being as prepared as she could be when the bomb dropped.

The bosses had already sent the balloon up, and the satellite office that she had been alone in was awash with personnel as hurried preparations were made to break the news as soon as they could. For her part, Fiona dug through historic footage that brought back vivid memories of a time when the nation had held their breath and watched as the local police in Beachbrook searched for a killer in their midst. That they'd been found wanting had left an indelible stain on the town that had only cleaned itself as time passed by.

She read of the police having forensic evidence, but not what the nature of it was. Typical, she thought, but not in a bad way. Let the public know that there are clues, that not everything ends in a cul-de-sac, but not giving away what the actual evidence is.

She read of the DNA mass screenings, of queues and queues of men waiting for hours to have their samples taken, so keen were they not to be associated with the crime. She read of groups of men who didn't want theirs taken, citing human rights and the like. It was those, she guessed, who the police would have been dialled into.

And she did the maths. Steve would've been only fifteen then. Just a kid himself. Her heart had skipped a beat when she'd thought of his age at the time of the crime, of the law around reporting restrictions for those under eighteen and whether they applied retrospectively, but a quick check on the CPS website made her breathe a sigh of relief. Those restrictions ceased when the child hit adulthood.

Essentially, what everything boiled down to was a simple decision. To name him, or not. It was a choice that was being mulled over at the highest levels, and she wasn't privy to any of that. Questions of ethics, of morals, whether it was legally sound, where they stood from a litigation perspective – all of that and so much more. Executive decisions were more than strategic; they were about reputational risk and financial exposure, should they be sued as a result. All she could do was to make sure that everything was ready, if the chips landed in her favour.

She could only imagine the clamour in other newsrooms around the country, as the news of an arrest had cleared schedules and turned into rolling news. Everyone would be tapping up sources, trying to roll a copper, doing whatever it was they could to identify the suspect. That she'd played the game before made it no easier to deal with. All she could do was sit and bide her time.

She had the ammunition, and the barrels were loaded. All she was waiting for was authority to pull the trigger.

The crescent moon stared down at her from the night sky as she looked out of the window. It was true that the office she was sitting in was usually without soul, without character, but not now. The soft hum of a team all pulling in the same direction, the buzz of chatter where the voices were calm and composed but excited too, the energy that spilled from every last one of them at the prospect of not just leading the news, but lapping everyone else in the race . . . And all of it contained within four walls, with no means of escape, no dilution of the atmosphere, ramped it up by the minute.

She drummed her fingers on the table as she force-read report after report after report, processing them until they stuck. This was the side of journalism that the public didn't see, the bit that separated the good from the great. Confidence came from being on top of one's brief, and she knew just how important it was especially with a story like that. Forearmed is forewarned, and all that, she said time and again to any trainee she came across, and it was something that had served her well across the years.

Finally . . . FINALLY . . . her phone rang. A FaceTime. Her boss, on the other end, with a curious grin on his face.

'Anything from the press office?' he asked.

'Not yet,' she replied.

'Stuff it,' he said, 'it's too big to sit on.'

Fiona smiled. She knew what was coming.

'Go for it,' her boss said, 'and make it fly.'

Chapter 37

STEVE

He circled around town, his mind blank one moment and working over-capacity the next. His skin prickled as the cool air rushed in through the open window. Isabella may have passed through, but the storm clouds of his own making were only just beginning to circle overhead. He was on a road to nowhere, driving aimlessly and without purpose. There was no end destination, just a circle that kept repeating itself.

It was no good. Everything that he'd always feared the most had come to fruition. Nightmares, coming to life. Visions of losing everything, being realised right in front of him, an unwilling participant with a front-row seat at the movie where his life was ripped apart.

And yet . . . at the heart of it, was a young girl. An innocent girl. Every time his angst grew too strong, he forced himself to take a step back. To think. To find some kind of clarity in the fog of self-indulgence that was drifting through his consciousness.

As he found himself at the top of the slope down to Coffee and Cream, his journey there a total mystery to him as he'd navigated the roads on autopilot, he climbed from his car and looked up to the sky. A sliver of moon on a black canopy was above him, but that's not what he was staring at. He was looking beyond the physical, to what religious people would call the heavens.

He tried to find words, but none seemed apt. He tried to think of something to communicate what he was thinking, something that he could share with Charlotte, to get across just how he felt. Nothing came, though. Only a sinking feeling, that started in his forehead and radiated to every extremity, through his arms and fingers, and his legs and toes. The tremors that followed weren't a product of the cold air, of the still night, of anything physical, in fact. No. They were a consequence, an after-shock. They were the result of a decades-old skeleton being dragged from the closet.

He stared and stared upwards, willing the cloudless sky to drop a deluge of rain on him, a fork of lightning, something, anything, but it was flat calm. He breathed through his nose slowly and deliberately, but the air around him tasted different, somehow. It was the same as it had always been but, now, it was tainted. Just like everything else, it seemed, nothing would ever be the same.

Time drifted by as he crawled around corners in his car once more, the evening passing well off into night before he realised. He couldn't go home. In fact, there was only one place to go that he could think of. Only one place of sanctuary that he had left.

As he knocked on the door, a sudden thought crossed his mind. Phil had been at his house, hadn't he? What if he wasn't there . . .

'Steve, thank God,' Phil said, as he opened the door and nearly yanked his arm off as he pulled him inside, slamming the door shut behind them both.

'Em,' Phil shouted, 'Steve's here.'

Emma was standing at the top of the stairs and bundled down to stand with them both.

'Steve, love?' she said, taking hold of his hand. 'You're freezing.'

His shoulders remained hunched, defeated, and he didn't answer. Instead, he walked into their lounge. The television was on, and tuned in to Anchor News.

At the bottom of the screen, the BREAKING NEWS caption was flashing boldly.

BREAKING: BEACHBROOK HERO, OR MURDER SUSPECT?

Fiona Strevens was on the screen. Of course she was. She had the only scoop that was going to keep Storm Isabella from the headlines. She was sitting in a studio and was talking directly to the camera. Her appearance was polished, her hair smooth and her skin flawless. The windswept reporter who had stood on the other side of the road to him only hours before had buffed up well for another moment in the sun. She was reaching out to everyone, everywhere, sitting in their homes and taking in the news with huge dollops of salacious intrigue. Fiona's broadcast was on the left-hand side of a split-screen, with a photo of Steve adorning the right. A big and bold question mark covered his face.

'So what do we know, Fiona?' an off-screen voice asked.

'Well,' Fiona began, her voice oozing calm and controlled professionalism, 'we know that Steve Minchin ran into a burning building and saved that little baby. Everyone knows that, and we have all been in awe at his heroic act.'

'But there's more to this story than meets the eye?' the off-screen voice prompted, as if from a script.

Steve could feel the eyes of both Phil and Emma burning into him. He couldn't turn around to face them. The explanation that he owed them was being delivered by proxy, and their yawning silence from behind him turned his stomach.

'There is, yes,' Fiona said.

If Phil and Emma's eyes were burning him from behind, then Fiona's were searing him from in front. They weren't cold, they weren't unfriendly, but they were mentally dissecting him piece by piece. There was no escape. Every word that she delivered, another nail in his coffin.

'Mr Minchin has always seemed distant, indeed reticent, and certainly not keen to appear on camera,' she continued. 'It may be that there's a story hidden behind all this, a reason for his apathy.'

Steve's breath was short and sharp, his lungs filled with razors as he forced air into them. Her words were ripping through him and tearing him apart.

'So what do we know?' the off-screen voice asked.

The screen cut from Fiona to the footage that she had recorded earlier. Steve watched, hand over mouth, as Storm Isabella raged, and his house came into shot from the pavement outside. It was him. An out-of-body experience, of sorts. Him, in handcuffs. Him, being led down his pathway. Police cars everywhere, both marked and unmarked. And him, being sick on the pavement. Fiona's studio commentary provided the soundtrack to it, and he felt the same wave of nausea pass over him now that had forced the contents of his stomach up earlier until, moments later, DS Willmott's words cut through the rain and the winds, and detonated a bomb inside of him.

'. . . we have forensic evidence that links you to the murder of Charlotte Hitch. Your arrest is necessary to allow us to investigate it promptly and effectively, and to allow for further forensic evidence to be obtained, namely an evidential sample of DNA. Understand?'

The image of Fiona Strevens in the studio filled the screen once more.

'Police say they arrested a forty-one-year-old local male today on suspicion of murder.'

She looked directly into the camera once more. This time, though, it seemed she was reaching out to each and every single person watching individually, crossing the divide between television set and living room in houses up and down the country. It was a very specific skill, to turn off the professional and stray into the personal, and Fiona seemed to have it down to a T.

'Look,' she said, 'I was there, at Mr Minchin's house earlier today. I was actually going there to see if I could tee up some kind of interview with him, to reveal the man behind the story a couple of weeks ago, the hero who ran into the fire. And I saw him being arrested. I saw . . . it all.'

Steve didn't have a clue about journalistic integrity, nor the questions surrounding ethics or standards involved in what was broadcast or not. He wasn't clued up on the rights or wrongs of it, the legality involved, or if what Fiona was doing was even allowed. Public interest? The respect for truth and the public's right to information? Accountability? Integrity? Responsibility? They were all just buzzwords in a game of bullshit bingo to him.

What he DID know, though, was that he didn't have a leg to stand on. Everything she was saying was accurate.

'I've got a feeling this is going to be a story that runs and runs,' the voice off screen said.

'I'll second that,' Fiona said, 'back to you in the studio.'

Steve grabbed at the remote control and turned the TV off. A yawning silence deepened further, until it was unbearable. The steady tick, tick, ticking of a clock on the mantelpiece played chaos with Steve's sense of time. They weren't seconds. They were much, much longer. Yet still, as those elongated seconds passed, he couldn't turn to face Phil and Emma. He knew they were there, of course, but he just couldn't look at them.

That incessant tick, tick, ticking. It wouldn't stop. It was like being in that cell all over again, the four walls of the house closing in on him until his mind threatened to shut down his senses. Breathe, he thought. Breathe.

'It's true, isn't it?' Phil asked.

'Yeah,' Steve whispered.

Silence fell once again, as Steve stared out of the window. The ghosts of his past were circling, and they were all that he could see. The spectre, of Charlotte. The ruins, of his life. Oscar and Gracie, no doubt crying for their daddy at that very moment. And Sarah, who had flinched when he'd touched her. She'd given him short shrift, and he'd deserved it. He knew that. Phil too, though? Emma? Who would he have left?

'It's all right, mate,' Phil said, reaching out and touching Steve's shoulder.

It may have been the merest of contact but, to Steve, it was everything. He clamped his eyes shut, squeezing every last drop of anguish from them, and swivelled on his feet to face the friend who had always been there and, it seemed, always would. Both men looked at each other and, as Phil blinked away tears of his own, he began to nod. Steve reciprocated.

And then they squeezed each other tightly, an embrace born of years of familiarity and companionship. It was a show of togetherness. Of affection. Of loyalty.

And the tears flowed.

Chapter 38

KEVIN

Steve wasn't the only one watching. Kevin had expected the news of the arrest to make the news, but this was a bolt out of the blue. A lightning rod, smacking directly into his heart.

His mouth was wide as Fiona transported herself into his living room. He was a passenger on a listing ship, struggling to stay buoyant in the face of an onslaught. When Fiona spoke of the historic murder of a thirteen-year-old girl, it was HIS thirteen-year-old girl. Historic? Not in his eyes. Not in his world. When she spoke of a sense of grief being reawakened, it was HIS grief. It was his loss, his angst, his heartache, his anguish. And, as he stared at the picture of Steve on the TV screen he didn't just tremor. No way. Instead, he shook with an uncontrollable ire to the sound of Fiona's voice, as she told him EXACTLY who it was who had been arrested. It had been HIS DNA under Charlotte's nails, HIS blood that had contaminated what was once pure. HE had been there. HE had done it.

'You . . .' he whispered.

His phone rang. It might've been a withheld number,

but who else was it going to be. He took a breath before answering.

'Sue?' he said.

'Are you watching?' she asked.

He said nothing as, in the background, Fiona's voice continued to bleed into his ears and into the phone.

'I guess so,' Sue said. 'So now you know.'

'Now I know,' he replied, each word slow. Measured. Deliberate.

'It's . . . not ideal,' she said.

'You're gonna get him, right?' It wasn't so much a question, more a command.

'No stone unturned, you know that.'

His heart was racing, but he was keeping a lid on it. His breathing was slow. Regulated. He had to trust in her. He HAD to.

'Press might come calling.'

'What do I say?'

Sue sighed. He was getting fed up of her non-answers.

'Probably best not to say anything prejudicial, don't want to jeopardise anything,' she said, but there was no meat behind her words. She was just saying them because her job dictated so. If he scratched just a bit beneath the surface, he was sure her instruction would be different. *Tell them what you really think. Tell them all about Charlotte, about her art, about how it still hangs on your walls. Tell them about the years of outright misery, waiting for a breakthrough, waiting for news. Tell them all about how no person who walked the earth was worthy of even lacing Charlotte's shoes, how her being gone had ripped a happy family to broken little pieces. Tell them how you dreamt of her, of finding out who had done it, of what you wanted to do to them . . .*

'Gotcha,' he said, oh so quietly. 'I'll be bland.'

'Thank you,' she said. 'It's only natural to feel angry, upset, whatever. I mean, here we are, all this time later, and it's going to be everywhere again. It's just . . . I worry about you, you know? Bottling it up.'

'Don't need to worry about me,' he mumbled, quietly embracing the petrol that was indeed filling his bottle. All it needed was a rag stuffed in the neck and a match to light it.

It was a natural point to end the conversation, but neither of them said goodbye. Neither of them hung up. Instead, Fiona's commentary filled both of their ears, as she spoke with precision and confidence about all things related to Charlotte, things that hadn't been dredged up for years.

'In Year Eight at Beachbrook High School. The school put out a statement at the time, saying that their Charlotte was a bright, quiet girl who excelled in art and would have gone on to great things.'

Kevin grimaced. He remembered that statement way back when, of how it had so rankled him that the school had referred to her as 'their' Charlotte.

'Still there?' DS Willmott asked.

'Still here,' Kevin replied.

'Remember what I said to you all those years ago?' she asked.

Kevin closed his eyes, and forced his mind to travel back in time.

PC Willmott looked so young. Too young to wear the uniform. If Charlotte had brought her home on some kind of teenage playdate, if that was even a thing, then Kevin wouldn't have been surprised at the sight of her in his house.

Yet, there she was. The face of the police. The one who seemed to be there the most and, who at the very end of

231

life as they knew it, was holding their hands. Physically and metaphorically.

Charlotte's breaths grew shallow. 'Shouldn't take long,' they'd been told.

'It's okay, love,' he said, stroking his baby girl's hair, 'go be free.'

And free, she became.

There were tears. There was sobbing. And there was PC Willmott.

'I'll always be here,' she said. Hollow words? Probably. But right at that moment, they were spoken as if pure poetry poured from her lips.

'I remember,' Kevin said. Even now, some twenty years and more down the line, she'd never broken her word. As his senses fired with every new word that Fiona barked on the telly, with every image of Charlotte that filled the screen, he remembered just how naïvely sincere that young police officer had been, and just how warming her words had been in the face of the iciest of realities.

'Just know, I'm still here,' Sue said, 'if you need anything. Anything at all. I'll always be here.'

Chapter 39

STEVE

After the storm, a calmness arrived, in meteorological terms at least. For, as Steve lay in the spare room of Phil and Emma's house, the winds of change were still howling around him.

Morning had arrived, and it had been a long night, punctuated by fits of sleep that had been woken from no sooner had they been drifted into. Through it all, his mind wandered, flitting from all the seminal moments in his life. Sarah's rage – her utter dismissal of him – was another dropped stitch in the tapestry of life. It wasn't so much a case of asking himself when the whole lot would unravel, more an internal interrogation as to what fabric was left in the first place.

'You up, Steve?' Emma asked, knocking gently on the bedroom door.

'Yeah,' he called.

She walked in, holding her phone in her hand.

'You need to read this,' she said, handing the device to Steve.

He squinted, adjusting his eyes to the brightness of the screen before reading the message. It was from Sarah.

I can't get hold of Steve. The press have set up outside and they're not going anywhere. Can you get him to call me ASAP xx

'God's sake,' Steve muttered, throwing the duvet off and jumping out of the bed.

He hadn't even considered a media scrum at his house.

'Stupid,' he said to himself. 'Stupid, stupid, stupid.'

He'd seen it coming, but had been too wrapped up in himself to confront it in his mind. Wasn't it blindingly obvious that the wolves would have come knocking? Of course it was, and he had left Sarah and the kids there alone to deal with it. While he had been basking in the refuge of protection that Phil and Emma's house provided, they had been in the eye of the media storm. Unforgivable? In his eyes, totally.

He ran down the stairs, where he found Phil standing in the lounge, remote control in hand and the television turned up loud. Fiona Strevens was on screen. Of course she was. Like a dog with a bone, and she wasn't going to give it up until it had been chewed out of shape and devoured. Behind her? Steve's house, and a sizeable crowd filled with journalists, camera crews and members of the public. Where the media assembled, the public followed, moths attracted to the head of a flame. Steve stood next to Phil, his knuckles clenching by his sides.

'Gotta be there,' he mumbled.

It was surreal. Truly, he felt he was living outside of his skin, completely detached from reality. His mind tried to catch up, to process what was being said.

LIVE: PUBLIC REACTION TO BEACHBROOK FIRE RESCUER: HERO OR VILLAIN?

'We're here outside Mr Minchin's house,' Fiona said, 'and we are hoping to hear from him. In the meantime, I've been speaking to members of the public and getting their views on what he did, and, in a wider context, whether past transgressions can ever be atoned for and forgiven. With me now is a friend of Mr Minchin.'

The camera panned around. John was standing next to her, with Lex sitting beside him.

'I understand you're a regular customer at his coffee shop,' Fiona continued. 'What is your take on it?'

'I don't think it takes anything away from what he did,' John said. His voice was belligerent, his face unmoved. 'All right, he might have done something terrible in the past, but he saved a baby's life, for crying out loud. Shouldn't we all cut him some slack, really?'

Steve's eyes, still raw, once again stung as they filled with tears. Such loyalty, from a man he barely knew.

'And what would you say to him, if he was here?' Fiona asked.

'You're still a hero in my eyes,' John replied immediately, staring into the camera.

Steve stood, frozen to the spot. His mouth still hung wide, gaping in disbelief as Fiona turned to another member of the public.

'Jane, I understand you've got a different view?' Fiona said.

'Yes,' Jane said. 'Look, I get that everyone has a past, but where do you draw the line? Bottom line, for me, is that he killed a child. Doesn't matter what he did afterwards, nothing can make that right.'

'So you don't think that what he did in the fire compensates for it in any way?' Fiona asked.

'No,' Jane replied, bluntly. She was not for swaying.

The camera panned back to Fiona, who turned away from her panel of interviewees.

'Well there you go,' she said. 'Emotions are clearly running high in the local community, and there are vastly conflicting views on this story amongst the everyday folk here in Beachbrook. Back to you in the studio.'

Phil turned the television off and turned to look at Steve.

'I've got to get home,' Steve said. He was quiet but resolute.

He was out of the door and in his car before Phil could even begin to articulate a list of reasons why that was a terrible idea. He drove by instinct, unable to focus on the roads but, regardless, navigating a route based on nothing but intuition. As he drove past his road, he saw the media scrum in the distance. Even though his tortured mind told him to swing onto the driveway, to get to his family, to be the shield that protected them from the onslaught, he retained a modicum of clarity. He knew the layout of the local roads, the rat runs and – more importantly – the alleyways. He drove past slowly, anonymously, and parked in an adjacent cul-de-sac. The alleyway that led from it was underused, and the foliage from the gardens that backed onto it was overgrown, but as an alternative means of access to the rear of his house, it was perfect. The adrenaline that coursed through his veins lightened his legs and helped him to float over the fence. He stood still. Silence. He was in his back garden, alone and undetected.

He rapped his knuckles on the patio doors. The blinds were closed, and the curtains pulled. He couldn't see inside and, in the absence of a key to the rear, was reliant on Sarah looking out, praying to God that she wouldn't assume he was a member of the press pack without scruples who was trespassing on her property. Upstairs, a curtain twitched. Moments later, a hand appeared from behind the blinds in front of him and unlocked the patio door. He slipped in under the radar and out of sight of the mob on the other side of the house.

His eyes took a second to adjust to the gloominess within. As they focussed, the image that presented itself to him was devastating. Sarah stood with Oscar in her arms and Gracie tucked in next to her, sucking her thumb. All three of them had the reddest of cheeks from the rivers of tears that had burned their skin raw. Sarah's tears were because of what she knew. The children's were because of what they didn't. Confused, he knew. Scared, he guessed. It was the weekend, but they weren't dressed and doing fun things. Their daddy had disappeared suddenly. The house was dark, and Mummy was upset. They weren't allowed to look out of the windows. Scary? It must have been beyond terrifying. Any lingering wind that might have remained in Steve's sails was ripped away. Those pains in his chest? They were his heart breaking.

His first instinct was to walk towards them, to cuddle them, to hold them and tell them that everything would be okay, but, as he moved towards them Sarah backed away. She flinched, once more.

'They've been here since it was dark,' Sarah said, her voice dripping with anger.

'I'll try to get rid of them,' Steve said. Every word tremored but, though he didn't know how, he had to do something. He'd put his family in this situation. It was on him to get them out of it.

He had no plan but, as he walked to the front door and opened it, he had no reservations. He had no misgivings. Doubt wasn't plaguing him. Instead, it was a fresh dose of adrenaline that hit him in wave after wave as he did something that he'd sworn always to do: protect his family, come what may. Protect his family, whatever the cost. His shoulders were draped in a cloak of courage as he opened his front door and faced the media caravan head on.

'Mr Minchin, Mr Minchin,' various voices shouted, clamouring for attention.

The flashes of multiple cameras made him shield his eyes, as microphones were thrust in front of him. Journalists of all branches of the media jockeyed for position as Steve took a deep breath. They became silent as he spoke without script, and without pause.

'I can't talk about anything that's been happening, as I'm sure most of you know.'

He paused and looked around. He saw Fiona, standing in the background. She raised half a smile at him. His eyes narrowed as he held her gaze. Her greeting wasn't reciprocated.

'What I will say is that there are two kids in my house, and they're absolutely terrified,' he continued. 'There will come a time when things need to be said, but this isn't it.'

He breathed deeply.

'You don't need to be here,' he concluded. 'My family are inside, and they don't deserve . . . all this.'

With that, he turned and walked inside, ignoring the waves of questions that followed him. The clamour for more words seemed to have intensified and, as he closed the door behind him and the shouts became muffled, he wondered if he had done the right thing.

He sat alone, his back against the front door, and waited. For the commotion to dim. For his heart rate to come down. For the adrenaline to subside. For his appeals for familial privacy to be heeded.

For the wolves to scarper, without their appetites being sated.

Chapter 40

SARAH

She heard the front door open and, about a minute or so later, close again. Everything in the middle though? She'd stayed hidden away upstairs, a child either side of her as they sought refuge behind a closed door in a room that had, less than twenty-four hours ago, been stained by her husband's confession.

Sitting on the marital bed, with Oscar burrowed into her right ribs and Gracie her left, she maintained the same placid smile on her face. No matter the turmoil behind it, no matter the mayhem in her mind, the kids came first. Always had, and always would.

'It'll be all right, kiddos. Daddy's asking them all to go away.'

They may have been her words, but it wasn't her voice. Not the one that she recognised, anyway. There was just a bit of bite, when she'd said 'daddy'. There was the tiniest undercurrent of turbulence attached to each syllable, undetectable to the kids, she hoped, but present, nonetheless.

Sure, she'd flinched. Once, when he'd touched her the day before. Again, when he'd moved towards them, only minutes prior. Who wouldn't have, though? The hand that had brushed against her shoulder . . . Had it been the one that he'd killed a child with? She shuddered at the very thought of it, but checked herself before those tremors radiated to her kids. They remained unmoved, each perhaps wrapped up their own cocoon of worry. She tightened her grip on them. There, they were safe. In her embrace, no one could touch them.

And yet, Steve remained at the forefront of her mind. The man who she'd said 'I do' to. The man who had given her the two kids she was cradling. The man who had been there for her time and again as the years had passed. The man who had rushed into a building being torn apart by flames, and rescued a baby. But the man with a secret. A dark secret. A terrible secret. The worst kind of secret. And one that had remained hidden, a festering sore lurking just beneath the surface for twenty-something years.

Her head was spinning as the two distinct acts crashed head on against each other, sending shards of pain to every corner of her skull. Was there a boundary where wickedness and integrity met? Was it blurred? Could they coexist? For now, it was unresolved in her mind.

As the day drifted by, and the kids fought for space on Steve's side of the bed, next to the iPad chargers, Sarah crept out of the bedroom door. She tiptoed across the landing and looked down the stairs, where Steve sat at the base of the front door, his knees bent and his head tucked in between them. There's no way he wouldn't have heard the creaking of the floorboards, no matter how thick the carpet was that padded them, but he didn't look up. Whatever was running through his head had switched him off to the world around him and, as the clamour at the front door had reduced to the point of near-quiet, it was as if he'd downed tools and clocked off.

She stared, and stared, and stared at him. A broken man? Maybe. But he deserved it. Didn't he? Around and around, in the quagmire of her mind, she spun.

'Mummy?'

Oscar's voiced roused her from her internal tumult and, it seemed, Steve too. He looked up at her, at Oscar, and though his smile was forced, it was something that her boy needed to see.

'Daddy,' he shouted, running past her and near launching himself down the stairs. Gracie was only a couple of paces behind him as they trampled a path to their daddy.

'Hey, bud. All right, princess,' Steve said, clinging onto his kids as though his life depended on it. He looked up at Sarah and his smile endured, but her face was granite in return. He didn't deserve a smile. Not yet. Not at all. Yet, she trod down a stair. Then, another. Thirteen of them, and she was in the downstairs hallway, next to Steve, Oscar and Gracie. Next to her kids.

And next to the man who had the blood of a child on his hands. Once more, she flinched.

She crept into the living room and peeked out from behind the net curtains. There were still some reporters there, but the posse had dwindled to a mere few, a couple of whom were packing up too. They soon melted away, leaving just one. The woman. The one from the TV. The one who had broken the news. Fiona something or other. Steve looked, too, and walked away with the shake of his head, as the kids charged upstairs. Normal service had resumed, for them at least.

'Bitch,' Sarah whispered, as she retreated into the heart of the room, safe from the lenses, protected from inquisitive eyes. No sooner had she done so than there was a knock at the door. Soft knuckles on wood. Dainty fingers, no doubt.

She knew exactly who it was. Steve did too, it seemed, for in an instant, he'd snatched at the door handle, ripping it open.

The news woman was alone. Beyond her, there was a cameraman. He wasn't looking at them, though. He was facing away, the tools of his trade pointing at the ground as much for show as comfort, Sarah surmised. She couldn't see Steve's face. She could guess what it looked like, though.

'What?' Steve hissed.

'How is everyone?' Fiona asked.

'How do you think?' Steve spat back. 'They're petrified.'

'Sorry to hear that,' Fiona said. She was passive. Though she still wore the warpaint of a journalist in character, her words were soft. She wasn't 'on'. In spite of who she was, and what she did, she seemed . . . normal?

'What do you want?' Steve said. His words sizzled and popped, her presence adding fuel to the fire that Sarah had been watching rage.

Fiona smiled. It wasn't a patronising one. It wasn't pity, either. It was something else . . . Something that Sarah couldn't quite decipher.

'Off the record,' Fiona said, 'I just wanted you to know that I've never seen a story like this. In our world, we talk about things cutting through with the public. This has done exactly that. I just wanted to tell you that.'

Steve, it seemed, had heard enough. Sarah winced as he slammed the door with such ferocity that it shook the house from the footings upwards, and she watched as Fiona turned and walked away slowly. They each stood in silence, Steve's breathing audibly ragged. Those gasps of air grew yet more volatile as his shoulders hunched and rose repeatedly. The sniffles that followed extended into more protracted weeping as the seconds passed, his head resolutely facing away from hers, staring into God only knew what abyss that existed inside his head.

'Sarah?' Steve said.

She looked up, then down.

'Sarah?'

'Yeah,' she whispered.

'I need to talk to you.'

She forced her head up and faced him. He was standing in the doorway and took a step towards her with his hands raised. It screamed, 'I'm not a threat, I promise,' and he stopped a respectful distance short of her. Five feet, she guessed, separating her and the man she'd married. In that moment, though, it might as well have been a mile.

He'd killed a child.

He was a child killer.

A child killer.

A CHILD KILLER.

'So talk,' she said.

'I'll tell you what happened,' Steve said, fixing his gaze on her and not letting it shift. It wasn't so much a battle of wills, but Sarah didn't avert her stare either.

'What I need to tell you first, though, is why.'

Chapter 41

STEVE

Steve stared at his wife. Her hands were by her sides, her knuckles white where she was clenching her fists so tightly. He raised his eyebrows and half-smiled uncertainly, but pursed lips were all that was returned.

'I just . . . I don't know,' he said, his words failing him.

'Talk to me,' she instructed.

And he wanted to. He really, truly was desperate to. But, as he fumbled for the necessary words to impress upon her exactly what had happened to him, why he had been the broken child that he was, he was unable to unlock the sentences that might be able to do it. Every time he closed his eyes and tried to crack those memories open, a sea of darkness washed across him.

He blinked away tears of despair, as he tried again and again, but nothing would come. And when he opened his eyes and focussed on Sarah, she wasn't giving an inch. Her face screamed at him 'tell me, tell me, tell me' from her raised eyebrows to her pursed lips, but his tongue was tied. His brain wasn't functioning. The synapses weren't firing.

In those five feet that separated him and his wife, a chasm

had formed and to take one step towards her would have been to breach the very edge of a precipice.

It was a pressure he'd never borne before. There he was, aware with every burning second that passed that he was in a fight to save his marriage, his life, his everything, but being a passenger standing by, unable to influence it. He closed his eyes once more, but it was just darkness.

Seconds turned into minutes and, apart from the faint stomps on the floorboards above them as the kids played some game or another, there was silence. It was like his brain was short-circuiting, refusing to allow any words to form and be spoken aloud. He opened his eyes one last time, and looked to the floor. As silent admissions of defeat went, it was absolute.

He tried hard to look at her, but terror flooded him every time he lifted his head. She was his wife, his life, and it was all slipping away from him. Still, though, he couldn't find the words.

Her sigh was quiet but strong. He had to look up. *Had to*. And he did, but she just looked away. There were tears pooling in her eyes as she looked up to the ceiling.

'I need you to leave.'

Her voice cracked as the last word slipped from her lips.

'Please, just go.'

She turned on her heels and walked into the kitchen.

His knees buckled under the unbearable weight of it all, and he groped at the hallway wall to prevent himself from toppling over. Sarah didn't look back. Not even once. As she closed the kitchen door, he was left alone with only those dull thumps from above to keep him company.

His kids.

His babies.

Oblivious to it all, to what was going on downstairs.

How he wanted to race up there, to take them in his arms, to envelop them in the warming embrace that was uniquely his, but he didn't. He couldn't. Sarah had asked him to leave and, though there was a razor blade slicing slivers of his heart with every move he made, he turned around. He unlocked the front door. He opened the latch, and he crossed the threshold where family home met cruel world.

The media had picked up and moved off, and he was alone on his driveway. That his neighbours were openly staring at him from their windows was lost on him, his focus being on putting one foot in front of the other as he traipsed towards his car.

Left foot, right.

Left foot, right.

Muscle memory counted for a lot but, when the fundaments of life had been stripped away, nothing was left unaffected. He climbed in through the driver's door and drove away, his engine revving and his car jerking as his right foot twitched involuntarily.

At least he had Phil. At least he had Emma. And as he stumbled through their front door, bringing his own cloud of misery into their four walls, he was oblivious to the atmosphere that they'd managed to create in his absence.

Phil was in the kitchen, sitting on a barstool with his leg tapping furiously on the floor, while Emma sat in the front room in silence. Yet . . . Steve didn't notice a thing. He didn't say a thing. The clock may have barely passed 3 p.m., and the light may still have been natural, but he walked up the stairs and closed the door to the spare bedroom behind him. Was this it, he wondered? Was this his lot? Destined to spend whatever time he had left in his friend's spare room? Praying that the press didn't turn up and hound his loved ones here, too? Prison came next, he was sure.

The afternoon passed into evening and beyond in fits and starts, as he lay on the single bed tossing and turning. It wasn't sleep he was seeking. The years gone by had taught him that, if it wasn't going to come, then it wasn't to be forced. Instead, it was the seeds of a plan that began to sow in his mind as he lay there, staring at the ceiling.

Morning came but, in the absence of his phone or a watch, it was only the rising of the sun that gave him any clue what the time was. Phil knocked on the door a while later and walked in with a steaming mug.

'Not up to your standard,' he said, handing it to Steve.

'You're right,' Steve replied, as he tilted it up to his lips.

'Any sleep?'

'Not a wink.'

Steve set the mug down on the bedside table as he climbed from the bed and stretched his arms above his head. Those seeds of a plan from the night before had begun to shoot.

'It's messed up, mate,' he said.

'Sarah?'

'Sarah, yeah, but what I did. Messed up.'

Steve looked Phil squarely in the eye. In many ways, his friend was imploring him to carry on, just as Sarah had the day before, but this was a different conversation to the one he'd tried to have with her.

'I've got to get my head around it, you know? What happened. It's just . . . I can't process it. I can't even quite remember it. The reasons, who I was, what I was. I keep coming up against a block when I try and think about it.'

Phil moved towards him, until there were only inches between them. Where there'd been a chasm with Sarah, there was a bridge with Phil.

'I've got to go there,' Steve whispered.

'Where?' Phil asked.

'Back to Finisham. Where I grew up. See if I can . . . I dunno . . . Make sense of it all. It's just a mishmash in my mind. Like, I can't explain it. I know what's up there, what happened and all, I just . . . can't process it. Make sense?'

'Kinda,' Phil replied. 'Whatever it takes, mate, whatever it takes.'

'I've got to sign on at the police station tomorrow, bail condition or something. Do you think . . . Can you help me book something for after? Train and hotel. I haven't got my phone or anything.'

'Course, mate.'

Steve sat down on the bed. To think of it was one thing. To plan it, another. To go through with it, though? To confront everything that had come before? To unlock those repressed doors in his mind that had been slammed shut and double-bolted for a reason? It was something else entirely.

'Can you let Sarah know for me?' he asked, ever so quietly.

'What do you want me to say?' Phil replied.

'Just . . . that I've gone away for a couple of days, that I need to go there to figure out where this all started so I can give her some answers. She'll understand.'

Chapter 42

DS SUE WILLMOTT

It was the start of another working week and, as DS Willmott sat in front of her computer, she pulled up the online bail signing-on forms from the intranet. The front counter had opened not twenty minutes before, but Steve had already been into the police station and signed on. She puckered her lips, and shut the form down with a click on the mouse that was just a little firmer than it needed to be.

Whether it was a help or a hindrance, it was part of DS Willmott's genetic make-up that she cared. Too much? Sometimes, and even she would admit to it. To take it away, though, to remove it from her toolkit would be to amputate what it was that set her apart.

She sat in her chair, with the door to the main office closed to keep the noise out, and chewed idly on the end of a pen as she flicked through her day book. It was her bible, her opus, the place where theories were made, where evidence was recorded and decisions made.

She knew it all in her mind, but the list of outstanding enquiries were listed in ink on the pages in bullet-point form. Some of them relied on those who worked Monday to Friday and, now that Monday had arrived, it was time to fire off some emails and make some phone calls. No sooner had she begun to do so than Vinny bustled in, with his phone in his hands. DS Willmott didn't need to look at the screen to know that it was Fiona who was reporting something or another on it. Her voice carried across the room and, as Vinny approached her, his eyebrows were raised. A short inhalation of breath followed. He knew what was coming, it seemed. Alas, DS Willmott didn't.

'What's up?' she asked.

'Just about to find out,' he replied.

He placed the phone on the table in front of her and stood behind her shoulder. The screen may have been small, but Fiona's presence filled it. She was sitting on a lounge chair that DS Willmott recognised, but couldn't quite place. It was homely. A normal lounge, in a normal house, in what was presumably a normal road. Normal. Everything screamed it. And yet . . .

'I'm here with some very special guests,' Fiona said, with that silky voice DS Willmott had heard her employ before when she'd interviewed Steve at the beach, 'Bob and Pam, and little baby Jack . . .'

'You're kidding me?' DS Willmott muttered.

'. . . and I'd like to thank you so much for taking the time to speak with me today,' Fiona continued, as the camera panned out from her and revealed Bob, Pam and Jack sitting on a three-piece sofa next to her. No wonder DS Willmott had recognised it. Not a week or so before, she'd been sitting in it.

'Thanks for having us,' Bob replied, as baby Jack bounced up and down on his knee. The coos that sprung from his mouth could melt hearts and, DS Willmott guessed, probably would be, up and down the country.

'First things first,' Fiona said, 'how's Jack doing?'

The camera panned in on the baby who, as if recognising his name, shot a smile at Fiona. In spite of the pulses of pain that were beginning to form in her head at the thought of exactly where this interview was likely to be heading, DS Willmott couldn't help but smile. Who could resist a baby's grin, after all? It took a few seconds before she checked herself, and her steely grimace returned.

'He's doing good, aren't you, mate,' Bob replied, gently tickling his grandson and eliciting a giggle.

'And you two?' Fiona asked. 'How are you both doing?'

'We're okay,' Pam said. 'It's good that we've got the little man to keep us occupied.'

It was all preamble, DS Willmott thought. Fiona wasn't there to check up on them, nor was she really there to broadcast Jack's giggles and coos, no matter how cute they were. She was a reporter. There was news to be had, stories to be spun, and THAT's why she was there, no matter what angle she'd gone at it from with Bob and Pam. Sure enough . . .

'Great to hear,' Fiona continued, 'and I'm sure that Jack's so very glad to have you here, too. It was such a tragic thing, the fire, but I'm sure there were crumbs of comfort for you all in the way the public responded to that tragedy, not least the way that Steve Minchin ran into the flames and brought Jack back to you.'

'Forever grateful,' Bob said. His voice was firm, his words resolute.

'And then, the story evolves,' Fiona said, as Jack cooed once more. This time, though, she didn't stop. She didn't play up to the babyish charm. Now, DS Willmott knew, it was business.

The camera was fixed on all four of them and, as Fiona

spoke, DS Willmott surveyed Bob and Pam's faces as best she could on a six-inch screen. The grief was still there for both of them, barely concealed behind their eyes and partially hidden in frown lines. It was there, though, for sure.

'And we find out . . . things . . . about Mr Minchin that maybe wouldn't have come out otherwise.' It wasn't a question, but it was treated as such by Bob. A question, in fact, that deserved short shrift.

'The man's a hero,' he said, barely allowing Fiona to finish her words before he put his point across in the bluntest possible way, 'and that's all there is to say about that.'

'Whatever way it's all shook out in the end,' Pam chimed in, 'we wouldn't have this little man with us without him. And, for us, that is that.'

'But,' Fiona interjected, 'what about the other side of the coin? What about what he's . . . alleged . . . to have done? I guess the question is, does an act of good counteract one of bad? Can the ledger of life be righted, I suppose, the books balanced? It's a question of philosophy as much as anything else, isn't it?'

'Call it what you like,' Bob replied, gruffly, 'all I know is that Steve Minchin is a hero and I'll be damned if anyone tries to tell me otherwise.'

As the interview finished, DS Willmott turned to Vinny with frown lines of her own on display.

'I guess they didn't tell you they were doing that?' she asked.

'Absolutely not.'

It wasn't so much what they'd said that had thrown a spanner in DS Willmott's proverbial works, it was who they were. Grieving parents, who had lost a child and a son-in-law. It was unspoken of in any and all circles of criminal justice that public opinion held a certain amount of sway when it came to investigations as high profile as those they were in the middle of, but it was true. The public had clout and, when the winds were blowing in a certain direction, it was difficult to beat them back. Bob and Pam's opinion mattered, and it counted for a lot. There had already been some noise from the usual Twitterati, calling for the investigation to be halted on account of Steve's heroism. Conversely, there were those who were adamant that the book should be thrown at him, irrespective of deed.

All she could do was track the evidence, to cross the i's and dot the t's, and to follow her nose wherever it led.

An interview like that? All it did was muddy a body of water that was already murky to begin with.

Chapter 43

STEVE

Steve stood on the platform of Beachbrook train station, shaded from the sun and letting the cool air seep through his clothes. He had a long journey ahead of him. Even if the connections ran smoothly, it would take about six hours. Plenty of time to cement the game plan in his mind. Phil had booked him a chain hotel in the middle of town. It hadn't been there all those years ago, and he wondered how much the landscape had changed in those intervening years. Would he still recognise it, he wondered?

A train pulled into the station. His train. The first leg on his journey and, as he climbed on board a feeling of nausea rose from the pit of his stomach until it sat at the top of his throat. It took every ounce of fortitude not to turn around, to get off the train, to give up and run back the safety of the single bed in Phil's spare room.

Sarah, though.

Gracie.

Oscar.

THAT's why he was doing it. THEY were the reason. His reason. His everything. He forced those waves of queasiness back from whence they'd come and watched as the door to the train carriage closed behind him. This one would take him to the capital. Then, a tube across town, before another train north. He settled into his seat and looked out of the window as the train slowly pulled away. Beachbrook was soon behind him, a dot in the distance. Ahead of him? The past, where the roots of his downfall lay.

The train rolled onwards and Steve counted down the stops until they reached the capital. He had always wanted to take the kids there, to see the sights and sounds, but he'd dreaded the thought of doing the journey, of being any closer to Finisham than he had to be.

Five stops left. Then four. He looked out at the little worlds that accompanied each station, and the towns and villages that were hives of activity before they gave way to oceans of emptiness as the train carved its way through the countryside between them.

They pulled into the terminating station and in stark contrast to the relative serenity of Beachbrook, the capital was positively bustling. Steve found his way to the tube station, from where it was a short ride north without any changes and, as he emerged from the gloomy warren of tunnels that pulsed like veins under the skin of the capital, he had already completed two of the three legs of his journey. Next came the longest. The northbound train, servicing so many towns and cities on the way. For all the talk of faster services into the capital, the north still seemed so far isolated from the south. And that's just the way Steve had liked it.

This train was certainly busier than on his first leg of the journey and, as he took the aisle seat next to an elderly lady, he nodded at her and forced a smile. She did likewise, and he breathed a sigh of relief. Though he was wearing a baseball cap and his stubble had grown into something of a beard over the week gone by, he felt as nakedly exposed as if his clothes had been stripped from his body.

He sat back in his chair and closed his eyes. Up until now, save from the nausea that had enveloped him as he'd boarded the train in Beachbrook, he had been feeling calm, but each time the train pulled into a station and ground to a halt, it was another step closer. Each time, as the train slowly pulled away and reached cruising pace, a knot of anxiety deep within his stomach grew. He tried to cast it aside with placatory thoughts. He had to do this. He had to, he had to, he had to. Even so, as the journey continued and concrete urbanity transformed into picturesque vistas outside the window, his back grew wet through a sweat that wasn't born of the cool, air-conditioned train carriage. He found himself tapping his foot on the floor and his hand on his knee, his head nodding up and down to an invisible beat of the train bouncing over the railway sleepers. It reached a crescendo when the automated Tannoy system made an announcement.

'This is a northern service. The next station is Finisham.'

Time had flown, and – as he looked out of the window – he remembered things that he had long since forgotten. Tennis courts. Parkland. Wasteland. The stalking grounds of his youth.

New structures, too. A brand-new housing estate. A new school. New supermarkets.

But it was the ghosts who had resided there decades before that he was there to confront. As he stared, and his memories came to life, there was another Tannoy announcement.

'We will shortly be arriving at Finisham.'

He looked around the carriage. No one stirred at the sound of the announcement but, as Steve stood up, those dribbles of sweat rolled down his back and pooled at the base of his spine. The metallic sound of grinding brakes cut through the air, and ripped through him, right to the core. The train pulled into the station and ground to a stop. Steve stood up, took a deep breath and alighted with his nerves on fire.

It was a generation later, sure, but he was back to walk once again in his shoes of the past. He strode with hesitant steps from the station, and hailed a cab from the rank outside.

They pulled up at a typical, non-descript chain hotel to the east of town, not too far away. He showered, washing away that mucky feeling that always came from a long journey, and solidified the battle plan that had been formulating in his mind. He stayed under the water for longer than he normally would, until his plan was set in concrete. The time spent cleansing his body had served to provide clarity in his mind. Keep it simple, he thought. He knew where he had to head first.

Dressed and in a bullish mood, he slipped out of his hotel room and found himself on Finisham Road. It was time to go back to where it all began, to where the seeds of his upbringing had been sown.

He stalked the streets of Finisham, finding roads and routes that he had long since forgotten. Sure, the aesthetics may have changed but, structurally, most things were as he remembered. A new roundabout here, a new building there, a new parade of shops grown as if from nowhere, but the layout of the streets that he walked was fundamentally the same. Lost in his mind, but not geographically, he was on autopilot as he made his way towards the housing estate where it all began.

How to adequately describe that estate? Probably best to say that, nearly four decades prior, even the police patrolled in groups and, all these years later, he guessed those rules still applied. From the thick stench of cannabis that cloyed the air around him, through to the bags of rubbish dumped beside some of the houses that had been nibbled on by one vulture or another and were spilling their load, the tightly packed rows of terraced houses simply oozed malice. An abandoned car with the number plates missing was dumped on the road outside the house he was there to see, and thumping garage music was blasting from inside. The closer he got, the more it shook his insides. There was no way he was going to knock, and he wasn't there to loiter. He just wanted enough time to watch, from a distance, and remember. Though hazy, those memories were the first that he could recall with anything approaching lucidity.

'The fuck have you done?' his dad slurred.

Drink or drugs? It could've been either. One always seemed to go hand in hand with the other. Regardless, the menace in his voice would soon be manifest in his actions.

'What now?' his mum screamed, her voice fighting to register above the blaring television that was spitting out swear words in the background.

'You need to learn a lesson, you little rat,' his dad said, as Steve ran from the kitchen.

He sought sanctuary upstairs in his bedroom, but he knew what was coming. His dad's deliberately slow ascent was foreshadowed by his heavy steps, and they were getting louder. In the background he could hear his mum shouting, but it was like white noise.

'What's he done?' his mum shouted.

She was seldom on her son's side.

'Little shit,' his dad replied.

Steve hadn't done anything. He'd played in the garden and got a bit muddy. That was all. He was a child, and he had been doing what any kid does. Playing. Trying to be *happy. Trying to be a normal little boy. Trying to escape his miserable existence for a few, fleeting minutes. His dad had walked out into the garden, spoiling for an argument. Steve was the target of his ire and it didn't matter what he was doing, or what he had done. His dad always found a reason.*

'Where are you, you little rat?' his dad shouted, clenching his knuckles in fists of rage.

Steve cowered in his wardrobe as he heard his bedroom door slam open. There wasn't enough furniture in his room to find a better hiding place, and his dad always knew where he was. Within seconds, he had been found. His dad grabbed a handful of his matted hair and yanked him roughly from the best hiding place that his bedroom could offer.

He was thrown on his bed where he felt his leg run wet. Four years old, and still unable to control his bladder. Who could blame him? His dad, for one. And he did. Something else to beat him for. Another lesson to be taught. His mum screamed as his dad's words rendered him motionless.

'I'll make a man out of you, you little . . .'

Steve knew what was coming. He closed his eyes, as his mother's screams faded away in the background and waited for what was to follow. Sometimes it was fists. Others, the hot end of a lighter. Today? It was the one he hated the most. The belt.

As the blows rained down, he whimpered. His fragile skin couldn't handle it. Those whimpers turned into screams, before everything went black.

Steve breathed deeply, as the vividity of his memories washed over him with stunning and brutal clarity. Being there, and physically seeing where his journey had begun, had somehow allowed him to access a power of recall that he would never have thought possible. He had lived it, but more than thirty years prior. Standing there, it could've been yesterday. He instinctively reached around to his back, checking for injury. The physical wounds may have healed, but the mental ones endured.

He knew what came next but, though he was there to confront such things, some didn't need to be rehashed. This was one of them. He still wore the scars of that particular incident, and it had been his screams that had caused the police to attend. Back then chastisement was an accepted practice, but even the veteran copper who handcuffed his dad had looked on in abject horror.

It was the last memory he had of either of his parents. He'd sometimes wondered what had happened to them but, as the years had passed, they had simply become non-entities to him. They were the very first ghosts of his past and, as he remembered what they had done to him and how they had shaped the early years of his childhood, his eyes burned with a rage that sent bolts of fire through his arms and legs. Gracie and Oscar had shown him everything that a child should be and, in turn, he'd been desperate to be everything that a father should.

Violence? Emotional detachment? Chaos? It was everything that a child should be protected from, and he'd been exposed to it when he'd been most vulnerable. The hatred for his parents may have dulled as the years had passed but, there and then, it all came flooding back. He didn't just hate them. He despised them.

Now, as the music from the house continued to blare, and the ominous sound of raised voices signalled a fight developing in the distance, Steve thought it wise to take his leave. The sun had fallen behind the houses over the horizon, anyway. It was no place to be in daylight hours, but as darkness fell it would be tantamount to self-harm. He turned to walk away, but took one last look at the place that had been his first house. He could only call it that, for it had never been a home. His resentment gave way to a feeling of sadness. No child should go through what he did. Thoughts of Gracie and Oscar flooded his mind, placating him as he knew they would never have to experience such terror.

He turned on his heels and walked apace back in the direction from whence he'd come, taking in all the sights and sounds that Finisham had to offer at dusk. It may have been half the country away from Beachbrook, but he was taken by how people still nodded at each other as they passed, how their heads were up and not buried in their phones, much as they did in his little slice of the world. Communities were built on the people within them, and he'd never before thought of Finisham like that. It'd always been . . . that . . . place, where evil lurked.

As the sun disappeared and a sharp, northern breeze chilled his damp forehead, Steve found himself back on Finisham Road and walking through the front door to his hotel. He hadn't known what to expect but, as he sat in his room and reflected, it felt strangely cathartic. He had to be there to experience it, his physical presence being the key to unlocking the memories of his past and ensuring their vividity. For the first time in a long time, he had remembered how it felt to be a boy. That boy. It had awoken the inner child in him, and all the suffering that had been attached, but the visceral reaction it had provoked – the prickling skin, the goose bumps, the tension, the apprehension as he'd stared and stared and stared at that house where some demons from his past had resided – was entirely necessary.

He skipped dinner, instead choosing to remain in his room with his thoughts for company. It had been hell back then.

Pure, living hell. It only served to heighten his appreciation for all that he held dear back in Beachbrook. His family, his friends, his life. The ones he was putting himself through all of this for. As he settled down into bed, he closed his eyes in the knowledge that tomorrow was going to be seismic.

The room was dark, and sleep came quickly. No nightmares. Just a welcome blankness that lasted until morning.

Chapter 44

KEVIN

His routines had already gone out of the window. The life that Kevin had lived for years, the man who grieved softly for the daughter forever trapped in time had been upended. However it was resolved, nothing was going to be the same again – of that he was certain.

Monday was normally his day for sitting on Charlotte's bench, with a stroll along the cliffs to keep the blood pumping, but not today. He knew he had to trust in the process, but he was restless for a result. It may have been on Sue to investigate but, after all the years, a man was on bail for Charlotte's murder. He was her dad. Her father. Her flesh and her blood. Doing nothing? Standing by? It gnawed away at his edges until they'd been devoured. Then, it moved on to his insides. How could he face Charlotte, with the spirit of her watching over him, while he stood by idly, doing nothing. Trust the process. Of course. But, at the same time, he'd been patient with the process for years. Decades. When would something have to give?

Instead, he sat with only his TV for company, surrounded by the paintings that he had kept across the years. He didn't need to look at them to know the brushstrokes, the colours, the patterns that they made, so indelibly imprinted on his mind were they. Each of them told a story, something either from Charlotte's imagination or that she had drawn from life.

Life.

Hers had been snatched away. Now, what was to become of the man who had done it?

He stood, then sat. Paced, then strode. Climbed the stairs and descended them. Over and over, around and around, he just couldn't remain still, not while things were happening, while investigations were taking place. That the case had come back to life had been a huge trigger for him. He'd always grieved, of course, sometimes harder than others, but it had always been there. Something else had been activated, though. A darkness that had lessened as time had gone by had returned, enveloping him in its cold embrace. The news on the TV had spoken of what had happened, rehashing news reports of those bleak days, splashing headlines from yesteryear's newspapers that had long been repressed deep inside of him.

COMMUNITY IN FEAR
FAMILY SEEK ANSWERS
FATHER'S RAGE
Those words were kryptonite.
FATHER'S RAGE
They hadn't been wrong, way back then.
They weren't wrong now, either.
But smothering the anger? Keeping a lid on it, preventing the flames of ire from burning? It'd been his way of dealing with it, a coping mechanism of sorts. His GP had referred him for therapy, but that hadn't worked. And he'd been doing it for so long, being the calm man in the face of

outright provocation, that he didn't know how to do anything else.

Dr Google had told him that it wasn't healthy. Suppressed anger was something real, something defined. Brought on by trauma, the websites had said. It didn't mean that his blood didn't boil, that his brow didn't sweat. He'd just become a pro at stifling how he presented it to others. The pressure, though . . . It was building with every second that passed.

And time . . . It marched on by. He stared out of the window, at the clifftops and beyond. Waiting. Waiting. Waiting for news, for something, for anything.

He'd seen those parents on the telly, with that reporter woman. How dare they? HOW DARE THEY? He'd felt sympathy for them back then, an empathy that only a parent who knew the cavernous depth of loss could. Now, though? They were blind to what Minchin had done to his little girl, and their cruel ignorance made his stomach churn.

The knock on HIS door hadn't materialised. No one had been to ask for HIS thoughts, no reporters clamouring for a soundbite from Charlotte's side of the coin. She was being marginalised, the side story, the sub-plot.

And it wounded him so.

Chapter 45

STEVE

Steve pulled open the curtains and his room was bathed in light. In spite of his having reopened the wounds of yesteryear, he'd slept without trouble, without interference. He had dreaded the prospect of sleep, sure in his mind that those repressed memories would confront him in the dark, but not a bit of it.

One more night to go. Two more days. It was time aplenty to do what he needed to but first, food. His stomach growled at him, having been ignored the night before.

Steve dressed and made his way downstairs, before heading out of the hotel in search of something greasy and unhealthy and, in a town like that, it didn't take long to find exactly what he was after. As he sat down he breathed in the smell, the ambience and the atmosphere that was universal in any greasy spoon, country wide. The clientele was the same as it would be anywhere else: a mix of locals and tradesmen. He almost felt at home. Almost.

He ordered a full English and looked around, his gaze being drawn instantly to a lone man sitting at a table nearby. It wasn't so much the person that caught his eye, though, more the newspaper that he was reading. A national rag, the type where headlines were sensationalist and carried in the boldest of fonts. This one screamed at him.

CHARLOTTE MURDER: FIRE PARENTS BACK SUSPECT

Underneath it was a photo of him, perhaps Photoshopped, that almost looked like a mugshot. His face was stern, his lips flatly horizontal as he frowned. It was, he was sure, taken when he'd walked out in front of the press gang outside his house, but it was just the silhouette of his head with no context behind, and it only served to make him look more sinister. He couldn't read the small print, but the headline told him what he needed to know.

Alas, as he shrunk into his chair and pulled his mirrored sunglasses over his face, the content provided no crumb of comfort. In the pit of his tummy, the knot that had loosened ever so slightly over the previous few hours tightened to the point of physical pain. He should have expected it. He should have known that he would still be making the headlines, but to see it there? In a place far removed from home? It just served to rip out the flimsiest of safety blankets from beneath him.

'Full English?' a waitress asked, as she popped a plate down in front of him.

He'd never eaten so quickly in his life and, in less than three minutes, he'd sated an appetite that had all but disappeared when he'd seen his face mirrored back at him in print form, before stumbling back out onto the street. He forced deep breaths into his lungs as his heart ran riot.

He trudged, step after step, walking slowly towards nowhere and trying to lift the fog that had set in around him. Each step helped. Every metre cleared just a bit more of the mist. He had a reason, a purpose for being there. Another step brought with it another reminder to himself. He was there not for absolution, not for redemption, but to begin a process. Healing? That might be a stretch. But he needed any help he could get to unlock the memories he'd repressed so deeply, to find reason, to seek answers amidst the chaos of his youth.

His first stop was out of town and necessitated a taxi ride, but the destination held the key to one of the biggest boxes that remained locked in his mind. The address, he knew by heart. It was one he would never, ever forget.

As the twenty-minute cab ride passed in the blink of an eye, he found himself standing on the pavement, in the shoes of the boy he had been when he was resident there. The building had been razed, and in its place stood some new, fancy apartments. But he knew where he was. He could feel those insidious forces all around him. He could taste the bitter evil that had been perpetuated there. His recollections flooded back, their clarity pure and intense. His knees trembled as any and all noises around him faded to nothing.

Memories. Festering, haunting memories. Among the agitations of his youth, these were perhaps the rawest.

A large sign boldly pronounced where he was. Hornley Boys Home. It was the last resort for children under the care of the state, and nine-year-old Steve was the latest arrival.

And it was okay to start with. He kept his head above water and even made some friends. Not the type of friends who would be there for a lifetime, but in the bubble that he found himself residing, they were a godsend.

He couldn't remember when or how it started. A strategically placed hand, perhaps. An ill-timed pat on the back that missed, too low. Someone being nice to him made a stark change from the years of hell that he had endured in the foster care system.

The first time wasn't actually something pronounced or different, because it was a gradual thing, a cumulative process. Those pats on the bottom turned to a lingering hand held there for too long, maybe. Then fingers, stroking a place that they shouldn't. A kiss. Affection. Any time someone took hold of his arm from behind, how he would flinch.

Then, it got worse.

It was systemic within the home. Steve wasn't singled out, nor was he spared. He was treated as others had been before him, and others were long after he was gone.

The mental scars that were inflicted on children within those four walls, in the place where they should have been safest, had far-reaching consequences. Suicides. Future lives, plagued with criminality. Drug taking. Overdoses. The normalisation of such abuse. It affected an entire cohort of boys remorselessly, stalking them in their worst nightmares and influencing entire lives.

Steve's liberation came of his own volition. He ran away after years of suffering, vowing never to tell another soul about his time there.

On the road to adulthood, Steve had yet to experience any of the joys of childhood. Instead, disillusioned and rankly abused, he had just existed. Life, and living, had been something out of his grasp.

It took his breath away. He could smell the stale, sweaty body odour. He could taste the alcohol that he had been plied with to make it easier. All of it, he could remember. He felt every touch, hitting him like a cattle prod.

Beachbrook hadn't just been him escaping from his past. He had been running from the hell that he had been subjected to, as well. Sins committed by him. Sins inflicted on him. Finisham was the root of it all.

A major police investigation had followed, accompanied by the usual promises of lessons learned, periodic reviews, safeguarding, yadda yadda yadda. Some of the staff had been convicted and sent to prison. Steve hadn't dug into the whys and wherefores, instead keeping those thoughts firmly locked away. There had been national appeals for survivors to come forward, but he had resolutely refused to countenance such an idea. It was in the past, he had reasoned, and that was where it would stay.

And there it had remained, until now. He had been groomed. Abused. Assaulted, sexually. And more.

He shook his head as haze filled his vision, aware of but ignoring a nausea that it provoked within him. The shakes of his head became more pronounced as the haze grew thicker until, in plain sight and full view of anyone who might be looking on, he began to sob. He gave in to the nausea and doubled over, leaning forwards and retching. Nothing came out, though. Instead, he began to shake, without control, without restraint. Remembering what had happened on the ground in front of him rendered him a quivering wreck. He was revolted. Totally, utterly sickened.

He stood and stared, wondering if the occupants of the new apartments knew what had once been there, and what misery had been inflicted upon children on the very space where they lived and breathed. They must have done. It had been headline news in years gone by.

He didn't get a taxi back. Instead, it took him several hours of rough navigation to find his way back to Finisham on foot. No matter how hard his feet stamped on the pavement, he couldn't shake the bitterness that oozed from his pores. He'd never had a chance, had he?

What was he doing there, reopening old wounds like that? Was it worth it? HOW could it be worth it? The clarity that had been present earlier was lost in a fog of self-doubt. Should he just go home? Give up and call it a day? As he arrived back at his hotel room and collapsed on the bed, he yearned for Sarah. He wanted her. He needed her, to tell her what he was going through. He didn't even have his phone with him, though. It was still sitting in Beachbrook Police Station, seized as evidence.

He tried to close his eyes and drift away into a sleep like he'd had the night before, but this time it seemed impossible. Instead, he drew pictures with his eyes in the dark, using the celling as a canvas to throw darts and more at those who had abused him. It was those images that, finally, sent him into an agitated, restive slumber.

'PLEASE, NO!'

He sat bolt upright in bed, with sweat pouring from him.

As he lay down, those sobs returned.

And there they remained, for the rest of the night.

Chapter 46

DS SUE WILLMOTT

Steve's phone wasn't sitting in Beachbrook Police Station. It had, instead, been sent to Central Headquarters for processing. DS Willmott didn't know any of the intricacies involved in how they retrieved data from it, but she had always marvelled at how the information was pulled together and presented in a legible document.

It was one of those items on her checklist that still hadn't been resolved. Instead, she turned to another.

In her inbox were the results of Intel checks. It had apparently been like getting blood from a stone, the Intel DS had complained, with every form in the world needing to be faxed off to the local authority to get them to release the names of all of those who had been resident at the care home on the clifftop at the same time that Steve had.

'*Who even uses a sodding fax machine anymore?*' he'd griped.

It mattered not. With a list of fifteen kids who'd been in care, she had something to go on at least. Names and dates of birth, if nothing else.

'Vinny,' she called, summoning him into her office.

'What's up, skip?' he asked.

'Give us a hand, will you?'

'What you got?'

'Kids to trace. Well, adults now. Possible witnesses. Might give us an angle on Minchin. He might've said something to one of them; they might've seen an injury on him or something.'

'Give us it here,' Vinny said, with a smile, one that DS Willmott was only too happy to mirror. While her expertise lay in the doing of police work, her technical proficiency lagged far behind the younger detectives in her charge.

Sure enough, less than two hours later, Vinny returned with a bundle of paperwork in his hand.

'Been through all the systems,' he said, 'local, PNC, voters, the lot. Found them all.'

DS Willmott whistled. 'Great stuff,' she said.

'Got phone numbers for most of them,' Vinny said. 'There's only one local who we don't have a number for.'

'Heads or tails?' DS Willmott asked, reaching for her purse and selecting a coin.

'What for?'

'To get on the phones or go out to that one.' She pointed at the paperwork in front of Vinny.

'Heads,' he said.

She spun the coin in the air and, just for a few fleeting moments, the shiny edges of the brand-new fifty-pence-piece sent shards of light all around her office as the sun bounced off it.

'Heads,' DS Willmott said.

'Phones for me,' Vinny replied.

DS Willmott nodded. It was fair enough. If she'd won, she'd have chosen the same. She climbed to her feet and looked out of the window before walking out of the office, carrying the paperwork that Vinny had given her. It wasn't a long drive from the police station, just a mile or so inland and, as she parked on the pavement outside, she checked she had everything in her bag that she might need. Statement forms, obviously. Pens. What she didn't have was a crystal ball, only a name and, as she walked up the pathway and knocked on the front door, it was a familiar face that answered.

'Are you Phil?' she asked, as she scanned her mind to locate the memory of him.

'I am,' he replied.

She looked at him and he at her. His frown told her he was worried but, then, she understood. She had her warrant card in her hand, and it was rare that a copper came bearing news of a lottery win.

'Where do I know you from?' she asked, as a million and one images of witnesses, victims and suspects flashed across her mind like a hard drive spinning a database.

'I met you at that fire,' he said, quietly.

Bingo.

'That's it! You're friends with Steve, right?'

'Friends . . . I'd say brothers.'

'Do you mind if I come in?' DS Willmott asked. 'I need to ask a few questions.'

Phil looked beyond her, as he moved to the side. As she passed him, she sensed unease. A tension, maybe. His shoulders were hunched and his face near-white, and neither of those traits resolved themselves as they sat in the lounge.

'Sorry to intrude,' she said, flashing a pearly smile, 'but I'm just following up on a few leads.'

Phil nodded but didn't reply.

'And I have been told that you and Steve may have spent some time together at a care facility here in Beachbrook when you were younger?'

'That's right,' Phil said, through bitten lips.

'I know you're friends, and I know you'll have seen what

has been written and reported on over the past few days, but would you mind if I take a statement from you, just covering background things and anything else you might be able to remember?'

'How long will it take?' He was muted.

'Not long. Is everything . . . okay?'

Phil sighed, and looked up to her. He had a tear in his eye, and those cheeks had yet to retain any of their colour.

'A lot of stuff happened to me when I was younger, and my wife doesn't know about it. She's due home in an hour.'

'We'll be wrapped up in forty-five minutes.' Her interjection was quick, and her retrieval of statement form and pen from her bag just as speedy.

Time, clearly, was of the essence. If there was anything to be gained, then she wasn't going to waste a second.

WITNESS STATEMENT
Criminal Procedure Rules, r 27. 2; *Criminal Justice Act 1967*, s.9; Magistrates' Court Act 1980, s, 5B
Statement of: Phillip ALLENBY
Age if under 18: Over 18
Occupation: computer technician

This statement is true to the best of my knowledge and belief and I make it knowing that, if it is tendered in evidence, I shall be liable to prosecution if I have wilfully stated in it, anything which I know to be false or do not believe to be true.

I was a resident at Clifftop Residential Home, located on Beach Road, Beachbrook, some twenty-five years ago or thereabouts. I don't have the exact dates as I moved around a lot when I was younger, from care home to care home, but I know that Clifftop was the last of all my residencies, so I would've been there from when I was about 15 to 17 years old.

I do not want to go into detail as to why I was placed into care but, suffice it to say, it was because of abuse inflicted upon me when I was young. That's as much as I'm willing to share about that.

When I was at Clifftop, I met Steve Minchin. I hadn't been there long when he arrived, and I can remember meeting him for the first time. It's weird. Neither of us spoke to each other about our past and, in all truth, we haven't in all the years since, but it's like there's a subconscious awareness that we are, in many ways, kindred spirits. I guess that's why we have remained the best of friends since. Brothers, in every way but blood, I always say.

I have no knowledge of Steve's involvement in any alleged crimes from our time at Clifftop. What I would like to place on record is that Steve was, and is, the most loyal of friends, a man who looks after all of those around him, who is a wonderful father and husband, and someone you can depend on with your life.

Later, as DS Willmott sat in her office with Vinny on the other side of the desk, they compared notes.

'Poor sod,' Vinny said, reading Phil's words twice and sliding the statement back over to her.

'Yeah,' she replied.

'Reckon there's anything in it?' he asked. 'Kindred spirits and all that? Minchin was abused too, maybe?'

'God knows. He clammed up, big time, told me three times that they never discussed their pasts.'

'Fair enough.'

'Anything your end?' she asked.

'Nothing that takes us forwards.'

She sighed as she popped Phil's statement into the file. It was a cul-de-sac, a road that she'd gone down hoping for answers but one where all she'd found was a dead end.

Chapter 47

STEVE

The night passed with those sobs returning in waves. That trip to Hornley had awoken something within, something that had lain dormant for so many years. To confront it had been to do a deep dive into the parts of his mind that had been inaccessible since that abuse had been inflicted, and it was tormenting him in ways he could never have imagined.

He climbed from his pit, washed and dressed, all before the clock had struck 05.00. There was one more thing to tick off the list, before his long journey back to Beachbrook.

He was out of the hotel door long before the night staff had handed over to the day shift and, as he made his way along the main road, the prevailing northern wind hit him squarely across the cheeks. His eyes widened as that chill crept up his face. The moon glistened on the windows around him and the sky was as clear as spring water. It was amazing the difference that a clear night sky could make to the temperature half a country away. He made his way around a warren of tight roads until, eventually, he was standing on the edge of a wasteland. Bricks and mortar littered the ground all around him as he poked and prodded at the footings of what had once been. It hadn't stood tall and proud but the derelict building that had been razed to the ground had been the place he'd found himself immediately after escaping the horrors of Hornley.

In some ways, it had been somewhere he might have called his first home.

'Who are you?' The voice wasn't aggressive, but it was tainted with an edge that wasn't exactly welcoming Steve through the door.

He'd heard whispers about the squat while he had been at Hornley, but it was almost something of an urban legend.

'When I get out of here, I'm going straight there,' someone had said.

'They'll look after you there.'

'Good 'uns, all of 'em.'

It had been enough for him to find his way there and, having absconded from the terrors that stalked him in Hornley, Steve found himself on the threshold looking in. He couldn't work out who had asked who he was – it was dark, and he could make out the silhouettes of various people inside. A dense smoke sat heavy in the air. It wasn't tobacco, but the pungent stench of cannabis.

'I'm Steve,' he said, trying to project himself with as much confidence as he could.

'Where you from, Steve?' someone else asked. 'Not a fed, are you?'

He was a malnourished, grimly abused, skinny rake of a teenager, about as far removed from a police officer or a plant as could be.

'No,' Steve replied. 'Come from Hornley.'

Someone approached him. It wasn't until they were a few feet away that he could see their face. A few years older than him, maybe, but he looked at Steve with a knowing expression. A kindred spirit.

'Boys' home?' he asked.

Steve nodded.

'I was there,' the other boy said. 'I'm Tony. Come on, bruv, let's get you sorted.'

Tony led Steve into the squat. As his eyes struggled to adjust to the dim fog of smoke he was meandering through, he stumbled. Rubbish here, furniture there, empty spirit bottles all over, everything was a trip hazard. People lay comatose on sofas with uncapped needles surrounding them and a carpet that had been used as an ashtray for God only knew how long. In spite of it all, Steve had never felt so at home.

Over the course of a few months, he settled in. The dregs of society who he found there became his family. He would do everything he could to fit in for, in a world where he had always been alone, he now had an identity. He'd been forever forgotten. Now, he was someone. Stealing, random muggings, any drug that was doing the rounds, nothing was off limits. He took to it like a duck to water and blended in as if he'd always been there.

Tony looked after him. Hornley boys, it seemed, looked after their own. After all they had been through, it was the least they could do for each other. In Tony, he had found a role model of sorts, someone he looked up to. In a life swimming with emptiness, and with a history of abandonment and abuse, he revelled in the company of someone who seemed to genuinely care.

A fractured child became a troubled teenager.

And, irrevocably, the wheels of devastation had been set in motion.

* * *

279

Steve didn't remember any other names. Only Tony. And he knew what had become of him. He didn't know where he was buried, and he wasn't there to pay his respects. He was just another statistic, another life cut short. It could so easily have been Steve's fate.

Instead, as he looked at the overgrown weeds that complemented the debris that was all that remained of the squat, and the recollections of all the things that he'd done and experienced on the very ground before him swamped his mind, he felt flushed with shame that he had thought of those who he'd run with as family.

Now, in real life, he knew what family was. It wasn't crime. It wasn't violence. It wasn't everything that he had thought it had been all those years before, when their reign of terror had brought misery to Finisham. No, it was warmth. It was affection. It was love. It only reaffirmed the thoughts that he'd wrestled with when he'd been sitting in the cell at the police station, only a few days before. What mattered the most? Family. Real family. True family.

It was everything that he had found in Beachbrook. Sarah, Gracie, Oscar, even Phil and Emma. They were all he would ever need. He turned around and walked away as thoughts of Tony and all the others melted away. Their stories were of their own making and, in truth, he didn't want to remember them. Instead, he filled his mind with thoughts of his wife, his babies, his best friend. It amazed him just how far he had come, and how much he needed them back where they'd always been – in the house they'd made a home, in the town he'd grown to love.

And, though the sun had yet to break through, to make its way beyond the horizon and take the chill out of the air around him, it was those thoughts of his wife, his babies, his best friend, that prompted him to turn around and march back from exactly where he'd come. He'd come, and he'd seen what he needed to. He hadn't conquered, not by any means, and the wounds that had been reopened just by being in the vicinity of Hornley still ran deep. Even so, he'd had to do it. Simply had to. In order to move forwards, those ghosts had needed exorcising and, though he'd only just begun to confront them in his mind, it was a step he'd not taken in some twenty years.

Way back when, it had taken a police raid for him to be found. And it hadn't been just a couple of coppers who had come knocking, looking for the missing child who had run away from Hornley. Totally the opposite, in fact.

'GET ON THE GROUND!'

It wasn't an entirely necessary instruction. The morning may have been near enough over, but the thick, black curtains kept the light out while everyone slept wherever they lay.

Steve was on the floor. Not quite sweet sixteen, and surrounded by young adults. By filth. By needles, capped and otherwise. He hadn't pinned himself yet, but it wouldn't have been long.

Coppers in riot gear swarmed the squat before anyone even had the chance to stir and, as the boys in blue kneeled firmly on the backs of those who lay on the floor, pinning them to the ground, handcuffs were slapped on everyone inside.

'Warrant under Section 23 of the Misuse of Drugs Act,' one of the coppers barked. 'No one move.'

Steve joined in with the abuse.

'Ain't you got a trough to eat from, pigs.'

'Fed twats.'

They weren't metal cuffs that he felt stinging his wrists behind his back. They were made of plastic, the type that the riot police used in a hurry. As he was dragged to his feet, he so nearly spat in the face of the copper who was manhandling him. It was only that his head was roughly bent forwards, his eyes facing his bare feet and the floor beneath him, that kept the phlegm contained within.

Outside, they were lined up for public consumption, no doubt a trophy being paraded in front of the very community that they had terrorised. Each of them sat on the kerb in between the meat wagons and the police cars that had been dumped on the road outside. The sneers continued, from Tony, from the others and from Steve.

Yet.

While all the others were led away in handcuffs.

And while they were read their rights, and hauled into the back of the wagons and cars.

Steve wasn't. He'd never been arrested. Never been caught. It looked like that streak was about to continue.

Instead, he faced down a social worker who he'd seldom seen, but who had apparently been looking for him and had turned up in the hurry when she'd been told he was there. Him being located was another box ticked, no doubt. Another problem solved. And, in seconds, it became clear that he was going to be someone else's issue very soon. The words rained down on him like acid from the skies.

'Delinquent.'

'Moving you.'

'Relocating.'

'Beachbrook, down south.'

Chapter 48

SARAH

Steve had been gone for four days, but it might as well have been a lifetime. Never before, in all their years together, had they spent more than a night apart. Others mightn't have thought it was healthy, but it's just the way they'd always been – thick as thieves, tight as a compressed spring. His absence wasn't just being felt by the kids, theirs not the only tears to have fallen at bedtimes and beyond. Sarah was suffering, too. Physically: school runs, packed lunches, dinners, washing, the bedtime routine, keeping their attention as she tried to get them to dial their iPads into Doodle Maths rather than YouTube. Mentally: with only herself for company long into the night, her mind ran rings around her as she tussled with the enormity of it all. Steve had killed a child. But he'd BEEN a child. And he'd SAVED a child. And emotionally: without him, she was only half of an equation that had always been the right answer to any questions that life had thrown at them. She might hate him, she might despise him. She might loathe what he'd done and that he'd kept the darkest of secrets hidden from her since forever. None of that took away from the fact that she loved him.

Phil had told her where Steve had gone, that he was without his phone. He'd told her that Steve had wanted to go and face his past, to figure out what had actually happened and find out the 'why'. And a huge part of her was hoping he found it. She needed answers. Desperately.

As she drove to Phil and Emma's after the school run, with Oscar unusually silent and Gracie staring out of the window behind her, there was none of the fizz of family life around her that she so loved. It was a grief that had hit them all, a stake through the heart of what had once been, and it was ripping her apart inch by inch by inch.

'Hey, Phil,' Sarah murmured, as he opened the door. Oscar stood by her side but Gracie was hiding behind, standing bum to bum with her and staring out to the road and beyond.

'Hey, guys,' Phil replied, offering his hand for high fives but receiving only a half-hearted, limp effort from Oscar. 'Come in.'

Sarah groped behind her, reaching for Gracie's hand and feeling resistance as she moved forwards. She turned around and looked at her daughter, joining her as they both locked eyes on nothing in particular. Gracie's little whimpers broke her heart.

'Daddy will be back soon,' she whispered, 'I promise.' She kept hold of Gracie's hand as they walked into the house, heading straight for the lounge where Phil and Emma were keeping up appearances.

'Oh hi!' Emma said, as a smile spread across her cheeks. Sarah saw through it like cling-film, but at least Gracie showed a flicker of placation. It wasn't half a smile, more a quarter, but it was something.

Phil sat on the sofa and nodded to Sarah. She was having doubts about leaving the kids for an hour, but she'd been bearing a load that was becoming unmanageable. Emma had finished work a couple of hours early just so they could get out for a coffee and a chat that she so desperately needed.

'Go on you two,' he said, waving his hand towards the door as if dismissing Sarah and Emma. 'We'll chuck a film on or something.'

Gracie turned on her heels and shot Sarah a look, her eyes wide and her top lip trembling, but Phil scooped her up before she could protest.

'Don't worry,' Sarah soothed, 'Mummy's not going to be long. I promise.'

'Don't want you to go,' Gracie cried, as she wriggled free from Phil's arms and wrapped herself up in Sarah's. Her little girl's heart was thumping, and Sarah got it. With one parent suddenly out of the equation, God only knew what was going through her seven-year-old mind at the prospect of the other not being there, too, no matter for how long.

'We'll stay here, sweetheart,' Sarah whispered, 'no dramas.' And it worked, like a charm. Gracie's tense shoulders loosened, and her heart rate lowered as Sarah's fingertips rubbed her back gently. 'All right if Mummy and Auntie Em go in the kitchen, for a chat?'

Gracie looked up, and around, presumably weighing the situation up. Eventually, she nodded and, as Sarah and Emma shuffled out of the room, she was sitting next to Oscar watching something or other on the television. Her thumb was still in her mouth, but she was content. There was no way that Sarah was going to tell her to take it out.

For her part, Sarah had been keeping it all in. No sooner had the kitchen door closed behind them than it all came pouring out. Silent tears. Soundless sobs. Her shoulders shuddered as she suppressed any noise. It was only when Emma took hold of her and her head was planted firmly into her best friend's chest that, finally, she let some wails out, those moans being muffled and absorbed by the silky fabric of Emma's top. One minute turned into two, until there were no tears left to fall.

Emma said nothing. She just held Sarah, and it was more appreciated than any words could have been.

As the clinch between the two of them finally came to an end, and Sarah looked across to Emma, she couldn't help but look down to her bosom. Over the years, she herself had worn plenty of snot, dribble and tears on her own clothes. It had always been the product of her kids, though, not a full-grown adult. She felt her cheeks flush as Emma pinched at the silk between her thumb and forefinger, pulling it away as it tried to cling onto her skin. That it was black only made the dampness and phlegm stand out more.

'Sorry,' Sarah said.

Emma looked down at her top once more, then up to Sarah and snorted. The laugh that followed brought warmth to Sarah's soul.

They sat next to each other on the stools at the breakfast bar, and though her thoughts were still spiralling, Sarah already felt a smidgen better for letting her emotions out to her best friend, after bottling them up for the sake of the kids.

'So how are things?' Emma asked.

'Shit,' Sarah replied. 'Just shit.'

'Have you been eating?'

'Don't need to eat, I did that last week.'

The two women smiled at each other, as Emma reached for a packet of custard creams that was lying atop the kitchen side. She pulled two out and dropped them in front of Sarah.

'Not gourmet dining, but it'll do for a starter,' Emma said. 'Cheers.'

Sarah picked one up and began to nibble at the edges but, in the same way that her view of the world had been warped by everything that had happened, so too were her taste buds affected. As she found her way to the cream inside the sandwich, it tasted rancid, and she set it back down in front of her.

'Have you heard from him?' Emma asked.

'Hasn't got his phone,' Sarah replied.

'Fair point . . . Do payphones still exist, even?'

'God knows.'

Sarah picked up the biscuit again and tried once more. It still tasted funny, but not as bad. She let a larger chunk settle in her mouth and forced it down the hatch.

'What are you gonna do, Sar?'

'Been asking myself the same thing.'

'You've got to talk to him, right?'

Sarah finished off the biscuit, and picked up the other. In two bites, it was gone.

'He killed a kid, Em.'

'I know. Has he . . . told you what happened? Why?'

'He tried, but . . . I don't know . . . He just couldn't. Hopefully when he's back, he'll give me some answers.'

She paused and looked at Emma.

'He'll have to.'

Her throat tightened, and her words were a whisper.

'I can't bear it.'

She looked around as her tummy rumbled. Emma reached across to the biscuits, and passed her the whole packet. She took another and began eating it.

They sat in silence for a minute, as Sarah worked her way through another couple of biscuits. She couldn't remember when she'd last eaten anything properly. It certainly wasn't that day. Nor, come to think of it, was it the day before.

'How are you, anyway?' she asked.

'Oh, we're fine' Emma replied, a bit too brightly. 'Besides, you don't need to hear about all that.' There was something in her voice. Something in the way she ground her teeth together, just for a split second, as she said it. And something in the way she narrowed her eyes as the words were delivered.

'Problems still?' Sarah asked, grateful for any distraction she could find.

Emma nodded, softly at first, then more protracted as her eyes filled. She was trying so hard to keep it in, Sarah knew, trying so hard to not make this about her. That's what good friends did.

'Our relationship has just completely broken down,' Emma cried.

'Broken things can be fixed,' Sarah whispered, doing whatever she could to soothe the pain that was manifest in every syllable that came from Emma's lips.

Emma looked up and met Sarah's gaze. 'I hope you're right,' she said, giving her friend a squeeze of the hand. 'For both of our sakes.'

Chapter 49

STEVE

It felt like it had been much, much longer than a two-night visit and, as Steve sat on the train while it slowly departed Finisham, he drank in the emotion, and basked in the profound relief at what he felt he had accomplished. It had been no small feat. He had gone there, alone, not knowing what to expect. As the train reached a steady, cruising pace, he settled back into his seat and closed his eyes. How would he ever explain to anyone the impact it had on him? He'd be able to formulate sentences to describe it. He would tell her about going to Hornley, standing amidst the wreckage that had been his upbringing. Sure, he'd exorcised some demons, but not all of them. That would take time . . . But he'd begun the process, and it was more than he could ever have hoped for.

One thing was for sure. To have experienced it, to have suffered the same wrench in the gut as he'd felt in the past, and to come out the other side with a renewed sense of liberation and emotional emancipation . . . It was something he'd never be able to put into words.

And yet, he must, he resolved. He owed it to Sarah. And

not just the lite version, the PG take. Everything. The whole lot. He just hoped it would be enough.

It had been life-changing, for sure, but it had been something else as well. He pulled his sunglasses tight to his nose as Finisham disappeared into the distance and, as he closed his eyes, he thought of her.

Of Charlotte.

Of the image of her that was enduring in his mind, on that clifftop on that day. So many times, he'd closed that snapshot down lest it bring on the pain, but not now. Not today. Instead, he looked at the outline of her against the backdrop of blue, and just let her linger there as his subconscious painted her face on top. Rosy cheeks. A few freckles dotted around her nose and cheeks. Tasselled light-brown hair at shoulder length. Blue eyes, and the smallest of shy smiles. The details may have been confirmed by all of the pictures in the papers across the years, but he could retrace it in his mind without any prompt.

There and then, he resolved to visit her. He knew where she was, where she'd been for all the years gone by, but he'd never dared to venture close to it. Now, though? His was a debt that could never be paid, but he'd never even been to say sorry. That much, he had to do.

And he thought of her dad, of the misery that he'd imparted and, no doubt, of the renewal of that very agony as the sores of the past had had salt rubbed in them over recent days. He was still local, Steve was sure, but twenty years and more had gone by. His was another portrait in Steve's mind, one from decades prior, of a man who had been stripped of everything he'd known to be right in the world. Would he still look the same, Steve wondered? Would the grief that he'd seen in the past be indelibly stained on his face for evermore? He could only imagine that pain, that torture. Being a dad himself . . . It didn't bear thinking about.

What would he do, in that situation? How would he react? It wasn't even a question, in his mind. Like every parent out there, he supposed, if someone hurt his children then . . . He shook himself away from those thoughts and, instead, closed his eyes. The broken sleep from the previous night was catching up with him. His head was in a different space to anything he could remember and, without realising it, he drifted away as the pitter-patter of the train on railway sleepers provided a melody to snooze to.

Steve slept until he felt his shoulder being gently rocked. The train had terminated, and a fellow passenger smiled as she woke Steve from his slumber. Momentarily confused, his senses quickly returned and he thanked her for letting him know. As he got up and slung his backpack over his shoulder, he caught a glimpse of her face as he turned to thank her once more before departing. Now, her eyes were squinting as she stared. Even behind his sunglasses, she recognised him. From where, though, it seemed she was stumped. Steve was in no mood to enlighten her, and instead he walked quickly from the carriage along the platform. He could feel her eyes burning into him from behind.

'Breathe,' he mumbled, as his heart rate spiked in tandem with his quickening stride.

He wasn't so naïve as to think that, while he was trying to deal with things on a personal level, that the noises on the outside might quieten down. Hell, there was still a strong possibility in his mind that he was going to be spending a fair chunk of the following years serving at His Majesty's pleasure. Even so, the stares of a stranger only served to exacerbate the whispers that were no doubt being spoken behind his back, the commentary he was sure existed on social media platforms that were beyond his understanding.

Yet, as he navigated the capital and was on the final leg of his long journey home, he trained his mind on one thing, and one thing only. All he could do was focus on what he could impact, to home in on the variables that he could affect. As the train rumbled on and he listened to the list of stations still to visit growing shorter as each stop passed by, his fingers tapped the window so quick that it sounded like a vibration. He was impatient to get back. He needed to be with his wife, to see her, to tell her everything that his mind had finally allowed him to remember. He'd found it in Finisham, and he had to share it. Whatever came after that, he would have to deal with. All he could do was his bit, and then see how the chips fell.

First, though, he had just one more thing to do. One more piece of the jigsaw to slot into place.

As the announcement came over the train Tannoy that the next station was Beachbrook, he hustled through the empty carriage to the door, jumping onto the platform as soon as the door opened and, in between all the smells of the train station, letting the unique aroma of Beachbrook wash over him. He was home.

It was a short drive from the train station to the clifftop. He drove past the slope down to Coffee and Cream, and meandered up the winding road that followed the outline of the cliffs. It seemed never-ending, much like it had when he'd first pitched up there, aged fifteen and full of anger.

'I'm just gonna run back up north,' Steve said, as the car crunched gravel beneath its wheels.

'Then we'll just bring you back,' the social worker replied. Her voice was calm, in the face of his rage. Annoyingly so.

'Whatever,' he muttered.

'This is a new start,' she replied as she applied the brakes and stopped at the side of the road. 'Here we are.'

Steve had never seen the sea before and, though it was dark, when he climbed from the vehicle, he heard it. Hell, under the light of the moon, he could just about make it out, the waves cresting and sending dull shards of light everywhere. Without meaning to, he sniffed and breathed it in, smelling that distinctive perfume of sand, sea and surf. In days to come, he'd even touch it, dipping his feet when no one was watching. Though he'd never admit to it, he was transfixed from the moment he climbed from the rear of the vehicle.

'Stinks here,' he said.

'That's fresh air,' the social worker replied.

He stormed up the path to the door, following as she led, leaving the sea behind them for now. Those cliffs behind him could tell stories aplenty, and it was only a matter of time before he gave them another tale to whisper about.

Steve stopped in the same spot his social worker had, way back when. He climbed from his car, breathing it all in, looking up at the care home that no longer had young children resident within. Like everything else, it seemed, it was now flats; a veritable assortment of short-term lets and Airbnbs, prime coastal real estate designed to maximise revenues. Even so, as he stood and stared, he could remember everything. How nervous he'd been, to be there for the first time, but how he'd slept like a log, on his first night. Sea air? Maybe. Or had it been the freedom from everything that had befallen him up north? For just a few, fleeting moments, he'd been . . . not quite comfortable in his own skin, but more so than he'd been before.

Those scars from Hornley lingered, though. What if . . . What if . . . What if, it happened again? He'd stayed on the periphery, a ghost looking in, not putting his head anywhere near the parapet. Scared? He was terrified, and more. One care home was like any other, wasn't it?

And so it was that, just a week or so after he'd arrived, he snuck out seeking solitude, but everything came to a head.

And it all crashed and burned around him.

Chapter 50

KEVIN

The itch had always been there but, across the years, he'd always been able to scratch it before he'd gone up into the loft and fetched that particular suitcase. Now, though, it was a burning rash in his mind and he simply couldn't sate it.

As he sat in his lounge poring over the news reports of yesteryear, looking at Charlotte's beautiful face staring back up at him, the fire inside was well and truly stoked. He hadn't laid eyes on them since it had happened, and the headlines screamed at him.

MURDER IN PARADISE
POLICE STUMPED
DNA HOPE FOR MURDER POLICE
HOPES FADING
CHARLOTTE KILLING UNRESOLVED

He flicked through the pages of one of them. Back then, his anger hadn't been suppressed. It'd been barely contained, in fact. It was one of those personal pieces, which had been suggested by the police when it appeared the investigation was stalling. A powder piece, to reinvigorate the public and to keep Charlotte in the public's consciousness. What he'd said, though? It probably wasn't what they'd been looking for.

On the three-month anniversary of Charlotte Hitch's death, her father Kevin sat down with us to discuss the investigation, and the impact that her killing has had on her family. Grief poured out of him as he spoke. These are his words, uncorrected and printed exactly as they were said to us and, please be warned, there is bad language from the outset.

'How has Charlotte's passing affected us? Imagine a boat, being rowed by two people with someone else as the skipper. Three people, pulling together to ensure smooth passage across the seas. Charlotte and I were on oars, and her mum was at the helm. Now take away one of the rowers. What do you do? Spin around in mindless circles, that's what you do. Charlotte has been taken away and all her mum and I are doing is spinning around, a circle from hell, with no destination in sight. And our boat? It's taking on water. It's sinking. And there's not a fucking thing we can do to stop it.

'Charlotte was a beauty. Was. Fucking was. I hate that, you know. Hate it so much. Talking about her as "was". Not "is". She was such a special girl. Loved her art, was good enough to make a career out of it, people said. And she was so good, such a sweetheart. Would always check that others were okay. The school told me that, you know? After. They said that she'd always been the one to go out of her way to help other people, to check in on her mates, on everyone.

'So yeah, I want people to know this about Charlotte. She was the best of us. She might have only been thirteen, but she was the best of the best. And now she's been ripped away, and our boat is spinning and spinning without her to straighten it up.

'Someone out there knows what happened. Someone out there knows who did this, who was responsible. And someone out there did it.

'What would I like to say to that person? What would I like to tell them? I'll tell you exactly what I'd like to say to them.

'Turn yourself in. You've got blood on your hands, the blood of my little girl. And I'll tell you what else, and I probably shouldn't say this but I really don't care anymore. You'd better hope and pray that the police get to you first, because if they don't . . .'

He could remember it so well. Reading the article in front of him, he was transported back in time to the living room that he was in now, with the reporter sitting opposite him and a Dictaphone in the middle. It was decorated the same, with the same furniture and the same television set. Back then, though, it had all been modern. No threads hanging off the chairs, clean walls that weren't full of Charlotte's pictures and paintings. Back then, it'd been a house that had only recently stopped being a home. Now, it was just a shell that he existed in.

He remembered those words as he'd spat them out. There'd been no suppressed anger back then, no checking himself before he spoke. It'd only been the intervention of whatever detective it was who'd sat in with them that had stopped him mid-sentence from saying EXACTLY what he'd do if he found out who'd killed Charlotte.

Now, as those feelings washed over him once more, he felt the same rage within, the same ire growing.

And the pressure? It just kept building.

Chapter 51

STEVE

Steve wasn't so naïve as to think that he could just waltz back home and tell Sarah everything that he'd been through up north, and that all would be forgiven. Her flinch was still fresh in his mind, so much more than her words had been when she'd told him to leave. Impatient though he was, turning up unannounced on the doorstep simply wouldn't do.

Darkness had fallen by the time he rolled to a gentle stop outside Phil and Emma's house and, as he slipped inside quietly, he walked to the lounge. His footsteps were so much lighter than they'd been a few days before.

'We can't carry on like this!' Emma shouted.

Her words may have come from the lounge, but they bounced off the walls in the hallway as they echoed in his ears. They were followed shortly after by the sound of something smashing. Glass? Maybe. Whatever, it made him stop dead in his tracks.

'You're mental,' Phil shouted back. 'This is nuts!'

What should he do? Turn around and walk out? While his brain prevaricated, his feet made up his mind for him.

'All right, guys?' he asked, as he crept into the lounge.

Emma was sitting on the sofa with her head in her hands, barely containing the sobs within them, while Phil was standing, looking out of the window. Next to him, on the floor, were the shattered remains of a picture frame, with the photo of the two of them that it had housed lying amongst the wreckage. Each of their faces shot across to him no sooner than he had spoken.

'You're back?' Phil said.

'I'm back.'

The atmosphere clung to his clothes as he stood there, a tension so deep and raw that it chilled him all the way to his bones.

'I'll be upstairs,' he mumbled, as he turned around and walked back out of the room. As he climbed the stairs at double pace, he heard pointed whispers coming from the lounge and, as he closed the door to the spare bedroom behind him, it only took a few seconds before there were footsteps getting closer to him. He'd barely sat down on the bed before there was a soft knock on the door. A moment later, Phil walked in. His face was a juxtaposed mishmash of anger and calm, raised eyebrows above squinting eyes and lips that were pursed yet puckering intermittently.

'Bad timing?' Steve asked.

Phil shook his head and looked away.

'How did it go?' he asked.

'It was . . . needed,' Steve replied. 'I'll be out of your hair soon, mate, one way or the other, all right?'

'No dramas.'

Phil looked over at him. He'd always been an open book to Steve and, in an instant, he knew there was something that needed to be said.

'What's up? You and Em? Need to chat?'

'No, nothing to do with that . . . We'll be fine. Something else, though.'

'Spill.'

Phil walked over to him and perched on the edge of the bed. It was only a single and, had it been anyone else, it might have felt uncomfortably close. Not them, though. Not him and Phil.

'That detective woman, she came here.'

The knot in Steve's stomach bounced from side to side. 'Willmott?'

'That's her.'

'What did she want?'

'Said she was doing background on Clifftop, just asked how we knew each other, did I know anything about anything, all that kinda stuff.'

Steve remained silent. It was one thing to be doing his own digging, but to have someone else drilling down on everything that had come before was something else entirely.

'What did you say?'

'She was asking about my past and stuff as well, didn't want to tell her about all that, but just said that we'd met there and been best mates since. The truth, you know?'

Steve nodded and lifted his head up. He stared at Phil, who met his gaze halfway.

'Sorry, mate.'

'Sorry for what?'

'That she came here, that you had to . . . tell her whatever.'

They'd never spoken of their times before Clifftop, but there'd always been something intrinsic there, something that connected them on a level far deeper than a friendship. It was a bond of brotherhood that transcended blood and, Steve knew, was based on shared experiences during their formative years. They'd never needed to speak of it. They'd

300

seen it in each other's eyes all those years before, and it had only served to cement their relationship across the years.

'S'all right,' Phil said, tapping his hand on Steve's knee. 'All good in the hood.'

The silence between them that followed wasn't uncomfortable. Instead, it gave Steve the time to think, to rationalise, to work out a plan moving forwards. First, though . . .

'You and Em,' he eventually said, 'all okay?'

Phil batted his enquiry away with a dismissive hand. 'What will be will be.'

'Gotcha. Anything I can do?'

'Nah, mate.'

'Fair enough.' Another silence, until . . . 'Can I borrow your phone? Need to message Sarah.'

'Course, mate. I'll leave you to it.'

Phil handed his phone to Steve, before tapping his knee once more and standing up. They nodded at each other with half a smile on each of their faces making one in total, and Phil walked out of the room, closing the door behind him. Steve took a deep breath as he opened WhatsApp, but it took an age to compose a message, and even longer to press send. It didn't matter, though, he had time enough to make it right, to make his words perfect. In every respect, it was the most important message he would ever send.

Hiya, it's Steve on Phil's phone. I know he told you that I haven't got my phone at the moment. The police took it, and that's why I haven't been in touch. I just needed to let you know that I've been away for a few days, up north, to where I grew up. It was something I just had to do, and I really hope that you'll understand why I've not been in touch. I did it, Sarah. I went back there. I faced up to everything that I grew up with. And I can talk about it now; I really feel like I can. Like, I

301

tried before, but the words were dry, you know? Now I just know that I can speak to you and it'll come out. I'm not asking you to forgive me. It's unforgivable, I know that, but I just want to tell you about it. That's all. Would that be okay? I miss my kids. I miss you. And I just want to give them a cuddle and to talk to you. All my love, Steve xxx

His breaths shook as one tick turned to two, then the colour turned blue as Sarah's moniker transitioned to 'online'. Moments later, there was a reply.

Come round tomorrow, midday.

No hello, no farewell, no query as to how he was or how his trip had been. No kisses on the end, either. But there was an olive branch. There was an instruction. There was a chance, and that mattered a million times more than anything else.

Chapter 52

DS SUE WILLMOTT

It was the start of another day and, as DS Willmott pulled up the online bail signing-on forms on the intranet, Steve's name already had the Thursday tick box showing as complete. He was an early bird, it seemed.

She picked up her phone to find a message waiting for her from her mum.

Lottie dropped off to school fine, hope you have a good day, love xxx

Her fingers typed a slow reply.

Thanks, Mum, you too. Love you xxx

She thought it might be the end of the conversation, but apparently not. Her mum was typing, and she watched and waited with a smile on her face as a couple of minutes passed by. She herself might be a bit sluggish with all things tech, but her mum had two paces: painful and funereal. She was half expecting a three-word 'love you too' entreaty after four solid minutes of typing but, instead, it was chapter and verse.

I've been thinking about you. On your own. Isn't it time to get back in the race? Have you heard of this online dating thing? Or something called speed-dating? Might be worth a look. Anyway, I'll keep my nose out if you want me to. I just want to see you happy is all. Love you too xxx

She rolled her eyes. It'd been a while coming, with little hints here and gentle nudges there, but this was the first time her mum had come out and explicitly said it. Still, she had a reply ready and waiting.

I will if you will xxx

Her mum fell silent. Checkmate. A smirk broke out across her cheeks, one that only fell away when she flicked across to her email inbox to catch up with everything that had flooded in from the day before and overnight.

There were a variety of emails. Some of them were the usual spammy ones, reminding her of training dates for different members of her staff, others informed her that some appraisals were due. One, though, leapt out at her.

MOBILE PHONE DATA EXTRACTION – R VS MINCHIN

It was like a nugget of gold in a field of dirt.

A report into the download of the contents of Steve's phone, sent not twenty minutes before. Everything else could wait. This is what she'd been waiting for, another one of those boxes in her day book that hadn't yet been ticked.

And the contents? The secrets that the report held within? It took her breath away.

'You're kidding me,' she said, holding a hand to her mouth, as she flicked through it.

304

Search after search in his phone browser, only hours after he was arrested for drink driving all those days before.

'Charlotte Hitch murder Beachbrook'
'Charlotte Hitch DNA'
'How long does it take police to process DNA'
'Can police take DNA if not charged'
'How long do you go to jail for killing someone'

'Vinny,' she called, summoning him into her office. He walked in and stood behind her, while she scrolled back to the top and began reading it again to make sure that everything was sinking in.

'Jesus Christ,' Vinny spluttered.

'Amen,' DS Willmott replied as she scrolled up and down to check that her eyes weren't deceiving her. These weren't searches that he'd done after he'd been arrested for Charlotte's murder, they were in the run-up to it. Why had he been searching for those things, unless . . .

'What's the plan?' Vinny asked.

DS Willmott puffed out her cheeks and rolled her shoulders, before forwarding the phone results to DCI Maine with an accompanying message . . . Not that one was needed, though. The results spoke for themselves.

'I think we need another little chat with our Mr Minchin, don't you?'

Chapter 53

SARAH

The school run, normally a shared rite, had been Sarah's domain for that week. Just the act of getting the kids up in the morning, getting them ready, doing packed lunches, making sure that teeth were brushed and hair was done, was exhausting enough. Factor in the emotional toll that everything was taking on her, the stares from other parents, the whispers that she couldn't hear but was sure were being mouthed around her, and it was all getting to be too much.

'Mummy will see you later, all right, kiddos?' she said, throwing the kids the best fake smile she could as they loitered on the pavement side of the school gate. Oscar nodded and ran into the playground, but Gracie hesitated.

'When's Daddy coming back?' she asked.

'Daddy's just sorting out a few things,' Sarah said, stroking Gracie's hair and making ringlets between her fingers. 'We'll see him very soon, I promise.'

'Pinkie?'

'Pinkie.'

They linked little fingers and Gracie's eyes filled. It was enough, it seemed, for Mrs Adams to wander over from her position standing sentry on the gate, where she'd met Gracie every morning that week. The school had stepped up, it had seemed. The news had hit every living room in the country, and Beachbrook wasn't immune from it. Not at all. One of their own had brought the attention of the nation to their doorstep and, as social media had shown Sarah when she'd dared to venture online, opinions were about as polarised as they could possibly be.

'Let's go, Gracie,' Mrs Adams said, sweeping her away under a protective arm.

As she watched teacher and student cross the pavement, Sarah couldn't help but feel that, for the first time, it was a pinkie promise she wasn't sure she could keep and, as it had been all week, her heart was empty.

She drove home slowly, eyes fixed and glazed while she navigated the roads. As she walked in through the front door, it felt cold. It felt empty. It was a loneliness that smacked her across the cheeks, as though the soul of their family home had been ripped out and replaced by a hollow void.

She slumped into the sofa and, through habit, reached for her mobile phone. Even the firms that she worked for had gone silent, no one messaging to ask for this update or the other. Instead of logging into one of the many corporate accounts she had on her social media, she instead opened her personal one.

Just a few scrolls made her wish she hadn't.

Some of the tweets took her off guard. Open discussions were taking place between members of the blue-tick community, with prominent celebrities insisting that Gracie and Oscar should be taken away from them. Sarah's eyes bulged as a growing rage grew inside her, a maternal fury at the thought of a stranger saying such a thing. They didn't know her. How dare they?

Still, the tweets came, and she saw some light. Some positive. Some with faint praise, some fulsome. The negative may have outweighed the positive, but it was nearly a fifty-fifty divide. Those who supported Steve spoke of his heroism and bravery; those who denounced him spoke of his villainy and cowardice. As had been evident elsewhere, opinions were polarised. You were either totally for, or absolutely against. There was no grey area, no room for fence sitting. To some, there was no smoke without fire. To others, there was no fire to begin with.

'Would you trust him to look after your kids?'
'Should've been castrated straight away.'
'Killed a girl, saved a baby. Paid his debt.'
'I think he has more than atoned. Obviously a good man now.'

She dropped her phone down next to her. How long was the nightmare going to endure? How loud were the whispers in the echo chamber going to get before everything came to a head? No sooner had the phone hit the fabric of the sofa next to her, though, than its ringtone stifled her ruminations in their tracks. She picked it up, and looked at the screen, at the caller ID.

School.

'Hello?'

'Mrs Minchin?' The voice was low. Urgent.

'Yeah.'

We need you to come in. Gracie is . . . We need you to come in.'

'What's the matter with her?' It wasn't a screaming voice, but it wasn't a gentle enquiry either.

'She's upset. Very upset.'

'I'm on my way.'

She was out of the door so quickly that locking it as she left didn't even cross her mind. Into the car, retracing a route she'd driven only an hour or so before, only this time at warp speed. As she drove, she fumbled at her phone. In the cold light of day, she might have had reservations about making the call but, guided only by instinct, she did what she would always have done whenever there was a problem.

She flicked to her speed-dial screen, her list of favourites, and called Steve. Straight to answerphone. Of course, of course, of course. No phone. She scrolled down two, her attention divided between the tarmac under her wheels and her need to get through to her husband, and clicked on Phil's name. She only hoped that he was working from home, and that Steve was with him.

Chapter 54

STEVE

'Steve,' Phil called, 'it's Sarah.'

Steve strolled at a fair pace into Phil's home office, where he took the phone from him.

'Sarah?'

'Get to the school. Something's up with Gracie.'

His heart didn't just skip a beat. It missed a whole bar.

'What's the matter with her?'

'I don't know, Steve, just get over there.'

'On my way.'

His fingers quivered as he handed the phone back.

'What's up? Phil asked.

'Gracie, something's up with Gracie.'

'What?' Phil asked, as his cheeks grew flushed with concern.

'I don't know, Sarah doesn't know, got to get to the school.'

Phil dropped a piece of paper that he was holding onto the desk and shut the lid of his laptop.

'I'll drive,' he said, 'come on, let's go.'

Sarah may have had the jump on them, but Phil was no slouch behind the wheel. However quickly he drove, it would never have been fast enough for Steve. As they swung into the school gates and Phil slammed on the brakes, bringing stares and scowls from a couple of members of staff who were in the vicinity, Sarah was only just emerging from her car in front of them. The three of them ran up the pathway to the office, matching each other stride for stride.

'Where's Gracie Minchin? I've just had a call from someone,' Sarah barked with flustered haste at the receptionist who looked up, startled.

She was about to reply when Mrs Adams walked into the reception area.

'Mr and Mrs Minchin,' she said, looking at them both with a degree of urgency. 'Come this way please.'

'They need to sign in,' the receptionist called.

Steve and Sarah ignored the request as they followed Mrs Adams through the doors leading into the school's main corridor, with Phil in close company behind them.

'Later,' Mrs Adams shouted back.

'What's going on?' Steve asked.

'I don't know,' Mrs Adams replied. 'We can't get to the bottom of it. She just started lashing out at everyone and won't say why.'

Steve looked at Sarah, their faces wearing mirrored expressions of worry. This wasn't Gracie. She didn't do that. Something was bitterly wrong.

'Where is she?' Steve asked.

'In the classroom,' Mrs Adams replied. 'The rest of the class are in the playground.'

As they walked down the corridor and the classroom

grew closer, Steve heard a soothing adult voice. In response, he heard Gracie's high-pitched, agitated replies. More than once they heard something being thrown across the floor.

'No,' Gracie screamed, 'leave me alone.'

As Steve opened the door and walked in, he stared at Gracie, at her face streaked red where tears had been falling, and at the disarray on the floor. A vice gripped hold of his heart, and he ran over to his daughter, wrapping his arms around his baby girl, and squeezing her into the safety of a daddy embrace that had been missing in action over recent days. Gracie reciprocated and, as the paternal love flowed, seven-year-old whimpers poured out.

'What's up, baby?' Steve whispered.

Gracie didn't reply. Instead, those whimpers turned into the kind of sobs that, in the absence of words, instructed her daddy to hold her tighter still.

'Daddy's here, sweetheart,' he whispered. 'Daddy's here.'

No matter how old she was, or how big she got, a little girl would forever remain exactly that to a parent. Steve picked Gracie up and held her, just as he had done from the day she'd come into his life, and just as he always would in the future. His girl. His world.

'Tell me what happened, princess,' Steve whispered, as Gracie's sobs became stifled.

Gracie looked beyond him, at Sarah and Phil who were standing no more than a pace behind them and, though her lips tremored, she didn't say a word.

'I've done my best to keep a lid on it,' Mrs Adams said, in a quiet but assertive tone, 'but . . . I don't know.'

'Don't know what?' Sarah barked back at her.

'I mean . . . It's been on the news everywhere, right, and kids are like sponges,' Mrs Adams said. 'There must have been something said . . .'

Steve turned around, keeping Gracie held tight against his chest as he looked at Mrs Adams. It wasn't quite contempt that was emanating from her; she was far too professional for that, he reasoned. Still, it wasn't sympathy for HIS plight, that was for sure.

'Do you want to talk about it, Gracie, love?' Mrs Adams continued, her voice transitioning with ease to the soft, teacherly one that Steve had heard so many times before.

The shake of Gracie's head was resolute and, as Sarah took her from Steve's arms, it felt like a piece of him had been forcibly detached. He watched on, as a growing sense of apprehension prickled its way from somewhere deep within until it was manifest in little twitches on his skin. Sarah stormed out of the classroom, as Steve and Phil stood shoulder to shoulder.

'So she's being bullied?' Phil asked.

'Sorry,' Mrs Adams replied, 'you are?'

'It's all right,' Steve said, 'he's family.'

'I hadn't noticed it,' Mrs Adams replied, 'but kids . . .'

'I know,' Steve interjected, 'they're like sponges.'

He could take it no longer and, as he stumbled through the upturned tables and chairs that a raging Gracie had left in her wake, he ran down the corridor, catching up with his wife and daughter as they walked through the reception office. The receptionist called after them to sign out, but neither Steve nor Sarah broke their stride as they bundled through the exit door. As Sarah loaded Gracie into the back seat of her car, she looked across to Steve.

'Can you get Oscar?' she asked.

He nodded. Of course he could.

'I'll see you back home,' she murmured and, as she drove away, Steve walked back into the reception area.

There was no argument from the head teacher, who had

arrived shortly after Sarah had whisked Gracie away. It was agreed that both children would remain at home until strategies were put in place for them to either come back to school, or for other arrangements to be put in place. Strategies? Arrangements? It hurt Steve's brain and stung his soul.

Their lives had been turned upside down.

And it was all his fault.

Oscar was silent as he sat in the back of Phil's car, his excitement at seeing his daddy arrive being replaced by a blurry confusion at having been so suddenly removed from his classroom where he had been playing with his friends. Steve sat next to him, his hand laying limply on his little boy's thigh as Phil drove slowly until, eventually, they arrived back home.

'I'll come in if you want?' Phil said, removing his seatbelt, but Steve shook his head and tapped him on the shoulder.

'This one's on me,' he said.

'You sure?'

'Sure.'

Sarah's car was on the driveway and, as he walked past it with Oscar squeezing his hand, he took a deep breath, before expelling it all from his lungs. Then, for good measure, he took another. Anything to slow his racing heart, to dull the razor-sharp edges of the anxiety that was threatening to engulf him. Before they reached the front door, and just as Phil pulled away with a faltering splutter of the engine that he rescued just before it stalled, Oscar stopped and looked up at him.

'Cuddle, Daddy,' he said, reaching up to find the paternal embrace of reassurance. Familiarity. Daddy. Always there.

Steve got it. He understood exactly what his little man was going through. He'd been plucked from the security of his classroom under a cloud of turmoil and, if it was unsettling for his forty-one-year-old mind, then God knows how it felt for his little man. He held him tightly and felt Oscar's arms wrap around his shoulders, his little fingers gently pinching the skin of his daddy's shoulder blades. He always did that, just like Gracie had before him, as though he found security in moulding his daddy's skin into shapes like putty. He carried Oscar in through the front door. It was his house, granted, but bricks and mortar didn't come into it. What he wanted more than anything, what he craved, what he yearned for above all else was for it to be his home again.

Father and son walked down the hallway and found mum and daughter in the lounge. Gracie was lying with her head on Sarah's lap. She had her eyes closed and Sarah was making ringlets in her hair. Was this a new trick, Steve wondered, that he wasn't privy to? Whatever, it seemed to work. Gracie seemed calm, and that was what mattered.

Sarah nodded at Steve, but her face was blank. He couldn't get a read of it, couldn't make out what her features were telling him. Taking a leap of faith, he walked into the room and sat down on the sofa next to them. Oscar nestled in tightly. He had so much to get off his chest, so much to say, but not there. Not then. This was time for the PG version, instead. Gracie and Oscar may have been sheltered from what he'd done in the confines of those four walls but, outside, people spoke.

Kids were sponges, he'd been told. And kids could be brutal, intentionally or otherwise. As much as he owed Sarah an explanation, he owed the kids one too. Why he'd been MIA. Why the media had been on their doorstep. Why . . . Why . . . Why . . . It was on him, and he had to step up.

And, it seemed, Sarah was on the same wavelength. Just as he was about to open his mouth, about to get the ball rolling, it was her soft, gentle words that crept out instead.

'You're very safe here, kids, you know that?' she said.

Both children nodded.

'And home will always be your safe place, no matter what,' Sarah continued. 'School should be as well, and if you ever have any problems then you go and tell your teacher straight away, okay?'

Again, she was answered with nods.

'You don't let things build up, Gracie darling, because that's when it all bubbles over. You talk to someone. Mrs Adams, Daddy, me, anyone, okay?'

Gracie took her thumb out of her mouth. She opened her mouth to speak but instead put her thumb back in.

'Is there anything you want to ask us?' Sarah said gently. 'Anything at all?'

Gracie looked at Oscar, who appeared entirely uninterested in the conversation. 'When's Daddy coming home again?' she whimpered. Steve's heart broke. How to deal with this in a way that they'd understand?

'I'd like to say something,' Steve interjected.

He had the floor. They had to be told. Solace could only be found in the truth, after all. He sat up straight but the enormity of what he was about to do gripped him like a vice. Instead of looking at his children, he stared at his feet.

'Daddy loves you both, okay?' he began. 'Always have, always will. But Daddy was a child once too. And when I was a boy, I wasn't the person I am now.'

He paused and looked up. Gracie and Oscar were staring at him. He rarely spoke with such depth and emotion but, now, he was letting it all out. He had started, and he owed it to his children to be straight with them. He didn't look back down, but instead maintained eye contact with each of his children in turn.

'When I was a boy, I did a lot of naughty things,' he

316

continued. 'Naughty, naughty things. Things that get you into real trouble with people like teachers and the police. And I won't lie to you and tell you that I didn't do some things that were really, really bad. Like I sometimes stole things that weren't mine, and I hung around with some people who I shouldn't have hung around with.'

It may have been his mind playing tricks on him, but neither of the kids seemed to blink.

'And Daddy did a terrible, terrible thing.'

'Someone said you killed someone,' Gracie said. Her words were so matter-of-fact, so blunt, that they left him momentarily without response.

Respond, though, he must. And respond, he did.

'That's right, sweetheart, a long time ago, when I was that person I just told you about, I did. I killed someone.'

Chapter 55

SARAH

The kids took it well. Too well? She wasn't to know. Either way, as Steve spoke, neither of them had broken down in tears, nor had they looked away, uninterested. Instead, they'd sat there and listened, taking it all in and watching as their daddy bared his soul. Had they been confused? She couldn't tell. They'd been so quiet, so still. She was sure there would be questions down the line but, right there and then, it was more than she could've asked for.

There didn't seem to be much of a playbook for this kind of thing. Even so, the truth was always a good starting point, no matter the situation, no matter the consequences. She had answers of her own that she wanted to get from Steve, but that could wait. It would have to. The kids came first to the exception of nothing.

An hour later, it was her turn. The kids were occupied by the glow of their respective iPad screens and, as Steve nodded in her direction, intimating towards the lounge door, she stood up and gently lowered Gracie onto the moulded impression in the sofa where she'd just sat. Gracie didn't say a word, simply swiping at something on YouTube, as she walked out of the room, Steve did the same with Oscar, provoking the same acquiescence. They made their way into the kitchen, where Steve once again maintained a respectful distance from her. This time, though, she didn't feel the same chills within. She didn't feel the chasm in the floor between them. There may have been a bridge to be erected, but it didn't feel insurmountable.

'So . . .' She dreaded what came next, knowing that whatever came out of his mouth she would never be able to unhear. And yet she needed to know it.

'So . . .' he replied. 'I've got so much that I need to tell you.'

She watched as he blinked away any tears that might threaten to fall as, finally, he let it all come out. Everything. Every last detail, sparing nothing.

Everything that had been hidden, everything that had been concealed, everything that had made him who he was. He bared his soul, and told her of the beatings and the abuse, of how his formative years had been full of the unspeakable. He recalled being a child apart, being utterly alone and only finding acceptance in the wrong places. His experiences while under the care of the state. How he'd been a victim, before he'd made Charlotte one. How everything from the 'troubled child' manual of behaviours and actions had been manifest in him.

How his teenage years were spent resenting everything and everyone. And how, when it all came to a head, he had found himself on that clifftop, in that situation, with that beautiful girl who was forever trapped in time because of him.

'My biggest regret? Who I was. My biggest mistake? Not telling you everything from the start. You, the kids, you're everything to me.'

Sarah's head was nodding back and forth but, at some point in the process, she'd turned away from him and closed her eyes just as they'd sprung leaks. What he'd been through . . . What he'd witnessed . . . What he'd had inflicted upon him . . . It made her feel sick. Not just nauseous. Sick, to the pit of her stomach.

'Everything,' he repeated.

She turned to face him, those big and bulbous tears still channelling down her cheeks until they reached her chin and fell in streams.

'What can I do to make it right?' he asked.

How could she answer that? There was no simple solution, no quick fix. Instead, she reached for a piece of kitchen towel, and dabbed at her eyes as the images that his confession had provoked continued to sear into her consciousness.

'God knows,' she replied. Her voice was softer. Conciliatory? Who knew. Not her, least of all. What she DID know, though, was that the darkness that stalked him whenever she clamped eyes on him had brightened, just a touch.

His monologue had paused, but it wasn't yet finished. In the weeks and months after . . . it . . . had happened, something in him changed. Something snapped. In a world where he could so easily have been another Tony, pushing up daisies somewhere, he'd found another path. What had instigated it? Clifftop had been safe. Nurturing. And there, he'd found something that he'd never had before. A friend, who would go on to be like a brother. One who didn't ask bad of him, who didn't do bad with him. It gave him hope. It may have been a small thing from the outside looking in but, to him it had been everything.

'Phil?' Sarah gasped.

'Phil,' Steve confirmed.

'But . . .'

She cast her mind back to every conversation her and

Steve had ever had in the past, searching for one where they might have discussed how he and Phil had first met. All she came up with was a whole lot of blanks.

'You never said that's how you met,' she whispered.

'You never asked.'

Tears were still making tracks down her cheeks. She opened her mouth to speak but, it seemed, words failed her. Instead, she reached across and held his hand.

There was no way that someone could fake who they were for twenty years. Gracie and Oscar adored him and he, them. So too, her. Those twenty years, he was sure, showed her that.

Love was blind . . . most of the time.

Sometimes, though, it just needed perspective to find clarity.

Chapter 56

DS SUE WILLMOTT

It was supposed to be a quick phone call with DCI Maine but, as DS Willmott's feet tapped the floor beneath the table as her legs grew restless, all she could think of was getting Steve back into interview and getting her questions on the record. He'd 'no comment' her, she was sure, but it would be one step closer to getting the answers she needed. That Kevin needed. And that Charlotte deserved.

'I want you to invite him in,' DCI Maine said, leaving it in doubt that it was an instruction, not a request. 'After last time, with that reporter and everything, we're not going for another media scrum. Low-key please, Sue.'

'Absolutely, ma'am.'

There was nothing she'd love more than to go and slap the handcuffs back on his wrists, but an order was an order.

'When's he due back on bail?'

'Another few weeks yet.'

'And he's been signing on okay?'

'Yep, he's due in on Saturday morning, actually.'

'All right, try to get him in before then but, worst-case

scenario, you'll scoop him up at front counter on Saturday, okay?'

'Roger that, ma'am.'

As she made tracks back to her office from the conference room, only one thought consumed her. Like hell was she going to wait another two days to get him into interview. She'd do as the boss said. There was no way she'd go against a lawful order. But, equally, she wasn't going to rest on her laurels. She still had Steve's phone, of course. That was the evidence she was going to be presenting against him. But there were ways and means, she'd found out across the course of a career and, more often than not, if you couldn't find someone then you just leaned gently on those closest to them.

She reached for Phil's statement and flipped it over to find his phone number. In a matter of seconds, it was ringing.

'Hello?'

'Phil, DS Willmott here.'

There was a pause. 'Everything all right?'

'Everything's fine. I'm just wondering if you might know where Steve is. I need to have a chat with him.'

Nice and light-hearted. Keep it conversational. It always worked better that way.

'He's at home. There was some grief at school a while ago with their eldest.'

'Oh no.' She sounded sincere enough, she was sure. 'So he's there now?'

'Yeah.'

'You're a star – thanks so much.'

She flicked through her day book, way back to when she'd first met Steve and Sarah. It had barely been a couple of weeks since she'd found them both in the Accident and Emergency department of Beachbrook Hospital, the stale stench of smoke clinging to them both, but it felt like years prior. Sure enough, as she tracked her way back across the pages, reversing through scribbled essays containing thoughts, theories and ponderings, there was Sarah's name, address and phone number.

'Sarah?'

'Speaking.'

'It's DS Willmott here – nothing to worry about.'

'Okay.'

'Is Steve with you?'

'One second.'

The phone crackled as, she was sure, Sarah held her hand over the bottom, doing her best to prevent whatever she was saying to Steve from being inadvertently shared with her.

'Hello?'

'Steve, DS Willmott. Can you come into the station, please. We need a chat.'

Just a request, like DCI Maine had instructed. An invitation extended, even if her voice didn't quite give the impression that it was just that.

'Now?'

'If you wouldn't mind.'

'I'll be there.'

It may have taken a couple of hours but, as her office phone rang, and the front counter officer told her that he had arrived, she felt the familiar pang of nervous energy surge through her. The day that stopped, she'd always said, was the day she needed to stop being a detective. Now, though, it was flowing in abundance. So much, in fact, that the overflow made her steps quicker, her shuffles niftier as she descended the stairs and made her way along the corridor to where Steve was waiting.

'Mr Minchin?' she called.

He followed her in silence as she led him to an interview

room, the same one they'd used twice before. Third time, she hoped, it would be a charm.

She wasn't going to get to him straight away, though. Not until he'd been through the usual custody rituals. The wait for his solicitor was interminable, but necessary. No way was she going to have this one thrown out on a technicality.

As he sat in the holding cell, waiting for his brief to arrive, she looked at him. There was something different, something distinct in the way he carried himself from the way he'd been before. No nervous tics. Making eye contact. His eyes weren't fierce, nor was the way his lips rose at the edges a smirk or a sneer. It was just a placid, neutral expression that adorned his features, and she just couldn't interpret it. It wasn't confidence, far from it, but there was something that seemed to have settled him.

And it unsettled her.

Chapter 57

STEVE

He'd discussed it at length with Sarah before he'd left. Tell the truth, she'd said. Get the weight off his shoulders.

And yet, as he sat with his solicitor in tow – in a tiny, stuffy room that made the cells seem like rooms from a palace – his throat tightened as the magnitude of his solicitor's words sent his head spinning out of control.

When he'd been discussing it with Sarah, they'd been fanciful musings. *Unburden yourself*, she'd said, *they'll understand*, she'd assured him.

Now, though, as Mr Russell sat and went through it all point by agonising point, Steve was presented with some stark home truths.

'Depends on what you're in it for,' Mr Russell said, straightening up the papers in front of him, 'if you want to take your chances at court then tell them what you just told me. If you want to stay out of court altogether, then your best chance is to not say a word.'

'They need to know,' Steve replied. He may have sounded confident. Beneath that veneer, though, he was anything but.

'Let me put it another way,' Mr Russell said, peering at

Steve from above the rims of his glasses, 'just how much do you value freedom?'

Steve was about to answer, to say how much he valued integrity, valued being able to look at himself in the mirror, valued the truth, until Mr Russell hit him with a sledgehammer to the morals.

'How much do you value being at home with your kids, your wife, providing for them, seeing them grow?'

And just like that, any vestige of assurance that Steve retained in his aesthetic was rendered redundant. He closed his eyes, and broken images of his family overwhelmed him. Without him, the three of them all alone. Sarah, bringing up the kids without a buoy to keep her afloat. Gracie, those rumours and whispers persisting until she exploded time and time again. Oscar, playing football at Under 6, Under 7, Under 8, and the rest of the age groups without his daddy on the sidelines to cheer him on. The house, up for sale. Only one wage, not enough to keep up the mortgage repayments. Temporary accommodation. Sarah bereft. The kids turning into young adults. Bad habits forming. It was too much. Too, too much.

And all of it potentially avoidable, according to Mr Russell, if only he could put his moral compass to one side.

Much as before, it all boiled down to what mattered the most. No matter how it was framed, no matter what it meant to him on an ethically intrinsic level, he had a choice to make.

To sing like a canary, or to batten down the hatches and ride out the storm.

Chapter 58

KEVIN

'Hey, Kevin.'

'Sue.'

Her headlights had breached the dark evening once more and, as had become habit over the past week, he guessed it wasn't a social call.

'Come in,' he said.

She waited for him to lead the way, something she hadn't done for so many years. When she'd pitched up informally, as a friend, whatever, she'd be happy to wander in first. Now, though? This was business, pure and simple, and his every sense tingled with the most sickening of sensations.

'Can we sit?' she asked, as she followed him into the lounge.

'Be my guest,' he answered, gesturing to the sofa where they'd shared so many moments, from the benign to rage, and all in between.

Sue sat down, perched on the very edge of the fraying cushion beneath her, and Kevin sat atop the upright suitcase that housed all of the articles from long ago that he'd spent the days surveying. She didn't make a quip, no joke asking him if he was going on holiday, no query as to whether he wanted to sit next to her so they could chat.

As before.

All business.

'So, it's been a long road to where we are, right?' she said.

'Long road.'

If he parroted her, he couldn't say anything wrong. Anything questionable. Anything incriminating.

'And you know I've given it everything across the years.'

'Given it everything. I know.'

'So, today I had Ste— Mr Minchin . . . back in for another interview.'

She looked down to the floor, to his left and his right, above him and all around. Anywhere, it seemed, apart from in his eyes.

'Right.'

'He went no comment.'

She sat rigid, saddled with a tension in her shoulders that he'd not seen before.

'So I took it to CPS,' she continued, 'to get their advice as to whether we have got enough to charge him, and they've come back with a result.'

Now, she looked at him. Now, their eyes met. And now, he saw within her what she was so desperate to avoid telling him.

'They're not going to charge him?' he said, softly.

'They're not going to authorise charges, no,' she confirmed.

'Reasons?' Kevin asked.

'So we can prove he was there,' she said, still staring at him, 'but they're saying we can't prove what happened. Nothing more, nothing less. Without something else, they're saying that it doesn't meet the charging threshold.'

Kevin sucked down some air. No matter the rage that the

headlines had spoken of, no matter the bile that rose within his throat at the sheer injustice of it all, he kept the lid on the pot. He prevented it all from boiling over. He'd spent so long doing it, it was all he knew.

'So where do we go from here?' he asked.

'I'm sorry that I've not got him yet,' Willmott said, eyes fixed on him. 'But trust me, I'll keep plugging away,' she said, nodding to herself. 'I'll keep doing everything that I can. This isn't the end, far from it.'

Long after she'd gone, and deep into the darkest of nights, her words resounded time and again in his mind.

This isn't the end.

Far from it.

This isn't the end.

Far from it.

This isn't the end.

Far from it.

And she was right. More right, in fact, than she could ever know.

PART THREE

Fully Developed

Fire has spread over much if not all the available fuel; temperatures reach their peak, resulting in heat damage.

Source – www.nfpa.org

Chapter 59

SARAH

When all was said and done, family came first. No sooner had Steve walked back through the front door, looked her square in the face and told her what he'd done, she'd got it. Hiding behind the cloak of silence in interview mightn't have helped him liberate himself from everything that ailed him, but he hadn't been thinking of himself. He'd been thinking of the kids. He'd been thinking of her. Besides, he'd been through enough, hadn't he? To be a public punchbag was one thing, he didn't need it at home as well. And besides . . . the CPS had said there was no case to answer as a result.

He was Steve. He was the father of their kids. He was her husband. HER Steve. Of course she wasn't immune to those insidious thoughts of what he'd done. They'd sully her mind, leaving a blemish every time, when she wasn't expecting it. When she looked at his hand, had it been the one that had done . . . it? When he opened his mouth, was he saying words similar to the last ones Charlotte had ever heard? Even so, as Friday turned into Saturday and beyond, those images were blurring by the hour, and a question from Steve gave her something else to focus on other than the eternally young girl in her mind.

'You know what tomorrow is, don't you?' he asked, as a necessarily lazy Sunday passed them by. The kids had just left the room and bundled upstairs. Whatever was on the agenda, it obviously wasn't something for their ears.

A mental checklist came up blank. School? No way. Not yet. Coffee and Cream? It hadn't even been mentioned. No birthdays, no bank holidays, nothing.

'Go on,' she said.

'The funeral.'

Of course it was.

'And you want to go?'

He may have been looking in her direction but, she could sense, he was staring far beyond.

'I think we should,' he said. Monotone sometimes implied a lack of compassion, but Steve's neutral intonation was a result of the mill that she could see him finding his way through.

'Then we will,' she said.

She reached out and held his hand, fighting against the image that threatened to beat a path to her mind of it being the one that had killed Charlotte. No sooner had their fingers touched than he seemed to spark to life. His face rose, and his eyes lightened. She saw it all and, though Charlotte was still there, lingering behind her eyes, she forced a smile.

'We'll do it,' she said, 'you and me.'

Chapter 60

STEVE

'We won't be long,' Steve said, as Phil settled into the sofa.

'No bother,' Phil replied, waving him away with his hand and reaching for the remote control.

Steve walked out to the hallway where Sarah was waiting for him, and called up the stairs.

'See you in a while, kids, won't be more than an hour and a half.'

No reply.

He rolled his eyes at Sarah as he reached for his coat. Black, on black, on black. With a pair of sunglasses and a flat cap in hand to finish off his outfit, he was about as incognito as he could ever hope to be.

He slipped his phone into his pocket. It was only when he'd been without it for so long that he'd realised how much he relied on it. When DS Willmott had returned it to him a few days before and he'd turned it on, though, it had been tumbleweed that had greeted him. There'd only been one message, in fact, and an answerphone one at that. As he'd listened to it a few times, he'd taken grim delight in deleting it without a reply.

'Hey Steve, it's Fiona Strevens. I just wanted to get in

touch . . . I don't know why, really. Just to say that, if there's anything I can do for you in the future, then please do let me know. You take care, okay, and look after yourself and your family.'

She could go swivel.

The driveway to the crematorium was long and winding, lined by steep and imposing trees that had been witness to the final journey of many. Steve and Sarah arrived early and drove into the car park that sat parallel to the chapel. Get in quick, get out quicker, Steve had thought. No such luck, though. The car park was full.

The tragic and untimely deaths of Louise and Adam had obviously struck a chord. Steve reversed out of the car park and, as he drove slowly back to the main road, he looked at the broad oaks while they whispered a song of serenity to him. It didn't exactly soothe his soul, but he could feel a peace there that had been missing in abundance over recent days.

He parked up on the road outside the crematorium and waited. If it was a five-minute walk up the driveway, but he had no intention of making that journey until the very last minute. As was natural at any funeral, emotions would be running high. If one person, just one, had an issue with him and his past, then it was the very last place he wanted to be confronted about it.

'All right, love?' Sarah asked, reaching across and gently holding his thigh.

He nodded without replying. He was looking out of the car window, wondering when the right time would be to make the walk.

The minutes crawled by and, as Steve took in the gentle breeze from his open window, in the distance he finally saw the funeral cortège slowly rolling towards them. As it got closer, and the world around them ground to a respectful halt, Sarah patted him on the leg.

'Let's go,' she said.

The vehicles turned into the driveway before Steve and Sarah had crossed the road from their car. They walked slowly behind the convoy, maintaining a gap that was both respectful and preserved Steve's desire to remain incognito. Their hands were linked, the unity between them seeming to have somehow solidified by the twists and turns of the weeks gone by.

'We'll get through this,' she whispered. It never crossed his mind that she meant anything other than in relation to the funeral.

He nodded, again without words. Instead, his eyes were fixed on the vehicles about thirty metres in front of them, travelling at the same crawling pace that he and Sarah were walking. The autumnal breeze created a chorus of melancholy as it blew with alacrity, stripping bare the branches of the beautiful oaks. Those leaves fell to ground all around Steve and Sarah like brownish green confetti at the altar of grief. It felt appropriately funereal.

As they emerged from the winding driveway into the light beyond the trees, and the cortège approached the chapel in the distance, the milling crowds formed as one entity on a grassy area immediately opposite the entrance, awaiting the arrival of Louise and Adam. The sombre atmosphere that had accompanied Sarah and Steve on their walk through the falling leaves and the whistling trees was replaced by one of reverential celebration. In the distance, someone began clapping. Then someone else. A group of others joined in and, as the vehicles finally drew to a stop at the chapel doors, a thunderous and sustained round of applause had broken out. Steve hadn't been to many funerals, granted, but he had never experienced anything like the energy of the mourners in that moment.

Neither, it seemed, had Bob or Pam because, as they climbed from the vehicle that had transported them behind their baby girl and her partner on their final journey, they both wore smiles of gratitude.

Pam had baby Jack in her arms, and she held him closely as he stared wide-eyed at the masses who were providing the ovation. He didn't understand. He wouldn't remember. But, Steve was sure, he felt the love. How could he not? It permeated the air all around them, after all.

Steve held Sarah's hand and, as she began to walk towards the assembled masses, he held her back. She looked at him, and he at her. Her eyes said it was time to move, but his begged her to wait. Just a minute. Just a second.

The applause that had welcomed Louise and Adam stopped nearly as soon as it had started and, as the first coffin was being unloaded, a deep silence had swept across the congregation. It was only punctuated by the sound of muted cries as collective tears began to flow amongst those present. As one, their grief was unified. Steve looked across to Bob and Pam, him standing with a straight back, stoic in the face of his obvious heartache, and her misty eyes averted towards baby Jack as she quietly cooed and held her grandson's innocent gaze. They were dignity personified, the very essence of decorum in the most heart-breaking of circumstances.

It was barely a minute before both coffins were on the shoulders of pallbearers and, as the crowd of mourners followed the families of Louise and Adam into the chapel, Steve and Sarah slowly made their way towards the rear of the group. They were right at the back, just as he wanted, and would be the first to leave. By the time they had slowly filtered into the chapel, it was standing room only. Steve slipped into a tight spot in the corner, still hidden beneath the lenses of his sunglasses and the fabric of his hat. Soft, orchestral music was playing, candles flickered near the lectern at the front, and the congregated group was silent. It was peaceful. Steve bowed his head and a calmness swept across him. He'd never been religious but, at that moment, he felt something beyond words. Closing his eyes and soaking it up, he heard the celebrant ask for everyone to stand.

Chopin's 'Funeral March' began and, as he opened his eyes, the coffins were carried down the centre aisle. Steve didn't take his eyes off them as they were gently placed next to each other to the left of the lectern. Roses adorned each and, as the last few bars of music played, the candles around the room flickered. It was mesmerising. Stunning, but tragic.

The service that followed was just as beautiful, the celebrant expertly weaving together stories of Louise and Adam in happy times, and allowing those gathered to feel the love that they had shared. They may have been a young couple, but they had made a life. They had made memories. They had made a family and, as Bob took his place at the lectern to give a eulogy in memory of his precious, only child, Steve stared at him, unable to take his eyes away. Bob's eyes darted around, looking for something.

For someone.

'Louise and Adam had something,' he began, his voice unfaltering, 'something that most people can only aspire to. They had love. For two people of such tender years, it was a love that transcended their age. We couldn't have been prouder of them both, of who they were, of how they lived and the family that they created.'

He paused and again surveyed the room.

'Their Jack,' he continued, before hesitating. His voice was breaking as he tried to continue, and Steve willed him on from the sidelines. He understood. If he was standing up there for his little girl, then he'd want the words to come without hesitation or stutter. It was for Louise and Adam. It was their moment, their day. Their farewell. As Bob took two deep breaths, the words arrived and Steve nodded silently in the wings.

'Their Jack was everything to them. He was their reason.'

Again, he paused as he scanned the crowd. Then, finally, he saw Steve. His eyes locked on him, and they didn't move. It didn't matter about the sunglasses, nor the hat. Steve had been found.

'Now a lot has been said about what happened, and about the man who saved Jack. All I know is, without him, Jack wouldn't be with us now.'

Bob nodded gently towards Steve, as he peeled his sunglasses away from his face.

'No,' Steve mouthed, 'please no.' He screwed his face up so tightly that he couldn't see, and he could only hope that whatever Bob had been intending to do, he wasn't going to point him out.

'That man is a hero, in my eyes,' Bob said quietly, before resuming his seat.

'Bollocks,' someone sitting in front of Steve whispered, barely audibly, while a couple of others quietly snorted in derision.

'Murderer,' someone else mumbled.

Steve heard it. So too must Sarah, for she clenched his hand tightly as he shrunk further into the corner where he was standing and bowed his head.

The service was soon over and, no sooner had it finished than he fumbled for his sunglasses and reaffixed them over his eyes. Last in, first out.

He walked apace, Sarah's linked arm dragging her along with him as they retraced the route past the oaks and back to the car. Neither of them spoke until they were safely back in the confines of the car, with the world shut out and only each other for company.

He wasn't impervious to the comments, not in the least. It was more than he deserved. It was just that he didn't want it to be the norm, and especially not where Sarah and the kids were concerned. He'd been and confronted the demons that had stalked him across the years. He'd fronted up. Now it seemed he had to do the same, somehow and some way, in the present.

'You okay?' Sarah asked.

He looked at her and nodded. The soft smile that half formed on his face wasn't a mask to hide behind, more a signal of the whirring thoughts that were spinning around inside his head.

There was no plan.

Just an awareness that he needed to break free from the shackles.

Chapter 61

DS SUE WILLMOTT

It was fortnights like the one she'd just experienced that gave weight to her mum's suggestion that she find something, anything, to help take her mind off work.

But she couldn't.

It just wasn't in her make-up to do so.

Instead, her day off on Monday was spent firstly at the funeral of Adam and Louise, and then at home in her dining room, sifting through the boxes and boxes of evidence that had gathered twenty years' worth of dust, looking for a needle in the haystack that simply wasn't there. Crime in real life wasn't like crime in the movies. There wasn't always that hidden bit of evidence, that epiphany, that last-minute witness who was wheeled out of nowhere. Her chance at eureka had come with the phone evidence, but the CPS hadn't agreed.

And that, as they say, was that.

'What are you doing, Mummy?' Lottie asked, wandering in with a book in her hand.

'Just working, sweetheart,' DS Willmott said.

'You're always working.'

And she had a point.

'What are you reading?' DS Willmott asked.

'*The Secret Garden.*'

Lottie held the book up. It was a hardback, bound beautifully with a cover that DS Willmott didn't recognise.

'Where's that from?' she asked.

'Nanny bought it for me.'

Of course she did. A shard of ice formed in DS Willmott's gut, spearing her with a guilt that normally lay dormant within.

'Let's see it,' she said, taking the book from Lottie's hands and surveying it. On the back cover, there was a single quote.

'WHERE YOU TEND A ROSE MY LAD, A THISTLE CANNOT GROW.'

There was something about those words that reached out and grabbed her, squeezing her throat until a panic nearly set in. No sooner had it taken a grip on her though, it released. In its place, a rising sense of sadness filled her, one that, in that moment, couldn't be sated by mountains and mountains of timeworn paperwork.

'Can I read it with you?' DS Willmott asked.

'YES!' Lottie shouted back, taking hold of her hand and near-dragging her from the dining room.

And as they sat in the lounge, Lottie's head on her mummy's lap, and DS Willmott cradled her little girl, stroking the blonde hairs that were at odds with either her or Alfie's locks of their youth, the smile she wore was bittersweet.

Sweet, insofar as it was the first real mummy time she'd had since . . . She couldn't remember when.

And bitter, because she could only guess how Kevin was

dealing with everything that had been thrown his way. Had he spent moments like this with Charlotte on the sofa? Reading kiddies' classics, whiling away the hours while getting lost in a literary feast? She guessed so. She hoped so. And she hoped memories like that would sustain him as time went on.

Chapter 62

KEVIN

Charlotte Hitch
Taken far too soon.
Earth's loss is Heaven's gain.
Sleep tight, angel.

Kevin stood by the stone that sat proudly in Beachbrook Cemetery, reading it time and again. Yes, she was taken too soon. Yes, Earth's loss was indeed Heaven's gain. Sleeping tightly? He hoped so. An angel? That and so much more.

'They're not charging him,' he said, as the rays of sunlight made him squint.

He bent down and pulled a few errant blades of grass away from the edges of the stone, flicking them in the air and watching them fall in the breeze.

'They didn't get him,' he whispered.

It was so calm there. So tranquil. It was a space that had never been touched by spite, by malice. For him, it was pure. Somewhere he could always find a bit of peace when he needed it most.

He bent down once more. A weed, in close proximity. Too close. He ripped it out of the ground.

'Sorry, love,' he mumbled.

There was nothing to make his words echo, no chamber around him, no walls for them to bounce off. Still, they reverberated in his ears.

Sorry, love.

Sorry, love.

Sorry, love.

Had Sue failed her? He wasn't sure. Had he failed her? He'd long wrestled with THAT particular question.

In the 'before', he'd always clung onto the hope that there would one day be a reckoning, that everything would be resolved. Now, though, as he stood in front of whatever it was that was left of his baby girl, and that notion of failure coursed through his every sinew, his arms and legs shook in tandem.

The calm man. The placid man. The one who saw reason, who kept a lid on everything.

The weed was still in his hand.

His knuckles whitened.

And he ripped it to shreds in a fit of fury.

Chapter 63

STEVE

They arrived home from the funeral to find Phil in the same position on the sofa, and the kids still upstairs.

'Haven't heard a peep,' Phil said, as he stood up and flexed his hands in front of him, cracking his knuckles. 'Oh well, back to the hellhole.'

'Things no better?' Steve asked.

Phil raised his eyebrows and, as Steve looked closer, he saw the tiniest of bruises that filled the void between eye and hair.

'Is that . . .' he began to ask, peering in and pointing with a finger, before Phil cut him off.

'No.'

The shake of his head was firm and, as he walked out, Steve tried to say something. What, though, he didn't have a clue. Phil was out of the front door before his brain engaged and, as he watched from the lounge window and Phil got into his car and drove away, he grimaced. Phil had been there for him when he'd needed him most, now it was time to repay the debt.

He grabbed his recently returned phone from his pocket, and unlocked the screen. Flicking to WhatsApp, he sent a message to Phil.

As he watched Phil's car disappear into the distance, the kids bounded down the stairs and into the lounge.

'All right, kiddos?' he asked.

'We're hungry,' Oscar said, with a grin on his face that spoke only of mischief.

And so, something approaching normality returned. The kids, insistent that there should be an established meal between lunch and tea. Sarah, her head flicking between her laptop and her phone as she caught up with a couple of weeks' worth of work that had filtered her way all at once. And Steve, working out what came next for him.

First things first, a phone call to the school. The kids couldn't stay off forever. It was another step back towards real life, another step closer to putting everything that they could behind them.

He was nervous when he made the call. Of course he was. That his voice jittered when he asked to be put through to the head teacher was only to be expected, given they were talking about how his actions had impacted upon his kids. But, as they discussed it openly, and the head teacher spoke of interventions, of strategies, of making sure that the kids blended in while a dedicated teaching assistant watched on in the background, it settled those nerves. Phone call done, he nodded to Sarah with a smile. Arrangements had been made. He'd taken the step and, now, it was time to think of another.

Coffee and Cream. Tomorrow. He'd do the school run, he'd front up, and then he'd open the shutters. And not just for the money, but for the normality he craved.

As Monday ended and Tuesday morning came, Steve strolled down the stairs wearing a work polo shirt. He caught sight of himself in the mirror in the hallway, and stopped for just a second to take it in, holding the fabric of his top in his fingers. It was looser, that was for sure. They didn't have scales in their house, but in the time since he'd last worn it, he'd lost inches. And his face. A couple more frown lines. A lot more greys seeping into his stubble.

Yet . . .

There was an ease contained within those lines, amongst that stubble, that he couldn't put his finger on. It was where the lines between the physical and the mental blurred, where the juxtaposition between a tangible trait and a perceptual feature blended. Taking away the philosophy, he looked like a weight had been lifted and that's just how it felt.

It wasn't until they were nearly at school that a few butterflies began to emerge from the chrysalis in his tummy. Though they fluttered their wings and tickled his insides to the point of distraction, he fought them away, sending messages from his brain to his stomach to flood them with acid.

Steve drove past the school gates. It was manic busy, and he had to park in an adjacent road. As he helped the kids get out of the car, he could already feel eyes focussing on him.

'Come on then, kiddos,' he said, as those butterflies morphed into a piece of string that knotted itself time and again. He had to do it. Had to. HAD TO.

He held their hands, one on each side of him as they walked slowly to accommodate Oscar's little legs. Steve made small talk with his kids, as the tortuous pace at which they were walking tied another loop in the knot.

Parents. The public. They were everywhere, and the shade that stalked him wasn't something he was imagining. It was real . . . It was striking . . . But, most importantly, the kids seemed oblivious to it.

Every dawdling step along the road was an event in its own right. As they reached the school gates, Steve kept his eyes high, almost daring someone to say something to his face. Parents were waving their kids off and into the playground, parents whom he knew. Parents, who knew him. Parents, who only recently, had burst into rounds of spontaneous applause at his deeds.

Parents, who noticed him now.

Parents, who stopped dead in their tracks and stared.

Steve cuddled his children at the gate, shutting out the noise that surrounded him. That it was silent didn't make any odds. As he let go, it was quiet no longer. He heard whispers. How could he not? They were within earshot, after all.

'Killed a kid.'

'I dunno.'

'Hero for me.'

'Murderer.'

He watched as Gracie and Oscar walked through the gate, and he stayed with his feet rooted to the spot as he watched them both cross the playground. The noise? It was still there. It hadn't gone away. The whispers, the murmurs, the gossip. It was happening all around him, but he tuned out as best he could. Watching his kids mattered so much more, and he wasn't leaving until he'd seen them off properly.

Mrs Adams wandered over to Gracie, and looked in his direction with half a smile and a wave. Oscar was straight into a game of dodgeball without missing a beat. Then, and only then, was Steve satisfied. He turned around and, head still held high, he walked through the middle of a gaggle of other parents who parted when he approached them. He nodded at each of them. Some were returned, others not.

Whatever.

It just served to sow further seeds in his mind that the restraints needed to be loosened.

350

Chapter 64

KEVIN

Demons, outside. Torment, within.

No matter where he looked, physically or otherwise, all he could see was a raging injustice, and it was eating away at his soul.

In his lounge, the suitcase of news clippings sat in the corner. He dare not open it, lest the headlines it contained consume just a bit more of the fabric that held him together. They'd screamed of the police hunt, of the search for clues, of DNA mass screenings and more.

Well, the police had hunted.

They had the clues in their possession.

They had the DNA they'd searched for across the years.

And still they hadn't sealed the deal.

And there he was, standing by, prevaricating.

He grabbed his coat, walked out of the front door and marched across the road to the grass area opposite, breathing in that fresh Beachbrook air but not feeling any of the peace that people came back for year upon year. He looked at Charlotte's bench, but just couldn't face the empty feeling that had sunk through him when he'd sat there the day before. Instead, he turned left and, with no destination in mind, he put one foot in front of the other and just walked.

'Morning.'

A nod.

'A bit chilly, isn't it?'

A murmur of assent.

'Winter's on its way.'

A faux shiver of the shoulders.

He could blend in when he wanted to, always had done. The footpath traced the same crescent shape of the cliff edge to his right and, as he walked on, following in footsteps that he'd walked a thousand times and more before, he had navigated the twenty-minute yomp to the end of that portion of cliffs in what had felt like seconds.

He stopped and turned around, staring out to the water and sucking down more of that sea air that still failed to quench his yearning for calm. He stared and stared at the sea, at the horizon, at the gulls and the boats in the distance. It all painted a wonderful canvas in his eyes, but it wasn't enough.

As his gaze shifted and his focus adjusted, he planted eyes on the sands beneath him. A few foolhardy souls were dipping their toes in the sea, testing the water, and a couple of others were hiding behind a windbreak with a flask of something. Out-of-towners, he assumed. You always got them.

And then, he looked to their left. To the promenade. To the café, where only a couple of weeks before, the owner had received a hero's reception and a television interview in front of the masses to boot.

The nerve. The absolute, bare-backed nerve.

The café was open, and Minchin was behind the counter. He'd only just got away with murder, and there he was, bold as brass, serving a man and his dog. Chatting to him. Laughing with him. LAUGHING. Shaking his hand, patting his dog, taking his money and waving him away.

'Morning.'

'Oh GO AWAY!' Kevin screamed, as he stalked away in the direction from whence he'd come. He slapped himself in the cheek, then followed it up with a solid punch to his jaw.

It was too much. His cheek stung and his jaw ached. He wasn't a young man, not by any stretch of the imagination, and things hurt a lot more than they used to.

He was young enough, though. He still had air in his lungs, blood in his veins, and a brain that retained a stunning clarity of thought.

He stopped dead in his tracks and turned around.

From a distance, he raised his index finger and pointed it down at the café.

Then, in his mind, he pulled the trigger.

Chapter 65

STEVE

What Steve had done that day would have been bread and butter only weeks before. The school run. A day at Coffee and Cream. Groundhog Day, in the past. Now, though, as he lay in bed, it had taken it out of him. It was barely 9 p.m., yet Sarah was already gently snoring next to him.

His eyes were shut and he was just approaching that point where the brain closed down and allowed inertia to take over, when something bright brought him back from the brink of sleep. He opened his eyes and squinted as he stared at his phone screen. It was too bright, and the message on the screen was a fuzz of blurred lines as he tried to focus. Closing his left eye meant that his right could open enough to read Phil's words.

It's all gone wrong here, mate. Can I come over? Got nowhere else to go. X

Steve sat up with a start and felt his elbow brush against Sarah's head. She murmured but didn't wake. Steve wasn't the quickest at composing messages, but he typed furiously.

Of course you can. What's up? Kids in bed so call me when you're here and I'll let you in. Is Emma okay? X

The sound of his finger jabbing against the glass display on his phone must've been louder than usual because, as he hit the green 'send' button, Sarah's eyes were open and staring at him.

'What's up?' she asked.

He turned the phone around, provoking an irritated grunt as the screen bathed her face in light. When she'd read it, though, she was out of bed and throwing on the clothes that had only recently been discarded. He did the same and, in a matter of minutes, they were both downstairs with the kettle on.

'If he's coming here, should I go over there?' she asked. 'What if something bad's happened?'

'Wait until he gets here, I suppose,' Steve replied.

Steve's mind was running away with itself. What could possibly have happened, he wondered?

After a couple more minutes, his phone vibrated in his hand, then stopped. He quick-stepped to the front door and quietly opened the latch.

Phil was there, and he was pacing up and down the driveway with his arms shaking and his knuckles white. He looked up at Steve and, with lips tight and his cheeks tight under the weight of stress that was etched all over him, he shook his head. Steve looked closer, and saw a welt on his cheek. It wasn't the same one as before.

'Come in, mate,' Steve mouthed silently, beckoning his friend forward.

Phil wasn't an angry person, and certainly never to the extent that he would be found with THAT look on his face. He was riled in every sense, in the way his legs moved without the flex of his knees, the way he grimaced as their eyes met and in the way he slammed the front door behind him.

'Phil! Kids!' Steve said in a low but firm voice, pointing upstairs.

Phil held his hands up, an act of contrition as some of the anger seemed to dissipate. He followed Steve into the lounge where they both sat on the sofa. Sarah appeared in the doorway and listened as they spoke.

'What's happened?' Steve asked.

'She said it's over,' Phil shot back.

'Why?'

'She thinks I'm having an affair.' Phil shook his head and, though he looked to the ceiling, he seemed to be staring far beyond it.

'Is she still at home?' Sarah asked.

Phil nodded, as he rubbed his temples.

'I'm going over there,' Sarah said and, before Phil could answer her, she was out of the door.

Steve looked at Phil, and sighed. Crises were like buses, it seemed.

'You're not, are you? Having an affair?'

The look of utter despair from Phil gave him his answer.

'Talk to me, then.'

There was silence for a moment. This time, it was awkward as Phil shuffled on the spot and his cheeks turned red.

'You don't have to have sex every day to have a healthy marriage,' Phil said, eyes to the ground.

'Well, no.'

'And she said I wipe my phone history every day,' Phil said. 'I'll leave it to your imagination why I might do that. Let's just say it has something to do with that lack of sex, and nothing to do with having an affair.'

'Oh,' Steve said.

'The truth?' Phil said, his voice reducing to a mere simmer. 'We've just drifted apart recently, and she's become obsessed with the idea I'm cheating on her. It's just . . . Everything's always an argument, you know? It's horrible. She's been . . . pretty aggressive about it all to be honest with you.'

'Aggressive?'

Phil looked to the floor and didn't answer, and the welt on his best friend's face seemed to glow as he focussed on it.

'Oh, mate,' Steve said. 'We'll get everything sorted, all right?' He didn't have a clue what getting everything sorted would actually look like, but that was kind of beside the point. A united front is what Phil needed and, with everything he had, it's what Steve was going to provide him.

'I'll find a hotel or something,' Phil whispered, still staring at the floor.

'Like hell you will.'

As Steve made a temporary bed for him on the sofa, his mind was already turning to a more semi-permanent solution. Gracie could go in with Oscar, maybe? Either way, there was no chance of him turfing Phil out.

One thing was clear: the chances of a reconciliation with Emma were slim to none, erring more towards the 'none' end of the spectrum.

Sarah was gone for little over an hour and, by the time she crept back through the front door, Steve was already upstairs. He'd left Phil in the lounge not long before and, as she joined him, and they sat on their bed, their voices were mere whispers as they exchanged notes.

'Emma's adamant he's shagging about,' she said.

'He's adamant he's not,' Steve replied.

'Wiping his phone, not interested in her, it all stacks up.'

'I don't need to paint a picture for why he's wiping his phone history, do I? No sex, but sex drive still . . .'

Sarah didn't immediately respond.

'I think she might have hit him,' Steve said, quietly.

'She's not the type, is she?'

'Who knows what goes on behind closed doors.'

Sarah sighed and, as a yawning silence enveloped them, Steve held her hand. How had their marriage survived given everything that had happened, he wondered, when Phil and Emma's appeared to be going down the pan? Life, and all its vagaries, worked in mysterious ways.

It was just past midnight when they finally turned the lights off. Sarah fell asleep quickly and, as Steve closed his eyes, he wondered if slumber would come easily. Almost within seconds, he had his answer.

He slept the sleep of the dead, but woke with a start. He fumbled for his phone and, once more, the bright light burned his retinas. It was 04.32.

His heart was thumping as his eyes darted around the room. Another loud thump on the front door gave him the answer as to why he had woken so suddenly. He got up quickly and, guided by the light from his phone, threw on Sarah's dressing gown that was lying on the floor. God only knew how, but Sarah hadn't woken. He stalked across the bedroom floor and quickly made his way downstairs, where Phil was just emerging from the lounge, rubbing his eyes.

No visit in the middle of the night can ever come to any good and, as Steve opened the front door, his hand shook. Sure enough, there were two police officers on the other side.

'Mr Minchin?' one of them asked.

'Yeah,' Steve replied. 'What's up?'

'Someone's had a pop at your kiosk,' the policeman replied.

'What's that?' Steve asked.

'It's on fire, mate,' the policeman said.

Chapter 66

KEVIN

The clouds above him were low, but they weren't releasing what they held. Instead, they kept everything in. Everything contained. The rains, bubbling away inside. Waiting. Waiting. Waiting, to let it all out. How apt, he thought, as he stood back and admired his handiwork.

He turned around and marched away, his back heating up like bread in a toaster. Along the promenade. Up the slope. A left turn, then along the footpath that led all the way up to the cliffs and beyond. It was only when he was safely out of range, out of sight, that he stopped and pivoted on his heels.

Those clouds were so low he could taste them and, as he reached out a hand, the silhouette of it dissolved against the black tapestry where the sky and the sea met in the distance. He closed his eyes and breathed. There was no peace, but there was a moment of calm. And that, for now, was okay. He'd got his fix and, as the fresh smell of smoke drifted his way, he lapped it up like a kid on bonfire night.

The orange glow was dim for a while. It may have only been wood, but it still retained some of the damp that Isabella had emptied upon it.

Indeed, as he crept ever closer to the edge of the cliff and sat down with his legs dangling on the very precipice where above met below, it took an almighty explosion for it to, literally, blow the roof off. The ice cream machine, maybe. Something with gas, or pressure. The coffee machine? He didn't know, nor did he care. All that mattered was that the fire in front of him was burning as brightly and intensely as the one within.

As he sat there and watched Minchin's business burn, he grinned. It was poetry in motion, an epic in its own right. The smile endured as his legs swung true and free.

'Burn, baby, burn,' he mumbled to himself, the lyrics out of time with the tune he wanted to sing.

And burn, it did. As the faintest of sirens rung out in the air, he climbed to his feet and stalked the clifftop path as he wound his way home. The sirens grew louder, and he walked faster.

How he'd have loved to have seen Minchin's face when he'd seen what had happened.

That smile?

That smug laugh?

It would've been wiped clean from it.

Chapter 67

STEVE

The roads were empty apart from the early morning brigade who were beginning their commute to work. Steve ignored traffic lights, giving way to no one. Coffee and Cream was more than just four wooden walls and some equipment. She had her own personality, her own soul. Steve spent more time with her than he did anyone else in those summer months and an attack on her was an attack on him.

The brake pads on his car smouldered, squealing in protest as he stamped on the middle pedal and abandoned ship on Beach Road. As he raced from the car to the slope, Sarah matching him stride for stride, the stench of smoke filled his nostrils. Gentle crackles filled the dark night air and the hairs on his neck prickled just as they had a couple of weeks before when he'd raced into the house fire. He shook those thoughts from his mind, and concentrated on putting one foot in front of the other.

Hidden by the cliffs, there had been a dim glow of orange softly illuminating the blackness beyond. As he descended the slope, and that glow showed itself in all its ruinous glory, his heart broke just a little. There, on the promenade in the distance, was the smouldering remains of what had been his pride and joy.

She was gone.

Her roof, burned to nothing, had dissolved into the flames below. Her wooden walls no longer protecting what was inside as, inch by inch, they had been devoured by the inferno. And the machines inside, molten shells of what they hand once been.

It was his Coffee and Cream, and it was being reduced to ash before his very eyes. There were police officers milling around, but no firefighters. She had just been left to burn and, now, there was nothing left except the simmering embers of what had once been.

Insurance? None. Insurance companies weren't crazy about providing indemnity for wooden structures next to the sea. As an asset, she was dust, but she was so much more than that. She had her own personality, her own aura, and it'd been incinerated along with everything else.

Steve could bear it no longer. His faltering steps increased in pace until the strides were almost a jog. Sarah struggled to keep hold of his hand as they lengthened further.

'Steve,' she said.

He was nearly at a sprint when she yanked on his fingers, making them click as they bent back against the joints.

'STEVE!'

It may have stopped him in his tracks, just short of the hastily erected police tape that guarded the scene, but it did nothing to quell the fire within.

'Is someone gonna do something!?' he shouted.

A police officer approached him.

'Yours?' the police officer asked, pointing towards the fire.

'Yeah,' Steve replied, 'where's the fire brigade?'

'On a call elsewhere,' the police officer said.

'God's sake,' Steve muttered.

'Can't get too close,' the police officer said, 'but there's something you should see.'

Steve stared at the copper.

'What?' he asked.

'Over here.'

Steve took hold of Sarah's hand as they followed the police officer beyond the cordon tape towards Coffee and Cream, stopping about five metres short of the smouldering residue. Steve saw it clearly, scrawled in chalk on the concrete floor that surrounded the fallen structure, illuminated by the glowing wreckage that was before them.

'MURDERER'

Life had a funny way of balancing the books.

Chapter 68

DS SUE WILLMOTT

It wasn't something that she'd normally turn out for. If there wasn't a body attached, then the night duty DC wouldn't dare to bother the on-call DS. Given that Vinny was in the chair, though, DS Willmott didn't blame him for dragging her from her pit.

She arrived long before the sun would even have threatened to breach the horizon and, as she met Vinny at the top of the slope, ash floated on whatever breeze there was around them.

'Let's have a look, then,' she said, leading the way down the slope.

Coffee and Cream was a carcass, a smoking and molten wreck where the flames that had blazed into the night sky were now just a seat of embers that glowed in the dark.

'Evening,' she said, to one of the officers standing guard in front of some scene tape.

'Skip,' he replied.

'Have the owners been down?' she asked, as she read the graffiti on the floor and winced.

'Been and gone.'

She nodded. She'd have to speak to them, but that was a conversation for the cold light of day. As she looked at the dull orange cinders in front of her, she shook her head before turning and walking away.

'I've had enough fires to last a lifetime,' she said.

'I hear ya,' Vinny replied. 'So, what do we reckon?'

She knew exactly what she reckoned. She wasn't a massive social media punter, but she'd snuck a look here and there as the events of the past few weeks had unfolded. It was safe to say that their list of suspects extended to half the country.

'I reckon . . . it's time you made me a coffee.'

'You not heading home?' he asked.

'Nah. No point. Wouldn't sleep anyway, might as well write this one up.'

The slope seemed steeper than normal, no doubt a product of the smoke that infiltrated her lungs and, when she reached the top, she could only assume that her huffing and puffing was exactly how a twenty-a-day smoker felt.

'Meet you back at the nick?' Vinny asked.

She nodded. 'Be a minute, just got an errand to run.'

'At half five in the morning?'

She raised an eyebrow, and shut down his question before he followed it up with another.

Back in her car, she looked at herself in the rear-view mirror, at the bulging bags that sat beneath her eyes, at the tiny red veins that made the sclera appear bloodshot, and the creases in her forehead that seemed exaggerated at stupid o'clock in the morning. She started the engine and, instead of performing a U-turn and heading back towards the police station, she instead took the turn onto Cliff Road, following the meandering road as it tracked the outline of the clifftops.

She drove for three minutes over gravel that she'd travelled along so many times before and, as she pulled up outside Kevin's house, she stared up at it.

He hadn't, had he?

It was in total darkness, with not a sign of life to be seen. She watched and waited for five minutes, veering in her mind from a policing hunch to encroach on Kevin's private angst, to the overriding position that he'd been through enough without being summoned from his pit in the small hours.

She ummed and aaahed until, finally, her heart won out.

The gravel under the tyres crackled as she performed a three-point turn and, as she looked at the house once more, it remained in darkness.

Later, she thought. Later, she'd speak to him.

Chapter 69

STEVE

The ash was dusted underfoot as, just a few hours later, Steve walked back along the promenade. As he stood amidst the remains of what had once been Coffee and Cream, all those thoughts of recent days, of breaking the shackles, of loosening the restraints, came back to roost.

He kicked at the residue of what had once been a worktop, and it disintegrated into a whole pile of nothing. It was a mess, all right, but one that was entirely of his own making.

Where would it end, he wondered? He wasn't so naïve as to think that the police closing their investigation was going to be the last hurdle to surmount, but this? Was it a precursor to what was to come?

He took a step here, a pace there, and felt something solid underfoot. He bent down to pick it up, but couldn't recognise the metal object that was still warm to touch. Whatever it was, whatever it had been, the fire had warped it beyond recognition. He laughed inwardly. How apt, he thought. How apt.

He kicked up yet more dust, more debris, as he tottered

around, his looping footprints in the embers a fitting parallel to the circles that his mind tracked on repeat.

Coffee and Cream? There was nothing salvageable.

In his own life, though? That was, perhaps, another matter entirely.

It was a simple case of putting up or shutting up. Fight or flight.

He had to put up.

He had to fight.

For himself. His wife. His kids. His life.

As he walked away, and the council refuse team went about their work, he didn't look back. He heard the twisting of metal as a digger truck scooped the molten remains of his machines into its claws, and heard them being unceremoniously dumped into the back of a tipper lorry that was parked up at the scene. Replacing it, rebuilding it, was another job, for another day. Right now, he needed to speak to Sarah, to Phil, to get their view on the plan that was slowly forming in his mind.

He drove home, thinking. Wondering. Mentally assessing. Slowly, as he took turnings he wouldn't normally take, and he extended his journey to allow that plan to take root with something approaching clarity, he finally settled on a resolution. His endgame. His penance, his pilgrimage.

The kids were at school when he sat Sarah and Phil down in the kitchen, and shared with them what he was thinking. That they questioned him was to be expected. They were, after all, questions that he'd been asking himself in the car, only moments before.

'Why don't you just tell the police?' Sarah asked.

'Because then people won't know,' Steve replied, 'to stop the whispers, the gossip, the bullying, people need to see it, to hear it.'

'What if . . . they come for you? The police?' Phil asked.

'Then they come.' Steve was quiet as he spoke. 'We can't go on like this. What if someone brings it here? What if it just gets worse? I can't live like this. WE can't live like this. Besides . . .' he looked at Phil, at Sarah, and then the floor '. . . we always preach to the kids about telling the truth, and I haven't done that.'

He took a deep breath, as the dark thoughts of the children being fatherless and Sarah being without a house over all their heads threatened to consume him, but he dispelled them with a sharp exhalation.

'Yet.'

Chapter 70

KEVIN

Kevin flicked through the various channels on the television, but there was nothing. Not even a mention in the local news. No mention of the fire and, as a result no mention of Charlotte.

She had been forgotten. Relegated. Not even mentioned in passing.

He flicked through the paper that had been delivered only that morning. Granted, it wouldn't have carried news of the fire, but there should have been something. Anything. A story, about Minchin getting away with it, a feature about the injustice that had been served upon Charlotte.

It should be headline news.

SHE should still be the story.

Instead, she was being overlooked once again.

Yesterday's news, today's chip shop paper.

He threw the paper at the wall, and it splayed into individual pieces as it fell to the floor, then he punched himself on the cheek to stop the twitches that the fury had provoked.

The taste of blood filled his mouth from a sharp cut on the inside of his cheek and, as a growl escaped from his mouth, he licked his lips with relish.

Chapter 71

FIONA

'Steve? What can I do for you?'

She'd have expected a phone call from the Pope before one from him, given all that had happened.

'We need to have a chat.'

And at the end of that chat, she could've been knocked over with a feather. Rarely, if ever, did someone offer something up like THAT.

'What's the catch?' she asked.

'No catch,' Steve replied, 'just don't edit what I'm going to say.'

No sooner had the phone call ended, she was on the phone to her boss. THIS wouldn't need executive sign-off.

'What have you got?'

'You're not gonna believe this,' she said, barely believing it herself, 'but Steve Minchin wants us to do an interview. Nothing off limits.'

'You're kidding?'

'Not kidding.'

'When?'

'Tonight.'

'Jesus.'

There was a silence as Fiona waited for what she knew was inevitable.

'Tee it up. I'll clear an hour in the schedule.'

Chapter 72

STEVE

Steve drove with Sarah in the front and Phil squashed between the kids in the back as they navigated the slow roads of Beachbrook. They'd picked up the kids early. Family emergency, they'd said, and the school receptionist hadn't argued. The ice cream they'd promised Gracie and Oscar seemed to make up for the short-notice news that Mummy and Daddy were going to be away for the night.

Before the ice cream shop in town, though, Steve had a quick stop to make. He pulled to the side of the road, and jumped out of the car outside one of the many convenience shops that had sprung up all over Beachbrook.

That it was corner-shop flowers he emerged with wasn't the point; it was what they signified that counted. He had never been one for gooey shows of emotion, and Sarah's face was a picture when he climbed into the car with a bunch of roses that probably had a two-day shelf life.

'For me?' she asked.

He plucked one from the bunch and handed it to her. She didn't question who the others were for. He was sure she could guess.

Sure enough, as he meandered across town, taking roads and routes that he'd long since avoided, her grip on his thigh tightened. It wasn't quite a pinch, but it was enough to leave nail marks in his skin.

'Won't be a minute,' he said, as he trundled to a gentle stop.

'Want me to come?' Sarah asked.

He shook his head. This was one for him alone.

'Daddy will be back in a minute,' he said, turning to the kids in the back. Gracie was staring out of the window, and a chuckling Oscar was being dug in the ribs by Phil.

'What's a symmetry?' Gracie asked, trying to pronounce a word on the sign at the side of the car that was probably a year beyond her grasp.

'A cemetery,' Steve replied. 'Mummy will explain it to you.' With that, he climbed from the car, roses in hand, and closed the door gently behind him. His heart rate was spiking, but he didn't even think about it. This wasn't about him, after all. This was about her. About Charlotte.

They were footsteps he'd taken before. More than twenty years prior, he'd gone there and found her grave, trying but failing to find closure in the mind of a teenage boy who had struggled to deal with what he'd done. Now, he was there to try again.

Straight down the main pathway, turn right, then on his left. A simple task but, as he put one foot in front of the other, they were lead-weighted. Maybe it was the fact that he felt so calm, that the peace that permeated around him was completely at odds with the violence that had put her there. Maybe it was the thought of him seeing her at rest, knowing that she was there because of him. Or maybe, just maybe, he was scared. Either way, as he willed himself forwards and forced himself to put one foot in front of the other, to approach her resting place and to face her, it was a simple case of mind over matter. He had to do it. He HAD to.

And he did.

He looked down at the white granite stone, with words inscribed in a delicately stylish font. It was so clean, so tidy, that no one would've ever guessed it had been laid decades before. The inscription was simple, but he'd forgotten it from when he'd visited as a boy, struck from his mind and compartmentalised in a place he'd never tried to access.

Charlotte Hitch
Taken far too soon.
Earth's loss is Heaven's gain.
Sleep tight, angel.

Steve breathed deeply as his eyes filled with tears that threatened to flow.

'Hi, Charlotte,' he whispered, placing the flowers gently next to her.

He tried so hard to say everything that he wanted to. He wanted so much for her to hear it from him, for her to know that his life hadn't followed the same path of destruction that he had been on when it had happened. He wanted her to know about his family, about how he had lived his life in the shadow of what he had done, and how he was trying to set himself free of that. With her blessing, he wanted to move on. He wanted to tell her everything.

But he couldn't.

'I'm so sorry,' was all that he could say, as the tears that had lurked in the corners of his eyes began to fall.

He'd come prepared, though, for this exact scenario. He was going to get through this, come hell or highwater, and he reached for a piece of paper in his pocket. Everything he needed was on there. With his voice quivering, and hands shaking in tune with those trembles, he began to read words that he'd written only an hour earlier.

'For what I did, and who I was, I'm so sorry,' he began. They may have been whispers seeping from his lips, but they were loud and clear. 'It can't be forgiven. I just wanted to let you know that I have changed. The boy who did that awful thing doesn't exist anymore. Unlike you, he had a second chance and my heart aches that you didn't.'

He breathed slowly, and felt the stillness of the surroundings infuse itself into him.

'I've got a little girl, you know,' he said, as the words that had been so absent finally found their way out. 'Gracie – goes to the same school you did. A little boy too – Oscar.'

It was so calm there. So tranquil.

'I hope that you've found peace,' he continued. 'It's what I'm trying to do and I hope you don't mind me coming. I'll leave you now. Again, I can't say anything other than I'm so, so sorry.'

He stood up straight, looking down at her one last time.

'Rest peacefully,' he said, leaving the flowers on her grave.

He turned around. Then, he was gone.

Chapter 73

KEVIN

The blood from the cut inside his cheek may have stopped flowing, but he'd got the taste for it. There was only one thing that could calm him, that could bring him down, and that was his girl. His Charlotte. As he sat in his chair, cradling a photo of her, though, the image of her didn't even touch the edges.

Across the road, and on the clifftop, the bench didn't have any effect, either.

There was only one other place he could think of, one other place where the quiet and the serenity could pacify his mind and soothe his soul.

It was a walk that he could do with his eyes shut and, with his restless legs, it flew by. He was impatient to be there, desperate to rid himself of the darkness that plagued him.

Three roads to go.

Then two.

One.

He walked around the final corner as, in the distance, someone walked out of the cemetery gates. He stopped and stared.

His eyes weren't what they once were but, even fifty

metres or so away, he recognised the strut in the person's step. He recognised the way their head lolled from side to side as they walked.

And, even at a distance, he recognised Minchin's face. As the car started, he ducked into an alleyway that filtered from the pavement. He heard the engine approaching and, as it drove past him, he stared in through the driver's window.

It was him. In the flesh.

'You . . .' Kevin whispered, eyes wild and mouth wide as he ran from the alleyway and in through the iron gates.

He couldn't catch his breath as he raced to her grave. There, he found flowers. Ugly, drooping roses. He snatched them from the ground and pulled them from their wrapping, the thorns tearing and slicing into his skin as he ripped the petals from the stems. They provided a macabre red confetti as he threw them to the ground.

That peace he'd always found there? Forever tainted.

That unique tranquillity? Forever fouled, forever polluted.

It had changed everything.

How dare he. How fucking dare he.

Chapter 74

FIONA

It had been a mad dash to get everything prepared. A car, to collect Steve and Sarah, to rush them up the motorway to the capital and get them into the studio. A room in the hotel next door, laid on for them to stay in. A plethora of last-minute graphics and teaser trailers, to promote the hell out of it in the hours running up to broadcast. And research. An absolute bucketload of research. It may have all been very last-minute, very 'breaking news', but that's where Fiona thrived.

Now, as she looked at the studio floor, she smiled. This was where the magic happened.

Two chairs. A table separating them. Water, in a jug with slices of lemons, and two glasses. Mood lighting. Plain décor. A backdrop, of the capital city outside a window. Perfect, Fiona thought as she affixed her microphone to a lapel on her blazer.

Steve was already sitting in his chair. They had met briefly when he'd arrived at the studio, but it had been an awkward few words of greeting as opposed to a conversation of any length. Fiona was keen that the interview be organic and, in order for it to flow in such a way, it was best that there were no preconceived or agreed topics of discussion. They could chat after, of course, but she doubted that would happen.

She took her seat opposite him, smiling and nodding. He returned the compliment. That it wasn't going to be broadcast live gave her team a couple of hours' breathing space to edit anything that needed to be. All he had asked was that they not cut any of his words. Condense the pauses, maybe. If he stuttered, or took too long to think about an answer, then trim it. But erasing words? Deleting context? He'd insisted on that not happening, and she'd readily agreed.

'Good to go?' she asked, as a make-up artist applied the final touches to her face.

'Good to go.' He nodded.

Fiona was used to the bright lights that shone on them, but Steve looked like a rabbit in headlights. She saw the beads of sweat forming on his forehead as he squinted to maintain eye contact with her but, with the prompt in her ear and the nod of the director, the cameras began rolling.

It was time.

FIONA: Steve Minchin, it's been quite a few weeks for you, hasn't it?

He sighed, almost shamefully, as he met Fiona's gaze and didn't shift from it.

STEVE: Yeah, you could say that.

FIONA: Let's go back to the start, if we can. Firstly, the fire. Now, I covered that in great depth and what you did, I think, touched the hearts of people up and down the country. Honestly, it resonated with so many people and the response we had was unlike anything I've ever seen before. How do you account for what you did?

Steve nodded, gently, and pursed his lips.

STEVE: Honestly? I don't know. It seems like such a long time ago, you know? I guess it was just instinct. I've got kids, you know.

FIONA: Do you think that, given what we know now, there may have been a part of you trying to atone for the past?

Again, Steve sighed. He broke eye contact and looked all around her. It was textbook, she thought. She'd seen people over the years searching their minds for an answer.

STEVE: That's something I've been asking myself, a lot. At the time, I just did it, you know, but afterwards, who knows? Maybe I did. Subconsciously, perhaps. It's not something I'll ever be able to answer, I think.

Fiona had hit her stride with consummate ease. Her way of relating to people, particularly under a spotlight as bright as the one shining on Steve, was unrivalled. Her voice remained soft, but authoritative.

FIONA: And have you been in touch with baby Jack since?

STEVE: I met his grandparents, and I went to the funeral of his parents, but nothing else. What with everything that has gone on since, it just hasn't happened.

FIONA: And, then, of course, news broke about your past, that there was something there that was hidden.

She was gently steering the interview along the path that she wanted. His act of heroism. His shameful past. Everything that had happened and why.

Steve bowed his head, before answering.

STEVE: Yep.

No sooner had she posed her question than he'd rammed home his response with the speed of someone intent on getting something off their chest. She'd expected to have to prise it out of him, to ask the question in a myriad of different ways to get an answer, but no. It took her off guard, and she shuffled her papers as she composed herself.

FIONA: Tell me what happened.

His head was high, his shoulders back. How long, she wondered, had he prepared what he was about to say? How long, had he practised the words over and over in the mirror, reciting them until they could be released as if by muscle memory?

STEVE: Can I qualify what I'm about to say, by saying I'm not trying to find an excuse. I'm really not. I just want you to know that, because anytime I see someone say something and then add a 'but' I roll my eyes. This isn't that. I won't be saying 'but'. What I did was . . .

He paused. Fiona wanted to help him, to find the word that he was searching for, but her every journalistic instinct told her that, in this case, silence was best. Let him do it. Let him figure it out.

STEVE: Devastating.

A fair summation, she thought.

FIONA: Go ahead, Steve.

The floor was his. She'd provided the platform, and would no doubt take the plaudits, but this was his show. His time. His chance to let it all out.

Chapter 75

STEVE

STEVE: I was brought up bad. My childhood was . . . broken. I think that's how it's best described. Broken. Troubled, I guess.

His eyes filled as those visceral memories exploded behind them, but just a couple of blinks prevented tears from falling. As much as this was about him, in equal measure it wasn't.

FIONA: Can you tell me what you mean by troubled?

STEVE: I could tell you a million things, but nothing would justify anything. What I will say is that I was in care and the home I was in isn't there anymore. Some of the staff are in jail. I still bear the scars of it. Inside and out.

FIONA: Please, carry on.

Steve's mind turned to his parents. Were they still out

there? Would they be watching? Did they even know what had become of him, what he had done?

STEVE: My parents were bad people. I got taken away from them when I was young. Four, I think. Drink, drugs.

He closed his eyes and flinched as he recalled his childhood house.

STEVE: Beatings. And worse. I used to hide, but my dad would always find me.

He looked at Fiona, finding her with mouth agape and without words. The floor, it seemed, was his.

STEVE: Then after some awful foster placements came that care home.

He sighed deeply. He had always intended for the abuse aspect to be implied. He was sure that mentioning the care home, and that several members of staff had been in jail, would be sufficient for people to draw their own conclusions. But as he sat there, and Fiona's eyes willed him on, there was no shame in having been a victim.

STEVE: What they did to me, to us, it just . . .

He wasn't floundering, and he wasn't playing for time. It was just . . . an explosion of images, of memories, of the feelings of nausea that had beaten him down the week before.

FIONA: Take your time, Steve.

STEVE: I was raped. I was abused. I was humiliated. It shaped who I was, I suppose. And then I moved away from it all.

FIONA: To Beachbrook?

STEVE: To Beachbrook.

His hands trembled as he reached for his glass of water, so much that it caused a dribble to run down his chin as he held it to his mouth. It was crunch time. THIS was the moment. And he was determined not to be found wanting.

FIONA: And what happened in Beachbrook?

They spoke funny down south. That was his first impression of Beachbrook. Once he got past the accents, though, some other things stood out to him.

People seemed to give a shit, there. He had his own room, his own space. And no one had tried to touch him.

Yet.

He didn't trust it, didn't trust them, not one bit. And why would he have? At every juncture of his upbringing, on every occasion when he should have felt protected, reassured, celebrated, he'd been shat on from the heavens.

Instead of embracing his new surroundings, he made a stand of sorts.

He didn't engage. He didn't play ball. He'd lie in his bed until lunchtime, then skulk around the home until the small hours. He had a 'look', one that told others to steer clear. He'd spent years perfecting it, and now it was deployed with maximum effect.

And yet . . . his was a room with a view. The cliffs and,

more strikingly, what lay beyond them. He'd been struck by the majesty of the sea when he'd first seen it, and it showed no sign of abating as the days strung together. Sometimes he'd just sit and stare, oblivious to the hours passing him by as distant boats traversed across the entire panorama, sometimes disappearing over the horizon where the sun would set. He'd found a drug that rivalled what those in the squat had plugged into their veins, and he was addicted.

And, as with every drug, a constant dribble would not be enough as the tolerance to it grew. So it was that, on one particularly warm day, he found that the safety fittings on his window had been disabled. The previous occupant of his room had obviously not liked being stuck inside, either.

He became expert at climbing out, shimmying down to the flat roof below, then sliding down a drainpipe. For a kid who'd spent their life prowling in the shadows, it was bread and butter. He'd lock his door and make a stealthy exit, day after day after day, repeating the process in reverse when he arrived back. Before long, the cliffs were home, the beach his refuge. And the sea? She was his release, the one he'd speak to when no one else would listen.

It was a day just like any other. Steve locked his door from the inside, climbed down to the flat roof, then to the ground, and made his way onto the cliffs. On that day, the sea had been flat calm, but she'd been breathing as she'd gently lapped into shore, and that's just how he liked her. Waves and rips weren't for him. It was, in every respect, the perfect day.

He walked along the clifftop, concentrating on putting one foot in front of the other as he strayed into the danger zone where the chalky surface crumbled near to the edge. He wasn't invincible, far from it, but he'd trodden so close to the precipice in the past that this was like a stroll in the park.

And then, a bench. He took a seat and didn't move.

Minutes came and went. An hour, perhaps. He wasn't wearing a watch, nor did he have a phone. And as he sat, he spoke, mumbling at first, before precise words flowed from his lips.

He asked why.

Why him?

He was still a boy, sure, but everything that he'd been through? Who else would've suffered that? Who else would've felt that pain, the type that you'd be willing to die to escape from?

He climbed to his feet, and paced up and down.

Why him?

He hadn't stood a chance, had he? He'd been born into a bear pit and, when he'd been rescued, they'd thrown him to the lions.

He stood, perilously close to the edge, murmuring questions and oblivious to the world around him. In his mind, he was back there. The beatings. The abuse. The touching. And the rapes. It flooded through him, eruptions of fear, of horror, of agony, all bundled into the consciousness of one terrified teenager.

'Hello?'

Her words didn't register.

It was torture. Unmitigated, pure, absolute torment, and he shook from head to toe.

'Hello? Are you okay?'

He was in a bubble, one where misery reigned. That he took another step ever closer to the edge barely registered in his mind.

'Excuse me? Are you okay?'

Grains of chalk crumbled beneath his feet and tumbled over the cliffs. He was millimetres away from joining those granules in the air and, as he stumbled, she reached out to grab his arm. What good a mere slip of a girl could do to prevent gravity from claiming another victim from those parts, he didn't know. Yet, as her fingernails dug into him, it was just like all those times before.

Someone grabbing his arm.

Fingers, on his skin.

It had always precipitated something bad, something torturous.

Instinct told him to react.

And, with his mind out of sync with his body, he did.

Turning on his heels, as yet more pellets of chalk from beneath his feet fell to a watery grave far beneath them, her fingers grew tense. As they scored his skin, it was one continuous motion that thrust them away from him, and pushed her backwards, taking a chunk of his DNA with them. It was a shove that was born of a bubbling apprehension, as the scared little boy in Steve revolted against everything that had come before. It wasn't her that he was pushing. Far from it. It was involuntary, a mere reflex to chase away the demons.

And yet, as the art folder that had been under her shoulder flew open, scattering blank paper into the air around them, he saw her.

It played out in slow motion.

She didn't stumble, and she didn't slip. He'd pushed her far too hard for that. Instead, she near flew through the air, her head tumbling backwards and her feet rising into the air. Just for a second, it was like she was floating, a passenger in the air, bathing in A3-sized confetti.

That slow motion became super slow-mo. She kicked her legs. No foothold. She grabbed at thin air. No traction. Nothing. Her face contorted as she floated, floated, floated, and her arms flailed, but it was no good. No use.

Her head cracked the corner of the bench behind her, the noise as loud as a shotgun. She crumpled beneath herself, her legs folding in ways that they shouldn't, and her head bent so violently at the neck that it almost looked like a cruel caricature of the little girl who the body belonged to.

Time sped up until it was on fast forward. Her fingers may have twitched but, as he looked into her eyes, they were dark. Empty. Devoid of anything and everything.

'Hello?' he whispered.

She didn't respond.

And he knew, there and then, what he'd done.

'PLEASE, NO!' he screamed. Words, that would haunt him across the years. Words that he'd heard himself cry in his nightmares every time he closed his eyes.

He turned around and ran. To where? Not even he knew. He had to get help. That much was obvious. Yet, as he passed houses and bungalows on his way, it didn't even occur to him to knock on any of the doors, to beg for a phone, to call an ambulance. Instead, he continued running. If he told the staff at the home, they'd sort it. Surely.

Muscle memory guided him up the drainpipe, into his room, and that's when he heard the first sirens. Faint at first. Then louder. Peeking out of his window, holding his breath, he saw police cars. An ambulance. He didn't need to get help anymore.

The cavalry was on their way, and he didn't tell a soul.

Chapter 76

KEVIN

No sooner had Kevin arrived home from the cemetery, with the bitter taste of vengeance on his palate, than Minchin's mug was emblazoned on the screen of the TV that he'd neglected to turn off earlier. It was tantamount to torture, enough to break the sanest of men.

A speck of scum formed at the corner of Kevin's mouth as he chewed on his bottom lip. That woman reporter was on the screen, wittering on.

'Join us tonight for an exclusive interview. Steve Minchin, who has been in the headlines in recent weeks for reasons spanning hero to zero, joins me, with nothing off limits. Tonight at seven, it's one not to be missed.'

He looked at his phone as it rang.

Sue.

He didn't want to talk to her. She had let him down and his faith in the justice system was well and truly dead.

He took his phone in his hand and launched it against the wall. As it shattered into debris on the floor, the speaker continued to ring, though it was warped. Squeaky. A distorted chiming that made his temples throb.

No sooner had it ended than he settled in for the day. Camping out on his chair, watching that news channel, growling whenever another trailer came on for 'the interview'.

And he waited.

Vengeance? No. It was a reckoning that was coming.

Chapter 77

FIONA

'That was . . . something,' Fiona said, as the lights dimmed.

Steve stared at her, but his face was blank, his eyes fixed on something far beyond the physical, burning holes through her as they searched for whatever it was his mind sought.

Sarah floated across the studio floor, her own cheeks streaked red with tear tracks, and stood next to Steve. Fiona watched as she tried to take hold of his hand, having to prise his white knuckles apart from the vice-like fist they found themselves balled into.

'You should be proud of him,' Fiona said. And she meant it, too. How many times in her career had something like THAT happened? She didn't even need one hand to count.

'What happens now?' Sarah asked.

'We edit,' Fiona replied, 'then it'll go out as planned in a few hours' time. You guys get off to your hotel. Rest up. I reckon it'll be a busy few days from here.'

'And what happens from here?'

'Like we discussed at the start, got to see how the chips fall.' Fiona looked at Sarah and smiled, and it wasn't just because she'd got the story that everyone else would've killed for. Deep down, she was rooting for Steve, for Sarah, for them. On screen, she was neutral, often the devil's advocate. This had been one of those stories that had cut through, though, and not just for the public. It had affected her, too. Deep down, she was on his side and as shots at redemption went, she'd done her bit for him.

Now, like she'd said, it was time to see how the land lay when everything was said and done.

Chapter 78

SARAH

Of course she was proud of her husband. Of course she would support him, down whatever path he took and whatever obstacles there would inevitably be on the way. Even so, as she'd watched on from the wings as the words had tumbled from his mouth and he'd shared it all, something inside her had screamed for them to stop, to take pause, to really think if this was the right thing to do.

And yet, with half a smile on her face, she'd let the moment pass. Behind the mask she was wearing, there had lain a petrified woman, one who worried what the fallout would be. They'd been questions that she'd asked of him at home. And not just her, but Phil too. He'd shot them down, though. He needed to do it, he'd said, to stop the noise, the whispers, the gossip, and everything else. This was the only way, he'd insisted, and she'd gone along with it, for him.

But what if . . . it broke them?

What if . . . all the reasons why he hadn't told the police in the first place came to fruition?

It wasn't that she didn't believe in the truth, in showing

the kids that the right thing to do didn't always mean taking the easy option but, in the cold light of day, family came first. Family was ALWAYS the right option. And she wasn't sure that Steve had taken it.

As she sat in the hotel room, though, watching him stare out of the window into the early evening sky, his silence was only amplified by the bustling life in the city beyond.

'All right, love?' she asked.

He had his back to her, his nod announced by the bouncing of the hair on the rear of his head. She could hear his breaths. Long. Drawn. Steady, though.

She looked at her phone. Dinner time had been and gone. McDonald's she guessed and, hopefully, now settled on the sofa at home with a film before bed. For once in her life, it seemed, there were no messages, no social media updates, just pure radio silence.

'You did great,' she said, tossing her phone onto the bed and walking towards him, 'really really great.' No matter what her belly was telling her, she was there for him.

Steve nodded again and, as she reached him, and she wrapped her arms around his waist while looking down from whatever floor it was that they occupied in the capital sky, he flinched. It was fleeting. It was quick. And, no sooner had he done it than his hands fell over hers.

'Really?' he asked.

'Really,' she confirmed.

Those steady breaths grew ragged very quickly.

'You think it'll do the job?'

'I hope so.'

Steve's nods were exaggerated. A manifestation, Sarah thought, of the winds of change that she could sense were buffeting him from within. It was a process, and he was working his way through it bit by bit.

'Heard from the kids?' Steve asked.

Sarah shook her head.

'Let's give them a FaceTime,' he said.

Sarah smiled, and walked back over to the bed as Steve shut the window, closing the hustle and bustle out. She picked up her phone and flicked to the FaceTime app, clicking Phil's name and waiting for it to connect. It wouldn't. Twice, three times, a fourth, but no joy.

'Let me have a go,' Steve said, reaching into his pocket, pulling his phone out and turning it on. A symphony of messages erupted as soon as he did so. Sarah looked over his shoulder.

Hope it's all going well. Kids all good. I'll be watching later. Xx

What is it with women? Xx

Emma won't leave me alone!!!! Xx

This is a copy and paste, of her last message to me: 'I'll ruin you if you don't reply to me. I'll find a way, trust me.' WOMEN!!!!!!!!!!!!

Sorry, just venting. Try to have . . . I don't know . . . a good night? Wrong choice of words I guess, but you get my meaning! Much love, and kids still being good. Xx

I've had enough of this. She. Just. Won't. Stop.

'Jesus,' Steve said.

She'd heard enough. 'Home?' she asked.

'Yeah.'

He pressed a couple of buttons on his screen and, as he hit the speaker button, Phil's face filled the screen. It went straight to answerphone.

And a little chisel carved the tiniest of dents into the core of her, wobbling her knees.

Phil always answered, never leaving for WhatsApp what could be said in person. Now though? His phone was off. It wasn't right, and especially with the messages that had preceded it.

In a matter of minutes, they packed up and were on their way to the train station. That it was the quickest link between the coast and the capital mattered not a jot. It was a couple of hours away. One hundred and twenty minutes. And it was interminable with each call that diverted straight to Phil's answerphone. No sooner had Steve tried to call him and got straight through to his answerphone than she'd try too with no luck.

As she dropped her phone onto the table separating her and Steve in frustration, the time on it barely registered with her: 18.59.

'I'll try Emma,' she said, shaking her head as it crossed her mind that she should have tried her long before.

'Hi, you're through to Emma, please leave a . . .'

She hung up, and dropped her phone on the table once more, the clock on the screen rolling over to 19.00 as it locked to black. It barely registered with her that, up and down the country, Steve's face would be beaming out across televisions at that very moment. Instead, as the train chugged through empty stations and barren countryside on its way down south, she just wanted to be home. She NEEDED to be back there.

Chapter 79

DS SUE WILLMOTT

'Watching?' Vinny asked, as he bustled into DS Willmott's office.

Watching? She'd stayed on late from an early turn to do just that. So heavily trailed had this sodding interview been over the hours gone by, that she'd been tempted to ring the network and ask if they were going to have mass screenings at cinemas up and down the country.

And Kevin. What the hell must he have been going through? She'd tried to call him as soon as she'd heard, but he must've turned his phone off, and when she'd gone to his house later in the day her knocks on the door had gone unanswered.

It wasn't that she'd been uneasy as she'd driven away for the second time in the day, but she'd heard the television blaring from inside. And yet, as she checked her phone one last time before setting it down in front of her, the WhatsApp messages that she'd sent him only had one grey tick. They'd not even been delivered.

'Here we go,' Vinny said, as Fiona's face appeared on the screen in front of them.

She was standing in an empty studio, with two chairs

next to her, and she spoke with an easy voice and a sombre smile.

'Good evening, and welcome to this special news programme. The nation has been transfixed by Steve Minchin, and we've all followed his story and his spectacular fall from the good graces of the public. Earlier today, Mr Minchin joined me here in the studio, where nothing was off limits. What we discussed . . . it was explosive. I must warn viewers that some of the topics covered are of a sensitive nature, so please be aware of this when watching. Here it is. My interview with Steve Minchin.'

The camera cut to those two same chairs but, now, they were filled by Fiona and Steve.

And so it began.

DS Willmott reached for her notepad and pen. Sure, she was going to spend hours poring over every word of his for the next day or more, trying to find a weak link in anything that he might say, any vulnerability that she could use to expose his pound of flesh, but making notes was what she did. It's how she worked.

As it turned out, she needn't have worried.

It was there.

It was ALL there.

An admission.

A confession.

An explanation as to how he'd escaped the mass DNA screenings, that he'd never been signed out of the care home and the police had taken the staff at their word that no one had been absent.

There was mitigation, sure.

But it was enough. SURELY it was enough.

An hour later, she dropped the pad onto the table, and seemed to breathe for the first time in those sixty minutes.

'That wasn't live, was it?' Vinny asked, as the screen faded away from Fiona and Steve.

As the picture transitioned to Fiona on her own, standing in front of the camera with the two chairs behind her empty, he had his answer.

'So there you go,' she said employing her matter-of-fact voice. 'Steve Minchin has given us the answers to the questions that we've all been desperate to ask. My two cents? I think it'll all work out for him.'

She paused, as if going off script.

'I hope so, anyway.'

DS Willmott clicked off the screen.

'Get your coat,' she muttered, standing up and marching out of the office.

Vinny matched her, step for step, as they made for the car park.

Chapter 80

KEVIN

Kevin wanted to turn it off, wanted to rip the power lead from the back of the telly, wanted to reach into it and drag Minchin through the fourth wall. With so much menace swarming and swamping his mind, he couldn't function. Couldn't move. He just sat there, stuck in his chair with Minchin's words ringing out from around him and polluting his thoughts even further.

Kevin watched.

His mouth dropped.

His mind, clouded by loathing, heard only what it wanted to. It justified his narrative and exaggerated his rage. He saw Minchin trying to rationalise what he had done. He heard him say that he only did it because of the way he was raised. His eyes grew wide and his heart blew gaskets as he listened to Minchin tell of how Charlotte had tried to help him, and how he had swatted her away. He had killed her. He'd KILLED HER.

Enough was enough.

No more words.

No more thoughts.

No more flirting with fires or raging in private.

He slipped into the kitchen, his feet light as a feather, and secreted a paring knife into his pocket. As he fumbled for the front door key, the blade sliced through his finger. He winced but, seconds later, it turned to a smile.

To feel pain was to feel something.

Chapter 81

STEVE

'Still nothing?' Sarah asked.

Steve shook his head, as they stopped at yet another deserted station in the middle of nowhere. His phone kept going straight through to Phil's answerphone, and he slammed it onto the table.

As he tried Phil, Sarah tried Emma, time and again. Same problem. Phone off.

Neither of them spoke. As the train trudged along with a purgatorial lack of haste, he dialled again and again. Every time, it was the same result.

'Phil here, leave a . . .'

'What's he doing?' Sarah asked.

Steve threw his hands in the air. If only he knew. Each time the train slowed to a stop, the hairs on the back of his neck curled up further. Something with Emma? Things had been bad between them. Was it something to do with that? Something related to those messages she'd sent him? That she'd *ruin him*? The smashed photo frame, the bruises on Phil, all those thoughts came to mind. The more he thought of it, the more dire his theories became.

It was an amalgamation of things, an accumulation of facts. Like ingredients that make a stew, on their own they're nothing. Together, they just make sense. The WhatsApp messages. The anger in them. And that his phone was off, when he was in charge of their kids. He never did that, ever.

Nor, for that matter, did Emma.

'He's probably just run out of battery or something,' Steve said, clutching at whatever straws he could muster.

'My charger's in the kitchen,' she replied. 'He always uses it.'

'Maybe he just left it in his car, then?' Steve said.

'It'd still ring, though,' Sarah replied.

For every rational explanation, she had an answer and, with each riposte, the tiny kernels of doubt that were in his mind grew, until they were fully established.

As he looked at his watch, and the train continued its merry trundle towards the coast, he'd been so preoccupied with Phil's switched-off phone that the hour had been and so nearly gone. His interview was being broadcast to the nation. At that very moment, people were hearing what he'd said, just hours before. His past laid bare. His confession, on the record. It was nearly over, and he hadn't even realised that it'd begun.

And those train sleepers? They growled as the carriages passed over them and, with their relentless, percussive beat ringing in his ears, and Phil's answerphone message playing on repeat, Steve's head began to throb in ways he didn't even know possible. Time was passing but, as the destination grew closer, with something amiss in the air, the seconds stretched into minutes gone by.

'*The next station is . . . Beachbrook . . . where this train will terminate.*'

'Let's go,' Sarah said as, finally, the train plodded into town.

She was off the carriage and gone as Steve threw a backpack onto each of his shoulders. They each ran from the platform, through the building and into the car park until, with Steve driving and Sarah passenger, they were heading to the house that they'd made a home.

Chapter 82

KEVIN

Kevin knew where he lived. He'd done his due diligence. It was a schlep across town, but it didn't matter.

It just focussed his mind.

Past Charlotte's bench.

Guided by moonlight.

Along the clifftop.

Past the slope down to the beach, where the carcass of Minchin's kiosk lay.

Then, inland.

Into town.

Through town.

And beyond.

It was a trek, all right, but as he twiddled the little blade of death in his pocket, and made fresh nicks on the tips of each of his fingers, his smile only grew.

This was for Charlotte.

Everything was for her.

Chapter 83

DS SUE WILLMOTT

The arteries that fed Beachbrook's suburbs were busy, with brake lights brightening the dark roads in every direction.

DS Willmott was in the driver's seat but wasn't doing much driving. It was stop, start, with a hell of a lot more emphasis on 'stop'.

'Sod this,' she said, pulling to the side of the road.

It wasn't like in the movies, where every unmarked police car was loaded with gadgets and gizmos and blue lights on tap. Instead, she turned around and ploughed a route the hundred metres back from whence they'd come.

'Getting a lift?' Vinny asked.

'You know it,' DS Willmott muttered, as she dived back into the police station and abandoned the car frontwards across two spaces.

She snapped her fingers at the first uniformed copper who walked out of the ground floor of the police station and, without so much as a dropped syllable, was in the passenger seat of their police car in a matter of moments. Vinny was in the back, the driver lighting the route in a sea of blue, playing a two-tone medley to the regular folk that they tore past in their wake.

Their destination? The Minchin house.

Chapter 84

KEVIN

He could taste the sweet smack of vengeance on his tongue and, as he swallowed it down, it added fuel to the fire within.

He prowled the streets as they morphed from the shops in the town centre to the burbs beyond, powerless to shed the images in his mind that Minchin had planted there.

She'd just tried to help. She'd just asked if he was okay. She'd just been her, been kind, been caring. And he'd grabbed her. She'd tried to get free, tried to resist, probably cried out for her daddy, for him, for HIM.

He gripped the blade until it sliced down deeper still, not once flinching as his steps made it saw just a bit further each time he moved.

The moon above burned down on him as Minchin's words forced him to replay the video in his imagination on loop.

Her, petrified. Minchin, overpowering his little girl. Her nails, digging into him. And Minchin, launching her into the bench like a rag doll.

Had she screamed?

What would her last thought have been? Where's my dad? Why didn't he stop this?

He doubled his stride and, as the blade shifted in his pocket once more, he released it from his grip. The fabric inside grew damp, then claggy as the blood poured from his fingers, but he didn't care. The pain that burned inside was too strong, too potent, to allow his synapses to register anything else.

The roar of an engine as it blazed past him barely registered with his ears. When he clamped eyes on it, though, they narrowed to the point of being nearly shut.

He'd seen it earlier in the day, at the cemetery.

Minchin's car.

Dashing towards home.

Perfect.

Chapter 85

STEVE

The screeching tyres as Steve rounded one corner after another drowned out the sound of Phil and Emma's voicemails on the car sound system as Sarah dialled them on repeat, but it didn't matter. They were so close to home.

He drove forwards onto the driveway at an angle that took it too close to Sarah's car. He may even have grazed it, he couldn't be sure, but that could wait. Instead, as he sprang from the driver's seat, he was already a good few paces behind Sarah, who'd got the jump on him.

She was first through the front door, closely followed by Steve. The lights were off, but the moon peered in through the windows. Upstairs, he could hear music. Loud, but muffled and, in their haste, neither of them shut the door behind them.

'Phil?' Sarah called.

No reply.

Steve ran up the stairs, with Sarah a few steps behind. The landing light was off but, as downstairs, the moon poured in through whatever windows it could find, bathing them in a dull white glow that shimmered all around.

The doors were closed.

'Phil?' Steve called.

There was no reply.

Chapter 86

KEVIN

Kevin rounded the corner to the smell of burnt rubber. Minchin's car was abandoned on the driveway with the lights still on and, as he squinted towards it from a fair distance away, he was sure he could see tiny wafts of smoke drifting into the sky from the four tyres. Overcooked rubber? Smoking brakes? What was going on?

All of that drifted from his mind when he saw that the front door was wide open, and the lights inside were on.

With a grin on his face, he caressed the knife in his pocket once more. The handle may have been sticky with blood, but it moulded into his fingers like two interconnecting pieces of a jigsaw.

One step. Then another.

Every pace towards Minchin's open front door was another stride towards a retribution that had been decades in the making.

Chapter 87

STEVE

Standing at the top of the stairs and calling out for Phil and Gracie, Steve's words were drowned out by the music that was thumping from Gracie's room. The frame glowed with soft light from within. A child's room. Innocence. The door, decorated in much the same way that baby Jack's had been in the fire. He'd never thought of it like that, until now. Everything that had happened since that moment in time flashed before his eyes in a millisecond . . . The triumph, the collapse, the highs and the lows, the peaks and the valleys. And as he shook it all away with one solid shudder, he pushed the door open and walked inside.

And time stood still.

Steve froze, as his brain processed what his eyes were telling him. Still, he didn't believe them.

'Daddy,' Gracie cried.

She had seen him come in, but Phil hadn't. His eyes were shut as, music blaring, he had one hand on Gracie and one hand on his naked self. He opened his eyes and his face contorted. No words came. The picture before Steve told him everything.

'It won't hurt, Steve. Trust me.'

'What. The. FUCK!?' Steve shouted.

Phil rolled over, and looked at him, one hand covering himself and the other raised to his face. Steve's eyes were wide as his brain still struggled to compute it all, and Sarah barged past him.

'You sick NONCE!' she screamed, as her blows rained down on him.

'Mummy.'

Gracie was crying. Shivering. Trembling.

And still Steve couldn't move.

Just our little secret, Steve. No one needs to know.

Sarah's punches were raining down upon Phil, and Steve just stood there. He was frozen in the present as nightmares of the past swarmed in the air around him.

If you breathe a word, we'll mess you up.

Phil?

PHIL!?

Sarah screamed, a rasping, animalistic wail as clumps of Phil's hair came away in her hands. She reached for anything in her arm space, ripping the Alexa from the bedside table and smashing it over the top of Phil's head, muting the music in an instant.

'Sarah!' Steve shouted, as his brain came to life. 'Get Gracie out of here!'

She scooped Gracie from the bed, wrapping her in the duvet all in one motion, and barged past Steve once again. He heard her walk into Oscar's room and, as her pounding steps ceased, he closed the door gently behind them.

It was just him and Phil. The man he'd known across the years, who'd always been there. As he looked at him, beyond the scratches and scrapes that Sarah had inflicted, his fingers twitched. His breaths grew ragged. And Gracie's voice from the days, weeks, months before filled his ears.

'*You weren't here, Daddy.*'

How had he been blind to it?

'*I want you to stay, Daddy.*'

Had she tried to tell him?

'*I wanted my own bed, Daddy.*'

'Steve, I . . .' Phil began to say, but Steve shushed him straight away, holding his hand in the air as a whine formed in his throat. It was soft at first, delicate. Then, as his head nodded and his eyes blinked all too quickly, it grew guttural.

He took a step towards Phil, fists by his sides and flexing his fingers from straight to a tightly formed fist on repeat.

'What have you done?' Steve whispered, as he took a step closer. He was in spitting distance, in arm's reach.

Phil's face fell to the floor.

'LOOK AT ME!' Steve screamed.

But he didn't. It was on Steve to make him, and he grabbed a handful of hair and yanked it upwards.

'What. The. HELL. Have you done!?' he shouted, tensing his hand and lifting Phil's head higher still.

In the distance, the faintest of sirens rang out, but Steve was too far gone to hear it, his brain spinning in circles beyond control as he worked out exactly how he was going to do what needed to be done.

Another inch of Phil's hair bounded around his fist as Steve's breaths grew more laboured. He'd taken a life before. He could do it again. It should be slow. Painful. Torturous.

'You . . . rabid . . .' His words grew louder as the darkness that had remained dormant for so long swamped him, overwhelming everything.

Releasing his grip on Phil's hair, he threw his naked body to the floor. Phil whimpered, but it was petrol to the blaze. Steve stood over him and looked at his shoes. Brogues. A solid heel. A sharp edge where it joined the sole. Enough, for sure, with the amount of adrenaline that was pumping through him. As he raised his foot, Phil extended his arms. Whatever. No defence was going to stop a father avenging his daughter.

His leg hovered, midair, and he willed it down, willed it to fall crashing into Phil's face time and time again, stomping the life out of him, that edge of his heel slicing and dicing him as the life flowed from his raping body. He wanted the blood, he wanted the pain, he wanted it all, and he wanted it now.

Instead, he stamped his foot down to the floor next to Phil, and collapsed into a seated position on the bed.

He'd killed before, all right, and knew what lay down that road. Something in the deepest caverns of him just wouldn't allow it. He wanted to. Was desperate to. But he couldn't.

He held his head in his hands as the siren outside grew louder still, as Phil scrabbled to his feet in front him, cupping his naked groin as the two men stared at each other.

'They'll sort you out,' Steve spat, 'and we all know what happens to nonces inside.'

Phil's lips were trembling, and he dabbed at his eyes with his spare hand, at the scuffs and cuts all around them.

'I . . .' he began, before Steve held his hand up once more.

'You're fucking dead to us,' Steve said.

No sooner had the words left his lips than the bedroom door flew open. And it all happened so quickly.

Sarah.

A glint as the bedside light reflected in the blade of the kitchen knife.

And, as Phil's eyes remained locked on Steve's, she plunged it into him.

Once.

Twice.

Too many times to count.

The blood flowed, just how Steve had wanted it to. On Sarah, on him, spraying on the pink walls, the bed, the floor, everywhere.

That Phil eventually went limp didn't seem to appease her. Sarah kept on stabbing the knife into Phil, crouched over his body as the blood ran over the carpet. It took Steve to wrestle the knife away, to look Sarah in the eye and bring her back into the real world, as the siren grew deafening before finally stopping outside the house.

Having prised the knife from Sarah's grip, the pair froze, motionless, and Steve experienced a moment of clarity unlike anything he had felt for the past weeks. In the blink of an eye, he knew what he had to do. He knew he was going to serve his time for Charlotte. But he'd be damned if he'd let his children live with both parents behind bars.

'I did this,' he whispered.

'What?' Sarah replied, looking from her shaking, blood-soaked hands to Phil's lifeless body on the floor.

'Look at me. It's got to be me. I did this,' he said, doing whatever it was they did in the movies, wiping the handle on his trousers before gripping it within his own hand. He bent down to Sarah's crouched position, took her other hand in his free one and squeezed tight, locking his tear-filled eyes onto her own. 'Trust me. It's better this way. When they come in, just say that I did it.'

He pulled Sarah up to her feet, and she stumbled back a few paces. Steve crouched back down and remained bent over Phil's lifeless body.

'POLICE!' a voice shouted, as heavy feet ascended the stairs.

Steve held the blade in position, just over Phil's back.

'What the . . . !?' DS Willmott screamed.

Steve plunged the knife into Phil's body, leaving the blade stuck between his ribs as he stood up and backed away slowly. He looked down at the body on the floor, and closed his eyes as his hands were grabbed and handcuffs applied.

That he hadn't protected Gracie was the worst crime he could ever imagine.

Chapter 88

KEVIN

Kevin heard screaming coming from within. He wasn't alone. Soon, the whole street was alive with people and, before long, police cars as well. He melted into the background, watching and waiting. His chance had gone, and he knew it. Still, he waited.

He watched as a blood-soaked woman and two children were escorted out of the house, and into the back of a police car. They were whisked away in the blink of an eye.

No sooner had they gone than Minchin was led away. He was handcuffed to the rear, and covered in so much blood it looked like he'd been butchering at an abattoir.

'Jesus,' Kevin whispered. It was Sue who put Minchin in the back of the meat wagon.

Kevin took a step further into the shadows and waited. It was only when the sun began to poke through, so many hours later, that a private ambulance arrived. It was black, non-descript but oh so shiny, and he knew exactly who was inside. It was the undertakers, and they'd come to collect some cargo.

The faces on everyone who came out of the house spoke

volumes. Whatever it was that had happened, it had been horrific.

It was supposed to have been *his* moment. He had worked it all out.

Someone had been destined to meet their fate that night, all right. That it wasn't Minchin stuck in the craw but, as he had learned across the years, life wasn't fair.

He walked away, shaking his head and mumbling without coherence. The knife in his pocket was soaked in blood that was developing a crust, but it wasn't Minchin's. He growled, as he stalked the roads back from whence he'd come hours earlier and, as he stumbled along the cliff path, with the sun fully formed over the horizon just beyond the sea, he stopped and stared until his eyes were temporarily blinded.

He'd been patient for years. He could always wait a bit longer.

PART FOUR

Decay

The fire consumes available fuel, temperatures decrease, fire gets less intense.

Source: www.nfpa.org

Twelve Months Later

Epilogue

Over Steve's dead body was his baby girl going to be put through anything else, least of all some kind of cross examination, no matter what special measures might be put in place. He'd retained the services of Mr Russell throughout and, during the many client and solicitor meetings that they'd had over the months, an agreement had been hashed out with the CPS.

He'd pled guilty to manslaughter, with mitigation that he'd lost control when Phil had been killed. That he'd not been the one to strike the fatal blow hadn't even been questioned, and he and Sarah had never broached the subject. The murder charge had been dropped, though it stuck in Steve's craw that he had to plead anything in relation to the monster who'd been lurking in plain sight.

Not only that, though. In unprecedented scenes at his plea hearing, the judge had granted him bail. *Exceptional circumstances*, he'd been told. *Mitigation of the highest order.* He'd barely digested it, months before. All he knew back then was that he was leaving the jail and going back home.

'Home' had been a new set of walls. In the ten or so

months that he'd been on remand, Sarah had managed to get rid of the house where the ghost of Phil prowled the hallways, and bought a new place on the other side of town. It was smaller in scale and more modest in space, but a fresh start away from the demons of the past. As soon as Steve had set foot inside, he'd loved it.

And Charlotte? He'd offered to plead guilty to her manslaughter too, but no charges had been forthcoming. In many ways, the court of public opinion had swayed the decision of the Crown Prosecutor and, as Mr Russell had advised him, what evidence was there? When the truth had come out, and the dust had settled, it had been an accident. Nothing more, but certainly no less.

He was going to do time. He knew that much. Precedent told him so. Mr Russell told him so. Sentencing guidelines told him so. Yet the final arbiter, the judge who'd granted him bail, had a decision to make and, as Steve sat in the back of a taxi with Sarah, and they made their way towards Beachbrook Crown Court for his sentencing hearing, he held her hand and felt at peace with everything that had happened.

As they stopped at the side of the road outside the court, the press pack descended upon them. Flashing bulbs, television cameras and microphones were thrust in his direction but he'd learned his lesson over the year gone by. Keep your head down, keep schtum, and keep moving forwards. It was sage advice to himself, and he followed it. With each step he took through the media scrum, though, he heard familiar voices by his side.

'We're with you, Steve,' John said. He was without Lex, but he was present. *That* mattered to Steve, more than anything.

'With you all the way,' Bob said, patting him on the shoulder as he matched Steve, stride for stride.

'All the way,' Pam affirmed, nodding at him and smiling. Steve looked up at her, and saw a composite picture of both baby Jack and Louise in her face. He smiled, and nodded.

'Me too,' Emma whispered, linking arms with him in a show of solidarity.

'Everyone's here, love,' Sarah said, squeezing Steve's hand as the assembled comrades formed a bubble of sorts around him. They ploughed forwards towards the court steps, where one last reporter was waiting.

Steve stopped, and looked directly at Fiona. Their eyes met, and the microphone that was in her hand dropped to her side, with the red light extinguished.

'Good luck,' she said, quietly, before putting her hand in front of the camera lens that was pointing squarely at them.

Steve nodded, and even threw her half a smile. He looked up to the courtroom, at the steps leading to its doors and, as he placed one foot in front of the other, he wondered just how long it would be before he once again breathed free air.

Kevin was just an anonymous man, in a crowd of dozens. He'd stood at the bottom of those court steps for hours, waiting for his moment.

In a flash, Minchin was right in front of him. Within reach.

Within striking distance.

The glow from the bulbs of the assembled press pack rained down on them, a spotlight that had eluded him as everything came out in the wash. Not now, though.

Now, it was his time.

His hand fidgeted in his pocket, as he stared deep into Minchin's eyes, not once blinking. Steve stared back at him, and seemed to cycle through every emotion. Shock, at Kevin's presence. Fear, at what he was there to do. And acceptance, that what will be will be.

Kevin's fingers may have healed from the wounds of all those months before, but the scars they bore still troubled him. It didn't matter, though. Not now. This was his moment. As he whipped his hand from his pocket, and thrust it towards Steve's chest, it wasn't the knife from a year before that was in his hand.

Instead, it was a photo.

A beautiful girl, forever trapped in time.

He handed it to Steve, and turned to walk away.

He would never forgive. He would never forget.

But he had followed the news. He had read what Steve had done. A grudging respect had grown, born of the one thing that he'd come to know that they both held in common:

A father's love.

Acknowledgements

The fabled 'difficult' second novel was actually not so tricky at all – I'd already written it in rough form long before my debut made its way to print!

First and foremost, I'd like to recognise and place on record once again just how grateful I am to my wonderful editor at Avon, Rachel Hart. Rachel's eye is beyond 20/20 when it comes to all things literary, and I am so lucky to have her in my corner, swinging from the batter's box and always knocking it out of the park. Thanks so much, Rach.

And my heartfelt thanks to the wider Avon and HarperCollins team, who work SO hard to make the books shine as best they can. To Jess Zahra on desk edits, Helena Newton on copy edits and Anne O'Brien on proofreads, thanks so much. To the sales team of Katie Buckley, Emily Scorer and Hannah Lismore, who make sure that the books get 'out there', you do a wonderful job. To Emily Hall and Jessie Whitehead in marketing, you both rock (and Emily has promised that she's going to let me read HER book in 2025. I'm writing this here so that I can hold her to it). To Francesca Tuzzeo in production, thank you. To Sean Garrehy who designed this wonderful cover – amazing work. To the international team, Angela Thomson who manages international sales, and Jean Marie Kelly, Emily Gerbner and Sophie Wilhelm on the US side of operations, a huge shout out and thank you. And to the rest of 'Team Avon', Kate Elton, Amy Baxter, Emma Grundy Haigh and Maddie Wilson, thanks so much for all that you do.

I'd like to give a special thanks to the boss, too. Helen Huthwaite has been there for so long that, as her bio on the website says, if you cut her open she would bleed Avon. That is so obvious from the way she treats everyone, from her team through to her authors. She is such a gem of a person and deserves all the credit in the world.

To Becky Hunter and Laura Sherlock, the best publicists in the entire world, a pleasure as always! You're the best.

To the book bloggers and reviewers, many of whom have become friends, thank you for everything you do. You are the lifeblood of this industry and – genuinely – I am so very grateful for your friendship, your words and your wisdom. Emily Portman, Jade Massie, Stu Cummins, Linda Hill, Tilly Fitzgerald, Nicola Winter, Jess Brown, Natalie Chapman, Emma Bowker, Aimee Johnson, Sarah Blackburn, Marianne Collins, Susie Green and Sam Johnson... To Sam Brownley who helps to run the UK Crime Book Club and Tracy Fenton with THE Book Club, and to Victoria Hyde (who does the BEST job of organising The Book Party with A.J. West), thank you all.

To the booksellers who do so much to help get our books out there, particularly those at my local branch of Waterstones, your support has been beyond anything I'd ever have expected. To Claire, who I actually studied A Level English with, and her wonderful team comprised of Karen, Liam, Molly, Georgie and Niamh, thanks so much for helping get my first book into the hands of readers, and selling so many copies of it! I can't wait for you all to get hold of this one.

To my wonderful family, thanks for all that you do. From dad's proof reading to mum keeping their (my) fridge stocked up... From Claire being the most conscientious nurse in the world, to Nicki being such a great teacher, thank you all.

To Georgia, who is going to be a superstar in whatever she does, and Charlie who is just the nicest young man you'd ever like to meet. And to Bella-boos, who is the most avid reader I know, and who will grow up to be a great author, keep working hard my lovely nieces and nephew.

To my wife, Naomi, thank you for loving me.

And to my babies, Florence and Sully, I love you mostest. Keep being 'you' and that will be more than enough.

And finally...

When I was in the last throes of writing *Into the Fire*, Graham Bartlett got in touch with me on a totally unrelated matter, and asked me if I might consider writing something for the Lucy Faithfull Foundation. The answer was 'yes', obviously – if a Chief Superintendent (retired or otherwise) asks for something, then they're generally going to get it, regardless. Trust me, I've learned that! Anyway, when I looked into the Foundation and what they do, I couldn't believe just how relevant their mission was to the story that I'd just written. Their aim is to stop child sexual abuse before it happens, and I'd love to share their website here: https://www.lucyfaithfull.org.uk/

Content Warning:

This novel contains themes that some may find upsetting, including: house fire, murder, abandonment, child death and bereavement, mental illness, and child sexual abuse and violence.

Don't miss the gripping debut crime novel in which a
child's tragic drowning rips a small community apart with
devastating consequences . . .

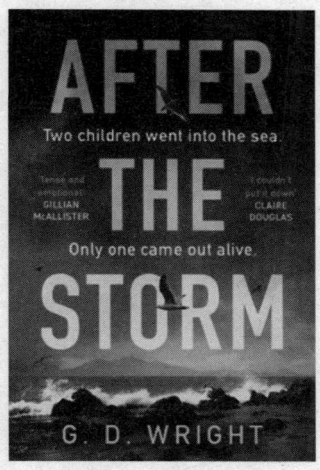

When Andrew and Sophie take their daughter and her
friend to the beach on a stormy day, they are momentarily
distracted and both children are washed out to sea.
Andrew dives in, but comes back ashore with only one
child – Maria, his own daughter. Joe, the son of his
best friend and local police officer, Chris, has drowned.
But it was just a tragic accident . . . wasn't it?

As Sergeant Mike Adams and DS Sue Willmott
investigate what really happened in the water that
afternoon, the ripple effects of the tragedy tear the
community apart. The detectives must discover the truth
before their colleague – bereaved and desperate father,
Chris – takes the investigation into his own hands . . .